ROBERT SILVERBE
They had claimed Cha
able to remember wha
this time he knew an
difference.

ROGER ZELAZNY
The Doors of his Face, the Lamps of his Mouth
'The one that got away' had destroyed his life once
before. Could he stand by and see it do the same to the
woman he had loved?

A. E. VAN VOGT *The Black Destroyer*
When the humans came, it was like an answer to his
prayers, for if he was careful, they could both sate his
hunger and give him the stars for his hunting grounds!

MICHAEL SHAARA *All the Way Back*
With fading hope, men had searched the starways in
search of other races and habitable worlds. Now their
dream was about to be fulfilled – in a way they could
never have anticipated.

Inside this book lurk these and seven more visions of the
alien terrors that have marked humanity as their prey.

Isaac Asimov's World of Science Fiction

MONSTERS

Edited by Isaac Asimov,
Charles G. Waugh and
Martin H. Greenberg

Robinson Publishing
London

Robinson Publishing
11 Shepherd House
Shepherd Street
London W1Y 7LD

First published in the UK by Robinson Publishing 1989

ISBN 1 85487 015 7

Printed by Wm. Collins & Sons Ltd., Glasgow

10 9 8 7 6 5 4 3 2 1

CONTENTS

ACKNOWLEDGMENTS

'Passengers' copyright © 1968 by Damon Knight. Reprinted by permission of the author and Agberg Ltd.

'The Botticeli Horror' copyright © 1960 by Ziff-Davis Publishing Company; copyright renewed © 1988 by Lloyd Biggle, Jr. Reprinted by permission of the author.

'The Shapes' reprinted by permission of the translator, Damon Knight.

'The Clones' copyright © 1969 by Ziff Davis Publishing Company. Reprinted by permission of the author.

'The Men in the Walls' copyright © 1963 by Galaxy Publishing Corporation, 1968 by William Tenn. Reprinted by permission of the author and the author's agent, Virginia Kidd.

'The Doors of His Face, the Lamps of His Mouth' copyright © 1965 by Mercury Press, Inc. Reprinted by permission of the author.

'Student Body' copyright © 1953, 1981 by Galaxy Publishing Corporation. Reprinted by permission of the author and the author's agents, Scott Meredith Literary Agency, Inc., 845 Third Avenue, New York, NY 10022.

'Black Destroyer' copyright © 1939 by Street and Smith Publications, Inc., copyright renewed © 1967 by A. E. van Vogt. Reprinted by permission of the author.

'Mother' copyright © 1953 by Standard Publications, Inc., copyright renewed © 1981 by Philip José Farmer. Reprinted by permission of the author and the author's agents, Scott Meredith Literary Agency, Inc., 845 Third Avenue, New York, NY 10022.

'Exploration Team' copyright © 1956, 1984 by Street & Smith Publications, Inc. Reprinted by permission of the author and the author's agents, Scott Meredith, Inc., 845 Third Avenue, New York, NY 10022.

'All the Way Back' copyright © 1952, 1980 by Street & Smith Publications, Inc. Reprinted by permission of the author and the author's agents, Scott Meredith, Inc., 845 Third Avenue, New York, NY 10022.

INTRODUCTION: MONSTERS

BY ISAAC ASIMOV

The word "monster" comes from the Latin *monere*, meaning "to warn." The ancients thought any unusual happening to be a warning from the gods. This was especially true if the unusual happening involved a life-form—let us say, if a two-headed calf were born.

As a result, a monster came to be narrowed down to any abnormal or misshapen creature. And since human beings, viewing events, had every right to expect the "warning" to be that of forthcoming disaster, the word monster was further narrowed down to any living thing that was abnormal, misshapen—and dangerous. Since large animals are bound to be more dangerous than small ones, a monster was, more often than not, expected to be very large.

It is not surprising, then, that the adjective "monstrous" came to mean something that was enormously evil, or enormously large, or both—as, for instance, America's monstrous national debt.

When one wants to make up a good story of heroism against danger, what better than to have a reasonably normal man fight against a monster? The easiest way to construct a monster is to think of something that is dangerous in itself and then imagine it to be much larger than normal.

Thus, Hercules' first labor was of slaying the Nemean lion, which was pictured as a monstrously large one. Simple size can be dramatic enough. The most successful monster in modern visual fiction was King Kong, who was merely a gorilla of enormous size. The sci-fi abominations of the 1950s abounded in giant spiders, giant crabs, giant dinosaurs, even giant women.

It is, however, a poor imagination that can work up only enlarged dimensions. Fantasies therefore arose in which monsters were enhanced by adding to their ugliness, their malignancy, or their powers. It was not enough to have mere giant men; one had to have ogres who were cannibalistic, or cyclops who were one-eyed ogres, and so on.

A giant crocodile wasn't enough. Add wings and it becomes a dragon. Or if you want a venomous snake, have it breathe fire instead, or have it kill not by a bite or even by a breath but by a mere glance, and you have a basilisk or cockatrice.

The octopus can become Medusa with snakes for hair, or Scylla with six dog-headed necks, or a Hydra that can grow two heads for every one cut off. Or you can combine creatures. A man's torso on a horse's body is a centaur; a woman's torso on a lion's body is a sphinx; an eagle's body on a lion's torso is a gryphon.

Such things come under the heading of "fantasy," however. No one with even a small degree of sophistication will think that a Medusa or a Cyclops or a sphinx literally exists. But can we imagine monsters that *don't* offend our modern sense of what is reasonable and possible? If so, we will end up not with fantasy monsters but with science-fiction monsters.

After all, some large and spectacular organisms were discovered by Europeans only comparatively recently. For instance, no European ever saw a living gorilla until the 1850s. The initial descriptions of its size and ferocity were greatly exaggerated and those exaggerations still live in popular thought—and lent considerable verisimilitude and plausibility to that exciting fantasy of King Kong, which I mentioned earlier.

Well, then, might it not be that other large primates might exist outside of Africa? Might there not be the yeti (or "abominable snowman") in the Himalayas, or Sasquatch (or "bigfoot") in the northwestern United States? The chances of this are virtually zero, but perhaps that's what people such as myself would have said about gorillas in 1845. So a story about the abominable snowman as a primate, perhaps even hominid, would be considered science fiction rather than fantasy.

Then again, there is the monstrous sea serpent. Actually, there is a kind of sea serpent that exits and was discovered in the nineteenth century. The giant squid lives at moderate depths in the ocean and has tentacles that when stretched out give it the length of a whale. Perhaps there are other large creatures in the ocean depths that we still know nothing about. Only in the 1930s did we first discover the coelacanth, which we were sure had become extinct when the dinosaurs trod the Earth.

We might therefore consider large sea creatures to be science-fiction monsters—even a plesiosaur in Loch Ness, for which I consider the chances to be about zero. (For that matter, some even talk about the possibility of a brontosaurus in the African rain forest—again about zero, in my opinion.)

It might even be possible to imagine a monstrous form of life starting from non-life here on Earth and creating a horror where none existed before. We have a story of that sort in this book.

Unquestionably, though, the best monsters that come under the heading of science fiction are creatures from other planets.

Up into the 1950s, it seemed possible that we might find extraterrestrial monsters within our own planetary system, and we have stories of *that* sort in the book, too. In the last third of a century, however, we have learned too much about our neighboring worlds, and life that would be anything like ours is not at all likely to be found on them. (The possibility still isn't entirely zero for Callisto or Titan perhaps, or even the upper gas layers of the atmospheres of Venus or the gas giants.)

That leaves us the possibility of life on planets circling stars other than our Sun, and those are represented, too.

To my way of thinking, science-fiction monsters are more frightening than fantasy ones. A dragon that we know doesn't exist isn't nearly as horrifying as a "black destroyer" that someday some explorers of the far distances might really encounter. In fact, a new subdivision of fantasy has arisen in which dragons and other such monsters are so presented as to gain our sympathy. I don't see that happening to science-fiction monsters—at least not as easily.

PASSENGERS

BY ROBERT SILVERBERG

There are only fragments of me left now. Chunks of memory have broken free and drifted away like calved glaciers. It is always like that when a Passenger leaves us. We can never be sure of all the things our borrowed bodies did. We have only the lingering traces, the imprints.

Like sand clinging to an ocean-tossed bottle. Like the throbbings of amputated legs.

I rise. I collect myself. My hair is rumpled; I comb it. My face is creased from too little sleep. There is sourness in my mouth. Has my Passsenger been eating dung with my mouth? They do that. They do anything.

It is morning.

A gray, uncertain morning. I stare at it awhile, and then, shuddering, I opaque the window and confront instead the gray, uncertain surface of the inner panel. My room looks untidy. Did I have a woman here? There are ashes in the trays. Searching for butts, I find several with lipstick stains. Yes, a woman was here.

I touch the bedsheets. Still warm with shared warmth. Both pillows tousled. She has gone, though, and the Passenger is gone, and I am alone.

How long did it last, this time?

I pick up the phone and ring Central. "What is the date?"

The computer's bland feminine voice replies, "Friday, December fourth, nineteen eighty-seven."

"The time?"

"Nine fifty-one, Eastern Standard Time."

"The weather forecast?"

"Predicted temperature range for today thirty to thirty-

12

eight. Current temperature, thirty-one. Wind from the north, sixteen miles an hour. Chances of precipitation slight."

"What do you recommend for a hangover?"

"Food or medication?"

"Anything you like," I say.

The computer mulls that one over for a while. Then it decides on both, and activates my kitchen. The spigot yields cold tomato juice. Eggs begin to fry. From the medicine slot comes a purplish liquid. The Central Computer is always so thoughtful. Do the Passengers ever ride it, I wonder? What thrills could that hold for them? Surely it must be more exciting to borrow the million minds of Central than to live awhile in the faulty, short-circuited soul of a corroding human being!

December fourth, Central said. Friday. So the Passenger had me for three nights.

I drink the purplish stuff and probe my memories in a gingerly way, as one might probe a festering sore.

I remember Tuesday morning. A bad time at work. None of the charts will come out right. The section manager irritable; he has been taken by Passengers three times in five weeks, and his section is in disarray as a result, and his Christmas bonus is jeopardized. Even though it is customary not to penalize a person for lapses due to Passengers, according to the system, the section manager seems to feel he will be treated unfairly. We have a hard time. Revise the charts, fiddle with the program, check the fundamentals ten times over. Out they come: the detailed forecasts for price variations of public utility securities, February—April 1988. That afternoon we are to meet and discuss the charts and what they tell us.

I do not remember Tuesday afternoon.

That must have been when the Passenger took me. Perhaps at work; perhaps in the mahogany-paneled boardroom itself, during the conference. Pink concerned faces all about me; I cough, I lurch, I stumble from my seat. They shake their heads sadly. No one reaches for me. No one stops me. It is too dangerous to interfere with one who has a Passenger. The chances are great that a second Passenger lurks nearby in the discorporate state, looking for a mount. So I am avoided. I leave the building.

After that, what?

Sitting in my room on bleak Friday morning, I eat my scrambled eggs and try to reconstruct the three lost nights.

Of course it is impossible. The conscious mind functions during the period of captivity, but upon withdrawal of the Passenger nearly every recollection goes too. There is only a slight residue, a gritty film of faint and ghostly memories. The mount is never precisely the same person afterwards; though he cannot recall the details of his experience, he is subtly changed by it.

I try to recall.

A girl? Yes: lipstick on the butts. Sex, then, here in my room. Young? Old? Blonde? Dark? Everything is hazy. How did my borrowed body behave? Was I a good lover? I try to be, when I am myself. I keep in shape. At thirty-eight, I can handle three sets of tennis on a summer afternoon without collapsing. I can make a woman glow as a woman is meant to glow. Not boasting; just categorizing. We have our skills. These are mine.

But Passengers, I am told, take wry amusement in controverting our skills. So would it have given my rider a kind of delight to find me a woman and force me to fail repeatedly with her?

I dislike that thought.

The fog is going from my mind now. The medicine prescribed by Central works rapidly. I eat, I shave, I stand under the vibrator until my skin is clean. I do my exercises. Did the Passenger exercise my body Wednesday and Thursday mornings? Probably not. I must make up for that. I am close to middle age, now; tonus lost is not easily regained.

I touch my toes twenty times, knees stiff.

I kick my legs in the air.

I lie flat and lift myself on pumping elbows.

The body responds, maltreated though it has been. It is the first bright moment of my awakening: to feel the inner tingling, to know that I still have vigor.

Fresh air is what I want next. Quickly I slip into my clothes and leave. There is no need for me to report to work today. They are aware that since Tuesday afternoon I have had a Passenger; they need not be aware that before dawn on Friday the Passenger departed. I will have a free day. I will walk the city's streets, stretching my limbs, repaying my body for the abuse it has suffered.

I enter the elevator. I drop fifty stories to the ground. I step out into the December dreariness.

The towers of New York rise about me.

In the street the cars stream forward. Drivers sit edgily at their wheels. One never knows when the driver of a nerarby car will be borrowed, and there is always a moment of lapsed coordination as the Passenger takes over. Many lives are lost that way on our streets and highways; but never the life of a Passenger.

I begin to walk without purpose. I cross Fourteenth Street, heading north, listening to the soft violent purr of the electric engines. I see a boy jigging in the street and know he is being ridden. At Fifth and Twenty-second a prosperous-looking paunchy man approaches, his necktie askew, this morning's *Wall Street Journal* jutting from an overcoat pocket. He giggles. He thrusts out his tongue. Ridden. Ridden. I avoid him. Moving briskly, I come to the underpass that carries traffic below Thirty-fourth Street toward Queens, and pause for a moment to watch two adolescent girls quarreling at the rim of the pedestrian walk. One is a Negro. Her eyes are rolling in terror. The other pushes her closer to the railing. Ridden. But the Passenger does not have murder on its mind, merely pleasure. The Negro girl is released and falls in a huddled heap, trembling. Then she rises and runs. The other girl draws a long strand of gleaming hair into her mouth, chews on it, seems to awaken. She looks dazed.

I avert my eyes. One does not watch while a fellow sufferer is awakening. There is a morality of the ridden; we have so many new tribal mores in these dark days.

I hurry on.

Where am I going so hurriedly? Already I have walked more than a mile. I seem to be moving toward some goal, as though my Passenger still hunches in my skull, urging me about. But I know that is not so. For the moment, at least, I am free.

Can I be sure of that?

Cogito ergo sum no longer applies. We go on thinking even while we are ridden, and we live in quiet desperation, unable to halt our courses no matter how ghastly, no matter how self-destructive. I am certain that I can distinguish between the condition of bearing a Passenger and the condition of being free. But perhaps not. Perhaps I bear a particularly devilish Passenger which has not quitted me at all, but which merely has receded to the cerebellum, leaving me the illusion of freedom while all the time surreptitiously driving me onward to some purpose of its own.

Did we ever have more than that: the illusion of freedom?

But this is disturbing, the thought that I may be ridden without realizing it. I burst out in heavy perspiration, not merely from the exertion of walking. Stop. Stop here. Why must you walk? You are at Forty-second Street. There is the library. Nothing forces you onward. Stop awhile, I tell myself. Rest on the library steps.

I sit on the cold stone and tell myself that I have made this decision for myself.

Have I? It is the old problem, free will versus determinism, translated into the foulest of forms. Determinism is no longer a philosopher's abstraction: it is cold alien tendrils sliding between the cranial sutures. The Passengers arrived three years ago. I have been ridden five times since then. Our world is quite different now. But we have adjusted even to this. We have adjusted. We have our mores. Life goes on. Our governments rule, our legislatures meet, our stock exchanges transact business as usual, and we have methods for compensating for the random havoc. It is the only way. What else can we do? Shrivel in defeat? We have an enemy we cannot fight; at best we can resist through endurance. So we endure.

The stones steps are cold against my body. In December few people sit here.

I tell myself that I made this long walk of my own free will, that I halted of my own free will, that no Passenger rides my brain now. Perhaps. Perhaps. I cannot let myself believe that I am not free.

Can it be, I wonder, that the Passenger left some lingering command in me? Walk to this place, halt at this place? That is possible too.

I look about me at the others on the library steps.

An old man, eyes vacant, sitting on newspaper. A boy of thirteen or so with flaring nostrils. A plump woman. Are all of them ridden? Passengers seem to cluster about me today. The more I study the ridden ones, the more convinced I become that I am, for the moment, free. The last time, I had three months of freedom between rides. Some people, they say, are scarcely ever free. Their bodies are in great demand, and they know only scattered bursts of freedom, a day here, a week there, an hour. We have never been able to determine how many Passengers infest our world. Millions, maybe. Or maybe five. Who can tell?

A wisp of snow curls down out of the gray sky. Central

had said the chance of precipitation was slight. Are they riding Central this morning too?

I see the girl.

She sits diagonally across from me, five steps up and a hundred feet away, her black skirt pulled up on her knees to reveal handsome legs. She is young. Her hair is deep, rich auburn. Her eyes are pale; at this distance, I cannot make out the precise color. She is dressed simply. She is younger than thirty. She wears a dark green coat and her lipstick has a purplish tinge. Her lips are full, her nose slender, high-bridged, her eyebrows carefully plucked.

I know her.

I have spent the past three nights with her in my room. She is the one. Ridden, she came to me, and ridden, I slept with her. I am certain of this. The veil of memory opens; I see her slim body naked on my bed.

How can it be that I remember this?

It is too strong to be an illusion. Clearly this is something that I have been *permitted* to remember for reasons I cannot comprehend. And I remember more. I remember her soft gasping sounds of pleasure. I know that my own body did not betray me those three nights, nor did I fail her need.

And there is more. A memory of sinuous music; a scent of youth in her hair; the rustle of winter trees. Somehow she brings back to me a time of innocence, a time when I am young and girls are mysterious, a time of parties and dances and warmth and secrets.

I am drawn to her now.

There is an etiquette about such things, too. It is in poor taste to approach someone you have met while being ridden. Such an encounter gives you no privilege; a stranger remains a stranger, no matter what you and she may have done and said during your involuntary time together.

Yet I am drawn to her.

Why this violation of taboo? Why this raw breach of etiquette? I have never done this before. I have been scrupulous.

But I get to my feet and walk along the step on which I have been sitting until I am below her, and I look up, and automatically she folds her ankles together and angles her knees as if in awareness that her position is not a modest one. I know from that gesture that she is not ridden now.

My eyes meet hers. Her eyes are hazy green. She is beautiful, and I rack my memory for more details of our passion.

I climb step by step until I stand before her.

"Hello," I say.

She gives me a neutral look. She does not seem to recognize me. Her eyes are veiled, as one's eyes often are just after the Passenger has gone. She purses her lips and appraises me in a distant way.

"Hello," she replies coolly. "I don't think I know you."

"No. You don't. But I have the feeling you don't want to be alone just now. And I know I don't." I try to persuade her with my eyes that my motives are decent. "There's snow in the air," I say. "We can find a warmer place. I'd like to talk to you."

"About what?"

"Let's go elsewhere, and I'll tell you. I'm Charles Roth."

"Helen Martin."

She gets to her feet. She still has not cast aside her cool neutrality; she is suspicious, ill at ease. But at least she is willing to go with me. A good sign.

"Is it too early in the day for a drink?" I ask.

"I'm not sure. I hardly know what time it is."

"Before noon."

"Let's have a drink anyway," she says, and we both smile.

We go to a cocktail lounge across the street. Sitting face to face in the darkness, we sip drinks, daiquiri for her, bloody mary for me. She relaxes a little. I ask myself what it is I want from her. The pleasure of her company, yes. Her company in bed? But I have already had that pleasure, three nights of it, though she does not know that. I want something more. Something more. What?

Her eyes are bloodshot. She has had little sleep these past three nights.

I say, "Was it very unpleasant for you?"

"What?"

"The Passenger."

A whiplash of reaction crosses her face. "How did you know I've had a Passenger?"

"I know."

"We aren't supposed to talk about it."

"I'm broadminded," I tell her. "My Passenger left me some time during the night. I was ridden since Tuesday afternoon."

"Mine left me about two hours ago, I think." Her cheeks color. She is doing something daring, talking like this. "I was ridden since Monday night. This was my fifth time."

"Mine also."

We toy with our drinks. Rapport is growing, almost without the need of words. Our recent experiences with Passengers give us something in common, although Helen does not realize how intimately we shared those experiences.

We talk. She is a designer of display windows. She has a small apartment several blocks from here. She lives alone. She asks me what I do. "Securities analyst," I tell her. She smiles. Her teeth are flawless. We have a second round of drinks. I am positive now that this is the girl who was in my room while I was ridden.

A seed of hope grows in me. It was a happy chance that brought us together again so soon after we parted as dreamers. A happy chance, too, that some vestige of the dream lingered in my mind.

We have shared something, who knows what, and it must have been good to leave such a vivid imprint on me, and now I want to come to her conscious, aware, my own master, and renew that relationship, making it a real one this time. It is not proper, for I am trespassing on a privilege that is not mine except by virtue of our Passengers' brief presence in us. Yet I need her. I want her.

She seems to need me, too, without realizing who I am. But fear holds her back.

I am frightened of frightening her, and I do not try to press my advantage too quickly. Perhaps she would take me to her apartment with her now, perhaps not, but I do not ask. We finish our drinks. We arrange to meet by the library steps again tomorrow. My hand momentarily brushes hers. Then she is gone.

I fill three ashtrays that night. Over and over I debate the wisdom of what I am doing. But why not leave her alone? I have no right to follow her. In the place our world has become, we are wisest to remain apart.

And yet—there is that stab of half-memory when I think of her. The blurred lights of lost chances behind the stairs, of girlish laughter in second-floor corridors, of stolen kisses, of tea and cake. I remember the girl with the orchid in her hair, and the one in the spangled dress, and the one with the child's face and the woman's eyes, all so long ago, all lost, all gone, and I tell myself that this one I will not lose, I will not permit her to be taken from me.

Morning comes, a quiet Saturday. I return to the library, hardly expecting to find her there, but she is there, on the steps, and the sight of her is like a reprieve. She looks wary, troubled; obviously she has done much thinking, little sleeping. Together we walk along Fifth Avenue. She is quite close to me, but she does not take my arm. Her steps are brisk, short, nervous.

I want to suggest that we go to her apartment instead of to the cocktail lounge. In these days we must move swiftly while we are free. But I know it would be a mistake to think of this as a matter of tactics. Coarse haste would be fatal, bringing me perhaps an ordinary victory, a numbing defeat within it. In any event her mood hardly seems promising. I look at her, thinking of string music and new snowfalls, and she looks toward the gray sky.

She says, "I can feel them watching me all the time. Like vultures swooping overhead, waiting, waiting. Ready to pounce."

"But there's a way of beating them. We can grab little scraps of life when they're not looking."

"They're *always* looking."

"No," I tell her. "There can't be enough of them for that. Sometimes they're looking the other way. And while they are, two people can come together and try to share warmth."

"But what's the use?"

"You're too pessimistic, Helen. They ignore us for months at a time. We have a chance. We have a chance."

But I cannot break through her shell of fear. She is paralyzed by the nearness of the Passengers, unwilling to begin anything for fear it will be snatched away by our tormentors. We reach the building where she lives, and I hope she will relent and invite me in. For an instant she wavers, but only for an instant: she takes my hand in both of hers, and smiles, and the smile fades, and she is gone, leaving me only with the words, "Let's meet at the library again tomorrow. Noon."

I make the long chilling walk home alone.

Some of her pessimism seeps into me that night. It seems futile for us to try to salvage anything. More than that: wicked for me to seek her out, shameful to offer a hesitant love when I am not free. In this world, I tell myself, we

should keep well clear of others, so that we do not harm
anyone when we are seized and ridden.

I do not go to meet her in the morning.

It is best this way, I insist. I have no business trifling with
her. I imagine her at the library, wondering why I am late,
growing tense, impatient, then annoyed. She will be angry
with me for breaking our date, but her anger will ebb, and
she will forget me quickly enough.

Monday comes. I return to work.

Naturally, no one discusses my absence. It is as though I
have never been away. The market is strong that morning.
The work is challenging; it is mid-morning before I think of
Helen at all. But once I think of her, I can think of nothing
else. My cowardice in standing her up. The childishness of
Saturday night's dark thoughts. Why accept fate so pas-
sively? Why give in? I want to fight now, to carve out a
pocket of security despite the odds. I feel a deep conviction
that it can be done. The Passengers may never bother the
two of us again, after all. And that flickering smile of hers
outside her building Saturday, that momentary glow—it should
have told me that behind her wall of fear she felt the same
hopes. She was waiting for me to lead the way. And I stayed
home instead.

At lunchtime I go to the library, convinced it is futile.

But she is there. She paces along the steps; the wind slices
at her slender figure. I go to her.

She is silent a moment. "Hello," she says finally.

"I'm sorry about yesterday."

"I waited a long time for you."

I shrug. "I made up my mind that it was no use to come.
But then I changed my mind again."

She tries to look angry. But I know she is pleased to see
me again—else why did she come here today? She cannot
hide her inner pleasure. Nor can I. I point across the street
to the cocktail lounge.

"A daiquiri?" I say. "As a peace offering?"

"All right."

Today the lounge is crowded, but we find a booth somehow. There is a brightness in her eyes that I have not seen
before. I sense that a barrier is crumbling within her.

"You're less afraid of me, Helen," I say.

"I've never been afraid of you. I'm afraid of what could
happen if we take the risks."

"Don't be. Don't be."

"I'm trying not to be afraid. But sometimes it seems so hopeless. Since *they* came here—"

"We can still try to live our own lives."

"Maybe."

"We have to. Let's make a pact, Helen. No more gloom. No more worrying about the terrible things that might just happen. All right?"

A pause. Then a cool hand against mine.

"All right."

We finish our drinks, and I present my Cedit Central to pay for them, and we go outside. I want her to tell me to forget about this afternoon's work and come home with her. It is inevitable, now, that she will ask me, and better sooner than later.

We walk a block. She does not offer the invitation. I sense the struggle inside her, and I wait, letting that struggle reach its own resolution without interference from me. We walk a second block. Her arm is through mine, but she talks only of her work, of the weather, and it is a remote, arm's-length conversation. At the next corner she swings around, away from her apartment, back toward the cocktail lounge. I try to be patient with her.

I have no need to rush things now, I tell myself. Her body is not a secret to me. We have begun our relationship topsy-turvy, with the physical part first; now it will take time to work backward to the more difficult part that some people call love.

But of course she is not aware that we have known each other that way. The wind blows swirling snowflakes in our faces, and somehow the cold sting awakens honesty in me. I know what I must say. I must relinquish my unfair advantage.

I tell her, "While I was ridden last week, Helen, I had a girl in my room."

"Why talk of such things now?"

"I have to, Helen. You were the girl.".

She halts. She turns to me. People hurry past us in the street. Her face is very pale, with dark red spots growing in her cheeks.

"That's not funny, Charles."

"It wasn't meant to be. You were with me from Tuesday night to early Friday morning."

"How can you possibly know that?"

"I do. I do. The memory is clear. Somehow it remains, Helen. I see your whole body."

"Stop it, Charles."

"We were very good together," I say. "We must have pleased our Passengers because we were so good. To see you again—it was like waking from a dream, and finding that the dream was real, the girl right there—"

"No!"

"Let's go to your apartment and begin again."

She says, "You're being deliberately filthy, and I don't know why, but there wasn't any reason for you to spoil things. Maybe I was with you and maybe I wasn't, but you wouldn't know it, and if you did know it you should keep your mouth shut about it, and—"

"You have a birthmark the size of a dime," I say, "about three inches below your left breast."

She sobs and hurls herself at me, there in the street. Her long silvery nails rake my cheeks. She pummels me. I seize her. Her knees assail me. No one pays attention; those who pass by assume we are ridden, and turn their heads. She is all fury, but I have my arms around hers like metal bands, so that she can only stamp and snort, and her body is close against mine. She is rigid, anguished.

In a low, urgent voice I say, "We'll defeat them, Helen. We'll finish what they started. Don't fight me. There's no reason to fight me. I know, it's a fluke that I remember you, but let me go with you and I'll prove that we belong together."

"Let—go—"

"Please. Please. Why should we be enemies? I don't mean you any harm. I love you, Helen. Do you remember, when we were kids, we could play at being in love? I did; you must have done it too. Sixteen, seventeen years old. The whispers, the conspiracies—all a big game, and we knew it. But the game's over. We can't afford to tease and run. We have so little time, when we're free—we have to trust, to open ourselves—"

"It's wrong."

"No. Just because it's the stupid custom for two people brought together by Passengers to avoid one another, that doesn't mean we have to follow it. Helen—Helen—"

Something in my tone registers with her. She ceases to struggle. Her rigid body softens. She looks up at me, her tearstreaked face thawing, her eyes blurred.

"Trust me," I say. "Trust me, Helen!"

She hesitates. Then she smiles.

* * *

In that moment I feel the chill at the back of my skull, the sensation as of a steel needle driven deep through bone. I stiffen. My arms drop away from her. For an instant I lose touch, and when the mists clear all is different.

"Charles?" she says. *"Charles?"*

Her knuckles are against her teeth. I turn, ignoring her, and go back into the cocktail lounge. A young man sits in one of the front booths. His dark hair gleams with pomade; his cheeks are smooth. His eyes meet mine.

I sit down. He orders drinks. We do not talk.

My hand falls on his wrist, and remains there. The bartender, serving the drinks, scowls but says nothing. We sip our cocktails and put the drained glasses down.

"Let's go," the young man says.

I follow him out.

THE BOTTICELLI HORROR

LLOYD BIGGLE, JR.

Even from a thousand feet the town looked frightened.

It lay tense under the shimmering heat of midafternoon, a town of museum piece houses with smoke-blackened roofs that crowded closely upon one another, and of tree-lined streets that neatly sliced it into squares. It was a town out of a history book—the kind of town some people thought no longer existed.

But hundreds of such towns survived, and John Allen encountered them often, hidden away in remote valleys or rising up unexpectedly amidst rolling farm lands, like this town of Gwinn Center, Kansas. They were, all of them, so much alike that even their differences seemed similar.

Gwinn Center had other differences.

The streets were deserted. The clumsy ground vehicles that crept along the twisting black ribbon of roadway miles beyond the town were headed south, running away. Stretched across the rich green of the cultivated fields was a wavering line of dots. As Allen slanted his plane downward the dots enlarged and became men who edged forward doggedly, holding weapons at the ready.

The town was not completely abandoned. As Allen circled to pick out a landing place he saw a man dart from one of the commerical buildings, run at top speed along the center of a street, and with a final, furtive glance over his shoulder, disappear into a house. None of this surprised Allen. The message that had been plunked on his desk at Terran Customs an hour and a half before was explanation enough. The lurking atmosphere of terror, the fleeing townspeople, the grim line of armed men—Allen had expected all of that.

It was the tents that puzzled him.

They formed a square in a meadow near the edge of town, a miniature village of flapping brown and green canvas surrounding an amazing clutter of weirdly shaped contraptions of uncertain function and unknown purpose. Allen's message didn't account for the tents.

He circled again, spotted the white numbers of a police plane that was parked on one of the town's wider streets. A small group of men stood nearby in the shadow of a building. Allen completed his turn and pointed the plane downward.

Dr. Ralph Hilks lifted his nose from the scientific journal that had claimed his entire attention from the moment of their take-off and peered down curiously. "Is this the place? Where is everyone?"

"Hiding, probably," Allen said. "Those that haven't already left."

"What are the tents?"

"I haven't any idea."

Hilks grunted. "Looks as if we've been handed a hot one," he said and returned to his reading. .

Allen concentrated on the landing. They floated straight down and came to rest beside the police plane with a gentle thud.

Hilks closed his journal a second time. "Nice," he observed.

Allen cut the motor. "Thanks," he said dryly. "It has the new-type shocks."

They climbed out. The little group of men—there were four of them—had turned to watch them land. Not caring to waste time on formalities, Allen went to meet them.

"Allen is my name," he said. "Chief Customs Investigator. And this—" He paused until the pudgy, slow-moving scientist had caught up with him. "This is Dr. Hilks, our scientific consultant."

The men squared away for introductions. The tall one was Fred Corning, State Commissioner of Police. The young man in uniform was his aide, a Sergeant Darrow. A sturdy, deeply tanned individual with alert eyes and slow speech was Sheriff Townsend. The fourth man, old, wispy, with startlingly white, unruly hair and eyeglasses that could have been lifted from a museum, was Dr. Anderson, a medical doctor. All four of them were grim, and the horror that gripped the town had not left them unmarked, but at least they weren't frightened.

"You didn't waste any time getting here," the commissioner said. "We're glad of that."

"No," Allen said. "Let's not waste time now."

"I suppose you want to see the—ah—remains?"

"That's as good a place to start as any."

"This way," the commissioner said.

They moved off along the center of the street.

The house was one of a row of houses at the edge of town. It was small and tidy-looking, a white building with red shutters and window boxes full of flowers. The splashes of color should have given it a cheerful appearance, but in that town, on that day, nothing appeared cheerful.

The yard at the rear of the house was enclosed by a shoulder-high picket fence. They paused while the commissioner fussed with the fastener on the gate, and Dr. Hilks stood gaping at the row of houses.

The commissioner swung the gate open and turned to look at him. "See anything?"

"Chimneys!" Hilks said. "Every one of these dratted buildings has its own chimney. Think of it—a couple of hundred heating plants, and the town isn't large enough for one to function efficiently. The waste must be—"

The others moved through the gate and left him talking to himself.

At the rear of the yard a sheet lay loosely over unnatural contours. "We took photographs, of course," the commissioner said, "but it's so incredible—we wanted you to see—"

The four men each took a corner, raised the sheet carefully, and moved it away. Allen caught his breath and stepped back a pace.

"We left—things—just as they were," the commissioner said. "Except for the child that survived, of course. He was rushed—"

At Allen's feet lay the head of a blonde, blue-eyed child. She was no more than six, a young beauty who doubtless had already caused romantic palpitations in the hearts of her male playmates.

But no longer. The head was severed cleanly just below the chin. The eyes were wide open, and on the face was a haunting expression of indescribable horror. A few scraps of clothing lay where her body should have been.

A short distance away were other scraps of clothing and two shoes. Allen winced as he noticed that one shoe contained a foot. The other was empty. He circled to the other side, where two more shoes lay. Both were empty. Hilks was kneeling by the pathetic little head.

"No bleeding?" Hilks asked.

"No bleeding," Dr. Anderson said hoarsely. "If there had been, the other child—the one that survived—would have died. But the wounds were—cauterized, you might say, though I doubt that it's the right word. Anyway, there wasn't any bleeding."

Dr. Hilks bent close to the severed head. "You mean heat was applied—"

"I didn't say heat," Dr. Anderson said testily.

"We figure it happened like this," the commissioner said. "The three children were playing here in the yard. They were Sharon Brown, the eldest, and her little sister Ruth, who was three, and Johnnie Larkins, from next door. He's five. The mothers were in the house, and no one would have thought anything could possibly happen to the kids."

"The mothers didn't hear anything?" Allen asked.

The commissioner shook his head.

"Strange they wouldn't yell or scream or something."

"Perhaps they did. The carnival was making a powerful lot of noise, so the mothers didn't hear anything."

"Carnival?"

The commissioner nodded at the tents.

"Oh," Allen said, looking beyond the fence for the first time since he'd entered the yard. "So that's what it is."

"The kids were probably standing close together, playing something or maybe looking at something, and they didn't see the—see it—coming. When they did see it they tried to scatter, but it was too late. The thing dropped on them and pinned them down. Sharon was completely covered except for her head. Ruth was covered except for one foot. And Johnnie, maybe because he was the most active or maybe because he was standing apart a little, almost got away. His legs were covered, but only to his knees. And then—the thing ate them."

Allen shuddered in spite of himself. "*Ate* them? Bones and all?"

"That's the wrong word," Dr. Anderson said. "I would say—*absorbed* them."

"It seems to have absorbed most of their clothing, too," Allen said. "Also, Sharon's shoes."

The commissioner shook his head. "No. No shoes. Sharon wasn't wearing any, and it left the others' shoes. Well, this is what the mothers found when they came out. They're both in bad shape, and I doubt that Mrs. Brown will ever be the same again. We don't know yet whether Johnnie Larkins will recover. We don't know what the aftereffects might be when something like that eats part of you."

Allen turned to Hilks. "Any ideas?"

"I'd like to know a little more about this *thing*. Did anyone catch a glimpse of it?"

"Probably a couple of thousand people around here have seen it," the commissioner said. "Now we'll go talk to Bronsky."

"Who's Bronsky?" Allen asked.

"He's the guy that owned it."

They left Dr. Anderson at the scene of the tragedy to supervise whatever was to be done with the pathetic remains. The commissioner led the way through a rear gate and across the meadow to the tents.

Above the entrance a fluttering streamer read, JOLLY BROTHERS SHOWS. They entered, with Hilks mopping his perspiring face and complaining about the heat, Allen looking about alertly, and the others walking ahead in silence.

Allen turned his attention first to the strange apparatus that stood in the broad avenue between the tents. He saw miniature rocket ships, miniature planes, miniature ground cars, and devices too devious in appearance to identify, but he quickly puzzled out the fact that a carnival was a kind of traveling amusement park.

Hilks had paused to look at a poster featuring a row of scantily clad young ladies. "*They* look cool," he muttered, mopping his face again.

Allen took his arm and pulled him along. "They're also of unmistakable terrestrial origin. We're looking for a monster from outer space."

"This place is something right out of the twentieth century," Hilks said. "If not the nineteenth. Ever see one before?"

"No, but I've seen stuff like this in amusement parks. I guess a carnival just moves it around."

Sheriff Townsend spoke over his shoulder. "This carnival

has been coming here every year for as long as I can remember."

They passed a tent that bore the flaming title, EXOTIC WONDERS OF THE UNIVERSE. The illustrations were lavishly colored and immodestly exaggerated. A gigantic flower that Allen recognized as vaguely resembling a Venusian Meat-Eater was holding a struggling rodent in its fangs. A vine, also from Venus, was in hot pursuit of a frantic young lady it had presumably surprised in the act of dressing. The plants illustrated were all Venusian, Allen thought, though the poster mentioned lichens from Mars and a Luna Vacuum Flower.

"That isn't the place," the commissioner said. "There isn't anything in there but plants and rocks."

"I'd like to take a look," Allen said. He raised the tent flap. In the dim light he could see long rows of plastic display cases, each tagged with the bright yellow import permit of Terran Customs.

"I'll take another look later, but things seem to be in proper order," he said.

They moved on and stopped in front of the most startling picture Allen had ever seen. A girl arose genie-like from the yawning opening of an enormous shell. Her shapely body was—perhaps—human. Tentacles intertwined nervously where her hair should have been. Her hands were webbed claws, her facial expression the rigid, staring look of a lunatic, and her torso tapered away into the sinister darkness of the shell's interior.

"This is it," the commissioner said.

"*This*?" Allen echoed doubtfully.

"That's one of the things it did in the act."

Hilks had been staring intently at the poster. Suddenly he giggled. "Know what that looks like? There was an old painting by one of those early Italians. Da Vinci, maybe. Or Botticelli. I think it was Botticelli. It was called 'The Birth of Venus,' and it had a dame standing on a shell in just about that posture—except that the dame was human and not bad-looking. I wonder what happened to it. Maybe it went up with the old Louvre. I've seen reproductions of it. I may have one at home."

"I doubt that it has much bearing on our present problem," the commissioner said dryly.

Hilks slapped his thigh. "Allen! Some dratted artist has a fiendish sense of humor. I'll give you odds this *thing* comes from Venus. It'll have to. And the painting was called, 'The Birth of Venus.' From heavenly beauty to Earthly horror. Pretty good, eh?"

"If you don't mind—" the commissioner said.

They followed him into the tent. Allen caught a passing glimpse of a sign that read, "Elmer, the Giant Snail. The World's Greatest Mimic." There was more, but he didn't bother to read it. He figured that he was too late for the show.

Bronsky was a heavy-set man of medium height, with a high forehead that merged with the gleaming dome of his bald head. His eyes were piercing, angry. At the same time he seemed frightened.

"Elmer didn't do it!" he shouted.

"So you say," the commissioner said. "This is Chief-Inspector Allen. And Dr. Hilks. Tell them about it."

Bronsky eyed them sullenly.

"Do you have a photograph of Elmer?" Allen asked.

Bronsky nodded and disappeared through a curtain at the rear of the tent. Allen nudged Hilks, and they walked together toward the curtain. Behind it was a roped-off platform six feet high. On the platform was a shallow metal tank. The tank was empty.

"Where Elmer performed, no doubt," Allen said.

"Sorry I missed him," Hilks said. "I use the masculine gender only as a courtesy due the name. We humans tend to take sex for granted, even in lower life forms, and we shouldn't."

Bronsky returned and handed Allen an envelope. "I just had these printed up," he said. "I think I'll make a nice profit selling them after the act."

"If I were you," Allen said, "I'd go slow about stocking up."

"Aw—Elmer wouldn't hurt nobody. I've had him almost three years, an' if he'd wanted to eat somebody he'd started on me, wouldn't he? Anyway, he won't even eat meat unless it's ground up pretty fine, an' he don't care much for it then. He's mostly a vegetarian."

Allen took out the glossy prints and passed the top one to Hilks.

"Looks a little like a giant conch shell," Hilks said. "It's much larger, of course. What did it weigh?"

"Three fifty," Bronsky said.

"I would have thought more than that. Has it grown any since you got him?"

Bronsky shook his head. "I figure he's full grown."

"He came from Venus?"

Bronsky nodded.

"I don't recall any customs listing of a creature like this."

Allen was studying the second print. It resembled—vaguely—the painting on the poster. The shell was there, as in the first photo, and protruding out of it was the caricature of a shapely Venus. The outline was hazy but recognizable.

The other photos showed other caricatures—an old bearded man with a pipe, an elephant's head, an entwining winged snake, a miniature rocket ship—all rising out of the cavernous opening.

"How do you do it?" Hilks asked.

"*I* don't do it," Bronsky said. "Elmer does it."

"Do you mean to say your act is genuine? That the snail actually forms these images?"

"Sure. Elmer loves to do it. He's just a big ham. Show him anyone or anything, and the first thing you know he's looking just like that. If you were to walk up to him, he'd think it over for a few seconds and then he'd come out looking pretty much like you. It's kind of like seeing yourself in a blurred mirror. I use that to close my act—I get some guy up on the stage and Elmer makes a pretty good reproduction of him. The audience loves it."

Hilks tapped the photo of the distorted Venus. "You didn't find a live model for that."

"Oh, no," Bronsky said. "Not for any of my regular acts. I got a young artist fellow to make some animated film strips for me. I project them onto a screen above the stage. The audience can't see it, but Elmer can. He makes a real good reproduction of that one—the snake hair twists around and the hands make clawing motions at the audience. It goes over big."

"I'll bet," Hilks said. "What does Elmer use for eyes?"

"I don't know. I've wondered about that myself. I've never been able to find any, but he sees better than I do."

"Is it a water creature or a land creature?"

"It doesn't seem to make much difference to him," Bronsky said. "I didn't keep him in water because it'd be hard to tote a big tank of water around. He drank a lot, though."

Hilks nodded and called the commissioner over. "Here's how I see it. Superficially, Elmer resembles some of the

terrestrial univalve marine shells. That's undoubtedly decep-
tive. Life developed along different lines on Venus, and up
until now we've found no similarity whatsoever between
Terran and Venusian species. That doesn't mean that accidental similarities can't exist. Some of the Terran carnivores
produce an acid that etches holes in the shells of the species
they prey on. Then there's the common starfish, which
paralyzes its victim with acid and then extrudes its stomach
outside its body, wraps it around the victim, and digests it.
Something like that must have happened to the kids. An
acid is the only explanation for the effect of cauterization,
and the way their bodies were—absorbed, the doctor said, a
very good word—means that the digestive agent has a terrifying corrosive potency. The only puzzling thing about it is
how this creature could move fast enough to get clear of the
tent and all the way over to that house and surprise three
agile children. Frankly, I don't understand how it was able
to move at all, but it happened, and it isn't a pleasant thing
to think about."

"How did Elmer get away?" Allen asked Bronsky.

"I don't know. We'd just finished a show, and I closed the
curtains and saw the people out of the tent, and then I went
back to the stage and he was gone. I didn't know he could
move around. He never tried before."

"No one saw him after that?" Allen asked the commissioner.

The commissioner shook his head.

"May I see Elmer's license?" Allen asked Bronsky.

Bronsky stared at him. "Elmer don't need no license!"

Allen said wearily, "Section seven, paragraph nine of the
Terran Customs Code, now ratified by all world governments. Any extra-terrestrial life form brought to this planet
must be examined by Terran Customs, certified harmless,
and licensed. Terran Customs may, at its discretion, place
any restrictions it deems necessary upon the custody or use
of such life. Did Elmer pass Terran Customs?"

Bronsky brightened. "Oh. Sure. This guy I bought Elmer
from, he said all that stuff was taken care of and I wouldn't
have any trouble."

"Who was he?"

"Fellow named Smith. I ran into him in a bar in San Diego.
Told him I was in show business, and he said he had the
best show on Earth in this warehouse. He offered to show it
to me, and I walked into his room where there wasn't
nothing but a big shell, and the next thing I knew I was

looking at myself. I knew it was a natural. He wanted twenty-five grand, which was all the money I had, and I wrote him a check right on the spot. The very next day Elmer and I were in business, and we did well right from the start. As soon as I got enough money together to have the film strips made we did even better. I got a receipt from this guy Smith, and he certified that the twenty-five grand included all customs fees. It's in a deposit box in Phoenix."

"Did Smith give you a Terran Customs license for Elmer?" Bronsky shook his head.

Allen turned away. "Place this man under arrest, Commissioner."

Bronsky yelped. "Hey—I haven't done anything! Neither has Elmer. You find him and bring him back to me. That's your job."

"My job is to protect the human race from fools like you."

"I haven't done anything!"

"Look," Allen said. "Ten, twelve years ago there was a serious famine in Eastern Asia. It took all the food reserves of the rest of the world to keep the populations from starving. There was no harvest of cereal crops for two years, and it all happened because a young space cadet brought home a Venusian flower for his girl. It was only a potted plant— nothing worth bothering customs about, he thought. But on that plant were lice, Venusian lice. Not many Venusian insects would thrive in Earth's atmosphere, but these did, and they had the food supplies of Japan and China ruined before we knew they were around. By the time we stopped them they were working into India and up into the Democratic Soviet. We spent a hundred million dollars, and finally we had to import a parasite from Venus to help us. That parasite could eventually do as much harm as the lice. It'll be decades before the whole mess is cleaned up.

"We have dozens of incidents like this every year, and each one is potentially disastrous. Even if Elmer didn't kill those kids, he could be carrying bacteria capable of decimating the human race. This is something for you to think about in the years to come. The minimum prison term for having unlicensed alien life in your possession is ten years. The maximum is life."

Bronsky, stricken silent, was led away by Sergeant Darrow.

"Do you suppose there really was a Smith?" the commissioner asked.

"It's likely. There've been a lot of Smiths lately. It was a mistake for the government to dump those surplus space-ships on the open market. A lot of retired spacers picked them up expecting to make a fortune freighting ore. They couldn't make expenses, so some of them took to smuggling in anything they could pick up, figuring that there'd be a nice profit in souvenirs from outer space. Unfortunately, they were right. Who's this?"

A dignified, scholarly-looking man entered the tent and stood waiting by the entrance.

"Did you want something?" the commissioner asked.

"I'm Professor Dubois," the man said. "You probably don't remember me, but a short time ago you were asking if anyone had seen that perfidious snail. I haven't seen it, but I can tell you one of the places it went. It broke open one of my display cases and ate an exhibit."

"Ah!" Allen exclaimed. "You'll be from the Exotic Wonders of the Universe. You say the snail ate one of the 'Wonders'?"

"I don't know what else would have wanted it that badly."

"What was it?"

"Venusian moss."

"Interesting. The snail's been on Earth nearly three years, and it probably missed its natural diet. Let's have a look."

A plastic display case at the rear of the tent had been ripped open. Inside lay a bare slab of mottled green rock—Venusian rock.

"When did it happen?" Allen asked.

"I couldn't say. Obviously at a time when the tent was empty."

"None of your customers noticed that a Wonder was missing?"

He shook his head. "They'd think the rock was the ex-hibit. It's about as interesting as the moss. There wasn't much to it but the color scheme—yellows and reds and blacks with a kind of a sheen."

"And so friend Elmer likes moss. That's an interesting point, since Bronsky claims the snail was by preference a vegetarian. Thank you for letting us know. If you don't mind, we'll take charge of this case. We might be able to let you have it back later."

"It's ruined anyway. You're welcome to it."

"Would you look after it, Commissioner? Just see that no

one touches it until our equipment arrives. I want a close look at some of these Wonders."

The commissioner sighed. "If you say so. But I can't help thinking you two aren't acting overly concerned about this thing. You've been here the best part of two hours, and all you've done is walk around and look at things and ask questions. I've got three hundred men out there in the fields, and what we're mostly worried about is how we're supposed to handle this snail if we happen to catch him."

"Sorry," Allen said. "I should have told you. I have five divisions of army troops being flown in. They're on their way. The corps commander will place this entire county under martial law as soon as he touches down. Another five divisions are under stand-by orders for use when and if the general thinks he needs them. We have a complete scientific laboratory ordered, we've drafted the best scientists we can lay our hands on, and we're reserving one of the Venus frequencies for our own use in case we need information from the scientific stations there. Alien life is unpredictable, and we've had some bitter experiences with it. And—yes, you might say we're concerned about this."

From somewhere in the darkness came the snap of a rifle, and then another, and finally a rattling hum as the weapon was switched to full automatic.

"I didn't expect that," Allen said.

"Why not?" Hilks asked.

"These are regular troops. They shouldn't be shooting at shadows."

"Maybe word got around about what happened to the kids."

"Maybe." Allen went to the door of their tent. Corps Headquarters was a blaze of light; the remainder of the encampment was dark, but the men were stirring nervously and asking one another about the shooting. The full moon lay low on the horizon, silhouetting the orderly rows of tents.

"What were you muttering about just now?" Allen asked.

"I'm still trying to figure out how Elmer got his six-foot shell from one tent to another, and smashed that display, and ate the moss, and got himself across fifty yards of open ground and over a fence into that yard and grabbed off the kids before they saw him coming, and then got clean away. It's enough to make a man mutter."

"It was a much better trick than that," Allen said. "He also did it without leaving any marks. You'd think an object that large and heavy would crush a blade of grass now and then, but Elmer didn't. Which really leaves only one explanation."

"The damned thing can fly."

"Right," Allen said.

"How?"

"It's the world's greatest mimic. Bronsky says so. When it feels like it, it can make like a bird."

Hilks rejected the suggestion profanely. "It must be jet-propelled," he said. "Our own squids can do it in water. It's theoretically possible to do it in air, but in order to lift that much weight, it'd have to pump—let's see, cubic capacity, air pressure—what are you doing?"

"Going back to bed. I'd like to get some sleep, but between the army's shooting and your snoring—did you send a message to Venus?"

"Yes," Hilks said. "I asked for Elmer's pedigree."

"I'll give you two-to-one Venus has never heard of him."

Hilks reflected. "I think fifty-to-one would be fairer odds."

Allen closed his eyes. Hilks continued to mutter. He would not be able to sleep until he had reduced the jet-propelled Elmer to a satisfactory mathematical basis. Allen considered it a waste of time. He had no faith in Earth mathematics when applied to alien life forms.

Hilks turned on a light. A moment later his portable computer hummed to life. Allen turned over and kicked his blanket aside. The night was distressingly warm.

Footsteps crunched outside their tent. A tense voice snapped, "Allen? Hilks?"

"Come in," Allen said. Hilks continued to mutter and to punch buttons on the computer.

The tent flap zipped open, and a very young major stood blinking in at them. "General Fontaine would like to see you."

"Do we have time to dress, or is the general in a hurry?"

"I'd say he's in a powerful hurry."

Allen pulled on his dressing gown and slipped on a pair of shoes. Hilks was out of the tent ahead of him, shuffling along in his pajamas. The camp seemed suddenly wide awake, with voices coming from every tent.

They found General Fontaine in his operations headquarters pacing up and down in front of a map board. An overlay of colored scribbles identified troop positions. The general had aged several years since that afternoon. Obviously he had not been to bed, and he wore the weary, frustrated look of a man who has just realized that he might not get to bed.

Allen felt sympathetic. The general was young, but he seemed competent, and doubtlessly he had mastered command functions and the campaigns of ancient wars and thought himself ready to fight a war of his own, despite the fact that land warfare had gone the way of the internal combustion engine and the electric light.

Now fate had provided an opportunity, perhaps the only one that would come his way in his entire military career, and he found himself maintaining a defensive position against an oversized alien mollusk. It was enough to make a military man weep, and General Fontaine looked as though he would do that as soon as he found time.

"I've lost a man," he announced to Allen.

"How?" Allen asked.

"He's disappeared."

"Without a trace?"

"Not exactly," the general said. "He left his shoes."

Despite strict orders that sentries were to stand duty in pairs, the missing man, Private George Agazzi, had been posted alone on the edge of a small wood. Nearby sentries heard him shout a challenge and then open fire. They could not leave their posts to investigate, but Agazzi's sergeant was on the spot within minutes.

A patrol searched the wood and found no trace of the missing man. Reinforcements were called out, and the search was expanded. Half an hour later a staff officer found Agazzi's rifle, sundry items of equipment, and his shoes in tall grass less than six feet from his post. None of the searchers had seen them.

"Want to have a look?" the general asked.

Hilks shook his head. "In the morning, perhaps. We've already seen something similar, and I doubt that there's anything to be learned there tonight. Perhaps you'd better put three men on a post."

"You think this snail got Agazzi?"

"I'm sure of it."

"He wasn't the best-disciplined soldier in my corps, but he was tough, and he knew how to handle himself. He fired a full clip of atomic pellets, and that would make mincemeat out of any snail. It doesn't make sense. I'd be inclined to think he's gone A.W.O.L. if it weren't for one thing."

"Right," Hilks said. "He wouldn't have left his shoes."

They returned to their tent, and Allen lay awake with the camp stirring around him and sifted through the few facts he had collected. He could not fit them together. He examined each one carefully, testing it, pushing it aside, trying it again. Either he desperately needed more facts, or—could it be that he already had too many?

Patrols passed their tent, and occasionally the soldiers' muttered remarks were sharp enough to be understood. "How often does this thing get hungry?" one wanted to know. Allen wished he knew the answer. He lay awake until dawn, wearily projecting his thoughts against the rumble of Hilks's snoring and the vast restlessness of the camp. Finally reveille sounded, and a short time later he heard the crunch of marching feet as the soldiers went to breakfast.

Allen had worn his facts threadbare, and he could think of only one avenue of exploration still open to him. He had to interview young Johnnie Larkins, who had, through chance or agility, lost only his legs to the thing from Venus. Allen fervently hoped he had lived to tell about it.

General Fontaine established a "Contaminated Zone" centering about the town of Gwinn Center. The first problem, as he saw it, was to contain the thing within this zone. The second problem was to find it and destroy it.

He ringed the zone with armed men and attempted to move all civilians out. Some of the carnival people and a few other crotchety individuals refused to go, one of them being Dr. Anderson. Allen advised against the use of force, so the general contented himself with gloomily forecasting their probable fate and allowed them to remain.

Allen found Dr. Anderson in his home, which was also his office. The front room was a waiting room furnished with comfortable, antique-looking chairs. On the door to the inner office a small sign read, "Doctor is in. Please be seated." Allen ignored it and knocked firmly on the door.

Dr. Anderson emerged with a scowl of stern disapproval on his wrinkled face. "Oh," he said. "It's you. What d'ya want?"

Allen told him. The doctor's scowl deepened, and he

said, "Office hours. I couldn't leave before noon, and I'd
have to be back by two."

"I rather doubt that you'll be having any patients this
morning, Doctor. Gwinn Center's population has been reduced to something like two dozen and all of them are
staying home."

"Matter of principle," the doctor said.

"If this mess isn't cleared up, you may never have any
patients. I'm hoping that the boy can help us."

Dr. Anderson stroked one withered cheek and continued
to scowl. Finally, with an abrupt motion, he turned to the
sign on the door and reversed it. "Doctor is out," it read.

"I'll get my hat," he said.

They walked out to the street together, and Allen handed
the doctor into his plane. He turned for a last look about
the abandoned town and felt a twinge of alarm as somewhere far down the street a door slammed. "There should
be troops stationed in town," he told himself. "I'll speak to
the general about it."

They flew south. The doctor continued to grumble until
Allen patiently explained a second time that the boy would
undoubtedly feel more comfortable answering questions with
a familiar face present, and then he sulkily settled down to
watch the scenery.

Langsford was a modern city, with tall apartment buildings rising from its park-like residential sections. The hospital was part of a vast service complex at the center of the
city, a low, web-like structure with narrow, sprawling wings.
All of the inner rooms opened into plastic-domed parks.

They found the boy outside his room laughing gaily, a
squirrel perched on each arm of his powered chair and a
flock of brightly colored birds fluttering about him. The
birds flew into a nearby tree when they approached. The
squirrels remained motionless.

"Hello, Johnnie," Dr. Anderson said.

The boy smiled at the doctor and then turned large,
brown, extremely serious eyes on Allen.

"Found yourself a couple of pets, I see," the doctor said.

"They're my friends," Johnnie said and ceremoniously
offered each squirrel a nut.

"Mr. Allen wants to ask you some questions about your
accident. Do you feel like talking about it?"

"I don't know much about it," the boy said.

"Can you tell me what happened?" Allen asked.

The boy shook his head. "We were playing. Sharon and Ruthie and me. Then it grabbed me. I couldn't get away. It hurt."

"What did it look like?"

"A rug," the boy said.

Allen pondered that. "What sort of rug?"

"A real pretty rug. It was sailing through the air, and it landed on us."

"What color was it?"

The boy hesitated. "Lots of colors."

Allen scratched his head and tried to envision a sailing, multicolored rug. "A big rug?" he asked.

"Real big."

"As big as a blanket?"

The boy frowned. "Not a real big blanket, I guess."

Dr. Anderson spoke in a low voice. "You can pinpoint the size by the area it covered."

Allen didn't agree, but he smiled and continued his questions. "How high did it fly, Johnnie?"

"Don't know," the boy said.

"Was it attached to something?"

The boy looked puzzled.

"I mean, was it fastened onto something?"

"Don't know."

"Okay, Johnnie. We want to try and catch that rug before it hurts someone else. You've been a help. If you should remember anything else about it, you tell your doctor, and he'll see that I'm told."

They walked away and left the boy with the motionless squirrels.

"Dratted waste of time," Dr. Anderson said.

"Perhaps. There's the matter of colors to consider. Could Elmer make himself different colors? The photos I saw were black and white."

"He could," the doctor said.

"You're sure about that?"

"I was one of the people he did an imitation of. This fellow Bronsky called me up on that platform. I only went out of curiosity. Then that dratted snail did an imitation of me. Made me feel like a dratted fool. But I was wearing a black suit and a red necktie, and it didn't have any trouble with those colors. Showed me wearing a black suit and a red necktie."

"Then that part is all right. As for the part about flying

through the air—I wonder if it can come out of its shell and fly around. That would—perhaps—explain things."

"Don't see what there is to be explained," the doctor grumbled. "Catch the thing and do away with it before it eats someone else. Explain about it afterward if you think you have to."

The doctor had nothing more to say, not even when Allen landed him back in Gwinn Center. He shrugged off Allen's thanks and marched resolutely through his front door. Through the window Allen saw him reverse the sign to read, "Doctor is in. Please be seated." He disappeared into his inner office and closed the door firmly.

When Allen got back to base camp he found that the laboratory plane had arrived, a gigantic old converted transport. The scientists Hilks had requisitioned had also begun to report, but many of them would have little to do until someone brought in Elmer, dead or alive, for them to work on.

Hilks had set up an office for himself in what had been the navigation room, and he looked thoroughly at home as he waved a cigar with one hand and a piece of paper covered with alarmingly shaped symbols with the other. Two of the newly arrived scientists were waving their own symbols in reply.

"The trouble is," Hilks announced to Allen, "all the experts we need are on Venus, because if they stayed here they'd have so little Venusian life to study that they wouldn't be experts. And if we were to ask them to dash back here to help us cope with one so-called snail, they'd laugh us right out of the Solar System. Did you get anything?"

"Maybe," Allen said. He transferred a pile of books from a chair to the table and seated himself. "Elmer is more talented than we'd thought. He decks himself out in technicolor. The doctor saw him on display and verifies that. And the injured boy says Elmer looked like a pretty rug flying through the air."

"We figured he had to fly," Hilks said.

"Yeah. But that youngster is no dunce, and if he saw a big shell come whizzing through the air, I don't think he'd call it a rug."

"What do you want us to do?"

"We've got to come up with something that'll help Fontaine capture it and keep it captured."

"Uh huh," Hilks said, scowling. "I've been studying the report on Private Agazzi. He did empty a full clip at whatever it was he saw, and his officer thinks he was a good enough shot to hit what he aimed at. Add the fact that while you were gone a patrol spotted Elmer skimming across a field. They called is skimming. He vanished into a large grove of trees, and I do mean vanished. The general had a regiment standing by for just that contingency, and he dropped them around the grove in nothing flat. That was two hours ago, and they still haven't found anything."

"Are any of them missing?"

Hilks shook his head. "Maybe Elmer hasn't had time to get hungry again. We've come up with a thought that's somewhat less than pleasant. Elmer might be able to reproduce all by himself, and if he likes Earth enough to start populating the planet with baby snails, this continent could become a rather unpleasant place to live."

"Have you come up with anything at all?"

"Sure. One of the boys has designed a nifty steel net to be dropped out of a plane—if Elmer is ever spotted from a plane. We're also working on some traps, but it's a little hard to decide what to use for bait, since the only thing Elmer seems to like to eat is people. We might ask for volunteers and put cages inside the traps. Touchy proposition, we don't know what sort of a cage would keep Elmer out, just as we also don't know what sort of trap would keep him in."

"Did you do anything with that plastic display case Elmer broke into?" Allen asked.

"No," Hilks said. "I had it brought over here, but I completely forgot about it. Let's go look at it now. Meyers, find someone who knows something about Venusian moss and fungus and related subjects. Since Elmer likes that particular moss enough to break a display case to get it, maybe we could use it for bait."

"Never mind," Allen said. "We're slipping on this thing, Hilks. That exhibit was licensed, so Terran Customs will have a complete file on it. I'll ask for a report."

Allen copied the license number and called his office from the plane's communications room, using his own emergency channel. Ten minutes later he bounded wildly into Hilks's office.

"What's the matter?" Hilks demanded.

"Everything. Get this Professor Dubois over here and fast. That exhibit was never registered. The license is a forgery."

The professor waved his arms excitedly. "I never dreamed!" he exclaimed. "I have been extremely careful with all of my exhibits. It does not pay not to be careful. But you must admit that the license looks genuine."

"You say you bought the exhibit on the West Coast," Allen said. "Tell us about it."

"Let's see—it was maybe three years ago. I was showing in upstate California. Fellow came in one day and said he was breaking up his own exhibit and had a few things left to sell. He made them sound good, and I went all the way to San Diego to see what he had. It really wasn't bad stuff—it would have been a good basic collection for someone starting out, but there wasn't anything there that would have helped my collection. I took that one because I hated to waste a trip and he made me a good price. And it was a pretty thing."

"Could you describe this man?"

"I doubt it. It's been a long time. His name? Oh—that I remember. It was Smith."

"Describe this 'moss' again, please."

"Well, like I said, it was pretty stuff. Vivid colors, red and black and yellow and white without any special pattern. It had a nice sheen to it—looked like a hunk of thick blanket."

"Or a hunk of rug?" Allen suggested.

"Well, yes. I suppose you could say rug."

Allen backed over to a chair and sat down heavily. "The fact that it was small and thick means nothing. 'Thick' things sometimes unfold into objects many yards square. Hilks, take a look at that case. Take a good look. I want to know if it was smashed by something breaking into it, or by something breaking out of it."

Hilks bent over the case. "It bulges," he announced. "If the snail could apply suction, it might have made it bulge this way."

Allen went to have a look. "The sides bulge, too," he said. "It looks as though something inside applied force in all directions, and the top gave first."

Hilks nodded slowly. "Yes, it does look that way. Without a demonstration to the contrary by the snail, I'd say that something broke out of here."

Allen returned to his chair. For twenty years he had been studying Venus and all things Venusian, assimilating every scrap of information and every voluminous report that came his way. Now he could rearrange his facts, and this time he could make them fit.

"Ever hear of a Venusian Night Cloak?" he asked.

They shook their heads.

"You have now. Tell General Fontaine to call off his snail hunt. This problem may be a lot worse than we'd thought."

They sat around a table in the large upper room of the lab plane—Allen, Hilks, General Fontaine, and Professor Dubois. Hilks's scientists had crowded into the room behind them.

Allen started the projector. The screen erupted a Venusian jungle, its blanched vegetation having a revolting, curdled appearance through the steaming mist. The camera shifted upward, taking in a square of greenish sky. In the distance, just above the seething treetops, appeared a blob of color. It enlarged slowly as it sailed toward them, a multicolored flat surface that rippled and twisted and curled in flight.

"That's it!" the professor exclaimed. "The markings are just like my moss."

It came on until it filled the screen. Suddenly it plummeted away, and the camera followed it until it disappeared into the jungle.

Allen switched off the projector. "Officially that's the closest anyone has got to one," he said. "Now we know otherwise. My feeling is that a number of scientists missing and presumed dead in the Great Doleman Swamp got rather too close to a Night Cloak."

The professor looked stricken. "This—my moss—killed those innocent children?"

"None of our facts fit the snail. All of them fit the Night Cloak."

"Why do they call it a Night Cloak?" the general asked.

"It was first observed at night, and it seems most active then. It grows to an enormous size, and as far as anyone on Venus knows—and don't forget there's a lot of the planet to be explored yet—it is found only in the Great Doleman Swamp. That's the reason so little is known about it. A jungle growing in a swamp isn't the easiest place for field work, and a Venusian jungle is impossible. Stations on the edge of the swamp occasionally observe the Night Cloaks, but always from a distance. They seem to be a unique life form, and the scientists were naturally curious about them.

Twice expeditions were sent out to capture a specimen, and both parties disappeared without a trace. No one thought to blame the Night Cloaks—there are enough other things in that swamp that can do away with a man, especially some of the giant amphibians.

"This film strip was shot by a lucky pilot who happened to be hanging motionless over the swamp. A Night Cloak won't approach a moving plane. The scientific reports contain little but speculation. Frankly, gentlemen, we already know more about the Night Cloak than Venus does, and we're going to have to learn in a hurry something Venus hasn't discovered in a hundred years of field work: how to catch one."

"This fellow Smith caught one," Professor Dubois said.

"It was obviously a young one, and it's possible that they have periods of dormancy when one could be picked up easily—fortunately for Smith. Something about being transported and placed in Earth's atmosphere kept it dormant. It's our misfortune that it didn't die."

General Fontaine was drumming on the table with his fingers. "You say we know more about them than Venus knows. Just what do we know?"

"We know that you can't shoot one. Private Agazzi probably punched a lot of holes in it, but how would you aim at vital organs of a creature thirty feet square and who knows what fraction of an inch thick? We know that it has strength. It broke that plastic display case apart. We know a few unpleasant things about its diet and how it ingests food. We even know that its victims are likely to leave their shoes behind, which may or may not be a vital bit of information. And we know that our contaminated zone isn't worth a damn because a Night Cloak can fly right over the ground troops and probably already has."

"I'll have to call up all the planes I can get ahold of," the general said. "I'll have to reorganize the ground troops so I can rush them in when the thing is sighted."

"Excuse me, sir," said the young scientist named Meyers. "What was that you said a moment ago about shoes?"

"Just a little peculiarity of our Night Cloak," Allen told him. "It will totally consume a human body, and it doesn't mind clothing, but shoes absolutely do not appeal to it. It eats the feet and stockings right out of them, sometimes, but it leaves the shoes. I don't know what it means, but it's one positive thing we do know."

"Just a moment," Meyers said. He pushed his way out of the room and ran noisily down the stairway. He returned waving a newspaper. "I picked this up when I came through Langsford this morning," he said.

He passed the paper to Allen, who glanced at the headline and shrugged. "Monster still at large."

"That isn't exactly news to us," General Fontaine said.

"It's down at the bottom of the page," Meyers said. "A woman went for a walk last night and disappeared. They found her handbag in a park on the edge of Langsford, and a short distance away they found her shoes."

The general sucked in his breath sharply and reached for the paper. Hilks leaned back, folded his hands behind his head, and looked at the ceiling.

"Langsford," Allen said slowly. "Forty miles. But it also got Private Agazzi last night."

"If we make this public, it'll start a panic," General Fontaine said. "We'll have to evacuate the eastern half of the state. And if we don't make it public—"

"We'll have to make it public," Allen said.

"I'll have to order in my five reserve divisions. I'll need them for police work, and I'll need their transport to get the people out. God knows how far that thing may have gone by now."

"Message from Venus," a voice called. It was handed to Hilks, who read it and tossed it onto the table disgustedly.

"I asked Venus about the mollusk. They've checked all their records, and as far as they know it has no Venusian relatives. They ask, please, if we will kindly send it along to them when we're finished with it, preferably alive. They'd like to study it."

General Fontaine got to his feet. "Shall I take care of the news release?" he asked Allen.

"I'll handle it," Allen said and reached for a piece of paper. He studied a map for a moment, and then he wrote, "Notice to the populations of Kansas, Oklahoma, Arkansas, Missouri, Iowa, Nebraska, and Colorado."

For five days Allen sat at a desk in the lab plane answering inquiries, sifting through reports and rumors, searching vainly for a fact, an idea, that he could convert into a weapon. The lab's location was changed five times and he hardly noticed the moves.

The list of victims grew with horrifying rapidity. A farmer at work in his fields, a housewife hurrying along a quiet

street to visit a friend, a sheriff's deputy investigating a
report of looting in an abandoned town, an off-duty soldier
who left his bivouac area for reasons best known to himself—
Allen compiled the list, and Hilks added the shoes to his
collection.

"This may not be the half of it," Allen said worriedly.
"With so many people on the move, it'll be weeks before we
get reports on everyone that's missing."

General Fontaine's Contaminated Area doubled and
tripled and tripled again. On the third day the Night Cloak
was sighted near the Missouri-Kansas border, and the populations of four states were in panicky flight.

That same night old Dr. Anderson got a call through to
Allen from Gwinn Center. "That dratted thing is fussing
around my window," he said.

"That can't be," Allen told him. "It was sighted two
hundred miles from there this afternoon."

"I'm watching it while I talk to you," the doctor said.

"I'll send someone right away."

They found Dr. Anderson's shoes near a broken window,
directly under the sign that read, "Doctor is in."

The next morning an air patrol sighted an abandoned
ground car just across the Missouri border. It landed to
investigate and found mute evidence of high tragedy. A
family of nine had been fleeing eastward. The car had
broken down, and the driver got out to make repairs. At
that moment the horror had struck. In and around the car
were nine pairs of shoes.

Hilks was losing weight, and he had also lost much of his
good-natured nonchalance. "That thing *can't* travel that
fast," he said. "The car must have been sitting there for a
couple of days."

"Fontaine has traced it," Allen told him. "The family left
home yesterday afternoon, and it'd have reached the place
the car was found about ten o'clock last night."

"That's when the doctor called."

"Right," Allen said.

Lieutenant Gus Smallet was one small cog in the enormous observation grid General Fontaine hung over eastern
Kansas and western Missouri. His plane was a veteran road-
hopper, a civilian model pressed into service when the general received emergency authority to grab anything that

would fly. It was armed only with a camera that Smallet had supplied himself.

Smallet flew slowly in a straight line, his plane being one of a vast formation of slow-moving observation planes. It was his third day on this fruitless search, his third day of taking off into the pre-dawn darkness and flying until daylight faded, and he was wondering which he would succumb to first, fatigue or boredom. His head ached. Other portions of his anatomy ached worse, especially that which had been crushed against an uncomfortable, thinly padded seat for more hours than Smallet cared to remember. His movements had become mechanical, his thoughts had long since taken flight to other, more pleasant subjects than a Venusian Night Cloak, and he had stopped asking himself whether he would recognize the damned thing if he happened to see it.

Suddenly, against the dark green of a cluster of trees, he glimpsed a fleck of color. He slipped into a shallow dive, staring hypnotically as the indistinct blur grew larger and took on shape.

A bellow from his radio jolted Smallet back to reality. His sharp-eyed commanding officer, whose plane was a speck somewhere on the horizon, was telling him to stop horsing around and keep his altitude.

"I see the damned thing!" Smallet shouted. "I see—"

What he did see so startled him that he babbled incoherently and did not realize until afterward that he had instinctively flipped the switch on his camera. It was well that he had done so. His story was received with derision, and his commanding officer sniffed his breath suspiciously and muttered words that sounded direly like *Courts-Martial*.

Then the developed film was brought in, and what Smallet had seen was there for all to gape at.

Not one Night Cloak, but five.

It was dark by the time the transports started pouring ground troops into the area. They lost seven men that night and saw nothing at all.

Solly Hertz was an ordinance sergeant with ability, imagination, and a commanding officer who sought to hide him under the proverbial bushel. Good ordinance men, as the old saying went, did not come off assembly lines.

So when Hertz told his captain that he wanted to go to division ordinance to discuss an idea he had about these Night Cloak things, the captain paled at the thought of losing the one man who could keep his electronic equipment operating. He confined Hertz to the company area and mopped his brow over the narrow margin of his escape.

Hertz went A.W.O.L., by-passed division and corps and army, and invaded the sanctuary of the supreme air commander. That much-harassed general encountered Hertz through the accident of seeing a squad of military police leading him away. Fortunately he had enough residual curiosity to inquire about the offense and ask Hertz what he wanted.

"One of your guys sees one of these Night Cloaks," Hertz said. "What's he supposed to do about it?"

"Blast it," the general said promptly.

"Won't do any good," Hertz said. "Slugs and shrapnel just punch holes in it, and that don't bother it none. And a contact fuse wouldn't even go off when it hit. It's like shooting at tissue paper."

"You think you can do something about that?" the general asked.

"I got an atomic mini-rocket with a proximity fuse. It'll trigger just before it hits the thing. It'll *really* blast it."

"You're sure it won't go off at the wrong time and cost me a pilot?"

"Not the way I got it fixed."

"How many have you got?"

"One," Hertz said. "How many do you want?"

"Just for a starter, about five thousand. Tell me what you need and get to work on it."

Captain Joe Carr took off the next morning equipped with two of Hertz's rockets. Before he entered his plane he crossed fingers on both hands and spat over his left shoulder. And once inside the plane he went through a brisk ceremony of clicking certain switches on and off with certain predetermined fingers. Having thus dutifully sacrificed to the goddess of luck, he was not at all surprised an hour later when he sighted a Night Cloak.

It was a big one. It was enormous, and Carr glowed with satisfaction as he made a perfect approach, fired one rocket, and circled to see if another was needed.

It was not. The enormous, rippling surface was suddenly seared into nothingness—almost. The rocket hit it dead center, and when Carr completed his turn he saw the Night Cloak looking, as he said later, like the rind off a piece of bologna.

But even as he yelped news of his triumph into the radio, the rind collapsed crazily and parted, and four small, misshapen Night Cloaks flew gently downward to disappear into the trees.

Private Edward Walker was thinking about shoes. Night Cloaks never ate shoes. Flesh and bones and clothing and maybe even metal, but not shoes. That was official.

"All right," Walker told himself grimly. "If one of those things comes around here, I'll kick the hell out of it."

He delivered a vicious practice kick and felt very little the better for it; and the truth was that Private Edward Walker had excellent reason for his uneasiness.

His regiment was deployed around a small grove of trees. Two Night Cloaks had been sighted entering the trees. The place had been kept under observation, and as far as anyone knew they were still there, but the planes hovering overhead, and the cautious patrols of lift-equipped soldiers that looped skittishly over the grove, from one side to the other, had caught no further glimpse of them.

Walker had put in an hour of lift-patrolling himself, and he hadn't liked it. He had the uncomfortable feeling, as he floated over the trees and squinted down into the shadows, that someone was using him for bait. This was maybe excusable if it promised to accomplish anything, but so far as anyone knew these Cloaks had the pernicious habit of taking the bait and never getting caught. The casualty list was growing with appalling speed, the Cloaks were getting fat—or at least getting bigger—and not one of them had been destroyed.

But the brass hats had tired of that nonsense and decided to make a stand. This insignificant grove of trees could well be the Armageddon of the human race.

Walker's captain had been precise about it. "If these things go on multiplying, it means the end of humanity. We've got to stop them, and this is the place and we're the guys to do it."

The men looked at each other, and a sergeant was bold enough to ask a question. "Just how are we going to knock them off?"

"They're working that out right now," the captain said. "I'll let you know as soon as I get the Word."

That had been early morning. Now it was noon, and they were still waiting for the Word. Private Walker felt more like bait with each passing minute. He looked again at his indestructible shoe leather. "I'll kick the hell out of them," he muttered.

"Walker!" his sergeant bellowed. "You going off your nut? Sit down and relax."

Walker walked toward the sergeant. "It's true, isn't it? That business about the Cloaks not eating shoes?"

Sergeant Altman took a cautious glance at his own shoes and nodded.

"Shoes are made out of leather," Walker said. "Why don't we make us some suits out of leather? And gloves, too?"

The sergeant scratched his head fretfully. "Let's talk to the captain."

They talked to the captain. The captain rushed the two of them off to see a colonel, and in no time at all they were in the hallowed presence of a general, a big, intense man whose glance chilled Walker to the soles of his feet and who paced irritably back and forth while Walker stammered his fanciful question about leather suits and gloves.

When he finished, the general stopped pacing. "Congratulations, Private Walker," he said. "Someone should have thought of this three weeks ago, but no one did. It's men like you who make our army great. I'll see that you get a medal for this, and I'll also see that you get all the leather you want."

They saluted and turned away, both of them stunned at the realization that they'd been granted the honor of testing Walker's idea. It didn't help when they heard the general say, just before they passed out of hearing, "Darned silly notion. Do you think it'd work?"

Dusk was dropping down on them when the "leather" arrived. Walker slipped on a leather jacket and boots that reached his knees. He wrapped pieces of leather around his upper legs and tied them on with strips of leather. He fashioned a rough leather skirt for himself, ignoring the snickers of those watching. Five others did the same—three privates, the sergeant and the captain. The captain tossed leather hats to them, and gloves, and Walker carefully worked the sleeves of his jacket down into the gloves.

"All right," the captain said. "This will have to do. If it works they'll design a one-piece leather suit with something to protect the face, but we'll have to show them that it works. Let's get in there before it's too dark to see."

The grove was already ringed with lights that laced the half-darkness with freakish shadows as far as they were able to penetrate. The captain arranged them in a tight formation, himself in the lead and the sergeant bringing up the rear. A quick glance to see that all was ready, a nod, and they worked their way forward.

After an advance of ten yards the captain held up his hand. They stopped, and Walker, in his position on the right flank, looked about uneasily—up, down, sideways. A light breeze stirred the treetops high overhead. From the sky came the hollow buzz of a multitude of planes. The noise had a remote, unreal quality.

The captain signaled, and they moved on. Someone stumbled and swore, and the captain hissed, "Silence!"

They reached the far side of the grove and turned back. The tension had lifted somewhat; they spread out and began to walk faster. Walker suddenly realized that he was perspiring under the leather garments, that his inner clothing was sopped with sweat.

"I could do with a bath," he muttered, and the captain silenced him with a wave of his hand.

At the center of the grove they wheeled off at an angle. Walker became momentarily separated from the others when he detoured around a dense clump of bushes. There was a warning shout, and as he whirled the Night Cloak was upon him.

He shielded his face with one arm and swung a clenched fist. His hand punched a gaping hole, and he withdrew it and swung again. There was almost no resistance to his blows, and he riddled the pulsating, multicolored substance that draped over him. He had a momentary feeling of exultation. The leather worked. It was protecting him, and he would fix this Cloak but good. He punched and clawed and tore, and huge pieces came away in his grasp. Someone was beside him trying to tear the Cloak away, and he had a glimpse of a furious battle with the other Night Cloak taking place a short distance away.

Then he was completely enveloped, and he screamed with agony as a searing, excruciating pain encircled one knee and then the other. There were several hands fumbling about him, now, pulling shreds of Night Cloak from his struggling body. He raised both arms to protect his face and became aware for the first time of a vile odor. Then the thing flowed, slithered around his arms and found his face, and he lost consciousness.

He awoke gazing at the restful pale gray ceiling of a hospital.

Someone in the next bed chuckled. "Came around, did you? It's about time."

He turned. Sergeant Altman sat on the edge of the bed grinning broadly. Both of his wrists were bandaged; otherwise he seemed unhurt. "How do you feel?" he asked.

Walker felt the bandage that covered most of his face. "It hurts like the devil," he said.

"Sure. You got a good stiff dose of it, too—around your knees and on your face. But the doc says you'll be as good as new after some skin grafts, and you're a hell of a lot better off than Lyle. It didn't get your eyes."

"What happened?" Walker asked.

"Well, the leather works good. None of us got hurt except where we weren't protected or where the Cloaks could get underneath the leather. So now they'll be making those one-piece leather suits with maybe a thick plastic to protect the face. All of us are heroes, especially you."

"What happened to the Cloaks?"

"Oh, we tore them into about a hundred pieces each."

Walker nodded his satisfaction.

"And then," Altman went on, "the pieces flew away."

Hilks had a scientific headquarters set up near what had been a sleepy little town north of Memphis. It was a deserted town, now, in a deserted countryside where no living thing moved, and the bustling activity around the lab plane seemed strangely inappropriate, like a frolic at a funeral.

John Allen dropped his plane neatly into a vacant spot among the two dozen planes that were parked nearby. He stood looking at the lab plane for a moment before he walked toward it, and when he did move it was the uncertain step of the outsider who expects at any moment to be ordered away.

At this moment the Night Cloaks were, as a general had put it that very morning, none of his business.

Two weeks previously his assignment had been cancelled and his authority transferred to the military high command. It was not to be considered a demotion or a reprimand, his superiors told him. On the contrary, he would receive a citation for his work. His competence, and his years of devotion to duty, had enabled him to quickly recognize the menace for what it was and take the best possible action. He had identified the Night Cloak on the sketchiest of evidence, and no one could suggest anything that he should have done but didn't.

But control of the investigation was passed to the military because the Night Cloaks had assumed the dimensions of a national catastrophe that threatened to become international. The nation's top military men could not be placed under the orders of a civilian employee of an extra-national organization.

"Can I continue the investigation on my own?" Allen demanded.

"Take a vacation," his chief said with a smile. "You've earned it."

So Allen had taken vacation leave and immediately returned to the zone of action. Unfortunately, he was temperamentally unsuited to the role of observer. He made suggestions, he criticized, and he attempted to prod the authorities into various kinds of action, and that morning a general had ordered him out of the Contaminated Zone and threatened to have him shot if he returned.

The lab plane was inside the Contaminated Zone, but word of Allen's banishment seemed not to have reached it. A few scientists recognized him and greeted him warmly. He went directly to Hilks's office, and there he found Hilks sitting moodily at his desk and gazing fixedly at a bottle that stood in front of him.

Allen exclaimed, "Where did you get it?"

In the bottle lay a jagged fragment, splotched red and yellow and black, that twisted and curled and uncurled.

"Didn't you hear about the great leather battle?" Hilks asked.

"I heard," Allen said.

"Great fight while it lasted. One small infantry patrol managed to convert two Cloaks into about a hundred cloaks, and this thing—" He nodded at the bottle. "This thing got left behind. It was only an inch long and a quarter of an inch wide, and it was too small to fly. I think one of the men must have stepped on the edge of a Cloak and pinched it off. Anyway, it was found afterward, so we've been studying it. I started feeding it insects, and then I gave it a baby mouse, and the thing literally grows while you watch it. Now it's grown big enough to fly, so I've stopped feeding it."

"But this is just what you needed!" Allen exclaimed. "Now you can find a way to wipe the things out!"

"Yeah? How? We've tried every poison we could think of, not to mention a nitric acid solution that Ferguson dreamed up. It seems to like the stuff. We've tried poison gases, including some hush-hush things the military flew in. You can see how healthy it looks. Now I have my entire staff trying to think up experiments, and I'm just sitting here hating the thing."

"Anything new from Venus?"

"Yeah. They found a cousin of Elmer the snail, so they kindly let us know that we could keep ours. Good joke, eh? I sent them my congratulations and told them the Night Cloaks have already eaten Elmer. Since the Cloaks absorb bones, they probably can absorb snail shells, too. Elmer's kind may be one of their favorite foods."

"What does Venus have to say about the Night Cloaks?"

"Well, they're very interested in what we've been able to tell them, and they thank us for the information. They're going to keep their research teams out of the Great Doleman Swamp until we can tell them how to cope with the things. Other than that, nothing."

"Too bad. I'd hoped they might know something."

"It's a lot worse than you realize. Venus has been so damned smug about the whole catastrophe that some of our politicians have decided to resent that. There's a movement afoot to ban travel to Venus and close down all the Venusian scientific stations. The other planets may be next, and then perhaps even the moon. After triumphantly moving out across the Solar System and hopefully taking aim at the stars, man crawls ignominiously back into his shell. Some of the pessimists think it may take us generations to handle the Cloaks, and in the meantime the Mississippi basin will become uninhabitable as far north as Minnesota and perhaps above the Canadian border in summer. Whatever happens, I'm betting that the well-dressed man will be wearing a lot of leather. The well-dressed woman, too. Do you have any bright ideas for us to work on?"

"I ran out of bright ideas on the third day," Allen said.

"If your mind isn't occupied with anything else, you might work on this one: Where are all the Night Cloaks?"

"The military seems to be keeping good track of them. That's one thing it does well."

"We have a rough tabulation of the minimum number

that should be around, and we have records of all of the sightings. As far as we can tell, about ninety percent have disappeared."

"We figured they had periods of dormancy."

"Sure. But if they're going dormant on us, why hasn't someone found a dormant Night Cloak somewhere? We're worried because we have no notion of what their range is. If they ever get established in the Central and South American jungles, it *will* take us generations to root them out."

"Do you mind if I hang around?" Allen asked. "The last friend I had on the general staff just ordered me out of the Contaminated Zone, but I don't think he'll come here looking for me."

Hilks grinned. "What have you been up to?"

"I keep giving advice even when I'm not supposed to. I raised a ruckus because I didn't see much sense in picking Night Cloaks apart just to make more and smaller Night Cloaks. And then they were designing a new leather uniform to be used in Cloak hunting, and I suggested that instead of wearing such ghastly uncomfortable armor they just give everyone a bath in tannic acid, or whatever the stuff is they use to make leather, and soak their clothing in it at the same time. That was when he threw me out. He said he had ten million scientists telling him what to do, and he had to put up with them, but he didn't have to put up with me. So—what's the matter?"

"Tannic acid?" Hilks said.

"Isn't that the stuff? Probably it'd dry up or evaporate or something and not work anyway, but I thought—"

Hilks was already on his way to the door. "Meyers!" he shouted. "Get your crew in here. We have work to do."

By coincidence Allen entered the room first. The general, looking up sharply from his desk, flushed an unhealthy crimson and leaped to his feet. "You! I told you—"

Hilks stepped around Allen. "Meet my assistant," he said. "Name of Allen."

The general sat down again. "All right. I have my orders. Hilks and three assistants. I have the protective clothing ready for you, and I have a place picked out for you and a patrol to take you there."

"Good," Hilks said. "Let's get going."

"My orders also say that I'm to satisfy myself as to the soundness of whatever it is you propose to do."

"We've developed a spray we'd like to try out on the Cloaks," Hilks said.

"What'll it do to them?"

"You know we have a specimen to work on? The spray seems to anesthetize it. Of course there's a difference between spraying a Cloak sliver in a bottle and spraying a full-sized Cloak in open air."

"You really don't know, then."

"Of course not. That's why we're making the experiment."

"You're asking me to risk the lives of my men—"

"Nope. All we want them to do is show us where the Night-Cloaks are and get out of the way. I'm not even risking the lives of my own men. Allen and I will do the testing."

The general stood up. "Tell me. I'm not asking for a prediction, damn it. Do you think this stuff might work?"

"We've had a lot of disappointments, General," Hilks said. "We're fresh out of predictions. But yes, we think it just might work."

"And if it doesn't?"

"The scientific staff will have a couple of openings. That's not much of a risk for a general to take, is it?"

The general grinned. "You're brave men. Anything you want, take it. And—good luck!"

As Allen dropped the plane into the small clearing, the pine forest took on an unexpectedly gloomy aspect. "Cover us while we're dressing," Allen said. He and Hilks climbed out and quickly slipped into the leather suits.

Meyers and another young scientist named Wilcox watched them anxiously. "Wasn't there a better place than this?" Meyers asked.

Allen shook his head. "All the other locations are swampy. Night Cloaks seem to be attracted to swamps, but I'm not. Also, they only saw two of them in this area. Two are enough for beginners like Hilks and me."

"Sure you don't want us to come along?" Meyers asked, as they donned their spray tanks.

Hilks shook his head. "One of the problems has been the total absence of witnesses. If we'd known exactly what happened with each victim, maybe we'd have solved this long ago. You're our witnesses. You're to record everything we say, and we'll try to describe it so you can understand what's happening. If we don't come back, you'll know what went wrong."

Meyers nodded unhappily. They fastened their plastic face guards, picked up the spray guns, and waved a cheerful farewell.

"No undergrowth," Allen observed as they entered the trees.

"It's a Co-op Forest," Hilks said.

"That means we're trespassing."

"So are the Night Cloaks."

They walked briskly for a couple of miles, turned, and started to circle back. "Better check in with Meyers," Allen said. "He'll be turning somersaults."

Hilks switched on his radio. "Haven't seen a thing," he announced.

"Man, you must be blind!" Meyers blurted at them. "There was one right overhead when you started out. It followed you."

They turned quickly and stared upward. For a moment they saw only the cloudless sky through the treetops, and then a blur of color flashed past.

"Okay," Hilks said. "It's flying above the trees—waiting for reinforcements, maybe. We'll keep moving toward the plane. When they attack we'll put a couple of nice big trees at our backs so they won't be able to get at us from behind. If I can find a tree as big around as I am, that is."

"Keep your radios on," Meyers said.

"Right."

They moved at a steady pace, keeping close together and taking turns looking upward.

"Two of them, now," Hilks announced. "They're circling. They look like small ones."

Two minutes later it was Allen's turn. "I just counted three," he said. "No, four. They're coming down—*get ready!*"

The Cloaks dropped through the trees with amazing speed. They plummeted, and Allen, backing up to a tree, had no time for more than the split-second observation that they were unusually small, one being no more than a yard across. All four of them curved toward him. He gave the first one the spray at ten feet and then cut it off. The Cloaks were gone.

Hilks was chuckling as he talked with Meyers. "They got one whiff of the stuff and beat it."

"Now we won't know what'll happen to the one I sprayed," Allen said.

Hilks swore. "I didn't think about that. The most we can claim is that they don't particularly like the stuff."

"Don't be too sure," Allen said. "Here they come again."

They were wary. They dipped down slowly, circled, sailed in and out among the trees. Only the small one ventured close, and it shot upward when Allen gave it a blast of spray.

"For what it's worth," Allen said, "the small ones are hungrier than the big ones."

"It figures," Hilks said.

Meyers, sitting far away in the plane, made unintelligible noises.

The Cloaks did not return immediately. Allen and Hilks peered upward searchingly, and finally Allen asked, "What do we do now?"

"Add the score and go home, I suppose. The stuff doesn't have the punch we hoped for, none of them dropped unconscious at our feet, but at the same time we can claim a limited success. It drives them off, which is more than anything else was able to accomplish. We can develop pressurized containers for self-defense and put the chemists to work making the stuff more potent. Shall we go back?"

"Not yet," Allen said. "Here they come again."

They came, and they continued to come. They seemed not to have noticed Hilks in their first rushes, but now they divided their attention and swooped down in pairs again and again. They were coming closer before they turned upward, flying through the clouds of spray. Once the small one brushed against Allen.

"They can't be *that* hungry," Hilks said.

"No. They're angry. That's what the spray does to them. It maddens them. Are you listening, Meyers?"

"We'd better get moving," Hilks said. "The spray won't last forever. Let's leapfrog. I'll cover you, and then you cover me."

Meyers cut in. "If you can find a clearing, I'll pick you up."

"We'll let you know," Hilks said. "In the meantime, keep a close watch on the forest. With them on our backs we might miss your clearing."

"Right," Meyers said.

Allen made a short dash, placed a tree at his back, and

turned to cover Hilks. The sudden movement seemed to infuriate the Cloaks. All four shot after Allen. Three of them turned away as he pointed the spray upward. The small Cloak hovered over him for a moment, taking the full, drenching blast. Then the pressure faded, the spray gun sputtered and cut off, and the Cloak fell upon Allen.

Allen thrust at it, but it encircled and clung to his arm. Hilks raced toward him, drenching both Allen and the Cloak with spray. Pain seared and stabbed at Allen's arm, and he staggered backward and fell. He must have blacked out, for he had no memory of the moment when the Cloak released him. He regained consciousness with Hilks standing over him and turning aside the Cloaks with blasts of spray. He pushed himself to a sitting position and stared down at the throbbing numbness that had been his arm.

"Are you all right?" Hilks asked anxiously. "Can you walk?"

"I—think so." Allen got up unsteadily. "My spray is gone."

"I know. You started before I did, but I can't have much left."

Allen was examining his arm.

"Bad?" Hilks asked.

"Clear to the bone in one place," Allen said. "Fortunately it's not bleeding."

"So we've learned another thing," Hilks said. "Even leather won't stop them when they're riled up or really hungry."

"Can we do anything?" Meyers asked.

"Just watch for us. We'll have to make a run for it. We'll start after their next rush. Ready?"

"Ready," Allen said.

They darted off through the trees.

But the Cloaks were after them in a fluttering rush. Hilks turned, warded them off, and they ran again.

"It's no good," Hilks panted. "My spray is almost finished. Not much pressure left. Any ideas?"

Allen did not answer. Hilks sprayed again, turned for another dash, and fell headlong over the protruding edge of a large rock. He scrambled to his feet and both of them stood staring, not at the circling Cloaks, but at the rock, which inexplicably humped up out of the ground and seemed to float away. After a dozen feet it bumped to the ground. Encrusted dirt fell away from it.

"The devil!" Allen breathed. "It's Bronsky's snail. And look at the size of it!"

"Here come the Cloaks," Hilks said. He aimed the spray gun.

But he did not use it. As the Cloaks dropped down through the trees, a tongue-like ribbon of flesh shot out from the enormous shell, broadened, folded back, and dropped to the ground with a convulsive shudder of satisfaction. And the Cloaks were gone.

They watched in fascination as the flesh heaved and twisted and finally subsided and began slowly to withdraw.

Meyers, screaming wildly into the radio, finally aroused them. "Are you all right?" he demanded.

"Sure," Hilks said. "Everything is all right now."

"What about the Cloaks?"

"They've just been eaten."

"What did you say? Beaten?"

"Eaten," Hilks said. "I have the picture now. All of it. How about you?"

Allen nodded. "The snail is the Cloak's natural enemy. Or the Cloak is its favorite food. This one was more or less happy with Bronsky until one day it smelled or otherwise sensed a Night Cloak in the vicinity. If we hadn't put an army to beating the woods and shooting at it, it probably would have eliminated the menace at once. As soon as we stopped bothering it, it started eating Cloaks, and it's been eating them ever since. That's where the missing Cloaks went. They aren't hibernating, or migrating, they're in the snail. Look how it's grown! How big did Bronsky say it was?"

"About six feet."

"It's ten feet now. At least. There's the answer to our Cloak problem. Forget the spray and the leather clothing. Clear everyone out and leave it to Elmer. Have Venus ship us the snail they have and as many more as they can find. Are you recording, Meyers?"

"Recording," Meyers said happily. "I got the whole thing. Just as the Cloaks were about to finish you off, that snail came galloping up and ate them."

"Not exactly," Allen said. "But close enough. What's Elmer doing now?"

"It sees us," Hilks said.

They watched. The pinkish flesh flowed out slowly, thickened, stood upright. Then, before their disbelieving eyes, it

suddenly took shape and color and became the snaky caricature of a once-lovely Venus.

"Allen!" Hilks hissed. "That thing has a memory! It has
the proportions wrong, but the image is still recognizable."

"It thinks we're an audience," Allen said. "So it's per-
forming. Bronsky said it was just a big ham." He walked
toward it.

"Watch yourself!" Hilks said sharply.

Allen ignored him. He approached the snail, stood close
to it, looked up at the wreathing head of Venus.

The Venus collapsed abruptly. The flesh quivered, thrust
up again, and became a hazy, misshapen caricature of John
Allen, complete with face mask, wounded arm, and dan-
gling spray gun. Somewhere behind him he heard Hilks
choking with laughter. Allen ignored him. He extended his
sound arm and solemnly shook hands with himself.

THE SHAPES

BY J. H. ROSNY AINE

(translated from the French by Damon Knight)

It was a thousand years before the beginning of that center of civilization from which Nineveh, Babylon and Ecbatana were later to spring.

The nomadic tribe of Pjehu, with its horses, asses and cattle, was crossing the wild forest of Kzur toward the west, through a slanting curtain of light. The edge of the setting sun swelled, hovered, dropped from its graceful perches.

Everyone being weary, they were all silent, searching for a good clearing where the tribe might kindle the sacred fire, prepare the evening meal and sleep in safety from wild animals, behind a double line of red-hot coals.

The clouds turned opalescent; illusory countrysides trailed away to the four horizons; the gods of night breathed their cradle song, and the tribe was still on the move. A scout came galloping back with word of a clearing and water, a pure spring.

The tribe gave three long shouts; everyone moved faster. Childish laughter rippled out; the very horses and asses, trained to recognize the nearness of a stopping-place by the return of the scouts and the nomads' cheers, raised their necks proudly.

The clearing came into view. Here, where the delightful spring had hollowed out its bed among mosses and shrubs, a phantasmagoria met the nomads' eyes.

It was, first, a great circle of translucent bluish cones, point uppermost, each nearly half the bulk of a man. A few clear streaks, a few dark convolutions were scattered across their surfaces; each one had a dazzling star near its base.

64

Farther distant, equally strange slabs stood on end, looking rather like birch bark, and spotted with varicolored elipses. Other Shapes, here and there, were almost cylindrical—some tall and thin, others low and squat, all of a bronzed color, tipped with green; and all, like the slabs, having the characteristic point of light.

The tribe stared in amazement. Even the bravest were frozen with superstitious fear, increasing still more when the Shapes began to sway in the twilight of the clearing. And suddenly, their stars wavering, flickering, the cones stretched higher, the cylinders and the slabs hissed like water thrown upon a flame, all of them moving toward the nomads with mounting speed.

Spellbound by the sight, the tribe did not move, but kept on watching. The Shapes fell upon them. The shock was terrible. Warriors, women and children fell in heaps, mysteriously struck down as if by lightning. Then the terrified survivors found strength to flee. And the Shapes, breaking their closed ranks, spread out around the tribe, implacably pursuing those who fled. Nevertheless, the frightful attack was not infallible; it killed some, stunned others, wounded none. A few red drops spurted from the nostrils, eyes and ears of the dying; but others, unhurt, soon arose and rejoined the fantastic rout.

Whatever might be the nature of the Shapes, they behaved like living creatures, not like elements of nature, having, like living creatures, an inconstancy and diversity of motion, evidently choosing their victims, not confounding the nomads with trees or shrubs, or even with animals.

In a short time the swiftest of the tribe noticed that no one was pursuing them any longer. Exhausted and in tatters, at last they dared retrace their steps toward the Mystery. Far away, between the tree trunks flooded with shadow, the resplendent chase went on. And the Shapes, seemingly by choice, ran down and massacred the warriors, often disdaining to attack the feeble, or the women and children.

Seen thus at a distance, in the night which had now fallen, the scene was more supernatural, more overwhelming to barbarian minds. About to take up their flight once more, the warriors made a vital discovery. It was this: whatever the fugitives did, *the Shapes abandoned the pursuit at a fixed boundary*. However weary and powerless the victim might be, even if he were unconscious, once he had crossed that invisible frontier, he was out of danger.

This reassuring discovery, soon confirmed by fifty observations, calmed the fugitives' frantic nerves. They dared to wait for their companions, their wives and their children who had escaped the butchery. One of them, indeed, their hero, who had been stunned at first, regained his spirit and lit a fire, blew on a buffalo horn to guide the fugitives.

Then one by one the pitiful survivors came. Many, cripples, dragged themselves by their hands.

The mothers, with indomitable maternal strength, had protected, gathered, and carried their children through the wild melee. And many asses, horses and cattle reappeared, less frightened than their masters.

A dismal night followed, passed in sleepless silence, while the warriors felt shivers run up and down their spines. But the dawn came, stealing pale through the heavy foliage; then the auroral fanfare of colors, of echoing bird cries, exhorted them to live, to cast off the terrors of darkness.

The hero, the natural leader, formed the crowd into groups and began counting the tribe. Half the warriors, two hundred, were missing. The loss of women was much less; of children, almost none.

When the counting was finished and the beasts of burden had been reassembled (few were missing, due to the superiority of instinct over reason during a crisis), the hero formed up the tribe as usual. Then, ordering everyone to wait for him, he walked, pale and alone, toward the clearing. No one dared follow him, even at a distance.

He went to where the trees were spaced out widely, a little inside the limit observed yesterday, and looked.

Far across the clearing, in the cool transparency of morning, flowed the pretty spring. Around the edges, reunited, the fantastic troop of Shapes shone resplendently. Their colors had changed. The Cones were more compact, their turquoise tint having turned greenish; the Cylinders were streaked with violet, and the Slabs looked like virgin copper. But each had its blazing star, dazzling even in daylight.

The outlines of these phantasmagorical Entities had also changed. The Cones tended to enlarge into Cylinders, the Cylinders to flatten and spread, while the Slabs curled slightly.

But suddenly, as on the night before, the Shapes swayed, their stars began to flicker; the hero, slowly, retreated beyond the borderline of safety.

The tribe of Pjehu halted at the doorway of the great nomad Tabernacle, where only chiefs might enter. In the starry depths, under the virile image of the Sun, sat the three high priests. Below them on the gilded steps, the dozen underpriests.

The hero stepped forward and recounted at length the fearful journey through the forest of Kzur; the priests listened very gravely, astonished, feeling their power dwindle before that inconceivable adventure.

The supreme high priest demanded that the tribes sacrifice to the sun twelve bulls, seven onagers, three stallions. He recognized divine attributes in the Shapes, and, after the sacrifices, he resolved upon a hieratic expedition.

All the priests, all the chiefs of the Zahelal nation, were to take part. And messengers were sent out over the mountains and the plains, for a hundred leagues around the place where later would rise Ecbatana of the magi. Everywhere the dark tale made men's hair stand on end; everywhere the chiefs responded quickly to the priestly call.

One autumn morning, the Male pierced the clouds, flooded the Tabernacle, reached the altar where the bleeding heart of a bull lay smoking hot. The high priests, the underpriests, fifty tribal chiefs raised a cry of triumph. A hundred thousand nomads, standing in the dew outside, took up the clamor, turning their tanned faces toward the miraculous forest of Kzur and shivering a little. The omen was favorable.

Thus, with the priests at their head, a whole people marched through the trees. In the afternoon, at about the third hour, the hero of the Pjehu halted the throng. The great clearing lay spread out in its majesty, glowing with autumn, a torrent of dead leaves covering its mosses. On the banks of the spring, the priests saw the Shapes which they had come to worship and appease. They were pleasant to the eye, under the shade of the trees, with their trembling color changes, the pure flames of their stars, their tranquil movements at the edge of the spring.

"We must make the offering here," said the supreme high priests, "that they may know we submit to their power!"

All the graybeards nodded. One voice was raised, nevertheless. It was Yushik, of the tribe of Nim, the young star-counter, the pale prophetic watchman, of recent fame, who boldly demanded to go nearer the shapes.

But the old men, white-haired in their wisdom, prevailed: the altar was built, the victim led forward—a dazzling white stallion. Then, in the silence of the prostrate people, the

bronze knife found the animal's noble heart. A great moan
went up. And the high priest intoned:

"Art thou appeased, O gods?"

Over there, among the silent trunks, the Shapes still moved
in a ring, brightening themselves, preferring places where
the sunbeams were thickest.

"Yea," cried the enthusiast, "they are appeased!"

And snatching up the stallion's warm heart, before the
high priest could say a word, he flung himself into the
clearing. Shouting, other fanatics followed him. The Shapes
gently swayed, crowding together, skimming the grass, then
suddenly hurled themselves on the daring ones, in a massacre that stunned the fifty tribes.

Six or seven fugitives, hotly pursued, managed to reach
the boundary. The rest were dead, Yushik among them.

"These are relentless gods!" solemnly spoke the supreme
high priest.

Then a council was held, the venerable council of priests,
elders and chiefs. They decided to put up a row of stakes
round the boundary line. In order to determine this line,
they would force slaves to expose themselves to attack by
the Shapes at one part of the perimeter after another.

And this was done. Under the threat of death, slaves
entered the ring. So careful were the precautions taken, that
few of them perished. The boundary was firmly established,
made visible to all by its line of stakes.

Thus the hieratic expedition ended successfully, and the
Zahelals believed themselves safe from the enemy.

But the preventive system advocated by the council was
not long in showing its flaws. The following spring, the
tribes of Hertoth and Nazzum, carelessly passing near the
ring of stakes, suspecting nothing, were cruelly assaulted
and decimated by the Shapes.

The chiefs who escaped the massacre told the great Zahelal
council that the Shapes were now much more numerous
than they had been the preceding autumn. Their pursuit was
still limited, but the boundary had been enlarged.

This news dismayed the people; there was great mourning
and many sacrifices. Then the council resolved to destroy
the forest of Kzur by fire.

In spite of all their efforts, they could burn no more than
the borders of the forest.

Then the priests, in despair, consecrated the forest and
forebade anyone to enter it. And many summers passed.

One October night, the sleeping encampment of the tribe
of Zulf, ten bowshots from the forbidden forest, was invaded by the Shapes. Three hundred more warriors lost
their lives.

From this day a dark, mysterious tale went from tribe to
tribe, a thing whispered by night, under the wide starry
skies of Mesopotamia. *Man was going to perish.* The *others*,
constantly expanding, in the forest, across the plains, indestructible, day by day would swallow up the overthrown
race of man. And this dark, fearful secret haunted the
brains of men, sapped their fighting strength and the confidence of their youth. The nomad, thinking such thoughts,
no longer dared take pleasure in the lush pastures of his
fathers. He turned his weary eyes upward, waiting for the
stars to halt in their courses. It was the millennial year of
this childlike people, the world's knell.

And in their distress, these thinkers turned to a bitter
cult, a cult of death preached by pale prophets, the cult of
Darknesses more powerful than the Stars, the Darknesses
which would engulf and devour the holy Light, the resplendent fire.

Everywhere at the edge of the wilderness were seen the
emaciated, immobile figures of the inspired ones, the men
of silence, who, passing from time to time among the tribes,
told of their terrible dreams, the Twilight of the great Night
to come, of the dying Sun.

Now in those days there lived an extraordinary man called
Bakhun, a member of the tribe of Ptuh and brother to the
supreme high priest of the Zahelals. In his youth he had
abandoned the nomadic life, had chosen a place in the
wilderness, between four hills, in a narrow green valley
where a spring poured out its pure song. He had built a
fixed tent of stones, a cyclopean habitation. With patience
and with the careful management of his horses and oxen, he
had achieved the opulence of regular harvests. His four
wives and thirty children lived the life of Eden there.

Bakhun professed unusual beliefs, for which he might
have been stoned, save for the respect of the Zahelals for
his elder brother, the supreme high priest.

First, he declared that the sedentary life was better than

the life of the nomads, conserving man's strength to the profit of his spirit.

Second, he believed that the Sun, the Moon, and the Stars were not gods, but luminous masses.

Third, he said that men should really believe only in those things tested by measurement.

The Zahelals credited him with magical powers, and the most daring of them sometimes risked consulting him. They never repented it. It was said that he had often helped unfortunate tribes by distributing food to them.

Now, in this dark hour, when men were faced with the melancholy choice of giving up their green lands or being destroyed by the inexorable gods, the tribes thought of Bakhun, and the priests themselves, after a struggle with their pride, sent to him a deputation made up of three of the greatest among them.

Bakhun listened with close attention to their accounts, asking them to repeat certain parts, asking many detailed questions. He asked for two days to meditate. When the time was up, he announced simply that he would dedicate his life to the study of the Shapes.

The tribes were a little disappointed, for they had hoped Bakhun might be able to deliver the land by sorcery. Nevertheless, the chiefs expressed their happiness at his decision, and hoped that great things would come of it.

Then Bakhun took up his station at the edge of the forest of Kzur, leaving it only when night fell, and all day long, mounted on the swiftest stallion in Chaldea, he watched. Soon, convinced of the splendid animal's superiority over the most agile of the Shapes, he was able to begin his bold and painstaking study to which we owe the great ante-cuneiform book of sixty tablets, the finest stone book bequeathed by the nomadic age to modern civilization.

In this book, admirable for its restraint and its patient observation, is the description of a form of life absolutely distinct from our animal and vegetable kingdoms, a form which Bakhun humbly admitted he had been able to analyze only in its grossest and most superficial features. It is impossible for a man to read without shuddering this monograph on the beings Bakhun called the Xipehuz; these dispassionate notes, never forced to fit into any system, of their actions, their modes of locomotion, of combat, of procreation —these notes which demonstrate that the human race was once on the brink of nothingness, that the Earth nearly became the patrimony of a *Kingdom* every trace of which has been lost.

The book should be read in Dessault's marvelous translation, full of unlooked-for discoveries in pre-Assyrian linguistics—discoveries unfortunately more admired in foreign countries, in England, in Germany, than in the author's native land. The eminent scholar has graciously made available the salient passages of this precious work, which are given in the following pages, and it is hoped that these passages will inspire the reader to look further into Dessault's superb translation.[1]

The Xipehuz are evidently living beings. All their motions reveal the free will, inpulsiveness, cooperation and partial independence which distinguish the animal from the plant and from nonliving matter. Although their mode of progression is impossible to describe in comparative terms—being a simple gliding motion across the ground—it is plain that it is under voluntary control. We see them stop suddenly, turn, pursue one another, stroll together by two and threes; they display preferences which will make them leave one companion to join another at a distance. They are incapable of climbing trees, but they succeed in killing birds after *attracting them* by undiscoverable means. They are frequently seen to surround forest animals or to lie in wait for them behind a bush; these they invariably kill and consume. It may be stated as a rule that they kill *all animals without distinction*, whenever they can catch them, and this without any apparent motive, for they do not devour them, but merely reduce them to ashes.

In doing so they make use of no funeral pyre; the incandescent point which each has at its base suffices them for this purpose. They form a circle of ten or twenty around the carcass of a large animal, and cause their rays to converge upon it. For small animals, birds for example, the rays of a single Xipehuz are sufficient to cause incineration. It should be noted that the heat they produce is not instantaneous in its effect. I have often received the irradiation of a Xipehuz upon my hand, and the skin began to feel warm only after a certain time.

I do not know if it is correct to say that the Xipehuz have

---

[1] *The Precursors of Nineveh,* by B. Dessault (Calmann-Levy). In the interests of clarity, I have converted the extract from the *Book of Bakhun* into modern scientific language.

different forms, for any one of them can successively transform itself into a cone, a cylinder and a slab, and this in the course of a single day. Their colors vary constantly, a fact which I believe can be attributed in general to the changes in the quality of the light from morning to evening and from evening to morning. Nevertheless certain variations seem to be due to the impulses of individuals, and in particular to their *passions*, if I may be permitted this term, and thus constitute genuine expressions of physiognomy, of which, in spite of ardent study, I have been utterly unable to identify any except by hypothesis. Thus, I have never been able to distinguish between an angry tint and a calm one, which surely would be the primary discovery in this field.

I have spoken of their *passions*. I have also remarked earlier upon their preferences, which I might term their *friendships*. They also have their *hatreds*. One Xipehuz continually keeps his distance from another, and vice versa. They seem to experience violent rages. They hurl themselves upon one another with movements identical to those observed when they attack men or large animals, and in fact it was these combats which taught me they are not immortal, as I had been at first disposed to believe, for two or three times I have seen Xipehuz succumb in these encounters, that is to say *fall, shrink,* and *petrify.* I have carefully preserved some of these bizarre cadavers,[1] and perhaps at some future time they may serve to reveal the nature of the Xipehuz. They are yellowish crystals, arranged irregularly, and streaked with blue filaments.

From the fact that the Xipehuz are not immortal, I was able to deduce that it should be possible to attack and defeat them, and at that point I began the series of martial experiments of which I shall have to speak later.

Since the Xipehuz's radiance is always sufficient to make them visible through underbrush and even behind large tree trunks—a wide halo emanates from them in all directions and warns of their approach—I was able to venture often into the forest, trusting myself to the speed of my stallion.

[1]The Kensington Museum in London, and Professor Dessault himself, have in their possession certain mineral fragments, similar in every way to those described by Bakhun, which under chemical analysis have been found impossible to *decompose* or to *combine* with other substances, and which, in consequence, cannot be assigned a place in any conventional nomenclature.

There, I tried to find out if they built shelters, but I confess to having failed in that research. They move neither stones nor plants, and appear to be strangers to any form of *tangible* and *visible* industry, the only sort which can be distinguished by human observation. Consequently they have no weapons, in the usual sense of that word. It is certain that they cannot kill at a distance: every animal which has been able to flee without coming into *direct* contact with a Xipehuz has invariably escaped, and I have witnessed this many times.

As the unfortunate tribe of Pjehu has already observed, they cannot cross certain intangible barriers; thus their movements are limited. But these limits continually expand from year to year, from month to month. I had to try to discover the cause of this.

Well, this cause appears to be nothing other than a phenomenon of *collective growth*, and like most Xipehuzian things, it is incomprehensible to the human mind. In brief, the governing principle is this: the limits of Xipehuzian movement enlarge in proportion to the number of living individuals, that is to say that when new beings are propagated, the frontiers are extended; but so long as their number does not increase, each individual is totally incapable of leaving the habitat determined—by natural forces?—for the race as a whole. This principle suggests a closer correlation between the individual and the group than that observed among other animals and men. Later we saw the reciprocal of this principle in operation, for when the numbers of Xipehuz began to diminish, their frontiers shrank in proportion.

Concerning the phenomenon of propagation itself, I have little to say, but this little is characteristic. To begin with, this propagation takes place four times a year, a little before the equinoxes and solstices, and only on very clear nights. The Xipehuz join in groups of three, and these groups draw together little by little until there is only one, tightly amalgamated and arranged in a very long ellipse. They remain so all night long, and until the Sun reaches the zenith on the following day. When they separate, vague forms arise, vaporous and *enormous*.

These forms slowly condense, dwindle, and transform themselves at the end of ten days into amber-tinted cones, considerably larger still than adult Xipehuz. It takes them two months and several days to reach their maximum development, which is to say diminution. At the end of this time, they become similar to other members of their race, their shapes and colors variable according to the weather, the time and the mood of the individual. A few days after their development of diminution is complete, the boundaries enlarge. Needless to say, it was shortly before this redoubtable moment that I kicked the flanks of my noble Kuath, in order to establish my camp farther away.

It is impossible to say whether the Xipehuz have senses as we understand the term. They certainly have organs which serve the same purpose.

The ease with which they detect the presence of animals, men above all, over great distances, makes it evident that their organs of perception are at least as efficient as our eyes. I have never seen them mistake a plant for an animal, even under circumstances in which I might well have fallen into this error, deceived by the light filtering through leaves, the color of the object, or its position. Their use of twenty to consume a large animal, whereas one alone incinerates a bird, indicates a correct understanding of proportions, and this understanding seems even more perfect when one considers that they make use of ten, twelve, fifteen, always in keeping with the relative size of the carcass. Still a better argument, either for the existence of sense organs analogous to ours, or for their intelligence, is their manner of attacking our tribes, for they give little or no attention to women and children, while they mercilessly pursue the warriors.

Now, the most important question—do they have a language? I am able to reply without the slightest hesitation, "Yes, they have a language." And this language is composed of signs, some of which I have even been able to decipher.

Suppose, for example, that a Xipehuz wishes to speak to another. For this, it suffices for him to direct the radiation from his star toward the other, a thing which is always perceived instantly. The one who is hailed, if he is in motion, stops and waits. The speaker then traces rapidly on the very skin of the listener—and it makes no difference on which side—a series of short luminous characters made by directing the radiation from his base, and these characters remain fixed a moment, then fade away.

The listener, after a short pause, responds.

As a preliminary to any action of combat or ambuscade, I have always seen the Xipehuz employ the following characters:

When I myself am in question—and this happens frequently, for they have done everything possible to exterminate us, my noble Kuath and me—the signs

have invariably been exchanged—among others, such as the word or phrase

above. The usual calling sign is

and this makes the receiving individual hasten up. When the Xipehuz are invited to a general meeting, I have never failed to observe a signal of this form

representing the triple appearance of these beings.

In addition, the Xipehuz have more complicated signs, not relating to actions similar to ours, but to a completely extraordinary order of things, and these I have been unable to decipher. One can hardly entertain any doubt of their ability to exchange *ideas* of an abstract order, probably the equivalents of human ideas, for they are capable of standing motionless for long periods, doing nothing but conversing, which indicates real accumulations of thoughts.

In spite of their metamorphoses (whose laws differ for each, only very slightly, but characteristically enough for a determined observer), during my long sojourn among them I learned to know a number of Xipehuz rather intimately by recognizing the peculiarities among their individual differences . . . should I say among their characters? I have known taciturn ones, who almost never traced a word; voluble ones who wrote veritable discourses; attentive ones, gossips who spoke at the same time, one interrupting the other. Some were of a retiring nature and preferred a solitary life; others obviously sought company; some were fierce, constantly hunting birds and beasts, and some merciful, often sparing animals and letting them live in peace. Does not all this open an enormous avenue to the imagination? Does it not lead us to imagine diversities of aptitude, strength, intelligence, analogous to those of the human race?

They practice education. How many times have I not seen an old Xipehuz, seated in the midst of many young ones, irradiating them with signs which they then repeated one after another, and which he made them do over when their repetition was imperfect!

These lessons were indeed marvelous to my eyes, and in all that concerns the Xipehuz, there is nothing that has more often fixed my attention, nothing that has preoccupied me more during my nights of insomnia. It seemed to me that here, in the morning of the race, the veil of mystery might open, that some simple, primitive idea might spring forth and illuminate for me a corner of this profound darkness. No, nothing discouraged me; year after year I watched that education, and I tried innumerable interpretations. How many times have I thought to grasp a fugitive glimmer of the essential nature of the Xipehuz, an invisible light, a pure abstraction, which, alas! my poor flesh-burdened faculties could never follow!

I have said previously that for a long time I believed the Xipehuz to be immortal. Having abandoned this belief, after seeing the violent deaths which followed some encounters between Xipehuz, I was naturally led to seek their vulnerable points, and devoted all my days from that time forward to the search for means of destruction; for the Xipehuz were growing in numbers, to such a point that, having emerged from the forest of Kzur in the south, west and north, they were beginning to encroach upon the plains in the direction of the levant. Alas! in a few cycles they would have dispossessed man from his earthly abode.

Accordingly, I armed myself with a sling, and whenever a Xipehuz emerged from the forest within my range, I took aim and hurled my stone at him. I obtained no result in this way, although I had struck my targets on every part of their surface, even including the luminous point. They appeared entirely insensible to my blows, and none ever turned aside to avoid one of my projectiles. After a month's trial I could only conclude that nothing could be done against them with the sling, and I abandoned that weapon.

I took up the bow. With the first arrows I shot, the Xipehuz betrayed an intense fear, for they turned aside, stayed out of range, and avoided me as much as possible.

For a week I did not succeed in striking one. On the eighth day, a party of Xipehuz, carried away I suppose by their enthusiasm for the hunt, passed fairly close to me in pursuit of a fine gazelle. I quickly shot several arrows, *without any apparent effect*, and the party dispersed, I pursuing them and using up my ammunition. I had barely shot my last arrow when they all turned back at full speed, from different directions, surrounding me on three sides, and I would have lost my life if not for the prodigious speed of my valiant Kuath.

This adventure left me full of hope and uncertainty; for a week I did nothing, lost in the oceanic depths of my meditations, in a subtle, absorbing, sleep-dispelling problem which filled me with joy and anguish. Why did the Xipehuz fear my arrows? Why, again, among the great number of projectiles with which I had struck the hunters, had none produced any effect? My knowledge of my enemy's intelligence ruled out the hypothesis of a terror without cause. On the contrary, everything I knew compelled me to believe that the *arrow*, under the proper conditions, must be a formidable weapon against them. But what were these conditions? What was the vulnerable point of the Xipehuz? And suddenly the thought came to me that it was the *star* that I must strike. For a moment I held this as a certainty, a blind, impassioned certainty. Then I was seized by doubt.

With the sling, had I not aimed at and struck this point many times? Why should the arrow be luckier than the stone . . . ?

Now the night had come, the measureless abyss, with its marvelous lamps strewn above the earth. And I sat lost in thought, my head in my hands, my spirit darker than the night.

A lion began to roar, jackals were running across the plain, and once again a spark of hope was born. It had just come to my mind that the single stone was relatively large, and the Xipehuz' star so tiny! Perhaps it was necessary to penetrate deeply, to pierce with a sharp point, and then their fear of the bow was understandable!

But Vega was turning slowly around the Pole, dawn was near, and for a few hours weariness conquered my thoughts with sleep.

In the days that followed, armed with the bow, I was in constant pursuit of the Xipehuz, as deep in their territory as prudence would permit. But they all avoided my assault, keeping at a distance, out of range. Lying in ambush was not to be considered; their mode of perception enabled them to detect my presence behind obstacles.

Toward the end of the fifth day, an event occurred which in itself proved that the Xipehuz, like men, are fallible and perfectible creatures. That evening, at twilight, a Xipehuz deliberately approached me, with that constantly accelerating speed which they use in the attack. Surprised, my heart beating fast, I drew my bow. He, steadily advancing, like a column of turquoise in the growing dusk, came almost within bowshot. Then, as I made ready to loose my arrow, I was stunned to see him turn his body, hiding his star, while he continued to hurtle toward me. I had barely time to put Kuath into a gallop, and retreat out of the reach of this formidable adversary.

Now this simple maneuver, which no Xipehuz appeared to have thought of before, in additon to demonstrating once more the individuality and personal inventiveness of the enemy, suggested two ideas: the first, that it was probable that I had reasoned correctly about the vulnerability of the Xipehuz star; the second, less encouraging, that the same tactic, if adopted by all, would render my task extraordinarily difficult, perhaps impossible.

Nevertheless, having labored so long to learn the truth, I felt my courage grow in the face of this obstacle, and I dared to hope that my ingenuity would be great enough to surmount it.[1]

I returned to my wilderness. Anakhre, the third son of my wife Tepai, was a potent maker of weapons. I ordered him to carve a bow of extraordinary size. He took a branch of the tree Waham, hard as iron, and the bow he made of it was four times stronger than that of the shepherd Zankann, the mightiest archer of the thousand tribes. No man living could have bent it. But I had thought of an artifice, and Anakhre having wrought according to my plan, it came about that the immense bow could be bent and loosed by a woman.

Now I had always been skilled in casting darts and ar-

---

[1]In the following chapters, of a narrative character, I have adhered closely to the literal translation of Professor Dessault, without, however, feeling bound to follow the tiresome division into verses of the needless repetitions.

rows, and in a few days I learned so perfectly the use of the weapon made by my son Anakhre that I never missed a target, be it as small as a fly or moving as swiftly as a falcon.

Having done all this, I returned to Kzur, mounted on my flame-eyed Kuath, and once more began to prowl around the enemies of man.

In order to give them confidence, I loosed many arrows with my customary bow, each time one of their parties approached the frontier, and my arrows fell far short of them. Thus they learned to know the exact range of the weapon, and from this to believe themselves absolutely out of danger at a certain distance. Nevertheless they remained mistrustful; this caused them to be mobile and agitated when they were not sheltered by the forest, and to hide their stars from my view.

By dint of patience I wore out their suspicions, and on the morning of the sixth day, a troop of them took up a position facing me, beneath a great chestnut tree, at a distance of three ordinary bowshots.

At once I loosed a cloud of useless arrows. Then their vigilance lessened more and more, and their movements became as free as in the earliest days of my sojourn.

It was the decisive moment. My heart beat so loudly that at first I felt myself strengthless. I waited for the future, hung upon a single arrow. If it failed to strike its target, never again, perhaps, would the Xipehuz offer themselves to my experiments, and then how would it be possible to know whether they were vulnerable to the blows of men?

Nevertheless, little by little my will triumphed, quieted my heart, made my limbs supple and strong and my eye steady. Then, slowly, I raised the bow of Anakhre. There, in the distance, a great cone of emerald stood motionless in the shade of the tree; its sparkling star turned toward me. The enormous bow bent; the arrow flew whistling across space . . . and the Xipehuz *fell, shrank and petrified*.

A resounding cry of triumph burst from my lips. Stretching out my arms in ecstasy, I gave thanks to the One.

So, then, they were vulnerable to humans weapons, these terrible Xipehuz! We could hope to destroy them!

Now, without fear, I let my heart murmur, I gave myself up to the beating of the music of gladness, I who had so greatly despaired of the future of my race, I who beneath the stars in their courses, beneath the blue crystal of the abyss, had so often calculated that in two centuries the vast world's limits would have burst before the Xipehuz invasion.

And yet when it came again, the well-beloved night, the pensive night, a shadow fell over my happiness, the sorrow that man and Xipehuz could not exist together, that the annihilation of one was the grim condition of the other's survival.

The priests, the elders and the chiefs had listened marveling to my story; couriers had carried the good news into the depths of the wilderness. The great Council had ordered the warriors to gather in the sixth moon of the year 22,649, in the plain of Mehur-Asar, and the prophets had preached a holy war. More than a hundred thousand Zahelal warriors came, and many members of foreign races, Dzums, Sahrs, Khaldes, came to offer themselves to the great nation.

Kzur was surrounded by a tenfold ring of archers, but all their arrows failed against the tactics of the Xipehuz, and incautious warriors perished in great numbers.

Then for several weeks great fear prevailed among men. . . .

On the third day of the eighth moon, armed with a sharp-pointed knife, I announced to the multitudes that I would go to fight the Xipehuz alone, in the hope of laying to rest the doubts which had begun to arise concerning the truth of my story.

My sons Lum, Demja and Anakhre were violently opposed to this project, and offered to go in my place. And Lum said, "You cannot go, for once you are dead, all will believe the Xipehuz are invulnerable, and the human race will perish."

Demja, Anakhre and many of the chiefs having echoed these words, I found their reasons good, and withdrew.

Then Lum, taking my horn-handled knife, crossed the frontier. The Xipehuz hastened up. One swifter by far than the rest, was about to rush upon him, but Lum, more agile than a leopard, sprang aside, circled the Xipehuz, then with a giant bound closed in again and stabbed with his sharp point.

The waiting throng saw his adversary *collapse, dwindle and petrify*. A hundred thousand voices rose to the blue dawn, and already Lum was returning, crossing the frontier. The glory of his name spread throughout the armies.

The year 22,649 of the world, the seventh day of the eighth moon.

At daybreak the horns sounded; hammers beat brazen

bells for the great battle. A hundred black buffalo and two hundred stallions were sacrificed by the priests, and my fifteen sons and I prayed to the One.

The globe of the sun was engulfed in the red dawn, the chiefs galloped in the forefront of their armies, the clamor of the attack swelled in the headlong rush of a hundred thousand warriors.

The tribe of Nazzum was first to encounter the enemy in bitter combat. Powerless at first, mowed down by invisible lightning bolts the warriors soon learned the art of striking the Xipehuz and destroying them. Then all the nations, Zahelals, Dzums, Sahrs, Khaldes, Xisoastres, Pjarvanns, roaring like oceans, invaded the plain and the forest, everywhere surrounding the silent enemy.

For a long time the battle was in chaos; messengers came continually to tell the priests that men were dying by hundreds, but that their deaths were being avenged.

In the heat of midday my swift-footed son Surdar, sent by Lum, came to tell me that for each Xipehuz destroyed, a dozen of ours had persished. My spirit was dark and my heart weak, but my lips murmured, "Let it be as the Father wills!"

In recalling to my mind the numbers of the armies, which added together gave a sum of a hundred and forty thousand, and knowing that the numbers of Xipehuz amounted to about four thousand, I told myself that more than a third of the vast army would perish, but that the earth would belong to man.

"It is a victory, then!" I murmured sadly.

But as I pondered on these things, the clamor of the battle shook the forest more violently; then great masses of warriors reappeared, all with cries of distress, fleeing toward the frontier.

Then I saw the Xipehuz emerge at the border, not separate from one another as they had been in the morning, but in groups of twenty formed into circles, with their stars turned inward. In this array, invulnerable, they advanced on our helpless warriors and massacred them.

It was defeat.

The boldest warriors thought of nothing but flight. Nevertheless, in spite of the sorrow that weighed down my spirit, I patiently observed the fatal encounters, in the hope of finding some remedy in the very heart of misfortune, for often the venom and the antidote are found side by side.

For this confidence in power of thought, destiny repaid me with two discoveries. I remarked, first, that in places where our tribes were massed in multitudes and the Xipehuz were in small numbers, the slaughter, immeasurable at first, lessened by degrees, that the strength of the enemy's blows grew less and less, many of the victims rising again after a moment's dizziness. The strongest resisted the shock completely, continuing to flee after repeated blows. The same phenomenon being in evidence at various parts of the field of battle, I dared to conclude that the Xipehuz were growing weary, that their powers of destruction were not unlimited.

The second observation which aptly complemented the first, was furnished to me by a group of Khaldes. These unfortunate men, surrounded on all sides by Xipehuz, and losing confidence in their short knives, pulled up bushes and made clubs of them, with which they tried to beat their way to freedom. To my great surprise, their attempt succeeded. I saw the Xipehuz topple by the dozen under these blows, and about half the Khaldes escaped through the hole they had opened in this way; but, curiously, those who made use of bronze implements instead of bushes (as in the case of several chiefs) killed themselves in striking the enemy. I must point out further that the blows from these clubs gave no apparent hurt to the Xipehuz, for those who fell rose again promptly and took up the pursuit. Nevertheless, I considered my double discovery of the greatest importance for future battles.

Meanwhile, the rout continued. The earth resounded to the flight of the vanquished; by nightfall, only our dead remained within the Xipehuz boundaries, and a few hundred warriors who had taken refuge in trees. The fate of these latter was terrible, for the Xipehuz burned them alive, concentrating a thousand fires in the branches which sheltered them. Their frightful cries echoed for hours under the vast firmament.

The next day, the tribes counted their survivors. The battle had cost nine thousand human lives or thereabout; a moderate estimate put the loss of Xipehuz at six hundred. Thus the death of each enemy had cost us fifteen men.

Despair settled in the hearts of the tribesmen, many crying out against the chiefs and talking of giving up the terrible enterprise. Then, under these complaints, I strode into the middle of the camp and loudly reproached the warriors for their faintheartedness. I asked them if it were better to let all men perish, or to sacrifice a part; I showed them that in ten years the Zahelal country would be invaded by the Shapes, and in twenty the country of the Khaldes, the Sahrs, the Pjarvanns and the Xisoastres; then, having reawakened their conscience in this way, I reminded them that already a sixth of the disputed territory had been reconquered, that on three sides the enemy had been driven back into the forest. Finally I told them of my observations, and made them understand that the Xipehuz were not tireless, that clubs of wood could topple them and force them to expose their vulnerable points.

Silence fell across the plain; hope returned to the hearts of the multitude who heard me. And to strengthen their confidence, I described the contrivances of wood which I had thought of, suited both for attack and defense. With renewed enthusiasm, the people applauded my words, and the chiefs laid their scepters of command at my feet.

In the days that followed, I had a great number of trees cut down, and displayed a model of a light, portable barrier, of which a brief description follows: a framework six cubits long and two cubits wide, fastened by crossbars to an interior framework one cubit wide and five long. Six men (two porters, two warriors armed with heavy, blunt wooden spears, two others also armed with wooden spears having sharp metal points, and furnished in addition with bows and arrows) could stand within it comfortably and could roam the forest, protected from the direct attack of the Xipehuz. Once within range of the enemy, the warriors armed with blunt spears were to strike and overturn them, force them to expose themselves, and the archer-spearmen were to aim at the stars, with bow or spear according to circumstance. Since the average height of the Xipehuz was a little more than a cubit and a half, I had arranged the crossbars in such a way that the exterior framework while being carried, would reach a height above the ground of no more than a cubit and a quarter, and for this it sufficed to incline somewhat the supports by which it was attached to the interior framework. In additon, since the Xipehuz were unable to surmount any steep obstacle, nor to move in any way except upright, the barrier thus devised was sufficient to give shelter against their direct assaults. Undoubtedly they would attempt to burn these new weapons, and in some cases they would succeed; but since their fires were almost ineffective out of bowshot, they would be forced to expose themselves in order to do so. Besides, since these fires did not take effect instantaneously, it would be possible to avoid them in many cases by rapid movement.

The year 22,649 of the world, the eleventh day of the eighth moon. On this day the second battle with the Xipehuz took place, and the chiefs gave me the supreme command. Then I divided the people into three armies. Shortly before dawn, I sent against Kzur forty thousand warriors armed with the barrier devices. This attack was less confused than that of the seventh day. The tribes entered the forest slowly, in small bands disposed in a good order, and the encounter began. During the first hour the advantage was entirely ours, the Xipehuz being caught off guard by the new tactics; more than a hundred Shapes were slain, while only a dozen of our warriors perished. But, once over their surprise, the Xipehuz applied themselves to burning the barriers. In some circumstances they were able to do so. A more dangerous maneuver was the one they adopted toward the fourth hour of the day: taking advantage of their swiftness, groups of Xipehuz, tightly pressed together, hurled themselves at the barriers and succeeded in overturning them. In this fashion great numbers of men perished; so many that, the enemy having regained the advantage, a part of our army fell into despair.

Toward the fifth hour, the Zahelal tribes of Khemar, Djoh, and part of the Xisoastres and Sahrs began to flee. Wishing to avert a catastrophe, I sent messengers protected by strong barriers to promise reinforcements. At the same time, I disposed the second army for the attack; but first I gave new orders: the barriers were to cluster in groups, as thickly as movement in the forest would permit, and to arrange themselves in compact squares whenever a large band of Xipehuz approached. This was to be done without giving up the offensive.

After this, I gave the signal, and in a short time I had the pleasure of seeing the battle turn in our favor. At length, toward the middle of the day, an approximate reckoning, which brought the number of our losses to two thousand men, and of the Xipehuz to three hundred, decisively showed the progress we had accomplished, and strengthened the hearts of all.

Nevertheless, the proportion changed somewhat to our disadvantage during the fourth hour, the tribes then having lost four thousand warriors, and the Xipehuz five hundred.

It was then that I sent in the third army. The battle reached its greatest intensity; the warriors' enthusiasm rose from minute to minute, until the hour when the sun was about to sink into the West.

At that moment, the Xipehuz took the offensive again to the north of Kzur; a retreat of the Dzums and Pjarvanns gave me uneasiness. Judging that in any case the darkness would be more favorable to the enemy than to us, I signaled the end of the battle. The troops returned calm and victorious; much of the night was passed in celebrating our successes. These were considerable; eight hundred Xipehuz had succumbed; their sphere of action was reduced to two thirds of Kzur. It is true that we had left seven thousand slain in the forest, but these losses were much smaller, in proportion to the result, than in the first battle. Thus, filled with hope, I dared to conceive the plan of a more decisive attack against the two thousand six hundred Xipehuz still living.

The year 22,649 of the world, the fifteenth day of the eighth moon.

When the red star rose over the eastern hills, the tribes were in battle array before Kzur.

With my heart full of hope, I gave my last instructions to the chiefs; the horns sounded, the bells set up their brazen clangor, and the first army marched against the forest.

Their barriers now were stronger and somewhat larger, enclosing twelve men instead of six, except for about a third which were constructed according to the old design. Thus they were more difficult either to set on fire or to overturn.

The beginning of the battle was promising; after the third hour, four hundred Xipehuz had been exterminated, and only two thousand men. Encouraged by the good news, I sent in the second army. The fury of the battle on both sides grew appalling, our warriors being flushed with triumph, their adversaries resisting with the stubbornness of a noble kingdom. From the fourth to the eighth hour, we sacrificed no less than ten thousand lives; but the Xipehuz paid with a thousand of theirs, so that only a thousand remained in the depths of Kzur.

From this moment, I knew that man would possess the world; my last misgivings faded.

Nevertheless, at the ninth hour, a great shadow fell over our victory. At this time, the Xipehuz appeared only in enormous masses in the clearings, concealing their stars, and it became almost impossible to overthrow them. In the

heat of the battle, many of our warriors hurled themselves
upon these masses. Then, with a rapid movement, a party of
Xipehuz would detach itself, overthrowing and slaughtering
these men.

A thousand perished thus, without any perceptible loss to
the enemy; seeing which, the Pjarvanns cried that all was
lost; a panic began which put more than ten thousand men
to flight, many being so imprudent as to abandon their
barriers in order to run faster. It cost them dear. A hundred
Xipehuz, pursuing them, cut down more than two thousand
Pjarvanns and Zahelals: terror was beginning to spread
throughout our lines.

When the messengers brought me this dismal news, I
knew that the day was lost unless by some swift maneuver
I succeeded in retaking the abandoned positions. At once I
gave the chiefs of the third army the order to attack, and I
announced that I would assume command. Then I quickly
brought these reserves to the place from which the others
had fled. Shortly we found ourselves face to face with the
pursuing Xipehuz. Carried away by the passion of their
slaughter, they did not regroup quickly enough, and in a few
moments we had surrounded them: few escaped; the great
acclamation for our victory went far to restore the courage
of our men.

From that time on, I had no trouble in re-forming the
attack; our methods were limited to detaching segments of
the enemy groups, then surrounding these segments and
annihilating them.

Soon, realizing how greatly these tactics worked to their
disfavor, the Xipehuz once more took up the assault in
small groups, and the massacre of the two kingdoms, neither of which could survive except by the annihilation of the
other, redoubled dreadfully. But all doubt of the final issue
had vanished from the faintest hearts. By the fourteenth
hour, there remained hardly five hundred Xipehuz against
more than a hundred thousand men, and this small number
of the enemy was more and more hemmed in by narrow
frontiers, about a sixth of the forest of Kzur, which greatly
facilitated our movements.

Meanwhile, the red light of sunset streamed through the
trees, and I broke off the battle.

The immensity of our victory swelled every heart; the
chiefs talked of offering me the kingship of the nations. I
counseled them never to confide the destinies of so many

men to one poor fallible creature, and to take *Wisdom* for their earthly master.

The Earth belongs to Man. Two days of combat have annihilated the Xipehuz; the whole domain occupied by the last two hundred of them has been razed, every tree, every plant, every blade of grass has been cut down. And I, aided by my sons Lum, Azah and Simho, have finished inscribing this history upon tablets of granite for the instruction of future nations.

And now I am alone, at the edge of Kzur, in the pale night. A coppery half-moon hangs over the West. Lions are roaring at the stars. The brook wanders slowly among the willows; its eternal voice speaks of time passing, of the melancholy of perishable things. And I have buried my face in my hands, and my heart mourns. For, now that the Xipehuz are no more, my soul laments for them, and I ask the One what Fatality demanded that the splendor of Life be tarnished by the Shadow of Murder!

THE CLONE

BY THEODORE L. THOMAS

clone, n. a Biol. The aggregate of individual organisms descended by asexual reproduction from a single sexually produced individual; . . . Webster's New International Dictionary, Second Ed.

Unknowing loomed the lovely city, gleaming softly in the dusk. The breezes drifted in from Lake Michigan, soaking up the heat of the day. Deep beneath the streets the cables hummed and the wires sang and the pipes gurgled. Here were the nerve fibers and the ducts of the city. And it was in the ducts that the Clone began to grow. Beneath every great city there flows streams of water rich in nutrients and minerals, and containing ample energy to supply the driving force for almost every conceivable chemical reaction. There are ground-up foods of all kinds, and soaps and detergents aplenty, and discarded medicines, spices, flavoring, colorings, inks, ointments, and cosmetics. The turbulent waters carry the astonishingly varied complex of chemical compounds that is the waste matter of any great city.

Buried under a busy intersection was a concrete collector box. Halfway up one side of the great box was a casting fault where an air bubble had become entrapped during the pouring of the concrete. In the course of time the thin shell of concrete separating the fault from the interior of the box had eroded away, leaving a cubic foot of sheltered area nestled in the wall. Here was the Pool, rock-hard womb for the Clone, kept warm by a high pressure steam line that passed near the exterior of the box.

The efforts of three widely separated people precipitated

what happened next. A bus boy scraped into the disposal unit of a restaurant a large volume of meat and vegetable scraps. In another building a late-working plumber poured into a drain his left-over muriatic acid. Two blocks away a scrubwoman dumped into a set tub the remnants of her floor-cleaning solution. All the materials coursed down through the pipes, and all entered the great collector box at the same time. A few seconds of swirling, an odd eddy, and the already rich waters of the Pool received a heavy charge of the mixture.

The Pool seethed with the stuff of life. The warm water approximated the "hot thin soup" that existed in the primordial oceans when the Earth was very young, but with some differences. The Pool waters contained materials already partially synthesized, and in greater concentration and variety. The chemical reactions started, and side by side, two microcosmic specks began to grow. In the hours that followed, the two specks grew into chromosomic chains encased in protoplasmic sheathing. The moment came when a minute thermal current in the Pool pushed the tiny flecks together; they blended and fused to become one. In that instant the Clone came into being. The time was 9:01 P.M.

The little cell divided, and then divided again. Daughter cells produced daughter cells in rapid succession, and by 12:48 A.M. the Pool was filled with nervous tissues. Differentiation began. Out over the lips of the Pool spread a quarter-inch-thick film of muscle tissue, creeping along the interior of the collector box. The fast-spreading film of tissue contained a network of tiny channels. Through the channels flowed a thin ichor containing a high concentration of two nameless enzymes. By 3:22 A.M. the collector box contained a complete lining of living tissue. The Clone entered the pipes that opened into the box and continued its growth along the pipe walls, growing with equal speed both upstream and downstream. Approximately 10 feet inside each pipe, at a joint, the Clone grew another mass of nervous tissue. The nervous tissue grew in annular shape to conform with the shape of the pipe, and its growth in no way interfered with the rapid extension of the main body; the two kinds of tissue grew simultaneously. Thenceforth, at about every 50 feet of its length the Clone produced the patch of nervous tissue.

At 6:18 A.M. a portion of the Clone turned off into its first building on the upstream side of the collector box. It grew slower—that portion of it—since there were fewer nutrients present. The character of the nervous tissue deposited inside the building was slightly different; diminished food made it so. The higher the Clone rose, the less food it found, and the more ravenous it became. It was 7:55 A.M. when the Clone made its first contact with human beings, and the incident passed almost unnoticed by others.

Maude Wendal stood scraping the breakfast dishes down the sink, and it was this that brought the Clone up the soil pipe to the Wendal apartment. The circle of tissue was not at all obvious as it ringed the sink outlet from the underside. Sunlight flooded through the window above the sink, and for the first time the Clone felt the impact of the energy in light. It was little enough, but it sufficed to activate the molecular structure of the muscular tissue. The film of tissue bulged out the opening, and the edges curved together to seal the drain. It was then that Maude Wendal saw it.

With a frown of annoyance she picked up the pot scraper and tried to push the greenish fluorescent mass out of the way. It resisted. Clicking her tongue in exasperation, she dropped the pot scraper. Then she prodded the mass with her finger.

Through the permeable cell walls flowed the enzyme-laden ichor. On contact with the proteinaceous matter of the finger the enzymes immediately broke down the existing protein and utilized the resulting amino acids to form the reversed-amide structure of the Clone itself. There was no sensation of pain in the finger, and it was several seconds before the woman realized that the finger had disappeared to be replaced by a different kind of matter. She screamed then, and lunged backward from the sink.

The Clone stretched as she pulled it away from the sink, and as it stretched, the linear polyamide structure of its body became oriented. The result was that the more the Clone stretched, the stronger it became. The woman was not able to move more than half a step back from the sink. The sudden halt jarred her, and it was a full second before she could adjust her eyesight to focus on her finger. The hand was gone, and the wrist, and part of the forearm. She screamed again.

*   *   *

Frank Wendal had been packing his sample kit, getting ready for another day of making calls. At his wife's first scream he straightened, shook his head and began to amble toward the kitchen. He came through the door at the second scream, and saw his wife pulling at what looked like a length of clothes line fastened to the bottom of the sink. "Oh for Pete's sakes," he said. He walked leisurely to her side and grasped the line with both hands.

He pulled on it, and tugged again, and then saw what was happening to his hands. Wide-eyed he looked at his wife. The Clone had taken the entire right arm and shoulder and part of the chest, and was about to engulf the head.

The human body structure contains approximately 60 percent by weight water. The structure of the Clone, on the other hand, contained only about 40 percent by weight water. As the Clone converted the nitrogen-containing materials, it utilized only that amount of water necessary to maintain its own structure. It rejected the rest. Therefore the rapidly advancing line of demarcation that separated human tissue from Clone tissue was particularly marked by large droplets of water that ran together and then flowed to the floor down Clone and human alike.

Wendal saw the dripping line disappear into his wife's dress, and he saw the dress grow gradually wetter downwards. The right upper side of the torso took on an odd shapelessness, and the dress began to collapse in on itself. The head disappeared, and she fell over. He screamed. The Clone had reached his chest.

In the next apartment the Knapps looked at each other, the screams still ringing faintly in their ears. George Knapp shook his head and said, "I don't know why they do it. Fight, fight, fight, all the time fight. Why do they put up with each other?" Shaking his head he turned back to his morning paper.

Two minutes passed. The wet clothes of the man and the woman lay on the floor of the Wendal apartment. The Clone rejected 36 pounds of water from the man, and 24 pounds from the woman, a total of 7.2 gallons of warm water. Too much to be absorbed by the clothes, the water spread out in a large puddle on the floor. The Clone took the nylon undergarments of the woman and the Dacron trousers of the man. It rejected the cotton dress of the woman and the cotton shirt and undergarments of the man. It took the shoes of both, and then there was nothing left to take. It briefly explored the polyethylene-containing wax on the floor, and the polyvinyl chloride floor tile before it swiftly withdrew to the drain. The time was 8:02 A.M.

In the buried pipes under the city, the Clone grew on. At intersections and distribution boxes it found more and more branches. It did not feed on the ample nutrients along the entire length of its body. Instead the bulk of its feeding was confined to those regions of its body which were actively engaged in growing; the static portions of its body took in relatively modest amounts of nutrition. There was, therefore, no shortage of nourishment even when the Clone underlay a full ten city blocks. It grew on with as much vigor as ever.

At 8:57 A.M. the Clone made its second contact with human beings. This time it came out of the drain in a kitchen in a restaurant. Harry Schwartz, dishwasher, stared at the actinic-activated ball of matter fluorescing greenly in the bottom of the tub. He pushed at it with his polyurethane sponge, and saw the sponge disappear into the ball. He looked around at his sidekick, Joe Martz, and said, "Hey looka this. Damn thing ate my sponge."

"Huh?" Martz stepped to his side and looked into the tub. "Why dontcha clean yer tub?" and Martz leaned over and scooped up the ball with both hands. He pulled at it and was brought up short, so he pulled again, harder. He tugged and hauled and tried to break the thin line that held him.

"Look atcha," shouted Harry Schwartz. "It's eating your hands."

Martz held his hands up before his face, and saw that they were almost gone. The band of water was advancing fast. With a yell Martz threw his weight against the Clone, and he began to run back and forth like a puppy at the end of a rope. The second cook and a bus boy and a waiter came over. Martz apparently was caught up in a sticky mass so they closed in to help him.

"Don't touch it," shouted Schwartz. "It'll eatcha."

Ignoring him, the three men grabbed the Clone and tried to pull it away from Martz. They knew immediately that they were caught, and the three men pulled with Martz to try to back away. But the Clone was growing rapidly, and it was able to pay off portions of its body so that no great strain was thrown on the rope-like section that stretched to the drain. The four men reeled across the kitchen to the far wall, and then they began to move along the wall. The Clone's body swept the kitchen, and caught the first cook and the pastry cook. Two waiters flung themselves onto the Clone and then began to struggle to get away. No one paid attention to Schwartz, dancing around the edges of the struggle yelling, "Don't touchit. Don't touchit. It'll eatcha. Don't touchit."

The noise brought other people to the kitchen. The manager took one look, and ran to telephone the police. The diners out in the dining room listened to the shouts and yells and crashes coming from the kitchen. They looked at each other nervously, and some left. Others went back to the kitchen to see what was happening that would cause so much chaos.

Water was everywhere. Martz's empty clothes were draped around a thick cylinder of greenly fluorescing material. Half consumed people lay in weird positions around the kitchen, some still struggling. Offshoots of the Clone rested on serving tables and counter tops where various foods had been, while water trickled off to the floor. It was then that the butcher entered the kitchen from the cold room. With horrified eyes he looked at the kitchen. From his position in a corner of the room two points seemed clear. All of the green matter was connected, and all of it seemed to stem from the dishwasher's tub. He stepped to the tub and was about to grasp the thin green line when Schwartz shouted to him from a corner, "Don't touchit. It'll eatcha."

The butcher stepped back and looked around. He picked up a meat cleaver and brought it down on the Clone where it passed over the edge of the dishwasher's tub. The thin green line parted.

Cut off from the nervous tissue lying back down in the pipeline, the portion of the Clone in the kitchen lost its purposefulness. It could no longer retreat down the drain. It simply lay in the kitchen continuing its absorption of nitrogen- and calcium-containing materials.

The policeman entered in time to see the last remaining portions of several bodies turn into Clone tissue. Wide-eyed he listened to Schwartz describe what had happened. Then he bolted to a phone and gave his report to the desk sergeant in some detail. Sergeant Alton listened and asked some questions, and then arranged to send several squads to the restaurant. Then he thought a moment and called the pathology department of a nearby hospital. He described what had happened to the Chief Pathologist. It was fortunate that Sergeant Alton was an intelligent man, because the telephone call to the Chief Pathologist was one of the last telephone calls that could be placed in the city. The time was 9:52 A.M.

The Clone by now had made a series of appearances. It had come out of the pipes in 22 private apartments, 10 restaurants, 25 food stores, an early morning movie house, 3 department stores, and various smaller shops, all over an eighteen-block area of the city. In the third grade room of a school an errant pupil surreptitiously poured his milk down the drain of the sink near the door. The Clone came to the drain and the pupil thrust his hand into it. In three minutes the water flooded the floor of the school room and poured over the sill and flowed down the hall and cascaded down the stairs.

The police stations, the firehouses, and the newspaper offices were jammed with telephone calls. The disbelief of the men handling the calls ended when the Clone made its appearance there.

By 10:00 A.M. some people had fled to the streets, driven out by the sights seen inside the buildings. Not knowing where to go they grabbed passersby and begged them to come and help, to do something, to do anything. Many of the people in the streets went into the buildings and were caught by the Clone, or saw others caught by the Clone.

When the Clone rose into the hospital the Chief Pathologist was one of the first to learn about it. In view of what he had learned from Sergeant Alton he immediately issued instructions over the hospital's public address system. "Leave it alone, and stay away from all plumbing. It can kill you, so leave it alone. Report to this office whenever you see it. But don't go near it."

Trained in the handling of emergencies, and used to working near death, the entire hospital staff went about its duties as though two doctors, a nurse, and two orderlies were still alive instead of being in the form of approximately fifteen gallons of warm water on the floor of Operating Room Number 2. The Chief Pathologist gathered his staff about him and spoke briefly. He split his group into three teams, and each team went to a different site in the hospital where the Clone was. For the first time the Clone was subjected to the close scrutiny of scientifically trained personnel. The time was 10:10 A.M.

Panic raged in the heart of the city. The streets were choked with people; vehicles could not pass. The radio and television stations were by this time broadcasting warnings about this thing that came out of the pipes. The Clone had entered all the broadcasting studios, and so the men doing the announcing had personal knowledge of that of which they spoke. Their emotion communicated itself to their listeners, and in the largest station of all, one of the announcers broke down on camera. The effect on the viewers was devastating.

Sound trucks manned by the police tried to bring order to the stampeding crowds, but it was no use. All the streets in the center of the city were filled with people trying to get away. In a strange community of consent, not a single person tried to use the subways. Some tried to carry with them a prized possession, a lamp, a strongbox, a set of china, a dress, only to drop it in the surging press of the crowds. It was worse for the children.

At 10:30 A.M. the mass of people had grown no thinner. The Clone now reached so far from the center of the city that it drove people out into the streets ahead of those in the center. Hot waves of panic spread in ever widening circles, nurtured by the announcements and ripened by the Clone itself. The disaster machinery of six states and the Federal Government slowly swung into action to care for the stricken city, even with no clear knowledge of what had happened. One factor stood out. The panic-driven stampede had to be brought under control.

Helicopters swung low over the jammed city streets, and powerful speakers blared at the crazed people, urging them to stop running, telling them there was no danger in the streets. Again and again the messages boomed forth, but the tearing screaming crowd could not heed. The copters landed troops on the roofs, and they immediately headed for the streets. Some were caught by the Clone, some ran back to the roofs and cowered there, and some got to the streets where they were swallowed up by the raging crowds.

At 11:02 A.M. the Chief Pathologist worked his way to the roof of the hospital and succeeded in waving down a copter. The Pathologist had with him a cotton-stoppered bottle containing a small piece of living Clone. Talking over the radio with Army headquarters he explained all he had learned about the Clone: it was a living organism; it lived in the waste pipes under the city; it absorbed nitrogen-containing and calcium-containing matter at fantastic rates of speed; and, most important of all, a solution of iodine in water killed it. Arrangements were made for the Chief Pathologist to fly to a university in another city. There a scientific group would be brought together to investigate the properties of the piece of Clone in the Pathologist's possession. The plan was put into immediate effect; the Pathologist climbed into the copter which then took off. Now the nature of the creature was known.

With all the people in the streets, nutrients no longer flowed through the waste pipes beneath the city. The Clone, grown to the outskirts, ceased growing farther. It lay dormant, save for those parts which had been pulled out of the pipes by unwary victims. But those parts kept the panic alive. The hysteria in the center of the city grew worse as more and more people saw the Clone feeding inside the buildings. At one street corner, stalled autos filled the intersection, rendering it difficult for people to pass on foot. Swarms of people clawed their way over the tops of cars and buses; others fought to get ahead of them. The regions between cars began to fill with the hurt and the maimed, and soon all the spaces between automobiles became jammed to car-top height with the bodies of those who fell. Throngs of people ran along the flesh and metal causeway.

Acts of heroism abounded. A groom, seeing what the Clone was doing to his bride and her father, nevertheless flung himself into the struggle and actually succeeded in parting the girl from the Clone. He lay sobbing over the half-wet white gown while the Clone, unnoticed, took him at the feet. An agile man, sprinting down the stairs past neighbors enmeshed in the Clone, stopped at the sight of a youth wonderingly watching the Clone climb up an arm. Seizing a chair the man fought to break the youth loose, but only succeeded in entangling himself. Father fought for son, brother for brother, and stranger for stranger. While most struggled blindly to save themselves, some men, some women, some children rose above the fearsome instinct for self-preservation and stayed to help another whenever it was possible.

Helicopters were everywhere, depositing soldiers on rooftops, carrying away helpless people who had sought refuge there, hovering low over the streets to try to bring the crowds under control.

At 1:43 P.M. the first technical teams began to move back into the city. Moving slowly and carefully against the droves of fleeing people, they spread out through the suburbs and worked their way into buildings. Once inside, the men poured iodine solution into drains; the counterattack had started. But down deep in the pipes the Clone protected itself. It formed a thick wall of tissue, completely blocking the pipes, damning up the material so poisonous to it. The teams learned what was happening when—too soon—the pipes overflowed and would not take any more solution. The radio communications net hummed with query and answer, and it became apparent that the Clone would have to be dug out, foot by foot, mile by mile.

But the iodine attack was not without effect. Water had almost ceased to flow, the nutrients were gone. Many of the pipes were closed with the Clone's own flesh, so the Clone grew frantic from lack of food. It developed a new tactic.

Forming a ball at the mouth of any drain, the light-activated fluorescent matter flung itself out into a long streamer. The streamer squirmed against floors and walls and furniture and fixtures. It sought nitrogen and calcium in the buildings in any amounts, however small.

The heavy crowds in the streets became drained of panic; numbness set in. For the first time the troops were able to direct intelligently the flow of traffic. In sodden silence the streams of people flowed from the city at a steady three miles per hour, heading for the safety of the countryside. It was then that buildings began to collapse.

Seeking the trace amounts of protein that occur in all wood, the Clone had penetrated floors and door frames. While it rejected the majority of the wood, it completely destroyed the structural strength of all wooden members. It followed the floors and frames into the studding, plates, and beams. Wooden buildings caved in, and the Clone explored the wreckage. It took many rugs and draperies. It took paints off the walls and adhesives out of joints. It reduced furniture to piles of shapeless splinters. Plaster, cement, and masonry were not immune. The calcium-seeking enzyme poured into walls, columns, and foundations, taking up more calcium than it needed and depositing the excess in the form of powdery calcium silicates. Buildings made of stone and ce-

ment began to fall apart, saved from complete collapse by
the steel framework.

At first there was no response from those in the streets;
they plodded onward ignoring the noise and the dust and
the occasional structural member that rolled into their midst.
Troops on roof-tops were swallowed up as buildings gave
way. The Clone pressed outward.

Thin films of it swarmed over the exterior walls of ruined
buildings. Mounds of it formed at windows and cracks, and
launched streamers out into the streets where the people
were. At a thousand places at once the Clone suddenly got
into the streets, and the panic this time was greater than
before. Mindless people tried to climb sheer walls and fight
their way through impassable wreckage.

Water wormed and flowed deep in the city streets. Cotton
clothes floated in the water and plugged the storm sewers;
the water level rose over the sidewalks and lapped against
what was left of the buildings. Men splashed knee-deep
through the water in futile attempts to escape the Clone.
Some fell exhausted and drowned.

At 3:35 P.M. the city was empty of life, save for the
Clone. The water began to drain away from the low areas,
leaving whitish salt deposits as it dried. The shining green
tissue that was the Clone covered 200 square miles of what
had been the lovely city.

The city was dead, and there remained the task of killing
the creature that had destroyed it. Armies of technical and
military personnel began the long job of digging and spraying.
In the ensuing months many theories were advanced to
explain the origin of the Clone. Among them was one that
placed the blame for the creature on a series of accidents of
chemistry. For beneath every great city there flow streams
of water rich in nutrients and minerals, and containing ample energy to supply the driving force for almost every
conceivable chemical reaction.

But no one listened.

THE MEN IN THE WALLS

BY WILLIAM TENN

I

Mankind consisted of 128 people.

The sheer population pressure of so vast a horde had long ago filled over a dozen burrows. Bands of the Male Society occupied the outermost four of these interconnected corridors and patrolled it with their full strength, twenty-three young adult males in the prime of courage and alertness. They were stationed there to take the first shock of any danger to Mankind, they and their band captains and the youthful initiates who served them.

Eric the Only was an initiate in this powerful force. Today, he was a student warrior, a fetcher and a carrier for proven, seasoned men. But tomorrow, tomorrow . . .

This was his birthday. Tomorrow, he would be sent forth to Steal for Mankind. When he returned—and have no fear: Eric was swift, Eric was clever, he would return—off might go the loose loin cloths of boyhood to be replaced by the tight loin straps of a proud Male Society warrior.

He would be free to raise his voice and express his opinions in the Councils of Mankind. He could stare at the women whenever he liked, for as long as he liked, to approach them even—

He found himself wandering to the end of his band's burrow, still carrying the spear he was sharpening for his uncle. There, where a women's burrow began, several members of the Female Society were preparing food stolen from the Monster larder that very day. Each spell had to be performed properly, each incantation said just right, or it

99

would not be fit to eat. It might even be dangerous. Mankind was indeed fortunate: plenty of food, readily available, and women who well understood the magical work of preparing it for human consumption.

And such women—such splendid creatures!

Sarah the Sickness-Healer, for example, with her incredible knowledge of what food was fit and what was unfit, her only garment a cloud of hair that alternately screened and revealed her hips and breasts, the largest in all Mankind. There was a woman for you! Over five litters she had had, two of them of maximum size.

Eric watched as she turned a yellow chunk of food around and around under the glow lamp hanging from the ceiling of the burrow, looking for she only knew what and recognizing it when she found it she only knew how. A man could really strut with such a mate.

But she was the wife of a band leader and far, far beyond him. Her daughter, though, Selma the Soft-Skinned, would probably be flattered by his attentions. She still wore her hair in a heavy bun: it would be at least a year before the Female Society would consider her an initiate and allow her to drape it about her nakedness. No, far too young and unimportant for a man on the very verge of warrior status.

Another girl caught his eye. She had been observing him for some time and smiling behind her lashes, behind her demurely set mouth. Harriet the History-Teller, the oldest daughter of Rita the Record-Keeper, who would one day succeed to her mother's office. Now there was a lovely, slender girl, her hair completely unwound in testament to full womanhood and recognized professional status.

Eric had caught these covert, barely stated smiles from her before; especially in the last few weeks, as the time for his Theft approached. He knew that if he was successful— and he *had* to be successful: don't dare think of anything but success!—she would look with favor on advances from him. Of course, Harriet was a redhead, and therefore, according to Mankind's traditions, unlucky. She was probably having a hard time finding a mate. But his own mother had been a redhead.

Yes, and his mother had been very unlucky indeed.

Even his father had been infected with her terrible bad luck. Still, Harriet the History-Teller was an important person in the tribe for one her age. Good-looking too. And, above all, she didn't turn away from him. She smiled at him, openly now. He smiled back.

"Look at Eric!" he heard someone call out behind him. "He's already searching for a mate. Hey, Eric! You're not even wearing straps yet. First comes the stealing. *Then* comes the mating."

Eric spun around, bits of fantasy still stuck to his lips.

The group of young men lounging against the wall of his band's burrow were tossing laughter back and forth between them. They were all adults: they had all made their Theft. Socially, they were still his superiors. His only recourse was cold dignity.

"I know that," he began. "There is no mating until—"

"Until never for some people," one of the young men broke in. He rattled his spear in his hand, carelessly, proudly. "After you steal, you still have to convince a woman that you're a man. And some men have to do an awful lot of convincing. An *awful* lot, Eric-O."

The ball of laughter bounced back and forth again, heavier than before. Eric the Only felt his face turn bright red. How dare they remind him of his birth? On this day of all days? Here he was about to prepare himself to go forth and Steal for Mankind . . .

He dropped the sharpening stone into his pouch and slid his right hand back along his uncle's spear. "At least," he said, slowly and definitely, "at least, my woman will stay convinced, Roy the Runner. She won't be always open to offers from every other man in the tribe."

"You lousy little throwback!" Roy the Runner yelled. He leaped away from the rest of the band and into a crouch facing Eric, his spear tense in one hand. "You're asking for a hole in the belly! My woman's had two litters off me, two big litters. What would you have given her, you dirty singleton?"

"She's had two litters, but not off you," Rick the Only spat, holding his spear out in the guard position. "If you're the father, then the chief's blonde hair is contagious—like measles."

Roy bellowed and jabbed his spear forward. Eric parried it and lunged in his turn. He missed as his opponent leaped to one side. They circled each other, cursing and insulting, eyes only for the point of each other's spears. The other young men had scrambled a distance down the burrow to get out of their way.

                              *   *   *

A powerful arm suddenly clamped Eric's waist from behind and lifted him off his feet. He was kicked hard, so that
he stumbled a half-dozen steps and fell. On his feet in a
moment, the spear still in his hand, he whirled, ready to
deal with his new opponent. He was mad enough to fight all
Mankind.

But not Thomas the Trap-Smasher. No, not that mad.

All the tension drained out of him as he recognized the
captain of his band. He couldn't fight Thomas. His uncle.
And the greatest of all men. Guiltily, he walked to the niche
in the wall where the band's weapons were stacked and slid
his uncle's spear into its appointed place.

"What the hell's the matter with you, Roy?" Thomas was
asking behind him. "Fighting a duel with an initiate? Where's
your band spirit? That's all we need these days, to be cut
down from six effectives to five. Save your spear for Strangers, or—if you feel very brave—for Monsters. But don't
show a point in our band's burrow if you know what's good
for you, hear me?"

"I wasn't fighting a duel," the Runner mumbled, sheathing his own spear. "The kid got above himself. I was punishing him."

"You punish with the haft of the spear. And anyway, this
is my band and I do the punishing around here. Now move
on out, all of you, and get ready for the council. I'll attend
to the boy myself."

They went off obediently without looking back. The Trap-
Smasher's band was famous for its discipline throughout the
length and breadth of Mankind. A proud thing to be a
member of it. But to be called a boy in front of the others!
A boy, when he was full-grown and ready to begin stealing!

Although, come to think of it, he'd rather be called a boy
than a singleton. A boy eventually became a man, but a
singleton stayed a singleton forever. He put the problem to
his uncle who was at the niche, inspecting the band's reserve
pile of spears.

"Isn't it possible—I mean, it is possible, isn't it—that my
father had some children by another woman? You told me
he was one of the best thieves we ever had."

The captain of the band turned to study him, folding his
arms across his chest so that biceps swelled into greatness
and power. They glinted in the light of the tiny lantern
bound to his forehead, the glow lantern that only fully

accredited warriors might wear. After a while, the older man shook his head and said, very gently:

"Eric, Eric, forget about it, boy. He was all of those things and more. Your father was famous. Eric the Storeroom-Stormer, we called him, Eric the Laugher at Locks, Eric the Roistering Robber of all Mankind. He taught me everything I know. But he only married once. And if any other woman ever played around with him, she's been careful to keep it a secret. Now dress up those spears. You've let them get all sloppy. Butts together, that's the way, points up and even with each other."

Dutifully, Eric rearranged the bundle of armament that was his responsibility. He turned to his uncle again, now examining the knapsacks and canteens that would be carried on the expedition. "Suppose there had been another woman. My father could have had two, three, even four litters by different women. Extra-large litters too. If we could prove something like that, I wouldn't be a singleton any more. I would not be Eric the Only."

The Trap-Smasher sighed and thought for a moment. Then he pulled the spear from his back sling and took Eric's arm. He drew the youth along the burrow until they stood alone in the very center of it. He looked carefully at the exits at either end, making certain that they were completely alone before giving his reply in an unusually low, guarded voice.

"We'd never be able to prove anything like that. If you don't want to be Eric the Only, if you want to be Eric the something-else, well then, it's up to you. You have to make a good Theft. That's what you should be thinking about all the time now—your Theft. Eric, which category are you going to announce?"

He hadn't thought about it very much. "The usual one I guess. The one that's picked for most initiations. First category."

The older man brought his lips together, looking dissatisfied. "First category. *Food.* Well . . ."

Eric felt he understood. "You mean, for someone like me—an Only, who's really got to make a name for himself—I ought to announce like a real warrior? I should say I'm going to steal in the second category—Articles Useful to Mankind. Is that what my father would have done?"

"Do you know what your father would have done?"

"No. What?" Eric demanded eagerly.

"He'd have elected the third category. That's what I'd be announcing these days, if I were going through an initiation ceremony. That's what I want you to announce."

"Third category? Monster souvenirs? But no one's elected the third category in I don't know how many auld lang synes. Why should I do it?"

"Because this is more than just an initiation ceremony. It could be the beginning of a new life for all of us."

Eric frowned. What could be more than an initiation ceremony and his attainment of full thieving manhood?

"There are things going on in Mankind, these days," Thomas the Trap-Smasher continued in a strange, urgent voice. "Big things. And you're going to be a part of them. This Theft of yours—if you handle it right, if you do what I tell you, it's likely to blow the lid off everything the chief has been sitting on."

"The *chief?*" Eric felt confused. He was walking up a strange burrow now without a glow lamp. "What's the chief got to do with my Theft?"

His uncle examined both ends of the corridor again. "Eric, what's the most important thing we, or you, or anyone, can do? What is our life all about? What are we here for?"

"That's easy," Eric chuckled. "That's the easiest question there is. A child could answer it:

"Hit back at the Monsters," he quoted. *"Drive them from the planet, if we can. Regain Earth for Mankind, if we can. But above all, hit back at the Monsters. Make them suffer as they've made us suffer. Make them know we're still here, we're still fighting. Hit back at the Monsters."*

"Hit back at the Monsters. Right. Now how have we been doing that?"

Eric the Only stared at his uncle. That wasn't the next question in the catechism. He must have heard incorrectly. His uncle couldn't have made a mistake in such a basic ritual.

"We will do that," he went on in the second reply, his voice sliding into the singsong of childhood lessons, *"by regaining the science and knowhow of our forefathers. Man was once Lord of all Creation: his science and knowhow made him supreme. Science and knowhow is what we need to hit back at the Monsters."*

"Now, Eric," his uncle asked gently. "Please tell me this. What in hell is knowhow?"

That was way off. They were a full corridor's length from the normal progression of the catechism now.

"Knowhow is—knowhow is—" he stumbled over the unfamiliar verbal terrain. "Well, it's what our ancestors knew. And what they did with it, I guess. Knowhow is what you need before you can make hydrogen bombs or economic warfare or guided missiles, any of those really big weapons like our ancestors had."

"Did those weapons do them any good? Against the Monsters, I mean. Did they stop the Monsters?"

Eric looked completely blank for a moment, then brightened. Oh! He knew the way now. He knew how to get back to the catechism:

The suddenness of the attack, the—"

"Stop it!" his uncle ordered. "Don't give me any of that garbage! *The suddenness of the attack, the treachery of the Monsters*—does it sound like an explanation to you? Honestly? If our ancestors were really Lords of Creation and had such great weapons, would the Monsters have been able to conquer them? I've led my band on dozens of raids, and I know the value of a surprise attack; but believe me, boy, it's only good for a flash charge and a quick getaway if you're facing a superior force. You can knock somebody down when he doesn't expect it. But if he really has more than you, he won't *stay* down. Right?"

"I—I guess so. I wouldn't know."

"Well, I know. I know from plenty of battle experience. The thing to remember is that once our ancestors were knocked down, they stayed down. That means their science and knowhow were not so much in the first place. And *that* means"—here he turned his head and looked directly into Eric's eyes—"*that* means the science of our ancestors wasn't worth one good damn against the Monsters, and it wouldn't be worth one good damn to us!"

Eric the Only turned pale. He knew heresy when he heard it.

His uncle patted him on the shoulder, drawing a deep breath as if he'd finally spat out something extremely unpleasant. He leaned closer, eyes glittering beneath the forehead glow lamp and his voice dropped to a fierce whisper.

"Eric. When I asked you how we've been hitting back at

the Monsters, you told me what we *ought* to do. We haven't been *doing* a single thing to bother them. We don't know how to reconstruct the ancestor-science, we don't have the tools or weapons or knowhow—whatever *that* is—but they wouldn't do us a bit of good even if we had them. Because they failed once. They failed completely and at their best. There's just no point in trying to put them together again."

And now Eric understood. He understood why his uncle had whispered, why there had been so much strain in this conversation. Bloodshed was involved here, bloodshed and death.

"Uncle Thomas," he whispered, in a voice that kept cracking despite his efforts to keep it whole and steady, "how long have you been an Alien-Science man? When did you leave Ancestor-Science?"

Thomas the Trap-Smasher caressed his spear before he answered. He felt for it with a gentle, wandering arm, almost unconsciously, but both of them registered the fact that it was loose and ready. His tremendous body, nude except for the straps about his loins and the light spear-sling on his back, looked as if it were preparing to move instantaneously in any direction.

He stared again from one end of the burrow to the other, his forehead lamp reaching out to the branching darkness of the exits. Eric stared with him. No one was leaning tightly against a wall and listening.

"How long? Since I got to know your father. He was in another band; naturally we hadn't seen much of each other before he married my sister. I'd heard about him, though; everyone in the Male Society had—he was a great thief. But once he became my brother-in-law, I learned a lot from him. I learned about locks, about the latest traps—and I learned about Alien-Science. He'd been an Alien-Science man for years. He converted your mother, and he converted me."

Eric the Only backed away. "No!" he called out wildly. "Not my father and mother! They were decent people— when they were killed a service was held in their name— they went to add to the science of our ancestors—"

His uncle jammed a powerful hand over his mouth.

"Shut up, you damn fool, or you'll finish us both! Of course your parents were decent people. How do you think they were killed? Your mother was with your father out in

Monster territory. Have you ever heard of a woman going along with her husband on a Theft? And taking her baby with her? Do you think it was an ordinary robbery of the Monsters? They were Alien-science people, serving their faith as best they could. They died for it."

Eric looked into his uncle's eyes over the hand that covered the lower half of his face. *Alien-science people . . . serving their faith . . . do you think it was an ordinary robbery . . . they died for it!*

He had never realized before how odd it was that his parents had gone to Monster territory together, a man taking his wife and the woman taking her baby!

As he relaxed, his uncle removed the gagging hand. "What kind of Theft was it that my parents died in?"

Thomas examined his face and seemed satisfied. "The kind you're going after," he said. "If you are your father's son. If you're man enough to continue the work he started. Are you?"

Eric started to nod, then found himself shrugging weakly, and finally just hung his head. He didn't know what to say. His uncle—well, his uncle was his model and his leader, and he was strong and wise and crafty. His father—naturally, he wanted to emulate his father and continue whatever work he had started. But this was his initiation ceremony, after all, and there would be enough danger merely in proving his manhood. For his initiation ceremony to take on a task that had destroyed his father, the greatest thief the tribe had ever known, and a heretical, blasphemous task at that. . . .

"I'll try. I don't know if I can."

"You can," his uncle told him heartily. "It's been set up for you. It will be like walking through a dug burrow, Eric. All you have to face through is the council. You'll have to be steady there, no matter what. You tell the chief that you're undertaking the third category."

"But why the third?" Eric asked. "Why does it have to be Monster souvenirs?"

"Because that's what we need. And you stick to it, no matter what pressure they put on you. Remember, an initiate has the right to decide what he's going to steal. A man's first Theft is his own affair."

"But, listen, uncle—"

There was a whistle from the end of the burrow. Thomas the Trap-Smasher nodded in the direction of the signal.

"The council's beginning, boy. We'll talk later, on expedition. Now remember this: stealing from the third category is your own idea, and all your own idea. Forget everything else we've talked about. If you hit any trouble with the chief, I'll be there. I'm your sponsor, after all."

He threw an arm about his confused nephew and walked to the end of the burrow where the other members of the band waited.

II

The tribe had gathered in its central and largest burrow under the great, hanging glow lamps that might be used in this place alone. Except for the few sentinels on duty on the outlying corridors, all of Mankind was here. It was an awesome sight to behold.

On the little hillock known as the Royal Mound lolled Franklin the Father of Many Thieves, Chieftain of all Mankind. He alone of the cluster of warriors displayed heaviness of belly and flabbiness of arm—for he alone had the privilege of a sedentary life. Beside the sternly muscled band leaders who formed his immediate background, he looked almost womanly; and yet one of his many titles was simply The Man.

Yes, unquestionably The Man of Mankind was Franklin the Father of Many Thieves. You could tell it from the hushed, respectful attitudes of the subordinate warriors who stood at a distance from the mound. You could tell it from the rippling interest of the women as they stood on the other side of the great burrow, drawn up in the ranks of the Female Society. You could tell it from the nervousness and scorn with which the women were watched by their leader, Ottilie, the Chieftain's First Wife. And finally, you could tell it from the faces of the children, standing in a distant, disorganized bunch. A clear majority of their faces bore an unmistakable resemblance to Franklin's.

Franklin clapped his hands, three evenly spaced, flesh-heavy wallops.

"In the name of our ancestors," he said, "and the science with which they ruled the Earth, I declare this council opened. May it end as one more step in the regaining of their science. Who asked for a council?"

"I did." Thomas the Trap-Smasher moved out of his band and stood before the chief.

Franklin nodded, and went on with the next, formal question:

"And your reason?"

"As a band leader, I call attention to a candidate for manhood. A member of my band, a spear-carrier for the required time, and an accepted apprentice in the Male Society. My nephew, Eric the Only."

As his name was sung out, Eric shook himself. Half on his own volition and half in response to the pushes he received from the other warriors, he stumbled up to his uncle and faced the chief. This, the most important moment of his life, was proving almost too much for him. So many people in one place, accredited and famous warriors, knowledgeable and attractive women, the chief himself, all this after the shattering revelations from his uncle—he was finding it hard to think clearly. And it was vital to think clearly. His responses to the next few questions had to be exactly right.

The chief was asking the first:

"Eric the Only, do you appy for full manhood?"

Eric breathed hard and nodded. "I do."

"As a full man, what will be your value to Mankind?"

"I will steal for Mankind whatever it needs. I will defend Mankind against all outsiders. I will increase the possessions and knowledge of the Female Society so that the Female Society can increase the power and well-being of Mankind."

"And all this you swear to do?"

"And all this I swear to do."

The Chief turned to Eric's uncle. "As his sponsor, do you support his oath and swear that he is to be trusted?"

With just the faintest hint of sarcasm in his voice, Thomas the Trap-Smasher replied: "Yes. I support his oath and swear that he is to be trusted."

There was a rattling moment, the barest second, when the chief's eyes locked with those of the band leader. With all that was on Eric's mind at the moment, he noticed it. Then the chief looked away and pointed to the women on the other side of the burrow.

"He is accepted as a candidate by the men. Now the women must ask for proof, for only a woman's proof bestows full manhood."

The first part was over. And it hadn't been too bad. Eric turned to face the advancing leaders of the Female Society,

Ottilie, the Chieftain's First Wife, in the center. Now came the part that scared him. The women's part.

As was customary at such a moment, his uncle and sponsor left him when the women came forward. Thomas the Trap-Smasher led his band to the warriors grouped about the Throne Mound. There, with their colleagues, they folded their arms across their chests and turned to watch. A man can only give proof of his manhood while he is alone; his friends cannot support him once the women approach.

It was not going to be easy, Eric realized. He had hoped that at least one of his uncle's wives would be among the three examiners: they were both kindly people who liked him and had talked to him much about the mysteries of women's work. But he had drawn a trio of hard-faced females who apparently intended to take him over the full course before they passed him.

Sarah the Sickness-Healer opened the proceedings. She circled him belligerently, hands on hips, her great breasts rolling to and fro like a pair of swollen pendulums, her eyes glittering with scorn.

"Eric the Only," she intoned, and then paused to grin, as if it were a name impossible to believe, "Eric the Singleton, Eric the one and only child of either his mother or his father. Your parents almost didn't have enough between them to make a solitary child. Is there enough in you to make a man?"

There was a snigger of appreciation from the children in the distance, and it was echoed by a few growling laughs from the vicinity of the Throne Mound. Eric felt his face and neck go red. He would have fought any man to the death for remarks like these. Any man at all. But who could lift his hand to a woman and be allowed to live? Besides, one of the main purposes of this exhibition was to investigate his powers of self-control.

"I think so," he managed to say after a long pause. "And I'm willing to prove it."

"Prove it, then!" the woman snarled. Her right hand, holding a long, sharp-pointed pin, shot to his chest like a flung spear. Eric made his muscles rigid and tried to send his mind away. That, the men had told him, was what you had to do at this moment: it was not you they were hurting, not you at all. You, your mind, your knowledge of self, were in another part of the burrow entirely, watching these painful things being done to someone else.

The pin sank into his chest for a little distance, paused, came out. It probed here, probed there; finally it found a nerve in his upper arm. There, guided by the knowledge of the Sickness-Healer, it bit and clawed at the delicate area until Eric felt he would grind his teeth to powder in the effort not to cry out. His clenched fists twisted agonizingly at the ends of his arms in a paroxysm of protest, but he kept his body still. He didn't cry out; he didn't move away; he didn't raise a hand to protect himself.

Sarah the Sickness-Healer stepped back and considered him. "There is no man here yet," she said grudgingly. "But perhaps there is the beginnings of one."

He could relax. The physical test was over. There would be another one, much later, after he had completed his theft successfully; but that would be exclusively by men as part of his proud initiation ceremony. Under the circumstances, he knew he would be able to go through it almost gaily.

Meanwhile, the women's physical test was over. That was the important thing for now. In sheer reaction, his body gushed forth sweat which slid over the bloody cracks in his skin and stung viciously. He felt the water pouring down his back and forced himself not to go limp, prodded his mind into alertness.

"Did that hurt?" he was being asked by Rita, the old crone of a Record-Keeper. There was a solicitous smile on her forty-year-old face, but he knew it was a fake. A woman as old as that no longer felt sorry for anybody. She had too many aches and pains and things generally wrong with her to worry about other people's troubles.

"A little," he said. "Not much."

"The Monsters will hurt you much more if they catch you stealing from them, do you know that? They will hurt you much more than we ever could."

"I know. But the stealing is more important than the risk I'm taking. The stealing is the most important thing a man can do."

Rita the Record-Keeper nodded. "Because you steal things Mankind needs in order to live. You steal things that the Female Society can make into food, clothing and weapons for Mankind, so that Mankind can live and flourish."

He saw the way, saw what was expected of him. "No," he

contradicted her. "That's not why we steal. We live on what we steal, but we do not steal just to go on living."

"Why?" she asked blandly, as if she didn't know the answer better than any other member of the tribe. "Why do we steal? What is more important than survival?"

Here it was now. The catechism.

"To hit back at the Monsters," he began. *"To drive them from the planet, if we can. Regain Earth for Mankind, if we can. But, above all, hit back at the Monsters. . . ."*

He ploughed through the long verbal ritual, pausing at the end of each part, so that the Record-Keeper could ask the proper question and initiate the next sequence.

She tried to trip him once. She reversed the order of the fifth and sixth questions. Instead of *"What will we do with the Monsters when we have regained the Earth from them?"* she asked, *"Why can't we use the Monsters' own Alien-Science to fight the Monsters?"*

Carried along by mental habit, Eric was well into the passage beginning *"We will keep them as our ancestors kept all strange animals, in a place called a zoo, or we will drive them into our burrows and force them to live as we have lived,"* before he realized the switch and stopped in confusion. Then he got a grip on himself, sought the right answer in his memory with calmness, as his uncle's wives had schooled him to do, and began again.

"There are three reasons why we cannot ever use Alien-Science," he recited, holding up his hand with the thumb and little finger closed. *"Alien-Science is non-human, Alien-Science is in-human, Alien-Science is anti-human. First, since it is non-human,"* he closed his forefinger, *"we cannot use it because we can never understand it. And because it is in-humane, we would never want to use it even if we could understand it. And because it is anti-human and can only be used to hurt and damage Mankind, we would not be able to use it so long as we remain human ourselves. Alien-Science is the opposite of Ancestor-Science in every way, ugly instead of beautiful, hurtful instead of helpful. When we die, Alien-Science would not bring us to the world of our ancestors, but to another world full of Monsters."*

All in all, it went very well, despite the trap into which he had almost fallen.

But he couldn't help remembering the conversation with his uncle in the other burrow. As his mouth reeled off the familiar words and concepts, his mind kept wondering how the two fitted together. His uncle was Alien-Science, and, according to his uncle, so had been his parents. Did that make them non-human, inhuman, anti-human?

And what did it make him? He knew his religious duty well: he should at this moment be telling all Mankind about his uncle's horrible secret.

The whole subject was far too complicated for someone with his limited experience.

When he had completed the lengthy catechism, Rita the Record-Keeper said: "And this is what you say about the science of our ancestors. Now we will find out what the science of our ancestors says about you."

She signaled over her shoulder, without turning her head, and two young girls—female apprentices—pulled forward the large record machine which was the very center of the tribe's religious life. They stepped back, both smiling shyly and encouragingly at Eric the Only.

He knew the smiles meant little more than simple best wishes from apprentices of one sex to apprentices of the other, but even that was quite a bit at the moment. It meant that he was much closer to full status than they. It meant that, in the opinion of unprejudiced, disinterested observers, his examination was proceeding very well indeed.

Singleton, he thought fiercely to himself. *I'll show them what a singleton can do!*

Rita the Record-Keeper turned a knob at the top of the squat machine and it began to hum. She flung her arms up, quiveringly apart, and all, warriors, women, children, apprentices, even the chief himself, all bowed their heads.

"Harken to the words of our ancestors," she chanted. "Watch closely the spectacle of their great achievements. When their end was upon them, and they knew that only we, their descendants, might regain the Earth they had lost, they made this machine for the future generations of Mankind as a guide to the science that once had been and must be again."

The old woman lowered her arms. Simultaneously, heads went up all over the burrow and stared expectantly at the wall opposite the record machine, waiting for the magic message.

"Eric the Only," Rita called, spinning the dial on the left of the machine with one hand and stabbing at it randomly with the forefinger of the other. "This is the sequence in the science of our ancestors that speaks for you alone. This is the appointed vision under which you will live and die."

He stared at the wall, breathing hard. Now he would find out what his life was to be about—*now!* His uncle's vision at this moment, years ago, had suggested the nickname he came to bear: the Trap-Smasher. At the last initiation ceremony, a youth had called forth a sequence in which two enormous airborne vehicles of the ancestors had collided.

They'd tried to cheer the boy up, but he'd known his fate was upon him. Sure enough, he had been caught by a monster in the middle of his Theft and dashed to pieces against a wall.

Even then, Eric decided, he'd rather have that kind of a sequence than the awful emptiness of a *blank* vision. When, every once in a while, the machine went on and showed nothing but a blinding white rectangle, the whole tribe knew that the youth being examined had no possibility of manhood in him at all. And the machine was never wrong. A boy who'd drawn a blank vision inevitably became more and more effeminate as he grew older without ever going out on his Theft. He tended to shun the company of warriors and to ask the women for minor tasks to perform. The machine of the ancestors looked at a boy and told exactly what he was and what he would become.

It had been great, that science which had produced this machine, no doubt about it. There was a power source in it which was self-contained, and which was supposed to be like the power behind all things. It would run almost forever, if the machine were not tampered with—although who could dream of tampering with it? In its visions were locked, not only the secrets of every individual human being, but enormous mysteries which the whole of Mankind had to solve before it could work out its salvation through the rituals and powers of the ancestral science.

Now, however, there was only one small part of Mankind that concerned Eric. Himself. His future. He waited, growing more and more tense as the power hum from the machine increased in pitch. And suddenly there was a grunt of awe from the entire burrow of people as a vision was thrown upon the wall.

He hadn't drawn a blank. That was the most important thing. He had been given an authentic ancestral vision.

"Scattergood's does it again!" a voice blared, as the picture projected on the wall showed people coming from all directions, wearing the strange body wrappings of the ancestors. They rushed, men, women, children, from the four corners of the glittering screen to some strange structure in the center and disappeared into its entrance. More and more poured in, more and more kept materializing at the edges and scrambling toward the structure in the center.

"Scattergood's does it again!" the vision yelled out at them. "The sale of sales! The value of values! Only at Scattergood's three stores tomorrow. Binoculars, tape recorders, cameras, all at tremendous reductions, many below cost. Value, value, value!"

Now the vision showed only objects. Strange, unfamiliar objects such as the ancestors used. And as each object appeared, the voice recited a charm over it. Powerful and ancient magic this, the forgotten lore of Ancestor-Science.

"Krafft-Yahrmann Exposure Meters, the best there is, you've heard about them and now you can buy them, the light meter that's an eye-opener, a price to fit every pocketbook, eight dollars and ninety-five cents, tomorrow at Scattergood's, absolutely only one to a customer.

"Kyoto Automatic Eight-Millimeter Movie Cameras with an f 1.4 lens and an electric eye that does all the focusing and gives you a perfect exposure every single time. As low as three dollars a week. The supply is limited, so hurry, hurry, hurry!"

Eric watched the sequence unfold, his hands squeezing each other, his eyes almost distended in reverence and concentration. This was the clue to his life, to what he might become. This was the sequence that the record machine of the ancestors, turned on at random, had vouchsafed as a prophecy of his future.

All knowledge was in that machine—and no possibility of error.

But Eric was getting worried. The vision was so strange. Sometimes there would be a vision that baffled even the wisest women. And that meant the youth who had called it forth would always be a puzzle, to himself and all of Mankind.

Let it not happen to him! O ancestors, O science, O record machine, let it not happen to him!

Let him only have a clear and definite vision so that his personality could be clear and definite for the rest of his life!

"Our special imported high-power precision binoculars,"

the voice roared on as a man appeared in the vision and
brought one of the strange objects up to his eyes. "If we told
you the manufacturer's name, you'd recognize it immediately. 7 x 50, only fourteen dollars and ninety-five cents,
with case. 10 x 50, only fifteen dollars and ninety-five cents,
with case. You see farther, you see clearer, you pay less.
You always pay less at Scattergood's. Rock-bottom prices!
Skyscraper values! Tomorrow, tomorrow, tomorrow, at Scattergood's annual week-after Hallowe'en Sale!"

There was a click as the vision went off abruptly to be
replaced by a white rectangle on the wall of the burrow.
Eric realized that this was all the clue there was to be to his
life. What did it mean? Could it be interpreted?

Anxiously, now he turned to Ottilie, the Chieftain's First
Wife. He turned to her as everyone else in Mankind was
now turning, Sarah the Sickness-Healer and Rita the Record-
Keeper amongst them.

Only Ottilie could read a vision, only short, squat, imperi-
ous Ottilie. The Chieftain's First Wife was her title of honor
and her latest title, but long before she had acquired that,
long before even she had become Head of the Female
Society, she had been Ottilie the Augur, Ottilie the Omen-
Teller, Ottilie who could walk in her mind from the homey
burrow of the present into the dark, labyrinthine corridors
of the future, Ottilie who could read signs, Ottilie who
could announce portents.

It was as Ottilie the Augur that she could pick out the one
new-born babe in a litter of three that had to be destroyed
because, in some way or other, it would one day bring death
to its people. It was as Ottilie the Augur that, upon the
death of the old chief, she had chosen Franklin the Father
of Many Thieves to take over the leadership of Mankind
since he stimulated the most propitious omens. In everything she had been right. And now, once again it was as
Ottilie the Augur that she threw her arms over her head and
twisted and swayed and moaned as she sought deep inside
herself for the meaning of Eric's vision, it was as Ottilie the
Augur and not as Ottilie the Chieftain's First Wife, for that
she had been only since Franklin had ascended the Throne
Mound.

The scratches and holes gouged in his body by Sarah the
Sickness-Healer had begun to ache badly, but Eric shrugged

off their annoyance. Could his vision be interpreted? And *how* would it be interpreted?

Whatever Ottilie saw in the vision would stick to him for the rest of his life, much closer than the dried blood upon his arms and legs and chest. How could you possibly interpret such a vision? Eric the Scattergood? That was meaningless. Eric the Value? No, that was a little better, but it was dreadfully vague, almost as bad as a blank vision.

He stared past Ottilie's writhing figure to where his uncle stood, surrounded by his band, a little to the left of the Throne Mound. Thomas the Trap-Smasher was watching Ottilie and grinning with all his teeth.

What did he find so funny, Eric wondered desperately? Was there nothing holy to him? Didn't he realize how important it was to Eric's future that his vision be readable, that he get a name to be proud of? What was funny in Ottilie's agony as she gave birth to Eric's future?

He realized that Ottilie was beginning to make coherent sounds. He strained his ears to listen. This, this was it. Who he really was. Who he would be, for all his life.

"Three times," Ottilie mumbled in a voice that steadily grew clearer and louder, "three times our ancestors gave Eric his name. Three repetitions they made. Three different ways they called on him to become what their science needed him to be. And all of you heard it, and I heard it, and Eric heard it too."

Which, Eric puzzled, which among the many strange magical statements had contained his name and his life's-work? He waited for the Augur to come out with it. He had almost given up breathing.

Her body relaxed now, her hands hanging at her sides, Ottilie was speaking to them in a sharp, authoritative voice as she stared at the wall of the burrow where the vision had appeared.

" 'A light meter that's an eye-opener,' the ancestor-science said," she reminded them. "And 'an electric eye that does all the focusing.' And 'you see farther, you see clearer, you pay less,' the Record-Machine told us of Eric. What the ancestors want of Eric is unmistakable, what he must be if we are to hit back at the Monsters and regain the Earth which is rightfully ours."

*   *   *

Thank the record machine, thank each and every ancestor! At least the message had been unmistakable. But what
precisely had it been?

Ottilie the Augur, the Omen-Teller, turned to face him
now where he stood apart from the rest of eagerly-watching
Mankind. He straightened up and stood stiffly to learn his
fate.

"Eric," she said. "Eric the Only, Eric the Singleton, you
go out now to make your Theft. If you are successful and
return alive, you will become a man. And as a man you will
no longer be Eric the Only, you will be Eric the Eye. Eric
the Eye, Eric the Espier, Eric who seeks out the path for
Mankind. Eric who hits back at the Monsters with his eye,
his open eye, his electric eye, his farther-seeing, clearer-
seeing, less-paying eye. For this is the word of the ancestors,
and all of you have heard it."

At last Eric could take a deep breath, and he did so now,
noisily, in common with the whole of Mankind who had
been hanging on Otillie's words. Eric the Eye—that was
what he was to be. If he was successful . . . and if he lived.

Eric the Eye. Eric the Espier. Now he knew about himself. It was fixed, and for all time. It was a good name to
bear, a fine personality to have. He had been very fortunate.

Rita the Record-Keeper and her daughter, Harriet the
History-Teller, rolled the record machine back into its accustomed holy place, the niche in the wall behind the Throne
Mound. Despite the sacred quality of the act in which she
was engaged, the younger woman could not take her eyes off
Eric. He was a person of consequence now, or at least
would be when he returned. Other young and mating-aged
women, he noticed, were looking at him the same way.

He began to walk around in a little circle before Mankind, and, as he walked, he strutted. He waited until Ottilie,
no longer the Augur now, no longer the Omen-Teller, but
once more the Chieftain's First Wife—he waited until she
had returned to her place at the head of the Female Society,
before he began to sing.

He threw back his head and spread out his arms and
danced proudly, stampingly, before Mankind. He spun around
in great dizzying circles and leaped in the air and came
down with wrenching spasmodic twists of his legs and arms.
And as he danced, he sang.

He sang out of the pride that racked his chest like a soul
coughing, out of the majesty of the warrior-that-was-to-be,

out of his sure knowledge of self. And he sang his promise
to his fellows:

I am Eric the Eye,
Eric the Open Eye,
Eric the Electric Eye,
Eric the Farther-Seeing, Clearer-Seeing, Less-Paying Eye.
Eric the Espier—
Eric who finds and points out the way.
Are you lost in a strange place?
I will show you the path to your home.
Does the burrow break off in too many branches?
I will pick out the best one and Mankind shall walk
through in safety.
Are there enemies about, hidden traps, unthought-of
dangers?
I will see them and give warning of them in time.
I will walk at the head of the line of warriors and see for
them,
And they shall be confident and they shall conquer—
For they have Eric the Espier to lead the way and point
the path!

So he sang as he danced before Mankind, under the enormous glow lamps of its great central burrow. He sang of his
mission in life as just a few short auld lang synes ago he had
heard Roy the Runner, at his initiation, sing of the fleetness
and swiftness that he would soon be the master of; as his
Uncle Thomas had sung long before that of his coming
ability to detect and dismantle traps; as once his own father
had sung of the robberies he was to commit, of the store-
rooms he would empty for the benefit of Mankind. He sang
and he leaped and he whirled, and all the while the watching host of Mankind beat time with its feet and hands and
played chorus in the litany of his triumph.

Then came a loud grunt from Franklin the Father of
Many Thieves. The noise stopped. Eric danced to a quivering halt, his body wet all over, his limbs still trembling.

"That is what is to be," Franklin pointed out, "once the
Theft has been made. But first, first comes the Theft. Always before manhood comes the Theft. Now let us speak of
your Theft."

"I will go into the very home of the Monsters," Eric
announced proudly, his head thrown back before the chief.
"I will go into their home alone, with no companion but my

own weapons, as a warrior should. I will steal from them, no matter what the danger, no matter what the threat. And what I steal, I will bring back for the use and enjoyment of Mankind."

Franklin nodded and made the formal reply. "That is good, and it is spoken like a warrior. What do you promise to steal from the Monsters? For your first Theft must be a promise made in advance and kept, kept exactly."

Now they were at it. Eric glanced at his uncle for support. Thomas the Trap-Smasher was staring off in a different direction. Eric licked his lips. Well, maybe it wouldn't be too bad. After all, a youth going off on his first Theft had complete freedom of choice.

"I promise to make my theft in the third category," he said, his voice trembling just a little.

The results were much more than he had anticipated. Franklin the Father of Many Thieves yelped sharply. He leaped off the Royal Mound and stood gaping at Eric for a while. His great belly and fat arms quivered with disbelief.

"The third category, did you say? The *third*?"

Eric, thoroughly frightened now, nodded.

Franklin turned to Chief Wife Ottilie. They both peered through the ranks of Mankind to where Thomas the Trap-Smasher stood in the midst of his band, seemingly unconcerned by the sensation that had just been created.

"What *is* this, Thomas?" the chief demanded, all ceremony and formality gone from his speech. "What are you trying to pull? What's this third category stuff you're up to?"

Thomas the Trap-Smasher turned a bland eye upon him. "What am *I* up to? I'm not up to a damn thing. The boy's got a right to pick his category. If he wants to steal in the third category, well, that's his business. What have I got to do with it?"

The chief stared at him for a few moments longer. Then he swung back to Eric and said shortly: "All right. You've chosen. The third category it is. Now let's get on with the feast."

Somehow it was all spoiled for Eric. The initiation feast that preceded a first Theft—how he had looked forward to it! But he was apparently involved in something going on in Mankind, something dangerous and unsavory.

The chief obviously considered him an important factor in

whatever difficulty had arisen. Usually, an initiate about to depart on a Theft was the focus of all conversation as Mankind ate in its central burrow, the women squatting on one side, the men on the other, the children at the far ends where light was dim. But at this meal, the chief made only the most necessary ritual remarks to Eric. His eyes kept wandering from him to Thomas the Trap-Smasher.

Once in a while, Franklin's eyes met those of Ottilie, his favored and first wife, across the feast that had been spread the length of the burrow. He seemed to be saying something to her, although neither of them moved their lips. Then they would nod at each other and look back to Eric's uncle.

The rest of Mankind became aware of the strained atmosphere: there was little of the usual laughter and gaiety of an initiation feast. The Trap-Smasher's band had pulled in tightly all around him; most of them were not even bothering to eat but sat watchful and alert. Other band captains—men like Stephen the Strong-Armed and Harold the Hurler—had worried looks on their faces as if they were calculating highly complex problems.

Even the children were remarkably quiet. They served the food over which the women had said charms much earlier, then scurried to their places and ate with wide eyes aimed at their elders.

All in all, Eric was distinctly relieved when Franklin the Father of Many Thieves belched commandingly, stretched, and lay back on the floor of the burrow. In a few minutes, he was asleep, snoring loudly.

Night had officially begun.

IV

At the end of the sleep period, as soon as the chief had awakened and yawned, thus proclaiming the dawn, Thomas the Trap-Smasher's band started on its trip.

Eric, still officially surnamed the Only, carried the precious loin straps of manhood in the food knapsack the women had provided for a possible journey of several days. They should return before the next sleep period, but when one went on an expedition into Monster territory anything might happen.

They stepped out in full military formation, a long, straggling single file, each man barely in sight of the warrior immediately ahead. For the first time in his military career,

Eric was wearing only one set of spears—those for himself. Extra weapons for the band—as well as extra supplies— were on the back of a new apprentice, a stripling who marched a distance behind Eric, watching him with the same mixture of fright and exhilaration Eric himself had once accorded all other warriors.

Ahead of Eric, momentarily disappearing as the dim corridor curved and branched, was Roy the Runner, his long, loose-jointed legs purposefully treading down the mile-age. And all the way in the lead of the column, Eric knew, was his uncle. Thomas the Trap-Smasher would be striding cautiously yet without any unnecessary waste of time, the large glow lamp on his forehead constantly shifting from wall to wall of the uninhabited burrow and then straight ahead, the heavy spear in each brawny hand ready for instant action, his mouth set to call the warning behind him if danger materialized.

To be a man—this was what it was like! To go on expeditions like this for the rest of one's life, glorious, adventure-charged expeditions so that Mankind might eat well and have weapons and live as Mankind should. And when you returned, triumphant, victorious, the welcoming dance of the women as they threaded their way through the tired ranks, giving you refreshment and taking from you the supplies that only they could turn into usable articles. Then, after you had eaten and drunk and rested, your own dance, the dance of the men, where you sang and acted out for the tribe all the events of this particular expedition, the dangers you had overcome, the splendid courage you had shown, the strange and mysterious sights you had seen.

The sights you had seen! As Eric the Eye, he would probably be entitled to a solo dance any time his band came across anything particularly curious. Oh, how high Eric the Eye would leap, how loudly, how proudly, how melodiously, he would sing of the wonders the expedition had encountered!

"Eric the Eye," the women would murmur. "What a fine, fine figure of a man! What a mate for some lucky woman!"

Harriet the History-Teller this morning, for example, before they started out. She had filled his canteen for him with fresh water as if he were already an accredited man instead of an initiate going out to face his ultimate trial. Before the eyes of all Mankind she had filled it and brought it to him, her eyes downcast and light purple blushes on the rosy skin of her face and body. She had treated him the way a wife treats a husband, and many warriors—Eric thought gleefully—many full warriors with their Thefts long behind them had observed that Eric was likely to join the ranks of the Male Society and the married men almost simultaneously.

Of course, with her unlucky red hair, her bustling, domineering mother, Harriet was not exactly the most marriageable girl in Mankind. Still, there were many full warriors who had not yet been able to persuade a woman to mate with them, who watched Franklin and his three wives with unconcealed hunger and envy. How they would envy Eric, the newest warrior of all, when he mated the same night he returned from his theft! Call him Only, then! Call him singleton, then!

They would have litter after litter, he and Harriet, large litters, ample litters, four, five, even six at a time. People would forget he'd ever been the product of a singleton birth. Other women, mates of other warriors, would wriggle to attract his attention as they now wriggled when they caught the eye of Franklin the Father of Many Thieves. He would make the litters fathered by Franklin look puny in comparison, he would prove that the best hope for Mankind's increase lay in his loins and his loins alone. And when the time came to select another chief . . .

"Hey, you damned day-dreaming singleton!" Roy the Runner was calling from the burrow ahead. "Will you wipe that haze out of your face and pay attention to signals? This is an expedition to Monster territory, not a stroll in the women's quarters. Stay alert, will you? The band captain's sent down a call for you."

Amid the chuckles ahead and behind him—damn it, even the new apprentice was laughing!—Eric took a firmer grip on his glow torch and sprinted for the head of the column. As he passed each man, he was asked the name of the girl he'd been thinking about and pressed for interesting details. Since he kept his mouth tightly shut, some of the warriors hypothesized out loud. They were painfully close to the truth.

His uncle wasn't much gentler with him. "Eric the *Eye*!" the Trap-Smasher growled. "Eric the Eyebrow, Eric the Closed Eyelash, you'll be known as, if you don't wake up! Now stay abreast of me and try to *act* like Eric the Eye. These are dangerous burrows and my vision isn't as sharp as

yours. Besides, I have to fill you in on a couple of things."
He turned. "Spread out a little farther back there," he
called out to the men behind him. "Spread out! You should
be a full spearcast from the backside of the man in front of
you. Let me see a real strung-out column with plenty of
distance between each warrior."

To Eric, he muttered, once the maneuver had been completed: "Good. Gives us a chance to talk without everyone
in the band hearing us. You can trust my bunch, but still,
why take chances?"

Eric nodded, with no idea what he was talking about. His
uncle had become slightly odd recently. Well, he was still
the best band captain in all Mankind.

They marched along together, the light from the strange
glowing substance on Eric's torch and his uncle's forehead
spreading a yellowish illumination some hundred feet ahead
of them. On either side, underfoot, overhead, were the
curved, featureless walls of the burrow. From the center of
the corridor, where they marched, the walls looked soft and
spongy, but Eric knew what tremendous labor was involved
in digging a niche or recess in them. It took several strong
men at least two sleep periods to make a niche large enough
to hold a handful of Mankind's store of artifacts.

Where had the burrows come from? Some said they had
been dug by the ancestors when they had first begun to hit
back at the Monsters. Others claimed the burrows had always been there, waiting for Mankind to find them and be
comfortable in them.

In all directions the burrows stretched. On and on they
went, interminably curving and branching and forking, dark
and silent, until human beings stamped into them with glow
lamp and glow torch. These particular corridors, Eric knew,
led to Monster territory. He had been along them many
times as a humble spear carrier when his uncle's band had
been dispatched to bring back the necessities of life for
Mankind. Other corridors went off to more exotic and even
more dangerous places. But were there any places which
had no burrows?

What a thought! Even the Monsters lived in burrows, big
as they were reputed to be. But there was a legend that
Mankind had once lived outside burrows, outside the branching corridors. Then what had they lived in? Just trying to
work it out made you dizzy.

They came to a place where the burrow became two burrows, each curving away from the other in opposite directions.

"Which one?" his uncle demanded.

Eric unhesitatingly pointed the right.

Thomas the Trap-Smasher nodded. "You have a good memory," he said as he bore in the direction that Eric had indicated. "That's half of being an Eye. The other half is having a feeling, a knack, for the right way to go. You have that too. I've noticed it on every expedition where you've been along. That's what I told those women—Rita, Ottilie—I told them what your name had to be. Eric the Eye, I told them. Find a vision for the kind that corresponds to it."

He was so shocked that he almost came to a halt. "You picked my name? You told them what kind of vision . . . That's—that's—I never heard of such a thing!"

His uncle laughed. "It's no different from Ottilie the Omen-Teller making a deal with Franklin to have a vision showing him as the new chief. He gets to be chief, she becomes the Chieftain's First Wife and automatically takes over the Female Society. Religion and politics, they're always mixed up together these days, Eric. We're not living in the old times any more when Ancestor-science was real and holy and it worked."

"It still works, Ancestor-science, doesn't it?" he pleaded. "Some of the time?"

"Everything works *some* of the time. Only Alien-science, though, works *all* of the time. It's working for Aliens, for the Monsters. It's got to begin working for us. That's where you come in."

He had to remember that his uncle was an experienced captain, a knowledgeable warrior. Thomas the Trap-Smasher's protection and advice had brought him, a despised single-ton, an orphaned child of parents that no one dared even talk about, to his present estate of almost full thieving status. It was very fortunate for him that neither of his uncle's wives had yet produced a son which survived into the initiate years. He still had a lot to learn from this man.

"Now," the Trap-Smasher was saying, his eyes still on the dimly illuminated corridors ahead. "When we get to the Monster burrows, you go in. You go in alone, of course."

Well, of course, Eric thought. What other way was there to make your Theft? The first time you stole for Mankind, you did it all alone, to prove your manhood, your courage, also the amount of personal luck you enjoyed. It was not like a regular band theft—or organized stealing of a large amount of goods that would last Mankind many sleep-periods, almost a tenth of an auld lang syne. In a regular band theft, assigned to each band in rotation, a warrior had to be assured of the luck and skill of the warriors at his side. He had to know that each one of them had made his Theft— and proved himself when completely alone.

Stealing from the Monsters was dangerous enough under the best of conditions. You wanted only the cleverest, bravest, most fortunate warriors along with you.

"Once you're inside, stay close to the wall. Don't look up at first or you're likely to freeze right where you are. Keep your eyes on the wall and move close to it. Move fast."

Nothing new here. Every initiate learned over and over again, before he made his Theft, that it was terribly dangerous to look up when you first entered Monster territory. You had to keep your eyes on the wall and move in the protection of it, the wall touching your shoulder as you ran alongside it. Why this was so, Eric had no idea, but that it was so he had long ago learned to repeat as a fact.

"All right," Thomas the Trap-Smasher went on. "You turn right as you go in. *Right*, do you hear me, Eric? You turn right, without looking up, and run along the wall, letting it brush your shoulder every couple of steps. You run forty, fifty paces, and you come to a great big thing, a structure, that's almost touching the wall. You turn left along that, moving away from the wall, but still not looking up, until you pass an entrance in the structure. You don't go in that first entrance, Eric; you pass it by. About twenty, twenty-five paces further on, there'll be a second entrance, a bigger one. You go in that one."

"I go in that one," Eric repeated carefully, memorizing his uncle's words. He was receiving directions for his Theft, the most important act of his life! Every single thing his uncle told him must be listened to carefully, must not be forgotten.

"You'll be in something that looks like a burrow again, but it'll be darker, at first. The walls will soak up light from your glow lamp. After a while, the burrow will open out into a great big space, a real big and real dark space. You go on in a straight line, looking over your shoulder at the light from the entrance and making sure it's always directly behind you. You'll hit another burrow, a low one this time.

Turn right at the first fork as soon as you go in, and there you are."

"Where? Where will I be? What happens then?" Eric demanded eagerly. "How do I make my Theft? Where do I find the third category?"

Thomas the Trap-Smasher seemed to have trouble continuing. Incredible—he was actually nervous! "There'll be a Stranger there. You tell him who you are, your name. He'll do the rest."

This time Eric came to a full stop. "A Stranger?" he asked in complete amazement. "Someone who's not of Mankind?"

His uncle grabbed at his arm and pulled him along. "Well, you've seen Strangers before," he said with a weak laugh. "You know there are others in the burrows besides Mankind. You know that, don't you, boy?"

Eric certainly did.

From an early age he had accompanied his uncle and his uncle's band on warfare and trading expeditions to the burrows a bit farther back. He knew that the people in these burrows looked down on the people in his, that they were more plentiful than his people, and led richer, safer lives—but he still couldn't help feeling sorry for them.

They were nothing but Strangers, after all. He was a member of Mankind.

It wasn't just that Mankind lives in the front burrows, those closest to the Monster larder. This enormous convenience might be counterbalanced, he would readily admit, by the dangers associated with it—although the constant exposure to dangers and death in every form were part of Mankind's greatness. They were great despite their inferior technology. So what if they were primarily a source of raw materials to the more populous but less hardy burrows in the rear? How long would the weaponsmiths, the potters and tanners and artificers of these burrows be able to go on with their buzzing, noisy industries once Mankind ceased to bring them the basic substances—food, cloth, metal—it had so gloriously stolen from fear-filled Monster territory? No, Mankind was the bravest, greatest, most important people in all the burrows.

But that still wasn't the point of it all.

The point was that you had nothing more to do with Strangers than was absolutely necessary. They were Strangers. You were Mankind. You stayed proudly aloof from them at all times.

Trading with them—well, you traded with them. Mankind needed spear-points and sturdy spear-shifts, knapsacks and loin-straps, canteens and cooking vessels. You needed these articles and got them in exchange for heavy backloads of shapeless, unprocessed stuff freshly stolen. Mating with them— well, of course you mated with them. One was always on the lookout for extra women who could add to the knowledge and technical abilities of Mankind. But these women became a well-adjusted part of Mankind once they were stolen, just as Mankind's women were complete outsiders and Strangers the moment they had been carried off by a foreign raiding party. And fighting with them, warring with them— next to stealing from the Monsters, that was the sweetest, most exciting part of a warrior's existence.

You traded with Strangers, coldly, suspiciously, always alert for a better bargain; you stole Stranger women whenever you could, gleefully, proudly, because that diminished them and increased the numbers and well-being of Mankind; and you fought Stranger men whenever there was more to be gained that way than by simple trading—and periodically they came upon you as you lay in your burrow unawares and fought you.

But otherwise, for all normal social purposes, they were taboo. Almost as taboo and not-to-be-related-to as the Monsters on the other side of Mankind's burrows. When you came upon an individual Stranger wandering apart from his people, you killed him quickly and casually.

You certainly didn't ask him for advice on your Theft.

Eric was still brooding on the unprecedented nature of his uncle's instructions when they came to the end of their journey, a large, blind-alley burrow. There was a line cut deep into the blank wall here, a line that started at the floor, went up almost to the height of a man's head, and then curved down to the floor again.

The door to Monster territory.

Thomas the Trap-Smasher waited for a moment, listening. When his experienced ears had detected no unusual noises in the neighborhood, no hint of danger on the other side, he cupped his hands around his mouth, faced back the way he had come, and softly gave the ululating recognition-call of the band. The four other warriors and the apprentice came up swiftly and grouped themselves about him. Then, at a signal from their leader, all squatted near the door.

They ate first, rapidly and silently, removing from their knapsacks handfuls of food that the women had prepared for them and stuffing their mouths full, the beams from the glow lamps above their eyes darting incessantly back and forth along the arched, empty corridor. This was the place of ultimate, awful danger. This was the place where anything might happen.

Eric ate most sparingly of all, as was correct for an initiate about to emerge upon his Theft. He knew he had to keep his springiness of body and watchfulness of mind at their highest possible pitch. He saw his uncle nodding approvingly as he returned the bulk of his food to the knapsack.

The floor vibrated slightly underfoot; there was a regular, rhythmic gurgling. Eric knew that meant they were directly over a length of Monster plumbing: upon his return, before the band started homewards, Thomas the Trap-Smasher would make an opening in the plumbing and they would refill their canteens. The water here, nearest to Monster territory, was always the sweetest and best.

Now his uncle got to his feet and called Roy the Runner to him. While the other warriors watched, tense and still, the two men walked to the curved line and laid their ears against it. Satisfied, finally, they inserted spear points into the door's outline on either side and carefully pried the slab back toward them. They laid it on the floor of the corridor, very gently.

A shimmering blur of pure whiteness appeared where the door had been.

Monster territory. The strange, alien light of Monster territory. Eric had seen many warriors disappear into it to fulfill their manhood tasks. Now it was his turn.

Holding his heavy spear at the ready, Eric's uncle leaned forward into the whiteness. His body twisted as he looked up, down, around, on both sides. He withdrew and came back into the burrow.

"No new traps," he said in a soft voice. "The one I dismantled last expedition is still up there on the wall. It hasn't been repaired. Now Eric. Here you go, boy."

Eric rose and walked with him to the doorway, remembering to keep his eyes on the floor. You can't look up, he had been told again and again, not right away, not the first time you're in Monster territory. If you do, you freeze, you're lost, you're done for completely.

His uncle checked him carefully and fondly, making certain that his new loin straps were tight, that his knapsack and back-sling were both in the right position on his shoulders. He took a heavy spear from Eric's right hand and replaced it with a light one from the back-sling. "If you're seen by a Monster," he whispered, "the heavy spear's not worth a damn. You scuttle into the closest hiding-place and throw the light spear as far as you can. The Monster can't distinguish between you and the spear. It will follow the spear."

Eric nodded mechanically, although this too he had been told many times, this too was a lesson he knew by heart. His mouth was so dry! He wished that it weren't unmanly to beg for water at such a moment.

Thomas the Trap-Smasher took his torch from him and slipped a glow lamp about his forehead. Then he pushed him through the doorway. "Go make your Theft, Eric," he whispered. "Come back a man."

V

He was on the other side. He was in Monster territory. He was surrounded by the strange Monster light, the incredible Monster world. The burrows, Mankind, everything familiar, lay behind him.

Panic rose from his stomach and into his throat like vomit. *Don't look up. Eyes down, eyes down or you're likely to freeze right where you are. Stay close to the wall, keep your eyes on the wall and move along it. Turn right and move along the wall. Move fast.*

Eric turned. He felt the wall brush his right shoulder. He began to run, keeping his eyes down, touching the wall with his shoulder at regular intervals. He ran as fast as he possibly could, urging his muscles fiercely on. As he ran, he counted the steps to himself.

Twenty paces. Where did the light come from? It was everywhere; it glowed so; it was white, white. *Twenty-five paces. Touch the wall with your shoulder. Don't—above everything—don't wander away from the wall. Thirty paces.* In light like this you had no need of the glow lamp. It was almost too bright to see in. *Thirty-five paces.* The floor was not like a burrow floor. It was flat and very hard. So was the wall. Flat and hard and straight. *Forty paces. Run and keep your eyes down. Run. Keep touching the wall with your shoulder. Move fast. But keep your eyes down. Don't look up. Forty-five paces.*

He almost smashed into the structure he had been told about, but his reflexes and the warnings he had received swung him to the left and along it just in time. It was a different color than the wall, he noted, and a different-textured material. *Keep your eyes down. Don't look up.* He came to an entrance, like the beginning of a small burrow.

Don't go in that first entrance, Eric; you pass it by. He began to count again as he ran. Twenty-three paces more, and there was another entrance, a much higher, wider one. He darted inside. *It'll be darker, at first. The walls will soak up light from your glow lamp.*

Eric paused, gasping. He was grateful for the sucking darkness. After that terrible, alien white light, the gloom was friendly, reminiscent of the familiar burrows now so horribly far away.

He could afford to take a breath at this point, he knew. The first, the worst part was over. He wasn't out in the open any more.

He had emerged into Monster territory. He had run fast, following instructions until he was safely under cover again. He was still alive.

The worst was over. Nothing else would be as bad as this.

Monster territory. It lay behind him, bathed in its own peculiar light. Now. Why not? Now, when he was in a place of comparative safety. He could take a chance. He *wanted* to take a chance.

He turned, gingerly, fearfully. He raised his eyes. He looked.

The cry that tore from his lips was completely involuntary and frightened him almost as much as what he saw. He shut his eyes and threw himself down and sideways. He lay where he had fallen for a long while, almost paralyzed.

It couldn't be. He hadn't seen it. Nothing was that high, nothing ran on and on for such incredible distances!

After a time, he opened his eyes again, keeping them carefully focused on the dark near him. The gloom in this covered place had diminished somewhat as his eyes had grown more accustomed to it. Yellowish light from his glow lamp was providing illumination now: he could make out

the walls, about as far apart from each other as those in a
burrow, but—unlike a burrow's walls—oddly straight and at
right angles to the floor and ceiling. Far off there was an
immense patch of darkness. *The burrow will open out into a
great big space, a real big and real dark space.*

What was this place, he wondered? What was it to the
Monsters?

He had to take another look behind, into the open. One
more quick look. He was going to be Eric the Eye. An Eye
should be able to look at anything. He had to take another
look.

But guardedly, guardedly.

Eric turned again, opening his eyes a little at a time. He
clamped his teeth together so as not to cry out. Even so, he
almost did. He shut his eyes quickly, waited, then opened
them again.

Bit by bit, effort by effort, he found he was able to look
into the great open whiteness without losing control of himself. It was upsetting, overpowering, but if he didn't look
too long at any one time, he could stand it.

Distance. Enormous, elongated, unbelievable distance.
Space upon space upon space—that white light bathing it
all. Space far ahead, space on all sides, space going on and
on until it seemed to have no end to it at all. But there,
fantastically far off, there was an end. There was a wall, a
wall made by giants that finally sealed off the tremendous
space. It rose hugely from the flat, huge floor and disappeared somewhere far overhead.

And in between—once you could stand to look at it this
much—in between, there were objects. Enormous objects,
dwarfed only by the greatness of the space which surrounded
them, enormous, terribly alien objects. Objects like nothing
you had ever imagined.

No, that wasn't quite true. That thing over there. Eric
recognized it.

A great, squat thing like a full knapsack without the
straps. Since early boyhood, many was the time he had
heard it described by warriors back from an expedition into
Monster territory.

There was food in that sack and the others like it. Enough
food in that one sack to feed the entire population of Mankind for unnumbered auld lang synes. A different kind of
food in each sack.

No spear point possessed by Mankind would cut through the fabric of its container, not near the bottom where it was thickest. Warriors had to climb about halfway up the sack, Eric knew, before they could find a place thin enough to carve themselves an entrance. Then the lumps of food would be lowered from man to man all the way down the sack, warriors clinging to precarious handholds every few paces.

Once the pile on the floor was great enough, they would clamber down and fill their specially large, food-expedition knapsacks. Then back to the burrows and to the women who alone possessed the lore of determining whether the food was fit for consumption and of preparing it if it were.

That's where he would be at this moment, on that sack, cutting a hole in it, if he'd chosen a first category Theft like most other youths. He'd be cutting a hole, scooping out a handful of food—any quantity, no matter how small, was acceptable on an initiatory Theft—and be preparing to go home to plaudits from the women and acceptance from the men. He'd be engaged in a normal, socially acceptable endeavor.

Instead of which . . .

He found that he was able to stare at the Monster room now from under the cover of his hiding place with only a slight feeling of nausea. Well, that in itself was an achievement. After only a short time, here he was, able to look around and estimate the nature of Monster goods like the most experienced warrior. He couldn't look up too high as yet, but what warrior could?

Well and good, but this wasn't getting him anywhere. He didn't have a normal Theft to make. His was third category. Monster souvenirs.

Eric turned and faced the darkness again. He walked rapidly forward into the straight-walled burrow, the glow-lamp on his forehead lighting a yellow path. Ahead of him, the great black space grew steadily larger as he pushed towards it.

Everything about his Theft, his initiation into manhood, was extraordinary. Thomas the Trap-Smasher telling the women about his special talents, so that he would be accorded a vision and a name which would fit with them. Visions were supposed to come from the ancestors, through the ancestor-science of the record machine. Nobody was supposed to have the slightest idea in advance of what the vision would be. That was all up to the ancestors and their mysterious plans for their descendants.

Was it possible, was it conceivable, that all visions and names were pre-arranged, that the record machine was set in advance for every initiation? Where did that leave religion? If that were so, how could you continue to believe in logic, in cause and effect?

And having someone—a Stranger, at that!—help you make your Theft. A Theft was supposed to be purely and simply a test of your male potential; by definition, it was something you did alone.

But if you could accept the concept of pre-arranged visions, why not pre-arranged Thefts?

Eric shook his head. He was getting into very dark corridors mentally: his world was turning into sheer confusion.

But one thing he knew. Making an arrangement with a Stranger, as his uncle had done, was definitely an act contrary to all the laws and practices of Mankind. Thomas's uncertain speech had underlined that fact. It was—well, it was *wrong*.

Yet his uncle was the greatest man in all Mankind, so far as Eric was concerned. Thomas the Trap-Smasher could do no wrong. But Thomas the Trap-Smasher was evidently leaning toward Alien-science. Alien-science was wrong. But again, on the other hand, his parents, according to the Trap-Smasher, his father and his mother had been Alien-sciencers.

Too much. There was just too much to work out. There was too much he didn't know. He'd better concentrate on his Theft.

The strange burrow had come to an end. The hairs rose on the back of his neck as he walked into the great dark area and sensed enormous black heights above him. He began to hurry, turning every once in a while to make certain that he was staying in a straight line with the light from the entrance. Here, his forehead glow lamp was almost no use at all. He didn't like this place. It felt almost like being out in the open.

What, he wondered again feverishly, was this structure in the world of the Monsters? What function did it have? He was not sure he wanted to know.

Eric was running by the time he came to the end of the

open space. He hit the wall so hard that he was knocked
over backwards.

For a moment, he was badly frightened, then he realized
what had happened. He hadn't taken his bearings for a
while: he must have moved off at an angle.

Groping along the wall with extended arms, he found the
entrance to the low burrow at last. It was quite low—he had
to bend his knees and duck his head as he went up to it. It was
an unpleasantly narrow little corridor. But then there was
an opening on his right—the fork his uncle had told him
about—and he turned into it with relief.

He had arrived.

There was a burst of light from a group of glow lamps.
And there were Strangers, there were *several* Strangers here.
Three of them—no, four—no, five! They squatted in a
corner of this large, square burrow, three of them talking
earnestly, the other two engaged in some incomprehensible
task with materials that were mostly unfamiliar.

All of them leaped to their feet as he trotted in and
deployed instantly in a wide semi-circle facing him. Eric
wished desperately he had been holding two heavy spears
instead of the single light one. With two heavy spears you
had both a shield and a dangerous offensive weapon. A light
spear was good for a single cast, and that was that.

He held it nevertheless in the throwing position above his
shoulder and glared fiercely, as a warrior of Mankind should.
If he had to throw, he decided, he would spring to one side
immediately afterward and try to pluck the two heavy spears
from his backsling. But if they rushed him right now—

"Who are you?" asked a strong-faced, middle-aged man
in the center of the semi-circle, his spear throbbing in an
upraised arm. "What's your name—what's your people?"

"Eric the Only," Eric told him quickly. Then he remembered to add: "I'm destined to be Eric the Eye. My people
are Mankind."

"He's expected, one of us," the middle-aged man told the
others who immediately relaxed, slung their spears and went
back to what they had been doing. "Welcome, Eric the
Only of Mankind. Put up your spear and sit with us. I am
Arthur the Organizer."

Eric gingerly dropped his spear into the back-sling. He
studied the Stranger.

A man about as old as his uncle and not nearly as hefty,

although well-muscled enough for normal warlike purposes. He wore the loin-straps of a full warrior, but—as if these were not enough honor for a man—he also wore straps laced about his chest and across his shoulders, though he was carrying no knapsack. This was the fashion of many Strangers, Eric knew, as was the strap at the back of the head that held the hair in a tight tail away from the eyes instead of letting it hang wild and free as the hair of a warrior should. And the straps were decorated with odd, incised designs—another weak and unmanlike Stranger fashion.

Who but Strangers, Eric thought contemptuously, would group us so in an alien place without setting sentries at either end of their burrow? Truly Mankind had good reason to despise them!

But this man was a leader, he realized, a born leader, with an even more self-assured air than Thomas the Trap-Smasher, captain of the best band in all Mankind. He was studying Eric in turn, with eyes that weighed carefully and then, having decided on the measure, made a definite placement, fitting Eric permanently into this plan or that plan. He looked like a man whose head was full of many plans, each one evolving inexorably through action to a predetermined end.

He took Eric's arm companionably and led him to where the others squatted and talked and worked. This was no tribal burrow of any sort: it was quite apparently a field headquarters—and Arthur the Organizer was Commander-in-Chief. "I met your uncle," he told Eric, "about a dozen auld lang synes ago, when he came to us on a trading expedition—back in our burrows, I mean. A fine man, your uncle, very progressive. He's attended our secret meetings regularly, and there's going to be an important place for him in the great burrows we will dig, in the new world we are making. He reminds me a lot of your father. But so do you, my boy, so do you."

"Did you know my father?"

Arthur the Organizer smiled and nodded. "Very well. He could have been a great man. He gave his life for the Cause. Who among us will ever forget Eric the—the—Eric the Storekeeper or something, wasn't it?"

"The Storeroom-Stormer. His name was Eric the Storeroom-Stormer."

"Yes, of course. Eric the Storeroom-Stormer. An unforgettable name with us, and an unforgettable man. But that's another story; we'll talk about it some other time. You'll have to be getting back to your uncle very soon." He picked up a flat board covered with odd markings and studied it with his glow lamp.

"How do you like that?" one of the men working with the unfamiliar materials muttered to his neighbor. "You ask him his people, and he says, 'Mankind.' *Mankind!*"

The other man chuckled. "A front-burrow tribe. What the hell do you expect—sophistication? Each and every front-burrow tribe calls itself Mankind. As far as these primitives are concerned, the human race stops at their outermost burrow. Your tribe, my tribe—you know what they call us? Strangers. In their eyes, there's not too much difference between us and the Monsters."

"That's what I mean. They don't see us as fellow-men. They are narrow-minded savages. Who needs them?"

Arthur the Organizer glanced at Eric's face. He turned sharply to the man who had spoken last.

"I'll tell you who needs them, Walter," he said. "The Cause needs them. If the front-burrow tribes are with us, it means our main lines of supply to Monster territory are kept open. But we need every fighter we can get, no matter how primitive. Every single tribe has to be with us if Alien-science is to be the dominant religion of the burrows, if we're to avoid the fiasco of the last rising. We need front-burrow men for their hunting, foraging skills and back-burrow men for their civilized skills. We need everybody in this thing, especially now."

The man called Walter put down his work and scowled at Eric dubiously. He seemed to be totally unconvinced.

These arrogant back-burrowers with their ornamented straps and unmilitary manners! Men from different tribes sitting around and talking, when—if they had any sense of propriety at all—they should be killing each other!

Suddenly, the floor shook under him. He almost fell. He staggered back and forth, trying to grab at the spears in his back-sling. He finally got used to it, managed to find a solid footing in the upheaval. The spear he held vibrated in his hand.

From far away came a series of ear-splitting thumps. The floor swung to their rhythm. "What is it?" he cried, turning to Arthur. "What's going on?"

"You've never heard a Monster walking before?" the Organizer asked him unbelievingly. "That's right—this is your Theft, your first time out. It's a Monster, boy. A Monster's moving around in the Monster larder, doing whatever Monsters do. They have a right, you know," he added with a smile. "It's their larder. We're just—visitors."

Eric noticed that none of the others seemed particularly concerned. He drew a deep breath and reslung his spear. How the floor and the walls shook! What a fantastic, enormous creature that must be!

As an apprentice warrior, he had often stood with the rear-guard on the other side of the doorway to Monster territory while the band went in to steal for Mankind. A few times there had been heavy, thumping noises off in the distance, and the walls of the burrow had quivered slightly. But not like this. It had never been remotely as awesome as this.

He raised his eyes to the straight, flat ceiling of the burrow above them. He remembered the dark space further back stretching up limitlessly. "And this," he said aloud. "This structure we're in. What is *this* to them?"

Arthur the Organizer shrugged. "A piece of Monster furniture. Something they use for something or other. We're in one of the open spaces they always leave in the bases of their furniture. Makes the furniture lighter, easier to move around, I guess." He listened for a moment as the thumps drifted further away and then died out. "Let's get down to business. Eric, this is Walter the Weapon-Seeker. Walter the Weapon-Seeker of the Miximilian people. Walter, what do you have for Eric's tribe—for, uh, for Mankind?"

"I hate to give anything even halfway good to a front-burrow tribe," the squatting man muttered. "No matter how much you explain it to them, they always use it wrong, they botch it up every single time. Let's see. This should be simple enough."

He rummaged in the pile of strange stuff in front of him and picked up a small, red, jelly-like blob. "All you do," he explained, "is tear off a pinch with your fingers. Just a pinch at a time, no more. Then spit on it and throw it. After you spit on it, get it out of your hands fast. Throw it as fast and as far as you can. Do you think you can remember that?"

"Yes." Eric took the red blob from him and stared at it in puzzlement. There was a strange, irritating odor: it made his nose itch slightly. "But what happens? What does it do?"

"That's not your worry, boy," Arthur the Organizer told him. "Your uncle will know when to use it. You have your third category theft—a Monster souvenir that no one in your tribe has ever seen before. It should make them sit up and take notice. And tell your uncle to bring his band to my burrow three days—three sleep-periods—from now. That will be the last time we meet before the rising. Tell him to bring them armed with every last spear they can carry."

Eric nodded weakly. There were so many complex, incomprehensible things going on! The world was a bigger, more active place than he had ever imagined.

He watched Arthur the Organizer add a mark to the flat board on which many symbols were scratched. This was another Stranger practice—made necessary, he knew, by the weak Stranger memory, so inferior to that of Mankind.

The Weapon-Seeker leaped up and stopped him as he was about to put the red blob into his knapsack. "Nothing wet in there?" Walter demanded, opening the bag and rummaging about in Eric's belongings. "No water? Remember, get this stuff wet and you're done for."

"Mankind keeps its water in canteens," Eric explained irritably. "We keep it here," he pointed to the sloshing pouch at his hip, "not splashing around loosely with our provisions." He swung the full knapsack on his back and stepped away with stiff dignity.

Arthur the Organizer accompanied him to the end of the burrow. "Don't mind Walter," he whispered. "He's always afraid that nobody but himself will be able to use the Monster weapons he digs up. He talks that way to everyone. Now, suppose I refresh your memory about the way back. We don't want you to get lost."

"I won't get lost," Eric said coldly. "I have a good memory, and I know enough to perform a simple reversal of the directions on the way here. Besides, I am Eric the Espier, Eric the Eye of Mankind. I won't get lost."

He was rather proud of himself as he trotted away, without turning his head. Let the Strangers know what you think of them. The snobs. The stuck-up bastards.

But still, he felt damaged somehow, made less—as when Roy the Runner had called him a singleton before the entire band. And the last comment he had heard behind him— "These primitives: so damned touchy!"—made it no better.

He crossed the dark open space, still brooding, his eyes

fixed on the patch of white light ahead, his mind engaged in a completely unaccustomed examination of values. Mankind's free simplicity against the Stranger multiplicity and intricacy. Mankind's knowledge of basics, the important foraging basics of day-to-day life, against the Stranger knowledge of so many things and techniques he had never even heard about. Surely Mankind's way was infinitely preferable, far superior?

Then why did his uncle want to get mixed up with Stranger politics, he wondered, as he emerged from the structure? He turned left and, passing the small entrance he had ignored before, sped for the wall which separated him from the burrows. And why did all these Strangers, evidently each from a different tribe, agree in the contempt with which they held Mankind?

He had just turned right along the wall, on the last stretch before the doorway, when the floor shook again, jarring him out of his thoughts. He bounced up and down, frozen with fear where he stood.

He was out in the open while a Monster was abroad. A Monster had come into the larder again.

VI

Far off in the dazzling distance, he caught sight of the tremendously long gray body he had heard about since childhood, higher than a hundred men standing on each other's shoulders, the thick gray legs each wider than two hefty men standing chest to chest. He caught just one wide-eyed, fear-soluble glimpse of the thing before he went into complete panic.

His panic was redeemed by a single inhibition: he didn't spring forward and run away from the wall. But that was only because it would have meant running directly toward the Monster. For one thoroughly insane moment, however, he thought of trying to claw his way through the wall against which his shoulders were pressed.

Then—because it was the direction he had been running in—he remembered the doorway. He must be about thirty, thirty-five paces from it. There lay safety: his uncle, the band, Mankind and the burrows—the blessed, closed-in, narrow burrows!

Eric leaped along the wall for the doorway. He ran as

he'd never in his life run before, as he'd never imagined he could run.

But even as he fled madly, almost weeping at the effort he was making, a few sane thoughts—the result of long, tiresome drills as an initiate—organized themselves in his screaming mind. He had been closer to the structure in which the Strangers were hiding, the structure which Arthur the Organizer explained was a piece of Monster furniture. He should have turned the other way, towards the structure, gotten between it and the wall. There, unless he'd been seen as the Monster entered the larder, he could have rested safely until it was possible to make his escape.

He had gone too far to turn back now. But run silently, he reminded himself: run swiftly but make no noise, make no noise at all. According to the lessons that the warriors taught, at this distance Monster hearing was more to be feared than Monster vision. Run silently. Run for your life.

He reached the door. It had been set back in place!

In disbelief and utter horror he stared at the curved line in the wall that showed where the door had been replaced in its socket. But this was never done! This had never been heard of!

Eric beat frantically on the door with his fists. Would his knuckles make enough noise to penetrate the heavy slab? Or just enough to attract the Monster's attention?

He twisted his head quickly—a look, a deliberately wasted moment, to estimate the closeness of his danger. The Monster's legs moved so slowly: its speed would have been laughable if the very size of those legs didn't serve to push it forward an incredible distance with each step. And there was nothing laughable in that long, narrow neck, almost as long as the rest of the body, and the malevolent, relatively tiny head on the end of the neck. And those horrible pink things, all around the neck, just behind the head—

It was much nearer than it had been just seconds ago, but whether it had noticed him and was coming at him he had no idea. Beat at the door with the shaft of a spear? That should attract attention, that might be heard.

Yes, by the Monster too.

There was only one thing to do. He stepped a few paces back from the wall. Then he leaped forward, smashing his shoulder into the door. He felt it give a little. Another try.

The floor-shaking thumps of the Monster's steps were

now so close as to be almost deafening. At any moment, a great gray foot might come down and grind out his life. Eric stepped back again, forcing himself not to look up.

Another leap, another bruising collision with the door. It had definitely moved. An indentation showed all around it.

Was he about to be stepped on—to be squashed?

Eric put his hands on the door. He pushed. Slowly, suckingly, it left the place out of which it had been carved long ago.

Where was the Monster? How close? How Close?

Suddenly, the door fell over into the burrow, and Eric spilled painfully on top of it. He scrambled to his feet and darted down the corridor.

He had no time to feel relief. His mind was repeating its lessons, reminding him what he had to do next in such a situation.

Run a short distance down the burrow. Then stop and wait on the balls of your feet, ready to bolt. Get as much air into your lungs as possible. You may need it. If you hear a hissing, whistling sound, stop breathing and start running. Hold your breath for as long as you can—as long as you possibly can—then suck another chestful of air and keep running. Keep this up until you are far away. Far, far away.

Eric waited, poised to run, his back to the doorway.

Don't look around—just face the direction you'll have to run. There's only one thing you have to worry about, only one thing you have to listen for. A hissing, whistling sound. When you hear it, hold your breath and run.

He waited, his muscles contracted for instant action.

Time went by. He remembered to count. If you counted up to five hundred, slowly, and nothing happened, you were likely to be all right. You could assume the Monster probably hadn't noticed you.

So the experienced warriors said, the men who had lived through such an experience.

Five hundred. He reached five hundred and, just to be on the safe side, still tense, still ready to run, counted another five hundred, up to the ultimate number conceived by man, a full thousand.

No hissing, no whistling sounds. No suggestion of danger.

He relaxed, and his muscles—suddenly set free—gave way. He fell to the floor of the burrow, whimpering with the release of tension.

It was over. His Theft was over. He was a man.

* * *

He had been in the same place as a Monster, and lived through it. He had met Strangers and dealt with them as a representative of Mankind. Such things as he would have to tell his uncle!

His uncle. Where was his uncle? Where was the band?

Suddenly fully aware of how much was wrong, Eric scrambled to his feet and walked cautiously back to the open doorway. The burrow was empty. They hadn't waited for him.

But that was another incredible thing! A band never gave an initiate up for lost until at least two full days had gone by. In the chief's absence, of course, this was measured by the sleep periods of the band captain. Any band would wait two days before giving up and turning homeward. And, Eric was positive, his uncle would have waited a bit longer than that for *him*. He'd been away for such a short time! Then what had happened?

He crept to the doorway and peeped outside. There was almost no dizziness this time. His eyes adjusted quickly to the different scale of distance. The Monster was busy on the other side of the larder. It had merely been crossing the room, then, not pursuing and attacking. Apparently it hadn't noticed him at all.

Fantastic. And with all the noise he had made! All that rushing back and forth, that battering-down of the door!

The Monster turned abruptly, walked a few gigantic steps and hurled itself at the structure in which Eric had met the Strangers. The walls, the floor, everything, shook mightily in sympathy to the impact of the great organism as it wriggled a bit and became still.

Eric was startled until he realized that the creature had done no more than lie down in the structure. It *was* a piece of Monster furniture, after all.

How had that felt to Arthur the Organizer and Walter the Weapon-Seeker and the others hidden in the base? Eric grinned. Those Strangers must be a little less haughty, a little more sober at this moment.

Meanwhile, he had work to do, things to find out.

He got his fingers under the slab of door and tugged it upright. It was heavy! He pushed against it, slowly, carefully, first one side and then the other, walking it back to the hole in the wall. A final push, and it slid into place tightly, only the thin, curved line suggesting its existence.

Now he could look around.

There had been a fight here—that much was certain. A brief, bitter battle. Examining the area closely, Eric saw unmistakable signs of conflict.

A broken spear shaft. Some blood on the wall. Part of a torn knapsack. No bodies, of course. You were not likely to find bodies after a battle. Any people of the burrows knew that the one unavoidable imperative of victory was to drag the bodies away and dispose of them. No one might ever leave dead enemies to rot where they would foul the corridors.

So there had been a battle. He had been right—his uncle and his uncle's band had not just gone off and left him. There must have been an attack by a superior force. The band had stood its ground for a while, · sustained some losses, and then been forced to retreat.

But there were a few things which didn't make sense. First, it was very unusual for a war party of Strangers to come this close to Monster territory. The burrows which were inhabited by Mankind, the natural goal of a war party, were much further back. At this point, you would not expect to find any group larger than a foraging expedition—a Stranger band at most.

His uncle's men, fully armed, operating under battle alert, could easily cope with a single band of weavers, weaponsmiths or traders from the decadent back burrows. They would have driven them off, possibly taking a few prisoners, and continued to wait for him.

That left only two possibilities. The unlikely war party—a two or three-band attack—and, even more unlikely, a band from another fierce, front-burrow people. But front-burrowers rarely went prowling at random near Monster territory. They would have their own door cut into it and would tend to feel hugely uncertain about one belonging to another people. They too would head for the inhabited burrows if they were on any business other than the important one of stealing for their tribe's needs.

And another thing. Unless his uncle's band had been wiped out to the very last man—a thought Eric rejected as highly improbable—the survivors were honor-bound, by their oath of manhood, after doing whatever the immediate military situation required, from pursuit to retreat, to return as soon as possible to the spot where an initiate was expected back from his Theft. No warrior would dare face the women if he failed to do this.

Possibly the attack had just come. Possibly his uncle's band was a short distance away, still fighting their way from burrow's end to burrow's end; and, once they had gotten clear of the enemy, would make their way back to him.

No. In that case, he should be able to hear the battle still going on. And the burrows were dreadfully still.

Eric shivered. A warrior was not meant to be abroad without companions. He'd heard of tribeless Strangers—once, as a child, he remembered enjoying the intricate execution of a man who'd been expelled from his own people for some major crime and who had wandered pathetically into the neighborhood of Mankind—but these people were hardly to be considered human: tribes, bands, societies, were the surroundings of human creatures.

It was awful to be alone. It was unthinkable.

Without bothering to eat, though he was quite hungry after his Theft, he began walking rapidly down the corridor. After a while, he broke into a trot. He wanted to get home as soon as possible—to be among his own kind again.

He reached into his back-sling and got a spear for each hand.

A nervous business going through the corridors all by yourself. They were so empty and so quiet. They hadn't seemed this quiet when he'd been on expedition with the band. And so fearfully, frighteningly dim. Eric had never before realized how much difference there was between the light you got from one forehead glow-lamp and the usual band complement of a half-dozen. He found himself getting more and more wary of the unexpected shadows where the wall curved sharply: he picked up speed as he ran past the black hole of a branching burrow.

At any one of those places, an enemy could be waiting for him, warned by the sound of his approaching footsteps. It could be the same enemy which had attacked his uncle's band, a handful of cruel and murderous Strangers, or a horde of them. It could be something worse. Abruptly he remembered legends of unmentionable creatures who lurked in the empty burrows, creatures who fled before the approach of a band of warriors, but who would come noiselessly upon a single man. Big creatures who engulfed you. Tiny creatures who came in their hundreds and nibbled you to pieces. Eric kept jerking his head around to look behind him: at least he could keep his doom from taking him by surprise.

It was *awful* to be alone.

And yet, in the midst of his fears, his mind returned again and again to the problem of his uncle's disappearance. Eric could not believe anything serious had happened to him. Thomas the Trap-Smasher was a veteran of too many bloody adventures, too many battles against unequal odds. Then where had he gone? And where had he taken the band?

And why was there no sound of him anywhere, no sign in all this infinity of gloomy, stretching, menace-filled tunnels?

Fortunately, he was an Eye. He knew the way back and sped desperately along it without the slightest feeling of doubt. The Record Machine was right: he would never be lost. Let him just get safely back to the companionship of Mankind and he would be Eric the Eye.

And there it was again: who had been right, the Record Machine or his uncle? The vision that named him had come from the Record Machine, but his uncle claimed that this was religious claptrap. The vision had been selected and his name proposed to the women well in advance of the ceremony. And his uncle was an Alien-sciencer, in touch with Strangers who were also Alien-sciencers. . . .

So many things had happened in the last two days, Eric felt. So much of his world had shifted. It was as if the walls of the burrows had moved outward and upward until they resembled Monster territory more than human areas.

He was getting close now. These corridors looked friendlier, more familiar. He made himself run faster, although he was almost at the point of exhaustion. He wanted to be home, to be officially Eric the Eye, to inform Mankind of what had happened so that a rescue and searching party could be sent out for his uncle.

That doorway to Monster territory: who had replaced it? If a battle had been fought, and his uncle's band had retreated, still fighting, would the attacker have stopped to put the door neatly back in its socket? No.

Could it be explained by a sudden onslaught and the complete extermination of his uncle's band? Then, before dragging the bodies away, the enemy would have had time to put the door back. A doorway into Monster territory was a valuable human resource, after all, valuable to Mankind and Strangers alike—why jeopardize it by leaving it visible and open?

But who—or what—could have been capable of such a sudden onslaught, such a complete extermination of the best-led band in all Mankind? He'd have to get the answer from one of the other band captains or possibly a wise old crone in the Female Society.

Definitely within the boundaries of Mankind now, Eric forced himself to slow to a walk. He would be coming upon a sentry at any moment, and he had no desire at all to have a spear flung through him. A sentry would react violently to a man dashing out of the darkness.

"Eric the Only," he called out, identifying himself with each step. "This is Eric the Only." Then he remembered his Theft proudly and changed the identification. "Eric the Eye. This is Eric the Eye, the Espier, the further-seeing, less-paying Eye. Eric the Eye is coming back to Mankind!"

Oddly, there was no returning call of recognition. Eric didn't understand that. Had Mankind itself been attacked and driven away from its burrow? A sentry should respond to a familiar name. Something was very, inexplicably wrong.

Then he came around the last curve and saw the sentry at the other end. Rather, he saw what at first looked like three sentries. They were staring at him, and he recognized them. Stephen the Strong-Armed and two members of Stephen's band. Evidently he had arrived just at the moment when the sentry on duty was about to be relieved. That would account for Stephen and the other man. But why hadn't they replied to his shouts of identification?

They stood there silently as he came up, their spears still at the ready, not going down in welcome. "Eric the Eye," he repeated, puzzled. "I've made my Theft, but something happened to the rest—"

His voice trailed off, as Stephen came up to him, his face grim, his powerful muscles taut. The band captain shoved a spear point hard against Eric's chest. "Don't move," he warned. "Barney. John. Tie him up. We've caught the little rat!"

VII

His spears taken from him, his arms bound securely behind his back by the thongs of his own knapsack, Eric was pushed and prodded into the great central burrow of Mankind.

The place was almost unrecognizable.

Under the direction of Ottilie, the Chieftain's First Wife, a horde of women—what seemed at first like the entire membership of the Female Society—was setting up a platform in front of the Royal Mound. With the great scarcity of any building materials that Mankind suffered from, a construction of this sort was startling and unusual, yet there was something about it that awoke highly unpleasant memories in Eric's mind. But he was pulled from place to place too fast and there were too many other unprecedented things going on for him to be able to identify the memory properly.

Two women who were accredited members of the Female Society were not working under Ottilie's direction, he noticed. Bound hand and foot, they were lying against the far wall of the great central burrow. They were both covered with blood and showed every sign of having undergone prolonged and most vicious torture. He judged them to be barely this side of death.

As he was jerked past, he recognized them. They were the two wives of Thomas the Trap-Smasher.

Just wait until his uncle got back! Someone would really pay for this, he thought, more in absolute amazement than horror. He had the feeling that he must keep the horror away at all costs. Once let it in and it would soak through his thoughts right into the memory he was trying to avoid.

The place was full of armed men, running back and forth from their band captains to unknown destinations in the outlying corridors. Between them and around them scuttled the children, fetching and carrying raw materials for the hard-working women. There was a steady buzz of commands in the air . . . "Go to—" "Bring some more—" "Hurry with the—" . . . that mingled with the smell of many people whose pores were sweating urgency. And it wasn't just sweat that he smelled. Eric realized as he was dragged before the Royal Mound. It was anger. The anger and fear of all Mankind.

Franklin the Father of Many Thieves stood on the mound, carrying unaccustomed spears in his fat hands, talking rapidly to a group of warriors, band captains and—yes, actually! —*Strangers.* Even now, Eric found he could still be astonished at this fantastic development.

Strangers in the very midst of Mankind! Walking around freely and bearing arms!

As the chief caught sight of Eric, his face broke into a

loose-skinned smile. He nudged a Stranger beside him and pointed at the prisoner.

"That's him," he said. "That's the nephew. The one that asked for the third category Theft. Now we've got them all."

The Stranger didn't smile. He looked briefly at Eric and turned away. "I'm glad you think so. From our point of view, you've just got one more."

Franklin's smile faded to an uncertain grin. "Well, you know what I mean. And the damned fool came back by himself. It saved us a lot of trouble, I mean, didn't it?" Receiving no answer, he shrugged. He gestured with flabby imperiousness at Eric's guards. "You know where to put him. We'll be ready for them pretty soon."

Again the point of a spear stabbed into Eric's back, and he was forced forward across the central space to a small burrow entrance. Before he could reach it, however, he heard Franklin the Father of Many Thieves call out to Mankind: "There goes Eric, my people. Eric the Only. Now we've got the last of the filthy gang!"

For a moment, the activity stopped and seemed to focus on him. Eric shivered as a low, drawn-out grunt of viciousness and hatred arose everywhere, but most of all from the women.

Someone ran up to him. Harriet the History-Teller. The girl's face was absolutely contorted. She reached up to the crown of her head and pulled out the long pin held in place by a few knotted scarlet hairs. About her face and neck the hair danced like flames.

"You Alien-sciencer!" she shrieked, driving the pin straight at his eyes. "You filthy, filthy Alien-sciencer!"

Eric whipped his head to one side; she was back at him in a moment. His guards leaped at the girl and grappled with her, but she was able to get in one ripping slash that opened up almost all of his right cheek before they drove her away.

"Leave something for the rest of us," one of his guards pleaded the cause of reason as he strolled back to Eric. "After all, he belongs to the whole of Mankind."

"He does not!" she yelled. "He belongs to me most of all. I was going to mate with him when he returned from his Theft, wasn't I, Mother?"

"There wasn't anything official," Eric heard Rita the Record-Keeper admonishing as he tried to stanch the flow of blood by bringing his shoulder up and pressing it against the wound. "There couldn't be anything official about it until he'd achieved manhood. So you'll just have to wait your turn, Harriet, darling. You'll have to wait until your elders are finished with him. There'll be plenty left for you."

"There won't be," the girl pouted. "I know what you're like. There won't be hardly anything left."

Eric was shoved at the small burrow entrance again. The moment he was inside it, one of his guards planted a foot in his back, knocking the breath out of him. The kick propelled him forward, staggering wildly for balance, until he smashed into the opposite wall. As he fell, unable to use his arms to cushion himself, he heard laughter behind him in the great central burrow. He rolled on his side dizzily. There was a fresh flow of blood coming down from his cheek.

This wasn't the homecoming he'd imagined after his Theft—not in the slightest! What was going on?

He knew where he was. A tiny, blind-alley burrow off Mankind's major meeting-place, a sort of little vault used mostly for storage. Excess food and goods stolen from Monster territory were kept here until there was enough accumulated for a trading expedition to the back burrows. Occasionally, also, a male Stranger, taken prisoner in battle, might be held in this place until Mankind found out if his tribe valued him enough to pay anything substantial for his recovery.

And if they didn't . . .

Eric remembered the unusual structure that the women had been building near the Royal Mound—and shivered. The memory that he'd suppressed had now come alive in his mind. And it fitted with the way Harriet had acted—and with what her mother, Rita the Record-Keeper, had said.

They couldn't be planning that for him! He was a member of Mankind, almost a full warrior. They didn't even do that to Strangers captured in battle—now *normal* Strangers. A warrior was always respected as a warrior. At the worst, he deserved a decent execution, quietly done. Except for— Except for—

"*No!*" he screamed "*No!*"

The single guard who'd been left on duty at the entrance turned around and regarded him humorously.

"Oh, yes," he said. "Oh, definitely yes! We're going to have a lot of fun with both of you, as soon as the women say they're ready." He nodded with ominous, emphatic slowness and turned back to miss none of the preparations.

Both of you? For the first time, Eric looked around the little storage burrow. The place was almost empty of goods, but off to one side, in the light of his forehead glow-lamp (how proud he had been when it had been bestowed on him at the doorway to Monster territory!) he now saw another man lying bound against the wall.

His uncle.

Eric brought his knees up and wriggled rapidly over to him. It was a painful business. His belly and sides were not callused and inured to the rough burrow floor like his feet. But what did a few scratches more or less matter any more?

The Trap-Smasher was barely conscious. He had been severely handled, and he looked almost as bad as his wives. There was a thick crust of dried blood on his hair. The haft of a spear, Eric guessed, had all but cracked his head open. And in several places on his body, his right shoulder, just above his left hip, deep in his thigh, were the oozing craters of serious spear wounds, raw and unbandaged.

"Uncle Thomas," Eric urged. "What happened? Who did this to you?"

The wounded man opened his eyes and shuddered. He looked around stupidly as if he had expected to find the walls talking to him. And his powerful arms struggled with the knots that held them firmly behind his back. When he finally located Eric, he smiled.

It was a bad thing to do. Someone had also smashed in most of his front teeth.

"Hello, Eric," he mumbled. "What a fight, eh? How did the rest of the band do? Anybody get away?"

"I don't know. That's what I'm asking *you*! I came back from my Theft—you were gone—the band was gone. I got here, and everyone's crazy! There are Strangers out there, walking around with weapons in our burrows. Who are they?"

Thomas the Trap-Smasher's eyes had slowly darkened. They were fully in focus now, and long threads of agony swam in them. "Strangers?" he asked in a low voice. "Yes, there were Strangers fighting in Stephen the Strong-Armed's band. Fighting against us. That chief of ours—Franklin—he got in touch with Strangers after we left. They compared notes. They must have been working together, been in touch with each other, for a long time. Mankind, Strangers, what difference does it make when their lousy Ancestor-science is threatened? I should have remembered."

"What?" Eric begged. "What should you have remembered?"

"That's the way they put down Alien-science in the other rising, long ago. A chief's a chief. He's got more in common with another chief—even a chief of Strangers—than with his own people. You attack Ancestor-science, and you're attacking their power as chiefs. They'll work together then. They'll give each other men, weapons, information. They'll do everything they can against the common enemy. Against the only people who really want to hit back at the Monsters. I should have remembered! Damn it all," the Trap-Smasher groaned through his ruined mouth, "I saw that the chief and Ottilie were suspicious. I should have realized how they were going to handle it. They were going to call in Strangers, exchange information—and unite against us!"

Eric stared at his uncle, dimly understanding. Just as there was a secret organization of Alien-sciencers that cut across tribal boundaries, so there was a tacit, rarely used understanding among the chiefs, based on the Ancestor-science religion that was the main prop of their power. *And* the power of the leaders of the Female Society, come to think of it. All special privileges were derived from their knowledge of Ancestor-science. Take that away from them, and they'd be ordinary women with no more magical abilities than was necessary to tell edible food from Monster poison.

Grunting with pain, Thomas the Trap-Smasher wormed his way up to a sitting position against the wall. He kept shaking his head as if to jar recollection loose.

"They came up to us," he said heavily, "Stephen the Strong-Armed and his band came up to us just after you'd gone into Monster territory. A band from Mankind with a message from the chief—who suspected anything? They might be coming to tell us that the home burrows were under attack by Strangers. Strangers!" He gave a barking laugh, and some blood splashed out of his mouth. "They had Strangers with them, hidden all the way behind in the corridors. Mobs and mobs of Strangers."

*   *   *

Eric began to visualize what had happened.

"Then, when they were among us, when most of us had reslung our spears, they hit us. Eric, they hit us real good. They had us so much by surprise that they didn't even need outside help. I don't think there was much left of us by the time the Strangers came running up. I was down, fighting with my bare hands, and so was the rest of the band. The Strangers did the mopping up. I didn't see most of it. Somebody handed me one hell of a wallop—I never expected to wake up alive." His voice got even lower and huskier. "I'd have been lucky not to."

The Trap-Smasher's chest heaved: a strange, long noise came out of it. "They brought me back here. My wives— they were working on my wives. Those bitches from the Female Society—Ottilie, Rita—this part of it is their business—they had my wives pegged out and they worked on them in front of me. I was blanking out and coming to, blanking out and coming to; I was conscious while they—"

He dropped to a bloody mumble again, his head falling forward loosely. His voice became clear for a moment, but not entirely rational. "They were good women," he muttered. "Both of them. Good, good girls. And they loved me. They had their chance to become more important. A dozen times Franklin must have offered to impregnate them, and they turned him down every time. They really loved me."

Eric almost sobbed himself. He'd had little to do with them once he'd reached the age of the warrior initiate, but in his childhood, they'd given him all the mother love he ever remembered. They'd cuffed him and caressed him and wiped his nose. They'd told him stories and taught him the catechism of the ancestral science. Neither had sons of his age who had survived the various plagues and the Monster-inflicted calamities that periodically swept through Mankind's burrows. He'd been lucky. He'd received much of the care and affection that their own sons might have enjoyed.

Their fidelity to the Trap-Smasher had been a constant source of astonishment in Mankind. It had cost them more than the large, healthy litters for which the chief had a well proven capacity: such eccentric, almost non-womanly behavior had inevitably denied them the high positions in the Female Society they would otherwise have enjoyed.

And now they were dead or dying, and their surviving

babies had been apportioned to other women whose importance would thereby be substantially increased.

"Tell me," he asked his uncle. "Why did the Female Society kill them? What did they do that was so awful?"

He saw that Thomas had lifted his head again and was staring at him. With pity. He felt his own body turn completely cold even before the Trap-Smasher spoke.

"You still won't let yourself think about it? I don't blame you, Eric. But it's there. It's being prepared for us outside."

"What?" Eric demanded, although a distant part of him had already worked out the terrible answer and knew what it was.

"We've been declared outlaws, Eric. They say we're guilty of the ultimate sacrilege against Ancestor-Science. We don't belong to Mankind anymore—you, me, my family, my band. We're outside Mankind, outside the law, outside religion. And you know what happens to outlaws, Eric, don't you? Anything goes. *Anything.*"

VIII

Ever since early childhood, Eric remembered looking forward to ceremonies of this sort. A Stranger would have been caught by one of the warrior bands, and it would be determined that he was an outlaw. Nine times out of ten, such a man was easy enough to identify. No one but an outlaw, for example, would be wandering the burrows by himself, without a band or at least a single companion to guard his back. The tenth time, when there was the slightest doubt, a request for ransom to his people would make the prisoner's position clear. There would be a story of some unforgivable sacrilege, some particularly monstrous crime that could be punished by nothing but complete anathema and the revocation of all privileges as a human being. The man had escaped the punishment being prepared for him. Do with him as you will, his people would say. He is no longer one of us; he is the same as a Monster; he is something non-human so far as we are concerned.

Then a sort of holiday would be declared. Out of the bits and pieces of lumber stolen from Monster territory and set aside by the women for this purpose, the members of the Female Society would erect a structure whose specifications had been handed down from mother to daughter for countless generations—all the way back to the ancestors who had built the Record-Machines. It was called a Stage or a Theater, although Eric had also heard it referred to as The Scaffold. In any case, whatever its true name, most of the details concerning it were part of the secret lore of the Female Society and, as such, were no proper concern of males.

One thing about it, however, everyone knew. On it would be enacted a moving religious drama: the ultimate triumph of humanity over the wickedness of the Monsters.

For this, the central character had to fulfill two requirements. He had to be an intelligent creature, as the Monsters were, so that he could be made to suffer as some day Mankind meant the Monsters to suffer; and he had to be non-human, as the Monsters were, so that every drop of fear, resentment and hatred distilled by the enormous swaggering aliens could be poured out upon his flesh without any inhibition of compunction or fellow-feeling.

For this purpose, outlaws were absolutely ideal, since all agreed that such disgusting creatures had resigned their membership in the human race.

When an outlaw was caught, work stopped in the burrows, and Mankind's warrior bands were called home. It was a great time, a joyous time, a time of festival. Even the children—doing whatever they could to prepare for the glorious event, running errands for the laboring women, fetching refreshment for the stalwart, guarding men—even the children boasted to each other of how they would express their hatred upon this trapped representative of the non-human, this bound and shrieking protagonist of the utterly alien.

Everyone had their chance. All, from the chief himself to the youngest child capable of reciting the catechism of ancestral science, all climbed in their turn upon the Stage—or Theater—or Scaffold—that the women had erected. All were thrilled to vent a portion of Mankind's vengeance upon the creature who had been declared alien, as an earnest of what they would some day do collectively to the Monsters who had stolen their world.

Sarah the Sickness-Healer had her turn early in the proceedings; thenceforth, she stood on the structure and carefully supervised the ceremony. It was her job to see that nobody went too far, that everyone had a fair and adequate turn, and that even at the end there was some life left in the victim. Because then, at the end, the structure had to be completely burned—along with its bloody occupant—as a symbol of how the Monsters must eventually be turned into ash and be blown away and vanish.

"*And Mankind will come into its own,*" she would chant, while the charred fragments were kicked out of the burrow contemptuously. "*And the Monsters will be gone. They will be gone forever, and there will be nothing upon all the wide Earth but Mankind.*"

Afterwards, there was feasting, there was dancing, there was singing. Men and women chased each other into the dimmer side corridors; children whooped and yelled around the great central burrow; the few old folks went to sleep with broad, reminiscent smiles upon their faces. Everyone felt they had somehow struck back at the Monsters. Everyone felt a little like the lords of creation their ancestors had been.

Eric remembered the things he himself had done—the things he had seen others do—on these occasions. A tremendous tic of fear rippled through his body. He had to draw his shoulders up to his neck in a tight hunch and tense the muscles of his arms and legs. Finally his nerves subsided.

He could think again. Only he didn't want to think.

Those others, those outlaws in previous ceremonies of this sort in auld lang synes long past—was it possible that they had experienced the same sick, bewildered dread while waiting for the structure to be completed? Had they trembled like this, had they also felt wetness running down their backs, had they felt the same pleading squirm in their intestines, the same anticipatory twinges of soft, vulnerable flesh?

The thought had never crossed his mind before. He'd seen them as things completely outside humanity, the compressed symbol of all that was alien. One worried about their feelings no more than about those of the roaches scurrying madly about here in the storage burrow. One squashed them slowly or rapidly—at one's pleasure. What difference did it make? You didn't sympathize with roaches. You didn't identify with them.

But now that he was about to be squashed himself, he realized that it did make a difference. He was human. No matter what Mankind and its leaders now declared him to be, he was human. He felt human fears; he experienced a desperate human desire to live.

Then so had the others been. The outlaws whom he'd helped tear to pieces. Human. Completely human.

They'd sat here, just as he did now, they'd sat and waited for the festival and its agonies . . .

Only twice in his memory had members of Mankind ever been declared outlaw. Both cases had occurred a long time ago, before he'd even been a warrior-initiate. Eric tried now to remember what they had been like as living people. He wanted to reach out and feel companionship, some sort of companionship, even that of the dead. The dead were better than this beaten, bloody man next to him who had subsided into half-insane mumbles, his battered head on his torn and wound-scribbled chest.

What had they been like? It was no use. In the first case, memory brought back only a picture of a screaming hulk just before the fire was lit. No recollection of a man. No fellow-human in Mankind. And in the second case—

Eric sat bolt upright, straining against his bonds. The second man to be declared an outlaw had escaped! How he had done it Eric had never found out: he remembered only that a guard was severely punished, and that bands of warriors had sniffed for him along far-distant corridors for a long time afterward.

Escape. That was it. He had to escape. Once declared an outlaw, he could have no hope of mercy, no remission of sentence. The religious overtones of the ceremony being prepared were too highly charged to be halted for anything short of the disappearance of its chief protagonist.

Yes, escape. But how? Even if he could get free of the knots which so expertly and so strongly tied his hands behind his back, he had no weapon to hand. The guard at the entrance would transfix him with a spear in a moment. And if he failed, there were others outside, almost the entire warrior strength of the people.

How? *How*? He forced himself to be calm, to go over every possible alternative in his mind. He knew there was not much time. In a little while, the structure would be finished and the leaders of the Female Society would come for him.

Eric began working on the knots behind him. He worked without much hope. If he could get his hands loose, perhaps he might squirm his way carefully to the entrance, leap up suddenly and break into a run. So what if they threw a spear through him—wouldn't that be better and quicker than the other thing?

But they wouldn't, he realized. Not unless he were very lucky and some warrior forgot to think straight. In cases like this, when it was a matter of keeping, not killing a prisoner, you aimed for the legs. There were at least a dozen men in Mankind with skill great enough to bring him down even at twenty or twenty-five paces. And another dozen who might be able to catch him. He was no Roy the Runner, after all.

Roy! He was dead and sewered by now. He found himself regretting the fight he'd had with Roy.

A Stranger passed by the storage burrow entrance, glancing in with only a slight curiosity. He was followed in a moment by two more Strangers, going the same way. They were leaving, Eric guessed, before the ceremony began. They probably had ceremonies of their own to attend—with their own people.

Walter the Weapon-Seeker, Arthur the Organizer—were they at this moment sitting in similar storage burrows awaiting the same slow death? Eric doubted it. Somehow he couldn't see these men caught as easily as he and his uncle had been. Arthur was too clever, he was certain of that, and Walter, well, Walter would come up with some fantastic weapon that no one had ever seen or heard of . . .

Like the one he had in his knapsack right now—that red blob the Weapon-Seeker had given him!

Was it a weapon? He didn't know. But even if it wasn't, he had the impression it could create some kind of surprise. "It should make them sit up and take notice," Walter had said back in Monster territory.

Any kind of surprise, any kind of upset and he might have a diversion under cover of which he and his uncle could escape.

But that was the trouble. His uncle. With his hands bound as thoroughly as he could now ascertain they were, he needed his uncle's help to do anything at all. And the Trap-Smasher was obviously too far gone to be at all useful.

He was talking to himself in a steady, monotonous, argumentative mutter, his upper body slumping further and further across his own lap. Every once in a while, the mutters would be broken by a sharp, almost surprised moan as his wounds woke into a clearer consciousness of themselves.

Most other men in his condition, Eric judged, would have been dead by now. Only a body as powerful as the Trap-

Smasher's could have lasted this long. And—who knew?—if they could escape, it was possible that his uncle's wounds, given care and rest, might heal.

If they could escape.

"Uncle Thomas," he said, leaning toward him and whispering urgently. "I think I know a way out. I think I've figured out a way to escape."

No response. The bloody head continued to talk in a low, toneless voice to the lap. Mutter, mutter, mutter. Moan. Mutter, mutter.

"Your wives," Eric said desperately. "Your wives. Don't you want to get revenge for your wives?"

That seemed to be worth a flicker. "My wives," said the thick voice. "They were good women. Real good women. They never let Franklin near them. They were real good women." Then the flicker was over and the mutters returned.

"Escape!" Eric whispered. "Don't you want to escape?"

A thin, coagulating line of blood dripped out of his uncle's slowly working jaws. There was no other answer.

Eric looked towards the entrance of the storage burrow. The guard posted there was no longer turning from time to time to glance at the prisoners. The structure outside was evidently nearing completion, and his interest in the final preparations had caused him to take a step or two away from the entrance. He was staring off to the left down the great central burrow in absolute fascination.

Well, that was something. It gave them a chance. On the other hand, it also meant that they had scant moments left to their lives. Any time now, the leaders of the Female Society would be coming to drag them to the torture ceremony.

With his eyes on the guard, Eric leaned against the rough burrow wall and began scraping the imprisoning knapsack thongs against the sharpest edges he could find. It wouldn't be fast enough, he realized. If there were only a spear point in this place, something sharp. He looked around feverishly. No, nothing. A few tumbled bags of food over which lazy roaches wandered. Nothing he could use to help him get free.

His uncle was his only hope. Somehow he had to rouse the man, get through to him. He squirmed up close, his mouth against the Trap-Smasher's battered ear.

"This is Eric, Eric the Only. Do you remember me,

Uncle? I went on the Theft, Uncle Thomas, I went on the Theft with you. Third category. Remember, I asked for a third category theft, just like you told me to? I did my Theft, I was successful, I made it. I did just what you told me to do. I'm Eric the Eye now, right? Tell me, am I Eric the Eye?"

Mutters, mumbles and moans. The man seemed beyond intelligibility.

"What about Franklin? He can't do this to us, can he, Uncle Thomas? Don't you want to escape? Don't you want revenge on Franklin, on Ottilie, for what they did to your wives? Don't you? *Don't you?*"

He had to cut through his uncle's confused mist of gathering delirium.

In complete desperation, he lowered his head and sank his teeth into a wounded shoulder.

Nothing. Just the steady flow of argumentative gibberish. And the thin blood dripping from the mouth.

"I saw Arthur the Organizer. He said he'd known you for a long time. When did you meet him, Uncle Thomas? When did you first meet Arthur the Organizer?"

The head drooped lower, the shoulders slumped farther forward.

"Tell me about Alien-science. What is Alien-science?" Eric was almost gibbering himself now in his frantic efforts to find a key that would unlock his uncle's mind. "Are Arthur the Organizer and Walter the Weapon-Seeker very important men among the Alien-sciencers? Are they the chiefs? What was the name of the structure they were hiding in? What is it to the Monsters? They talked about other tribes, tribes I never heard of. How many other tribes are there? Are these other tribes—"

That was it. He had found the key. He had gotten through.

Thomas the Trap-Smasher's head came up waveringly, dimness swirling in his eyes. "Other tribes. Funny that you should ask about other tribes. That *you* should ask."

"Why? What about them?" Eric fought to hold the key in place, to keep it turning. "Why shouldn't I ask about those other tribes?"

"Your grandmother was from another tribe, a real strange tribe in a faroff burrow. I remember hearing about it when I was a little boy." Thomas the Trap-Smasher nodded to himself. "Your grandfather's band went on a long journey, the longest they'd ever taken. And they caught your grandmother and brought her back."

"My grandmother?" For the moment, Eric forgot what was being prepared for him outside. He'd known there was some peculiar secret about his grandmother. She had rarely been mentioned in Mankind. Up to now, he'd taken it for granted that this was because she'd had a son who was terribly unlucky—almost the worst thing a person in the burrows could be. A one-child litter, after all, and being killed together with his wife in Monster territory. Very unlucky.

"My grandmother was from another tribe? Not from Mankind?" He knew, of course, that several of the women had been captured from other peoples in neighboring burrows and had the good fortune now to be considered full-fledged members of Mankind. Sometimes one of their own women would be lost this way, when she strayed too far down an outlying burrow and stumbled into a band of Stranger warriors. If you stole a woman from another people, after all, you stole a substantial portion of their knowledge. But he'd never imagined—

"Dora the Dream-Singer." Thomas's head waggled loosely: he dribbled words mixed with red saliva. "Did you know why your grandmother was called the Dream-Singer, Eric? The women used to say that the things she talked about happened only in dreams, and that she couldn't talk straight like other people—she could only sing about her dreams. But she taught your father a lot, and he was like her. Women were a little afraid to mate with him. My sister was the first to take a chance—and everyone said she deserved what she got."

Abruptly, Eric became conscious of a change in the sounds outside the burrow. More quiet. Were they coming for him now?

"Uncle Thomas, listen! I have an idea. Those Strangers—Walter, Arthur the Organizer—they gave me a Monster souvenir. I don't know what it does, but I can't get at it. I'll turn around. You try to reach down into my knapsack with the tips of your fingers and—"

The Trap-Smasher paid no attention to him. "She was an Alien-sciencer," he rambled on, mostly to himself. "Your grandmother was the first Alien-sciencer we ever had in

Mankind. I guess her tribe were all Alien-sciencers. Imagine—
a whole tribe of Alien-sciencers!"

Eric groaned. This half-alive, delirious man was his only
hope of escaping. This bloody wreck who had once been the
proudest, most alert band captain of them all.

He turned for another look at the guard. The man was
still staring down the length of the great central burrow.
There was nothing to be heard now but a terrifying silence,
as if dozens of pairs of eyes were glowing in anticipation.
And footsteps—were not those footsteps? He had to find a
way to make his uncle cooperate.

"Thomas the Trap-Smasher!" he said sharply, barely man-
aging to keep his voice low. "Listen to me. This is an order!
There's something in my knapsack, a blob of sticky stuff.
We're going to turn our backs to each other, and you're
going to reach in with your fingers and fish it out. Do you
hear me? That's an order—a warrior's order!"

His uncle nodded, completely docile. "I've been a warrior
for over twenty auld lang synes," he mumbled, twisting
around. "Six of them a band captain. I've given orders and
taken them, given them and taken them. I've never dis-
obeyed an order. What I always say is how can you expect
to give orders if you don't—"

"*Now,*" Eric told him, bringing their backs together and
hunching down so that his knapsack would be just under his
uncle's bound arms. "Reach in. Work that mass of sticky
stuff out. It's right on top. And hurry!"

Yes. Those were footsteps coming up outside. Several of
them. The leaders of the Female Society, the chief, an
escort of warriors. And the guard, watching that deadly
procession, was liable to remember his duties and turn back
to the prisoners.

"*Hurry,*" he demanded. "I told you to hurry, dammit!
That's an order, too. Get it out fast. Fast!"

And, all this time, as the Trap-Smasher's fumbling fingers
wandered about in his knapsack, as he listened with fright
and impatience to the sounds of the approaching execution
party—all this time, somewhere in his mind, there was won-
derment at the orders he was rapping out to an experienced
band captain and the incredible authority he had managed
to get into his voice.

"Now you're wondering where your grandmother's tribe
have their burrow," Thomas began suddenly, reverting to

an earlier topic as if they were having a pleasant conversation after a fine, full meal.

"Forget it! Get that stuff out. Just get it out!"

"It's hard to describe," the other man's voice wandered on. "A long way off, their burrow is, a long way off. You know the Strangers call us front-burrow people. You know that, don't you? The Strangers are back-burrowers. Well, your grandmother's people are the bottom-most burrowers of all."

Eric sensed his fingers closing in the knapsack.

The three women who ruled the Female Society came into the storage burrow. Ottilie the Omen-Teller, Sarah the Sickness-Healer and Rita the Record-Keeper. With them was the chief and two band captains, heavily armed.

IX

Ottilie, the Chieftain's First Wife, was in the lead. She stopped, just inside the entrance to the burrow and the others came to a halt around her.

"Look at them," she jeered. "They're trying to free each other! And what do they plan to do if they get themselves untied?"

Franklin moved to her side and took a long, judicious look at the two men squatting back to back. "They'll try to escape," he explained, continuing his wife's joke. "They'll have their hands free, they figure, and surely Thomas the Trap-Smasher and his nephew are a match, even bare-handed, for the best spearmen in Mankind!"

And then Eric felt the searching hands come up out of the knapsack to which his own arms were tied. Something fell to the floor of the burrow. It made an odd noise, halfway between a splash and a thud. He twisted around for it immediately with his mouth open, flexing his knees in a tight crouch underneath his body.

"You've never seen anything like the burrows of your grandmother's people," his uncle was mumbling, as if what his hands had just done was no concern of the rest of him. "And neither have I, though I've listened to the tales."

"He won't last long now," Sarah the Sickness-Healer commented. "We'll have to have our fun with the boy."

All you do, Walter the Weapon-Seeker had said, *is tear off a pinch with your fingers. Then spit on it and throw it. Throw it as fast and as far as you can.*

He couldn't use his fingers. But he leaned down to the red blob and nipped off a piece with his teeth. He brought his tongue against the strange soft substance, lashing saliva into it. And simultaneously he kicked at the burrow floor with curved toes, straightening his legs, jerking his thighs and body upward. Unable to use his arms for balance, he tottered erect and turned, swaying, to face the leaders of his people.

After you spit on it, throw it fast. As fast and as far as you can.

"I don't know what he's doing," someone said, "but I don't like it. Let me through."

Stephen the Strong-Armed stepped ahead of the group and lifted a heavy spear, ready for throwing.

Eric shut his eyes, bent his head far back on his neck and took a deep, deep breath. Then he snapped his head forward, flipping his tongue hard against the object in his mouth. He forced out his breath so abruptly that the exhalation became a wild, barking cough.

The soft little mass flew out of his mouth, and he opened his eyes to watch its course. For a moment, he was unable to find it anywhere; then he located it by the odd expression on Stephen's face and the fearful upward roll of his eyes.

There was a little red splotch in the middle of the band captain's forehead.

What was supposed to happen, he wondered? He had followed directions as well as he could under the circumstances, but he had no idea what the scarlet stain, made loose and moist by his saliva, was supposed to accomplish. He watched it, hoping and waiting.

Then Stephen the Strong-Armed brought his free hand up slowly to wipe the stuff off. Eric stopped hoping. Nothing was going to happen.

Strangers, he had begun to think despairingly, *that's what comes of trusting Strangers—*

The blast of sound was so tremendous that for a moment he thought the roof of the burrow had fallen in. He was slammed backwards against the wall and fell as if he'd been walloped with a spear haft. He remembered the cough with which he'd expelled the bit of red blob from his mouth. Had there been a delayed echo to his cough, a gigantic, ear-splitting echo?

He lifted his head from the floor finally, when the reverberations in the little storage burrow had rumbled into a comparative silence. Someone was screaming. Someone was screaming over and over again.

It was Sarah. She was looking at Stephen the Strong-Armed from the rear. She had been standing directly behind him. Now she was staring at him and screaming in sharp steady bursts.

Her mouth was open so wide that it seemed she was about to tear her jaws apart. And with each scream she lifted her arm rigidly and pointed to the back of Stephen's neck. She kept lifting her arm and pointing as if she wanted everyone present to know beyond the least doubt why and how she came to be screaming.

Stephen the Strong-Armed had no head. His body ended at the neck, and flaps of skin fell down to his chest in an irregular wavy pattern. A fountain of blood bubbled and spurted where his head had been. His body still stood up-right, feet planted wide apart in a good warrior's stance, one arm holding the spear ready for action and the other con-gealed in its upward motion to wipe the red blob away. It stood, incredibly straight and tall and alive.

Suddenly, it fell apart.

First the spear slid slowly forward out of the right hand and clattered to the floor. Then the arms began to fall loosely to the sagging knees and the entire great, brawny body slumped as if its bones had left it. It dropped aimlessly to the floor, an arm poking out here, a leg twisting out there, in a pattern as meaningless as if an oddly shaped bag of skin had been flung to one side of the burrow.

It continued to twitch for a moment or two, as the bubbling fountain of blood turned into a sluggishly flowing river. At last it lay still, a motionless heap of limbs and torso. Of the missing head there was no trace anywhere.

Sarah the Sickness-Healer stopped screaming and turned, shaking, to her companions. Their protruding eyes left the body on the floor.

Then they all reacted at once.

They yelled madly, wildly, fearfully, as if they were a chorus and she the conductor. Still bellowing, they made for the narrow entrance behind them. They got through in a pushing, punching scramble that at one point looked like a composite monster with dozens of arms, legs and swinging, naked breasts. They carried the guard outside with them, and with them, too, they carried their uncontrollable panic, screaming it into existence all along the great central burrow.

For a little while, Eric could hear feet pounding into the distant corridors. Then there was quiet. There was quiet everywhere, except for Thomas the Trap-Smasher's interminable mumbling.

Eric forced himself upright again. He was unable to imagine what had happened. That red blob—the Stranger, Walter, had said it was a weapon, but it didn't operate like any weapon he had ever in his life heard of. Except possibly in the times of the ancestors: the ancestors were supposed to have had things which could blow an object apart and leave no trace. But this was an alien artifact, a possession of the Monsters which Walter the Weapon-Seeker had somehow found and appropriated. What was it? How had it exploded the head of Stephen the Strong-Armed?

That was to be worked out another time. Meanwhile, he had his chance. It might not last long: he had no idea when the panic might subside and a patrol of warriors be sent back to investigate. He stepped carefully across the red stream flowing from the fallen man's neck. Squatting down in front of the dropped spear, he managed to get a grip on it with his bound hands and rose, holding it awkwardly behind him.

No time to cut his bonds. Not here.

"Uncle Thomas," he called. "We can get away. We have a chance now. Come on, get up!"

The wounded band captain stared up at him without comprehension. "—corridors like you've never seen or imagined," he continued in a low monotone. "Glow lamps that aren't on foreheads. Corridors filled with glow lamps. Corridors and corridors and corridors—"

For a moment, Eric considered. The man would be a heavy liability in fast travel. But he couldn't desert him. This was his last surviving relative, the only person who didn't consider him an outlaw and a thing. And, shattered as he was, also still his captain.

"Get up!" he said again. "Thomas the Trap-Smasher, get up! That's an order, a warrior's order. Get up!"

As he'd hoped, his uncle responded to the old command. He managed to get his legs under his body, and strained against them, but it was no use. He didn't have the energy to rise.

*   *   *

Casting apprehensive looks over his shoulder at the entrance to the storage burrow, Eric ran to the struggling man. Working backwards, he managed to get one end of the spear under the crook of his uncle's arm. Then, using his own hip as a fulcrum, he levered hard at the other end.

It was painful, slippery work, since he couldn't bring all of his muscles into play and it was difficult to see what he was doing. In between efforts, he gasped out orders to "Get up, get up, get *up*, damn you!" At last the end of the spear went all the way down. His uncle was on his feet, staggering, but at least on his feet.

Dragging the spear awkwardly, Eric urged and butted him out of the place. The great central burrow was empty of people. Weapons, pots and miscellaneous possessions lay strewn about where they had been dropped. The finished structure of the Stage stood deserted in front of the royal mound. And some time before, the bodies of his uncle's wives had evidently been removed.

The chief and the other leaders had bolted to the left once they had clawed their way out of the storage burrow. They had apparently run past the scaffold structure and picked up the rest of Mankind in their panic.

Eric turned right.

His uncle was a problem. Thomas the Trap-Smasher kept coming to a bewildered halt. Again and again he began the story of his long-ago journey to the burrows of the strange, distant tribe. Eric had to push against him to keep him moving.

Once they were in the outlying corridors, he felt better. But not until they had made many turns, passed dozens of branches and were well into completely uninhabited burrows, did he feel he could stop and saw himself free of his bonds on the point of the spear. He did the same for his uncle. Then, throwing the Trap-Smasher's left arm across his own shoulders and clutching him tightly about the waist, he started off again. It was slow going: his uncle was a heavy man, but the more distance they could put between themselves and Mankind, the better.

But distance where? Where should they go? He pondered the problem as they tottered together down the silent, branching corridors. One place was as good as another. There was nowhere that they would be welcome. Just keep going.

He may have muttered his questions aloud. To his surprise, Thomas the Trap-Smasher suddenly said in an entirely coherent but very weak voice: "The doorway to Monster territory, Eric. Make for the doorway to Monster territory where you went to make your Theft."

"Why?" Eric asked. "What can we do there?"

There was no answer. His uncle's head fell forward on his chest. He was evidently sliding into a stupor again. And yet, somehow, as long as Eric's encircling arm pulled at his body, the man's legs kept moving forward. There was some residual stamina and a warrior's determination in him yet.

Monster territory. Was there more safety for them there now than they could find among human beings?

Very well then. The doorway to Monster territory. They would have to come around in a wide arc through many corridors to get to it, but Eric knew the way. He was Eric the Eye, after all, he told himself: it was his business always to know the way.

But was it? He had not enjoyed the formal initiation into manhood that was the usual aftermath of a successful Theft. Without that, perhaps he was still Eric the Only, still a boy and an initiate. No, he knew what he was. He was Eric the Outlaw, nothing else.

He was an outlaw, without a home and a people. And, except for the dying man he pulled along, everyone's hand was henceforth against him.

X

Thomas the Trap-Smasher had been badly injured in the surprise attack that had wiped out his band. Ordinarily, he would have had his wounds carefully dressed by the cleverness and accumulated experience of Sarah the Sickness-Healer. Under the circumstances, however, Sarah had done the reverse.

Now, the strain of escape and the forced headlong flight that followed it had emptied his body of its last resources. His eyes were glazed and his strong shoulders hung slack. He was a somnambulist walking jerkily in the direction of death.

When they stopped to rest, Eric—after listening intently for any sounds of pursuit—had washed his uncle's wounds carefully with water from the canteens and had bound the uglier gashes with strips torn from a knapsack. It was all he knew how to do: warrior's first aid. A woman's advanced therapeutic knowledge was needed for anything more complicated.

Not that it would have made very much difference by this time. The Trap-Smasher was too far gone.

Eric felt desperate at the thought of being left alone forever in the dark, uninhabited corridors. He tried to force water and bits of food upon his uncle. The man's head rolled back, nourishment dribbling carelessly down from both sides of his mouth. He was breathing lightly and very rapidly. His body had grown quite warm by the time they stopped.

Eric himself ate ravenously: it was his first meal in a long, long while. He kept staring at his recumbent uncle and trying to work out a line of action that would do some good. In the end, he had thought of nothing better than to hitch the man's arm up over his shoulder again and to keep going in the direction of Monster territory.

Once erect, the Trap-Smasher's feet began walking again, but with a dragging, soggy quality that became more and more pronounced. After a while, Eric had to come to a halt: he had the feeling that he was hauling dead weight.

When he tried to lower his uncle to the floor of the burrow, he found that the body had become almost completely limp. Thomas lay on his back, his eyes staring without curiosity at the rounded ceiling upon which his forehead glow-lamp outlined a bright circular patch.

The heartbeat was very, very faint.

"Eric," he heard a weak voice say. He raised his eyes from his uncle's chest and looked at the painfully working mouth.

"Yes, uncle?"

"I'm sorry—about—what I got you into. I had—no right. Your life—after all—your life. You—my wives—the band. I led—death—everyone. I'm sorry."

Eric fought hard to hold back his tears. "It was for a reason, Uncle Thomas," he said. "We had a cause. It wasn't just you. The cause failed."

There was a hideous cackle from the prone man. For a moment, Eric thought it was a death rattle. Then he realized that it had been a laugh, but such a laugh as he had never heard before.

"A cause?" the Trap-Smasher gasped. "A cause? Do you know—do you—know what—the cause was? I wanted—wanted to be chief. Chief. The only—only way I could—do it—Alien-science—the Strangers—a cause. Everyone—the killings—I wanted to—to be chief. *Chief!*"

He went rigid as he coughed out the last word. Then slowly, like flesh turning into liquid, he relaxed.

He was dead.

Eric stared at the body a long time. It didn't make any difference, he found. The numbness in his mind remained. There was a great paralyzed spot in the center of his brain that was unable to think or to feel.

In the end, he shook himself, bent down and grabbed the body by the shoulders. Walking backwards, he dragged it in the direction of Monster territory.

Something he had to do. The duty of anyone who lived in the burrows when death occurred in his neighborhood. Now it filled time and used up energies that he might otherwise have expended in thoughts which were agonizing.

The energies which it demanded were almost more than he was capable of at this point. His uncle had been a heavy, well built man. Eric found that he had to stop at the end of almost every curving corridor and get his breath back.

He finally arrived at the doorway, grateful for the fact that his uncle had died so relatively close to it. He also felt he understood why this had been suggested as their destination. Thomas the Trap-Smasher had known he had little time left. His nephew would have the responsibility of sewering him. He had tried to make it as easy for Eric as possible by going the greater part of the distance on his own feet.

There was a fresh-water pipe in the wall near the doorway to Monster territory. And wherever there was a fresh-water pipe, the Monsters were likely to have laid a sewer pipe nearby. It was down this, probably, that the men killed in the battle with Stephen the Strong-Armed's band had been disposed of much earlier. And it was down this that Thomas had known his remains must also go—the closest point at which his nephew could sewer him in comparative safety.

This much, at least, he had done for Eric's benefit.

Eric located the fresh-water pipe without much difficulty. There was a constant low rumbling and gurgling underfoot, and—at the spot where it was most pronounced—he found the slab in the floor cut at the cost of infinite labor by some past generation of Mankind. Near it, after the slab was lifted, was another, much thicker pipe, large enough to carry two men abreast. Like the other one, the hard stuff of the burrow floor had been scraped away so that a joint lay exposed.

Opening the joint was another matter. Eric had seen it done many times by his elders, but this was his own first attempt. It was a tricky business of tugging a heavy covering plate first right, then left, and getting his fingers under the rim and pulling at just the right moment.

The joint opened at last, and the incredible stink of Monster sewage poured out as the liquid swirled darkly by. Death had always been associated in Eric's mind with this stink, since the pipe carried not only the Monster's waste matter but also that of Mankind, collected from its burrows every week by the old women who were too feeble for any other work. All that was not alive or useful was carried to the nearest Monster sewer pipe, all that might decay and foul the burrows. And that included, of course, the bodies of the dead.

Eric stripped his uncle's body of all useful gear as he had seen the women do many times. Then he dragged it to the hole in the burrow floor and held it by one arm for a moment as the current of the sewage caught it. He repeated as much of the ceremony as he could remember, concluding with the words: *"And therefore, O ancestors, I beg you to receive the body of this member of Mankind, Thomas the Trap-Smasher, a warrior of the first rank, a band captain of renown and the father of nine."*

There was usually another line or so—*"Take him to you and keep him with you until the time when the Monsters have been destroyed utterly and the Earth is ours again. Then shall you and he and all human beings who have ever lived rise from the sewers and joyously walk the surface of our world forever."* But this, after all, was a pure Ancestor-science passage; and his uncle had died fighting Ancestor-science. What was the Alien-science equivalent? And was it likely to be any more potent, any less full of falsehood? In the end, Eric omitted those last two lines.

He let go of the stiffening arm. The body shot away and down the pipe. Thomas the Trap-Smasher was gone, he was gone for all time, the way Eric reasoned now. He was dead and sewered, and that was that.

Eric closed the joint, pulled the slab down and stamped it into place.

He was completely alone. An outlaw who could expect

nothing from other human beings but death by slow torture. He had no companions, no home, no beliefs of any sort. His uncle's last words still lay, in all their stern ugliness, at the bottom of his mind. *"I wanted to—to be chief."*

It was bad enough to discover that the religion on which he had been raised was a mere prop to the power of the chieftainship, that the mysterious Female Society was completely unable to see into a person's future. But to find out that his uncle's thoughtful antagonism to such nonsense was based on nothing more substantial then simple personal ambition, an ambition murderously unscrupulous and willing to sacrifice anybody who trusted him—well, what was there left to believe in, to base a life upon?

Had his father and mother been any less gullible than the most naive child in the burrows? They had sacrificed themselves—for what? For one superstition as opposed to another, for the secret political maneuvers of this person as opposed to that.

Not for him. He would be free. He laughed, bitterly and self-consciously. He had to be free. There was no choice: he was an outlaw.

Eric walked a few steps and put his hands on the door to Monster territory. To shift it out of its socket was a hard job for one man. He strained and tore his fingers; finally he managed it. The door came away and he deposited it carefully on the floor of the burrow.

He stared at it for a while, trying to figure out a way of getting it back after he'd passed through the doorway. No, a single man just couldn't do that from the other side. He'd have to leave the doorway open, an incredible social crime.

Well, he couldn't commit a crime any more. He was beyond all rules made by human communities. Ahead lay the glaring white light that he and his kind feared so much. Into this he would go. Here, where there were no illusions to be found and no help to be expected, here he would make his solitary outlaw home.

Behind him lay the dark, safe, intricate burrows. They were tunnels, Eric knew now, in the walls that surrounded Monster territory. Men lived in these walls, and shivered, and were ignorant, and made fools of each other. He could no longer do these things: he had to face the Monsters. He wanted to face them and destroy them.

It was like one of the roaches in the storage burrow

declaring war on a cook who came in to make the evening meal for Mankind. The cook would roar with laughter at such a thought. Who knew what went on in the mind of a roach—and who cared? Yet the roach would enjoy two special advantages. He had once and for all stopped crawling greedily and aimlessly with his own kind; and the enemy he had selected could regard him with nothing more than heavy oblivious contempt. If he could ever for a moment find one usable weapon and one vital area on which that weapon could be used . . .

He hefted his two special advantages grimly. Then Eric the Only, the Eye, the Outlaw, Eric the Self-Aware Individual Man, stepped through the doorway into Monster territory.

THE DOORS OF HIS FACE, THE LAMPS OF HIS MOUTH

BY ROGER ZELAZNY

I'm a baitman. No one is born a baitman, except in a French novel where everyone is. (In fact, I think that's the title. *We are All Bait.* Pfft!) How I got that way is barely worth the telling and has nothing to do with neo-exes, but the days of the beast deserve a few words, so here they are.

The Lowlands of Venus lie between the thumb and forefinger of the continent known as Hand. When you break into Cloud Alley it swings its silverblack bowling ball toward you without a warning. You jump then, inside that firetailed tenpin they ride you down in, but the straps keep you from making a fool of yourself. You generally chuckle afterwards, but you always jump first.

Next, you study Hand to lay its illusion and the two middle fingers become dozen-ringed archipelagoes as the outers resolve into greengray peninsulas; the thumb is too short, and curls like the embryo tail of Cape Horn.

You suck pure oxygen, sigh possibly, and begin the long topple to the Lowlands.

There, you are caught like an infield fly at the Lifeline landing area—so named because of its nearness to the great delta in the Eastern Bay—located between the first peninsula and "thumb." For a minute it seems as if you're going to miss Lifeline and wind up as canned seafood, but afterwards—shaking off the metaphors—you descend to scorched concrete and present your middle-sized telephone directory of authorizations to the short, fat man in the gray cap. The papers show that you are not subject to mysterious inner rottings and etcetera. He then smiles you a short, fat, gray smile and motions you toward the bus which hauls you to the Reception Area. At the R.A. you spend three days proving that, indeed, you are not subject to mysterious inner rottings and etcetera.

Boredom, however, is another rot. When your three days are up, you generally hit Lifeline hard, and it returns the compliment as a matter of reflex. The effects of alcohol in variant atmospheres is a subject on which the connoisseurs have written numerous volumes, so I will confine my remarks to noting that a good binge is worthy of at least a week's time and often warrants a lifetime study.

I had been a student of exceptional promise (strictly undergraduate) for going on two years when the *Bright Water* fell through our marble ceiling and poured its people like targets into the city.

Pause. The Worlds Almanac re Lifeline: ". . . Port city on the eastern coast of Hand. Employees of the Agency for Non-terrestrial Research comprise approximately 85% of its 100,000 population (2010 Census). Its other residents are primarily personnel maintained by several industrial corporations engaged in basic research. Independent marine biologists, wealthy fishing enthusiasts, and waterfront entrepreneurs make up the remainder of its inhabitants."

I turned to Mike Dabis, a fellow entrepreneur, and commented on the lousy state of basic research.

"Not if the mumbled truth be known."

He paused behind his glass before continuing the slow swallowing process calculated to obtain my interest and a few oaths, before he continued.

"Carl," he finally observed, poker playing, "they're shaping Tensquare."

I could have hit him. I might have refilled his glass with sulfuric acid and looked on with glee as his lips blackened and cracked. Instead, I grunted a noncommital.

"Who's fool enough to shell out fifty grand a day? ANR?"

He shook his head.

"Jean Luharich," he said, "the girl with the violet contacts and fifty or sixty perfect teeth. I understand her eyes are really brown."

"Isn't she selling enough face cream these days?"

He shrugged.

"Publicity makes the wheels go 'round. Luharich Enterprises jumped sixteen points when she picked up the Sun Trophy. You ever play golf on Mercury?"

I had, but I overlooked it and continued to press.

"So she's coming here with a blank check and a fishhook?"

"*Bright Water,* today," he nodded. "Should be down by now. Lots of cameras. She wants an Ikky, bad."

"Hmm," I hmmed. "How bad?"

"Sixty day contract, Tensquare. Indefinite extension clause. Million and a half deposit," he recited.

"You seem to know a lot about it."

"I'm Personnel Recruitment. Luharich Enterprises approached me last month. It helps to drink in the right places.

"Or own them." He smirked, after a moment.

I looked away, sipping my bitter brew. After a while I swallowed several things and asked Mike what he expected to be asked, leaving myself open for his monthly temperance lecture.

"They told me to try getting you," he mentioned. "When's the last time you sailed?"

"Month and a half ago. The *Corning.*"

"Small stuff," he snorted. "When have you been under, yourself?"

"It's been awhile."

"It's been over a year, hasn't it? That time you got cut by the screw, under the *Dolphin?*"

I turned to him.

"I was in the river last week, up at Angleford where the currents are strong. I can still get around."

"Sober," he added.

"I'd stay that way," I said, "on a job like this."

A doubting nod.

"Straight union rates. Triple time for extraordinary circumstances," he narrated. "Be at Hangar Sixteen with your gear, Friday morning, five hundred hours. We push off Saturday, daybreak."

"You're sailing?"

"I'm sailing."

"How come?"

"Money."

"Ikky guano."

"The bar isn't doing so well and baby needs new minks."

"I repeat—"

". . . And I want to get away from baby, renew my contact with basics—fresh air, exercise, make cash. . . ."

"All right, sorry I asked."

I poured him a drink, concentrating on H_2SO_4, but it didn't transmute. Finally I got him soused and went out into the night to walk and think things over.

Around a dozen serious attempts to land *Ichthyform Leviosaurus Levianthus*, generally known as "Ikky," had been made over the past five years. When Ikky was first sighted, whaling techniques were employed. These proved either fruitless or disastrous, and a new procedure was inaugurated. Tensquare was constructed by a wealthy sportsman named Michael Jandt, who blew his entire roll on the project.

After a year on the Eastern Ocean, he returned to file bankruptcy. Carlton Davits, a playboy fishing enthusiast, then purchased the huge raft and laid a wake for Ikky's spawning grounds. On the nineteenth day out he had a strike and lost one hundred and fifty bills' worth of untested gear, along with one *Ichthyform Levianthus*. Twelve days later, using tripled lines, he hooked, narcotized, and began to hoist the huge beast. It awakened then, destroyed a control tower, killed six men, and worked general hell over five square blocks of Tensquare. Carlton was left with partial hemiplegia and a bankruptcy suit of his own. He faded into waterfront atmosphere and Tensquare changed hands four more times, with less spectacular but equally expensive results.

Finally, the big raft, built only for one purpose, was purchased at auction by ANR for "marine research." Lloyd's still won't insure it, and the only marine research it has ever seen is an occasional rental at fifty bills a day—to people anxious to tell Leviathan fish stories. I've been baitman on three of the voyages, and I've been close enough to count Ikky's fangs on two occasions. I want one of them to show my grandchildren, for personal reasons.

I faced the direction of the landing area and resolved a resolve.

"You want me for local coloring, gal. It'll look nice on the feature page and all that. But clear this— If anyone gets you an Ikky, it'll be me. I promise."

I stood in the empty Square. The foggy towers of Lifeline shared their mists.

Shoreline a couple eras ago, the western slope above Lifeline stretches as far as forty miles inland in some places. Its angle of rising is not a great one, but it achieves an elevation of several thousand feet before it meets the mountain range which separates us from the Highlands. About four miles inland and five hundred feet higher than Lifeline are set most of the surface airstrips and privately owned hangars. Hangar Sixteen houses Cal's Contract Cab, hop service, shore to ship. I do not like Cal, but he wasn't around when I climbed from the bus and waved to a mechanic.

Two of the hoppers tugged at the concrete, impatient beneath flywing haloes. The one on which Steve was working belched deep within its barrel carburetor and shuddered spasmodically.

"Bellyache?" I inquired.

"Yeah, gas pains and heartburn."

He twisted setscrews until it settled into an even keening, and turned to me.

"You're for out?"

I nodded.

"Tensquare. Cosmetics. Monsters. Stuff like that."

He blinked into the beacons and wiped his freckles. The temperature was about twenty, but the big overhead spots served a double purpose.

"Luharich," he muttered. "Then you *are* the one. There's some people want to see you."

"What about?"

"Cameras. Microphones. Stuff like that."

"I'd better stow my gear. Which one am I riding?"

He poked the screwdriver at the other hopper.

"That one. You're on video tape now, by the way. They wanted to get you arriving."

He turned to the hangar, turned back.

"Say 'cheese.' They'll shoot the close close-ups later."

I said something other than "cheese." They must have been using telelens and been able to read my lips, because that part of the tape was never shown.

I threw my junk in the back, climbed into a passenger seat, and lit a cigarette. Five minutes later, Cal himself emerged from the office Quonset, looking cold. He came over and pounded on the side of the hopper. He jerked a thumb back at the hangar.

"They want you in there!" he called through cupped hands. "Interview!"

"The show's over!" I yelled back. "Either that, or they can get themselves another baitman!"

His rustbrown eyes became nailheads under blond brows

and his glare a spike before he jerked about and stalked off. I wondered how much they had paid him to be able to squat in his hangar and suck juice from his generator.

Enough, I guess, knowing Cal. I never liked the guy, anyway.

Venus at night is a field of sable waters. On the coasts, you can never tell where the sea ends and the sky begins. Dawn is like dumping milk into an inkwell. First, there are erratic curdles of white, then streamers. Shade the bottle for a gray colloid, then watch it whiten a little more. All of a sudden you've got day. Then start heating the mixture.

I had to shed my jacket as we flashed out over the bay. To our rear, the skyline could have been under water for the way it waved and rippled in the heatfall. A hopper can accommodate four people (five, if you want to bend Regs and underestimate weight), or three passengers with the sort of gear a baitman uses. I was the only fare, though, and the pilot was like his machine. He hummed and made no unnecessary noises. Lifeline turned a somersault and evaporated in the rear mirror at about the same time Tensquare broke the fore-horizon. The pilot stopped humming and shook his head.

I leaned forward. Feelings played flopdoodle in my guts. I knew every bloody inch of the big raft, but the feelings you once took for granted change when their source is out of reach. Truthfully, I'd had my doubts I'd ever board the hulk again. But now, now I could almost believe in predestination. There it was!

A tensquare football field of a ship. A-powered. Flat as a pancake, except for the plastic blisters in the middle and the "Rooks" fore and aft, port and starboard.

The Rook towers were named for their corner positions— and any two can work together to hoist, co-powering the graffles between them. The graffles—half gaff, half grapple— can raise enormous weights to near water level; their designer had only one thing in mind, though, which accounts for the gaff half. At water level, the Slider has to implement elevation for six to eight feet before the graffles are in a position to push upward, rather than pulling.

The Slider, essentially, is a mobile room—a big box capable of moving in any of Tensquare's crisscross groovings and "anchoring" on the strike side by means of a powerful electromagnetic bond. Its winches could hoist a battleship the necessary distance, and the whole craft would tilt, rather than the Slider come loose, if you want any idea of the strength of that bond.

The Slider houses a section operated control indicator which is the most sophisticated "reel" ever designed. Drawing broadcast power from the generator beside the center blister, it is connected by shortwave with the sonar room, where the movements of the quarry are recorded and repeated to the angler seated before the section control.

The fisherman might play his "lines" for hours, days even, without seeing any more than metal and an outline on the screen. Only when the beast is graffled and the extensor shelf, located twelve feet below waterline, slides out for support and begins to aid the winches, only then does the fisherman see his catch rising before him like a fallen Seraphim. Then, as Davits learned, one looks into the Abyss itself and is required to act. He didn't, and a hundred meters of unimaginable tonnage, undernarcotized and hurting, broke the cables of the winch, snapped a graffle, and took a half-minute walk across Tensquare.

We circled till the mechanical flag took notice and waved us on down. We touched beside the personnel hatch and I jettisoned my gear and jumped to the deck.

"Luck," called the pilot as the door was sliding shut. Then he danced into the air and the flag clicked blank.

I shouldered my stuff and went below.

Signing in with Malvern, the de facto captain, I learned that most of the others wouldn't arrive for a good eight hours. They had wanted me alone at Cal's so they could pattern the pub footage along twentieth-century cinema lines.

Open: landing strip, dark. One mechanic prodding a contrary hopper. Stark-o-vision shot of slow bus pulling in. Heavily dressed baitman descends, looks about, limps across field. Close-up: he grins. Move in for words: "Do you think this is the time? The time he *will* be landed?" Embarrassment, taciturnity, a shrug. Dub something. —"I see. And why do you think Miss Luharich has a better chance than any of the others? Is it because she's better equipped? [Grin.] Because more is known now about the creature's habits than when you were out before? Or is it because of her will to win, to be a champion? Is it any one of these things, or is it all of them?" Reply: "Yeah, all of them." "—Is that why you signed on with her? Because your instincts say, 'This one will be it'?" Answer: "She pays union rates. I couldn't rent that damned thing myself. And I want in." Erase. Dub something else. Fade-out as he moves toward hopper, etcetera.

"Cheese," I said, or something like that, and took a walk around Tensquare, by myself.

I mounted each Rook, checking out the controls and the underwater video eyes. Then I raised the main lift.

Malvern had no objections to my testing things this way. In fact, he encouraged it. We had sailed together before and our positions had even been reversed upon a time. So I wasn't surprised when I stepped off the lift into the Hopkins Locker and found him waiting. For the next ten minutes we inspected the big room in silence, walking through its copper coil chambers soon to be Arctic.

Finally, he slapped a wall.

"Well, will we fill it?"

I shook my head.

"I'd like to, but I doubt it. I don't give two hoots and a damn who gets credit for the catch, so long as I have a part in it. But it won't happen. That gal's an egomaniac. She'll want to operate the Slider, and she can't."

"You ever meet her?"

"Yeah."

"How long ago?"

"Four, five years."

"She was a kid then. How do you know what she can do now?"

"I know. She'll have learned every switch and reading by this time. She'll be up on all theory. But do you remember one time we were together in the starboard Rook, forward, when Ikky broke water like a porpoise?"

"How could I forget?"

"Well?"

He rubbed his emery chin.

"Maybe she can do it, Carl. She's raced torch ships and she's scubaed in bad waters back home." He glanced in the direction of invisible Hand. "And she's hunted in the Highlands. She might be wild enough to pull that horror into her lap without flinching.

". . . For Johns Hopkins to foot the bill and shell out seven figures for the corpus," he added. "That's money, even to a Luharich."

I ducked through a hatchway.

"Maybe you're right, but she was a rich witch when I knew her.

"And she wasn't blonde," I added, meanly.

He yawned.

"Let's find breakfast."

We did that.

When I was young I thought that being born a sea crea-ture was the finest choice Nature could make for anyone. I grew up on the Pacific coast and spent my summers on the Gulf or the Mediterranean. I lived months of my life negoti-ating coral, photographing trench dwellers, and playing tag with dolphins. I fished everywhere there are fish, resenting the fact that they can go places I can't. When I grew older I wanted bigger fish, and there was nothing living that I knew of, excepting a Sequoia, that came any bigger than Ikky. That's part of it. . . .

I jammed a couple of extra rolls into a paper bag and filled a thermos with coffee. Excusing myself, I left the galley and made my way to the Slider berth. It was just the way I remembered it. I threw a few switches and the short-wave hummed.

"That you, Carl?"

"That's right, Mike. Let me have some juice down here, you double-crossing rat."

He thought it over, then I felt the hull vibrate as the generators cut in. I poured my third cup of coffee and found a cigarette.

"So why am I a double-crossing rat this time?" came his voice again.

"You knew about the cameramen at Hangar Sixteen?"

"Yes."

"Then you're a double-crossing rat. The last thing I want is publicity. 'He who fouled up so often before is ready to try it, nobly, once more.' I can read it now."

"You're wrong. The spotlight's only big enough for one, and she's prettier than you."

My next comment was cut off as I threw the elevator switch and the elephant ears flapped above me. I rose, settling flush with the deck. Retracting the lateral rail, I cut forward into the groove. Amidships, I stopped at a junc-ture, dropped the lateral, and retracted the longitudinal rail.

I slid starboard, midway between the Rooks, halted, and threw on the coupler.

I hadn't spilled a drop of coffee.

"Show me pictures."

The screen glowed. I adjusted and got outlines of the bottom.

"Okay."

I threw a Status Blue switch and he matched it. The light went on.

The winch unlocked. I aimed out over the waters, extended the arm, and fired a cast.

"Clean one," he commented.

"Status Red. Call strike." I threw a switch.

"Status Red."

The baitman would be on his way with this, to make the barbs tempting.

It's not exactly a fishhook. The cables bear hollow tubes; the tubes convey enough dope for any army of hopheads; Ikky takes the bait, dandled before him by remote control, and the fisherman rams the barbs home.

My hands moved over the console, making the necessary adjustments. I checked the narco-tank reading. Empty. Good, they hadn't been filled yet. I thumbed the Inject button.

"In the gullet," Mike murmured.

I released the cables. I played the beast imagined. I let him run, swinging the winch to simulate his sweep.

I had the air conditioner on and my shirt off and it was still uncomfortably hot, which is how I knew that morning had gone over its noon. I was dimly aware of the arrivals and departures of the hoppers. Some of the crew sat in the "shade" of the doors I had left open, watching the operation. I didn't see Jean arrive or I would have ended the session and gotten below.

She broke my concentration by slamming the door hard enough to shake the bond.

"Mind telling me who authorized you to bring up the Slider?" she asked.

"No one," I replied. "I'll take it below now."

"Just move aside."

I did, and she took my seat. She was wearing brown slacks and a baggy shirt and she had her hair pulled back in a practical manner. Her cheeks were flushed, but not necessarily from the heat. She attacked the panel with a nearly amusing intensity that I found disquieting.

"Status Blue," she snapped, breaking a violet fingernail on the toggle.

I forced a yawn and buttoned my shirt slowly. She threw a side glance my way, checked the registers, and fired a cast.

I monitored the lead on the screen. She turned to me for a second.

"Status Red," she said levelly.

I nodded my agreement.

She worked the winch sideways to show she knew how. I didn't doubt she knew how and she didn't doubt that I didn't doubt, but then—

"In case you're wondering," she said, "you're not going to be anywhere near this thing. You were hired as a baitman, remember? Not a Slider operator! A baitman! Your duties consist of swimming out and setting the table for our friend the monster. It's dangerous, but you're getting well paid for it. Any questions?"

She squashed the Inject button and I rubbed my throat.

"Nope," I smiled, "but I am qualified to run that thing-amajigger—and if you need me I'll be available, at union rates."

"Mister Davits," she said, "I don't want a loser operating this panel."

"Miss Luharich, there has never been a winner at this game."

She started reeling in the cable and broke the bond at the same time, so that the whole Slider shook as the big yo-yo returned. We skidded a couple of feet backwards. She raised the laterals and we shot back along the groove. Slowing, she transferred rails and we jolted to a clanging halt, then shot off at a right angle. The crew scrambled away from the hatch as we skidded onto the elevator.

"In the future, Mister Davits, do not enter the Slider without being ordered," she told me.

"Don't worry. I won't even step inside if I am ordered," I answered. "I signed on as a baitman. Remember? If you want me in here, you'll have to *ask* me."

"That'll be the day." She smiled.

I agreed, as the doors closed above us. We dropped the subject and headed in our different directions after the Slider came to a halt in its berth. She did say "good day," though, which I thought showed breeding as well as determination, in reply to my chuckle.

Later that night Mike and I stoked our pipes in Malvern's cabin. The winds were shuffling waves, and a steady spattering of rain and hail overhead turned the deck into a tin roof.

"Nasty," suggested Malvern.

I nodded. After two bourbons the room had become a familiar woodcut, with its mahogany furnishings (which I had transported from Earth long ago on a whim) and the dark walls, the seasoned face of Malvern, and the perpetually puzzled expression of Dabis set between the big pools of shadow that lay behind chairs and splashed in corners, all cast by the tiny table light and seen through a glass, brownly.

"Glad I'm in here."

"What's it like underneath on a night like this?"

I puffed, thinking of my light cutting through the insides of a black diamond, shaken slightly. The meteor-dart of a suddenly illuminated fish, the swaying of grotesque ferns, like nebulae—shadow, then green, then gone—swam in a moment through my mind. I guess it's like a spaceship would feel, if a spaceship could feel, crossing between worlds—and quiet, uncannily, preternaturally quiet; and peaceful as sleep.

"Dark," I said, "and not real choppy below a few fathoms."

"Another eight hours and we shove off," commented Mike.

"Ten, twelve days, we should be there," noted Malvern.

"What do you think Ikky's doing?"

"Sleeping on the bottom with Mrs. Ikky if he has any brains."

"He hasn't. I've seen ANR's skeletal extrapolation from the bones that have washed up—"

"Hasn't everyone?"

". . . Fully fleshed, he'd be over a hundred meters long. That right, Carl?"

I agreed.

". . . Not much of a brain box, though, for his bulk."

"Smart enough to stay out of our locker."

Chuckles, because nothing exists but this room, really. The world outside is an empty, sleet-drummed deck. We lean back and make clouds.

"Boss lady does not approve of unauthorized fly fishing."

"Boss lady can walk north till her hat floats."

"What did she say in there?"

"She told me that my place, with fish manure, is on the bottom."

"You don't Slide?"

"I bait."

"We'll see."

"That's all I do. If she wants a Slideman she's going to have to ask nicely."

"You think she'll have to?"

"I think she'll have to."

"And if she does, can you do it?"

"A fair question," I puffed. "I don't know the answer, though."

I'd incorporate my soul and trade forty percent of the stock for the answer. I'd give a couple years off my life for the answer. But there doesn't seem to be a lineup of supernatural takers, because no one knows. Supposing when we get out there, luck being with us, we find ourselves an Ikky? Supposing we succeed in baiting him and get lines on him. What then? If we get him shipside, will she hold on or crack up? What if she's made of sterner stuff than Davits, who used to hunt sharks with poison-darted air pistols? Supposing she lands him and Davits has to stand there like a video extra.

Worse yet, supposing she asks for Davits and he still stands there like a video extra or something else—say, some yellowbellied embodiment named Cringe?

It was when I got him up above the eight-foot horizon of steel and looked out at all that body, sloping on and on till it dropped out of sight like a green mountain range . . . And that head. Small for the body, but still immense. Fat, craggy, with lidless roulettes that had spun black and red since before my forefathers decided to try the New Continent. And swaying.

Fresh narco-tanks had been connected. It needed another shot, fast. But I was paralyzed.

It had made a noise like God playing a Hammond organ. . . .

And looked at me!

I don't know if seeing is even the same process in eyes like those. I doubt it. Maybe I was just a gray blur behind a black rock, with the plexi-reflected sky hurting its pupils. But it fixed on me. Perhaps the snake doesn't really paralyze the rabbit, perhaps it's just that rabbits are cowards by constitution. But it began to struggle and I still couldn't move, fascinated.

Fascinated by all that power, by those eyes, they found

me there fifteen minutes later, a little broken about the head and shoulders, the Inject still unpushed.

And I dream about those eyes. I want to face them once more, even if their finding takes forever. I've got to know if there's something inside me that sets me apart from a rabbit, from notched plates of reflexes and instincts that always fall apart in exactly the same way whenever the proper combination is spun.

Looking down, I noticed that my hand was shaking. Glancing up, I noticed that no one else was noticing.

I finished my drink and emptied my pipe. It was late and no songbirds were singing.

I sat whittling, my legs hanging over the aft edge, the chips spinning down into the furrow of our wake. Three days out. No action.

"You!"

"Me?"

"You."

Hair like the end of the rainbow, eyes like nothing in nature, fine teeth.

"Hello."

"There's a safety rule against what you're doing, you know."

"I know. I've been worrying about it all morning."

A delicate curl climbed my knife then drifted out behind us. It settled into the foam and was plowed under. I watched her reflection in my blade, taking a secret pleasure in its distortion.

"Are you baiting me?" she finally asked.

I heard her laugh then, and turned, knowing it had been intentional.

"What, me?"

"I could push you off from here, very easily."

"I'd make it back."

"Would you push me off, then—some dark night, perhaps?"

"They're all dark, Miss Luharich. No, I'd rather make you a gift of my carving."

She seated herself beside me then, and I couldn't help but notice the dimples in her knees. She wore white shorts and a halter and still had an offworld tan to her which was awfully appealing. I almost felt a twinge of guilt at having planned the whole scene, but my right hand still blocked her view of the wooden animal.

"Okay, I'll bite. What have you got for me?"

"Just a second. It's almost finished."

Solemnly, I passed her the wooden jackass I had been carving. I felt a little sorry and slightly jackass-ish myself, but I had to follow through. I always do. The mouth was split into a braying grin. The ears were upright.

She didn't smile and she didn't frown. She just studied it.

"It's very good," she finally said, "like most things you do—and appropriate, perhaps."

"Give it to me." I extended a palm.

She handed it back and I tossed it out over the water. It missed the white water and bobbed for awhile like a pigmy seahorse.

"Why did you do that?"

"It was a poor joke. I'm sorry."

"Maybe you are right, though. Perhaps this time I've bitten off a little too much."

I snorted.

"Then why not do something safer, like another race?"

She shook her end of the rainbow.

"No. It has to be an Ikky."

"Why?"

"Why did you want one so badly that you threw away a fortune?"

"Man reasons," I said. "An unfrocked analyst who held black therapy sessions in his basement once told me, 'Mister Davits, you need to reinforce the image of your masculinity by catching one of every kind of fish in existence.' Fish are a very ancient masculinity symbol, you know. So I set out to do it. I have one more to go. —Why do you want to reinforce *your* masculinity?"

"I don't," she said. "I don't want to reinforce anything but Luharich Enterprises. My chief statistician once said, 'Miss Luharich, sell all the cold cream and face powder in the System and you'll be a happy girl. Rich, too.' And he was right. I am the proof. I can look the way I do and do anything, and I sell most of the lipstick and face powder in the System—but I have to be *able* to do anything."

"You do look cool and efficient," I observed.

"I don't feel cool," she said, rising. "Let's go for a swim."

"May I point out that we are making pretty good time?"

"If you want to indicate the obvious, you may. You said you could make it back to the ship, unassisted. Change your mind?"

"No."

"Then get us two scuba outfits and I'll race you under Tensquare.

"I'll win, too," she added.

I stood and looked down at her, because that usually makes me feel superior to women.

"Daughter of Lir, eyes of Picasso," I said, "you've got yourself a race. Meet me at the forward Rook, starboard, in ten minutes."

"Ten minutes," she agreed.

And ten minutes it was. From the center blister to the Rook took maybe two of them, with the load I was carrying. My sandals grew very hot and I was glad to shuck them for flippers when I reached the comparative cool of the corner.

We slid into harnesses and adjusted our gear. She had changed into a trim one-piece green job that made me shade my eyes and look away, then look back again.

I fastened a rope ladder and kicked it over the side. Then I pounded on the wall of the Rook.

"Yeah?"

"You talk to the port Rook, aft?" I called.

"They're all set up," came the answer. "There's ladders and draglines all over that end."

"You sure you want to do this?" asked the sunburnt little gink who was her publicity man, Anderson yclept.

He sat beside the Rook in a deckchair, sipping lemonade through a straw.

"It might be dangerous," he observed, sunken-mouthed. (His teeth were beside him, in another glass.)

"That's right," she smiled. "It *will* be dangerous. Not overly, though."

"Then why don't you let me get some pictures? We'd have them back to Lifeline in an hour. They'd be in New York by tonight. Good copy."

"No," she said, and turned away from both of us.

She raised her hands to her eyes.

"Here, keep these for me."

She passed him a box full of her unseeing, and when she turned back to me they were the same brown that I remembered.

"Ready?"

"No," I said, tautly. "Listen carefully, Jean. If you're going to play this game there are a few rules. First," I counted, "we're going to be directly beneath the hull, so we

have to start low and keep moving. If we bump the bottom,
we could rupture an air tank. . . ."

She began to protest that any moron knew that and I cut
her down.

"Second," I went on, "there won't be much light, so we'll
stay close together, and we will *both* carry torches."

Her wet eyes flashed.

"I dragged you out of Govino without—"

Then she stopped and turned away. She picked up a
lamp.

"Okay. Torches. Sorry."

". . . And watch out for the drive-screws," I finished.
"There'll be strong currents for at least fifty meters behind
them."

She wiped her eyes again and adjusted the mask.

"All right, let's go."

We went.

She led the way, at my insistence. The surface layer was
pleasantly warm. At two fathoms the water was bracing; at
five it was nice and cold. At eight we let go the swinging
stairway and struck out. Tensquare sped forward and we
raced in the opposite direction, tattooing the hull yellow at
ten-second intervals.

The hull stayed where it belonged, but we raced on like
two darkside satellites. Periodically, I tickled her frog feet
with my light and traced her antennae of bubbles. About a
five-meter lead was fine; I'd beat her in the home stretch,
but I couldn't let her drop behind yet.

Beneath us, black. Immense. Deep. The Mindanao of
Venus, where eternity might eventually pass the dead to a
rest in cities of unnamed fishes. I twisted my head away and
touched the hull with a feeler of light; it told me we were
about a quarter of the way along.

I increased my beat to match her stepped-up stroke, and
narrowed the distance which she had suddenly opened by a
couple meters. She sped up again and I did, too. I spotted
her with my beam.

She turned and it caught on her mask. I never knew
whether she'd been smiling. Probably. She raised two fingers in a V-for-Victory and then cut ahead at full speed.

I should have known. I should have felt it coming. It was
just a race to her, something else to win. Damn the torpedoes!

So I leaned into it, hard. I don't shake in the water. Or, if

I do it doesn't matter and I don't notice it. I began to close the gap again.

She looked back, sped on, looked back: Each time she looked it was nearer, until I'd narrowed it down to the original five meters.

Then she hit the jatoes.

That's what I had been fearing. We were about halfway under and she shouldn't have done it. The powerful jets of compressed air could easily rocket her upward into the hull, or tear something loose if she allowed her body to twist. Their main use is in tearing free from marine plants or fighting bad currents. I had wanted them along as a safety measure, because of the big suck-and-pull windmills behind.

She shot ahead like a meteorite, and I could feel a sudden tingle of perspiration leaping to meet and mix with the churning waters.

I swept ahead, not wanting to use my own guns, and she tripled, quadrupled the margin.

The jets died and she was still on course. Okay, I was an old fuddyduddy. She *could* have messed up and headed toward the top.

I plowed the sea and began to gather back my yardage, a foot at a time. I wouldn't be able to catch her or beat her now, but I'd be on the ropes before she hit deck.

Then the spinning magnets began their insistence and she wavered. It was an awfully powerful drag, even at this distance. The call of the meat grinder.

I'd been scratched up by one once, under the *Dolphin*, a fishing boat of the middle-class. I *had* been drinking, but it was also a rough day, and the thing had been turned on prematurely. Fortunately, it was turned off in time, also, and a tendon-stapler made everything good as new, except in the log, where it only mentioned that I'd been drinking. Nothing about it being off-hours when I had a right to do as I damn well pleased.

She had slowed to half her speed, but she was still moving crosswise, toward the port, aft corner. I began to feel the pull myself and had to slow down. She'd made it past the main one, but she seemed too far back. It's hard to gauge distances under water, but each red beat of time told me I was right. She was out of danger from the main one, but the smaller port screw, located about eighty meters in, was no longer a threat but a certainty.

She had turned and was pulling away from it now. Twenty meters separated us. She was standing still. Fifteen.

Slowly, she began a backward drifting. I hit my jatoes, aiming two meters behind her and about twenty back of the blades.

Straightline! Thankgod! Catching, softbelly, leadpipe on shoulder SWIMLIKEHELL! maskcracked, not broke though AND UP!

We caught a line and I remember brandy.

Into the cradle endlessly rocking I spit, pacing. Insomnia tonight and left shoulder sore again, so let it rain on me—they can cure rheumatism. Stupid as hell. What I said. In blankets and shivering. She: "Carl, I can't say it." Me: "Then call it square for that night in Govino, Miss Luharich. Huh?" She: nothing. Me: "Any more of that brandy?" She: "Give me another, too." Me: sounds of sipping. It had only lasted three months. No alimony. Many $ on both sides. Not sure whether they were happy or not. Wine-dark Aegean. Good fishing. Maybe he should have spent more time on shore. Or perhaps she shouldn't have. Good swimmer, though. Dragged him all the way to Vido to wring out his lungs. Young. Both. Strong. Both. Rich and spoiled as hell. Ditto. Corfu should have brought them closer. Didn't. I think that mental cruelty was a trout. He wanted to go to Canada. She: "Go to hell if you want!" He: "Will you go along?" She: "No." But she did, anyhow. Many hells. Expensive. He lost a monster or two. She inherited a couple. Lot of lightning tonight. Stupid as hell. Civility's the coffin of a conned soul. By whom?—Sounds like a bloody neo-ex. . . . But I hate you, Anderson, with your glass full of teeth and her new eyes. . . . Can't keep this pipe lit, keep sucking tobacco. Spit again!

Seven days out and the scope showed Ikky.

Bells jangled, feet pounded, and some optimist set the thermostat in the Hopkins. Malvern wanted me to sit it out, but I slipped into my harness and waited for whatever came. The bruise looked worse than it felt. I had exercised every day and the shoulder hadn't stiffened on me.

A thousand meters ahead and thirty fathoms deep, it tunneled our path. Nothing showed on the surface.

"Will we chase him?" asked an excited crewman.

"Not unless she feels like using money for fuel." I shrugged.

Soon the scope was clear, and it stayed that way. We remained on alert and held our course.

I hadn't said over a dozen words to my boss since the last time we went drowning together, so I decided to raise the score.

"Good afternoon," I approached. "What's new?"

"He's going north-northeast. We'll have to let this one go. A few more days and we can afford some chasing. Not yet."

Sleek head . . .

I nodded. "No telling where this one's headed."

"How's your shoulder?"

"All right. How about you?"

Daughter of Lir . . .

"Fine. By the way, you're down for a nice bonus."

Eyes of perdition!

"Don't mention it," I told her back.

Later that afternoon, and appropriately, a storm shattered. (I prefer "shattered" to "broke." It gives a more accurate idea of the behavior of tropical storms on Venus and saves lots of words.) Remember that inkwell I mentioned earlier? Now take it between thumb and forefinger and hit its side with a hammer. Watch yourself! Don't get splashed or cut—

Dry, then drenched. The sky one million bright fractures as the hammer falls. And sounds of breaking.

"Everyone below?" suggested loudspeakers to the already scurrying crew.

Where was I? Who do you think was doing the loudspeaking?

Everything loose went overboard when the water got to walking, but by then no people were loose. The Slider was the first thing below decks. Then the big lifts lowered their shacks.

I had hit it for the nearest Rook with a yell the moment I recognized the pre-brightening of the holocaust. From there I cut in the speakers and spent half a minute coaching the track team.

Minor injuries had occurred, Mike told me over the radio, but nothing serious. I, however, was marooned for the duration. The Rooks do not lead anywhere; they're set too far out over the hull to provide entry downwards, what with the extensor shelves below.

So I undressed myself of the tanks which I had worn for the past several hours, crossed my flippers on the table, and

leaned back to watch the hurricane. The top was black as
the bottom and we were in between, and somewhat illuminated because of all that flat, shiny space. The waters above
didn't rain down—they just sort of got together and dropped.

The Rooks were secure enough—they'd weathered any
number of these onslaughts—it's just that their positions
gave them a greater arc of rise and descent when Tensquare
makes like the rocker of a very nervous grandma. I had
used the belts from my rig to strap myself into the bolted-
down chair, and I removed several years in purgatory from
the soul of whoever left a pack of cigarettes in the table
drawer.

I watched the water make teepees and mountains and
hands and trees until I started seeing faces and people. So I
called Mike.

"What are you doing down there?"

"Wondering what you're doing up there," he replied.
"What's it like?"

"You're from the Midwest, aren't you?"

"Yeah."

"Get bad storms out there?"

"Sometimes."

"Try to think of the worst one you were ever in. Got a
slide rule handy?"   •

"Right here."

"Then put a one under it, imagine a zero or two following
after, and multiply the thing out."

"I can't imagine the zeros."

"Then retain the multiplicand—that's all you can do."

"So what are you doing up there?"

"I've strapped myself in the chair. I'm watching things
roll around the floor right now."

I looked up and out again. I saw one darker shadow in
the forest.

"Are you praying or swearing?"

"Damned if I know. But if this were the Slider—if only
this were the Slider!"

"He's out there?"

I nodded, forgetting that he couldn't see me.

Big, as I remembered him. He'd only broken surface for a
few moments, to look around. *There is no power on Earth
that can be compared with him who was made to fear no one.*
I dropped my cigarette. It was the same as before. Paralysis
and an unborn scream.

"You all right, Carl?"

He had looked at me again. Or seemed to. Perhaps that mindless brute had been waiting half a millenium to ruin the life of a member of the most highly developed species in business. . . .

"You okay?"

. . . Or perhaps it had been ruined already, long before their encounter, and theirs was just a meeting of beasts, the stronger bumping the weaker aside, body to psyche. . . .

"Carl, dammit! Say something!"

He broke again, this time nearer. Did you ever see the trunk of a tornado? It seems like something alive, moving around in all that dark. Nothing has a right to be so big, so strong, and moving. It's a sickening sensation.

"Please answer me."

He was gone and did not come back that day. I finally made a couple of wisecracks at Mike, but I held my next cigarette in my right hand.

The next seventy or eighty thousand waves broke by with a monotonous similarity. The five days that held them were also without distinction. The morning of the thirteenth day out, though, our luck began to rise. The bells broke our coffee-drenched lethargy into small pieces, and we dashed from the galley without hearing what might have been Mike's finest punchline.

"Aft!" cried someone. "Five hundred meters!"

I stripped to my trunks and started buckling. My stuff is always within grabbing distance.

I flipflopped across the deck, girding myself with a deflated squiggler.

"Five hundred meters, twenty fathoms!" boomed the speakers.

The big traps banged upward and the Slider grew to its full height, m'lady at the console. It rattled past me and took root ahead. Its one arm rose and lengthened.

I breasted the Slider as the speakers called, "Four-eighty, twenty!"

"Status Red!"

A belch like an emerging champagne cork and the line arced high over the waters.

"Four-eighty, twenty!" it repeated, all Malvern and static. "Baitman, attend!"

I adjusted my mask and hand-over-handed it down the side. Then warm, then cool, then away.

Green, vast, down. Fast. This is the place where I am equal to a squiggler. If something big decides a baitman looks tastier than what he's carrying, then irony colors his title as well as the water about it.

I caught sight of the drifting cables and followed them down. Green to dark green to black. It had been a long cast, too long. I'd never had to follow one this far down before. I didn't want to switch on my torch.

But I had to.

Bad! I still had a long way to go. I clenched my teeth and stuffed my imagination into a straightjacket.

Finally the line came to an end.

I wrapped one arm about it and unfastened the squiggler. I attached it, working as fast as I could, and plugged in the little insulated connections which are the reason it can't be fired with the line. Ikky could break them, but by then it wouldn't matter.

My mechanical eel hooked up, I pulled its section plugs and watched it grow. I had been dragged deeper during this operation, which took about a minute and a half. I was near—too near—to where I never wanted to be.

Loath as I had been to turn on my light, I was suddenly afraid to turn it off. Panic gripped me and I seized the cable with both hands. The squiggler began to glow, pinkly. It started to twist. It was twice as big as I am and doubtless twice as attractive to pink squiggler-eaters. I told myself this until I believed it, then I switched off my light and started up.

If I bumped into something enormous and steel-hided my heart had orders to stop beating immediately and release me—to dart fitfully forever along Acheron, and gibbering.

Ungibbering, I made it to green water and fled back to the nest.

As soon as they hauled me aboard I made my mask a necklace, shaded my eyes, and monitored for surface turbulence. My first question, of course, was: "Where is he?"

"Nowhere," said a crewman; "we lost him right after you went over. Can't pick him up on the scope now. Musta dived."

"Too bad."

The squiggler stayed down, enjoying its bath. My job

ended for the time being, I headed back to warm my coffee with rum.

From behind me, a whisper: "Could you laugh like that afterwards?"

Perceptive Answer: "Depends on what he's laughing at."

Still chuckling, I made my way into the center blister with two cupfuls.

"Still hell and gone?"

Mike nodded. His big hands were shaking, and mine were steady as a surgeon's when I set down the cups.

He jumped as I shrugged off the tanks and looked for a bench.

"Don't drip on that panel! You want to kill yourself and blow expensive fuses?"

I toweled down, then settled down to watching the unfilled eye on the wall. I yawned happily; my shoulder seemed good as new.

The little box that people talk through wanted to say something, so Mike lifted the switch and told it to go ahead.

"Is Carl there, Mister Dabis?"

"Yes, ma'am."

"Then let me talk to him."

Mike motioned and I moved.

"Talk," I said.

"Are you all right?"

"Yes, thanks. Shouldn't I be?"

"That was a long swim. I—I guess I overshot my cast."

"I'm happy," I said. "More triple-time for me. I really clean up on that hazardous duty clause."

"I'll be more careful next time," she apologized. "I guess I was too eager. Sorry—" Something happened to the sentence, so she ended it there, leaving me with half a bagful of replies I'd been saving.

I lifted the cigarette from behind Mike's ear and got a light from the one in the ashtray.

"Carl, she was being nice," he said, after turning to study the panels.

"I know," I told him. "I wasn't."

"I mean, she's an awfully pretty kid, pleasant. Head-strong and all that. But what's she done to you?"

"Lately?" I asked.

He looked at me, then dropped his eyes to his cup.

"I know it's none of my bus—" he began.

"Cream and sugar?"

*   *   *

Ikky didn't return that day, or that night. We picked up
some Dixieland out of Lifeline and let the muskrat ramble
while Jean had her supper sent to the Slider. Later she had
a bunk assembled inside. I piped in "Deep Water Blues"
when it came over the air and waited for her to call up and
cuss us out. She didn't, though, so I decided she was sleeping.

Then I got Mike interested in a game of chess that went
on until daylight. It limited conversation to several "checks,"
one "checkmate," and a "damn!" Since he's a poor loser it
also effectively sabotaged subsequent talk, which was fine
with me. I had a steak and fried potatoes for breakfast and
went to bed.

Ten hours later someone shook me awake and I propped
myself on one elbow, refusing to open my eyes.

"Whassamadder?"

"I'm sorry to get you up," said one of the younger crew-
men, "but Miss Luharich wants you to disconnect the squiggler
so we can move on."

I knuckled open one eye, still deciding whether I should
be amused.

"Have it hauled to the side. Anyone can disconnect it."

"It's at the side now, sir. But she said it's in your contract
and we'd better do things right."

"That's very considerate of her. I'm sure my Local appre-
ciates her remembering."

"Uh, she also said to tell you to change your trunks and
comb your hair, and shave, too. Mister Anderson's going to
film it."

"Okay. Run along; tell her I'm on my way—and ask if
she has some toenail polish I can borrow."

I'll save on details. It took three minutes in all, and I
played it properly, even pardoning myself when I slipped
and bumped into Anderson's white tropicals with the wet
squiggler. He smiled, brushed it off; she smiled, even though
Luharich Completacolor couldn't completely mask the dark
circles under her eyes; and I smiled, waving to all our fans
out there in videoland.— Remember, Mrs. Universe, you,
too, can look like a monster-catcher. Just use Luharich face
cream.

I went below and made myself a tuna sandwich, with
mayonnaise.

*   *   *

Two days like icebergs—bleak, blank, half-melting, all frigid, mainly out of sight, and definitely a threat to peace of mind—drifted by and were good to put behind. I experienced some old guilt feelings and had a few disturbing dreams. Then I called Lifeline and checked my bank balance.

"Going shopping?" asked Mike, who had put the call through for me.

"Going home," I answered.

"Huh?"

"I'm out of the baiting business after this one, Mike. The Devil with Ikky! The Devil with Venus and Luharich Enterprises! And the Devil with you!"

Up eyebrows.

"What brought that on?"

"I waited over a year for this job. Now that I'm here, I've decided the whole thing stinks."

"You knew what it was when you signed on. No matter what else you're doing, you're selling face cream when you work for face cream sellers."

"Oh, that's not what's biting me. I admit the commercial angle irritates me, but Tensquare has always been a publicity spot, ever since the first time it sailed."

"What, then?"

"Five or six things, all added up. The main one being that I don't care any more. Once it meant more to me than anything else to hook that critter, and now it doesn't. I went broke on what started out as a lark and I wanted blood for what it cost me. Now I realize that maybe I had it coming. I'm beginning to feel sorry for Ikky."

"And you don't want him now?"

"I'll take him if he comes peacefully, but I don't feel like sticking out my neck to make him crawl into the Hopkins."

"I'm inclined to think it's one of the four or five other things you said you added."

"Such as?"

He scrutinized the ceiling.

I growled.

"Okay, but I won't say it, not just to make you happy you guessed right."

He, smirking: "That look she wears isn't just for Ikky."

"No good, no good." I shook my head. "We're both fission chambers by nature. You can't have jets on both ends of the rocket and expect to go anywhere—what's in the middle just gets smashed."

"That's how it *was*. None of my business, of course—"

"Say that again and you'll say it without teeth."

"Any day, big man"—he looked up—"any place . . ."

"So go ahead. Get it said!"

"She doesn't care about that bloody reptile, she came here to drag you back where you belong. You're not the baitman this trip."

"Five years is too long."

"There must be something under that cruddy hide of yours that people like," he muttered, "or I wouldn't be talking like this. Maybe you remind us humans of some really ugly dog we felt sorry for when we were kids. Anyhow, someone wants to take you home and raise you—also, something about beggars not getting menus."

"Buddy," I chuckled, "do you know what I'm going to do when I hit Lifeline?"

"I can guess."

"You're wrong. I'm torching it to Mars, and then I'll cruise back home, first class. Venus bankruptcy provisions do not apply to Martian trust funds, and I've still got a wad tucked away where moth and corruption enter not. I'm going to pick up a big old mansion on the Gulf and if you're ever looking for a job you can stop around and open bottles for me."

"You are a yellowbellied fink," he commented.

"Okay," I admitted, "but it's her I'm thinking of, too."

"I've heard the stories about you both," he said. "So you're a heel and a goofoff and she's a bitch. That's called compatibility these days. I dare you, baitman, try keeping scmething you catch."

I turned.

"If you ever want that job, look me up."

I closed the door quietly behind me and left him sitting there waiting for it to slam.

The day of the beast dawned like any other. Two days after my gutless flight from empty waters I went down to rebait. Nothing on the scope. I was just making things ready for the routine attempt.

I hollered a "good morning" from outside the Slider and received an answer from inside before I pushed off. I had reappraised Mike's words, sans sound, sans fury, and while I did not approve of their sentiment or significance, I had opted for civility anyhow.

So down, under, and away. I followed a decent cast about two hundred-ninety meters out. The snaking cables burned black to my left and I paced their undulations from the yellowgreen down into the darkness. Soundless lay the wet night, and I bent my way through it like a cock-eyed comet, bright tail before.

I caught the line, slick and smooth, and began baiting. An icy world swept by me then, ankles to head. It was a draft, as if someone had opened a big door beneath me. I wasn't drifting downwards that fast either.

Which meant that something might be moving up, something big enough to displace a lot of water. I still didn't think it was Ikky. A freak current of some sort, but not Ikky. Ha!

I had finished attaching the leads and pulled the first plug when a big, rugged, black island grew beneath me. . . .

I flicked the beam downward. His mouth was opened.

I was rabbit.

Waves of the death-fear passed downward. My stomach imploded. I grew dizzy.

Only one thing, and one thing only. Left to do. I managed it, finally. I pulled the rest of the plugs.

I could count the scaly articulations ridging his eyes by then.

The squiggler grew, pinked into phosphorescence . . . squiggled!

Then my lamp. I had to kill it, leaving just the bait before him.

One glance back as I jammed the jatoes to life.

He was so near that the squiggler reflected on his teeth, in his eyes. Four meters, and I kissed his lambent jowls with two jets of backwash as I soared. Then I didn't know whether he was following or had halted. I began to black out as I waited to be eaten.

The jatoes died and I kicked weakly.

Too fast, I felt a cramp coming on. One flick of the beam, cried rabbit. One second, to know . . .

Or end things up, I answered. No, rabbit, we don't dart before hunters. Stay dark.

Green waters finally, to yellowgreen, then top.

Doubling, I beat off toward Tensquare. The waves from the explosion behind pushed me on ahead. The world closed in, and a screamed "He's alive!" in the distance.

A giant shadow and a shock wave. The line was alive,

too. Happy Fishing Grounds. Maybe I did something
wrong. . . .

Somewhere Hand was clenched. What's bait?

A few million years. I remember starting out as a one-
celled organism and painfully becoming an amphibian, then
an air-breather. From somewhere high in the treetops I
heard a voice.

"He's coming around."

I evolved back into homosapience, then a step further
into a hangover.

"Don't try to get up yet."

"Have we got him?" I slurred.

"Still fighting, but he's hooked. We thought he took you
for an appetizer."

"So did I."

"Breathe some of this and shut up."

A funnel over my face. Good. Lift your cups and drink. . . .

"He was awfully deep. Below scope range. We didn't
catch him till he started up. Too late, then."

I began to yawn.

"We'll get you inside now."

I managed to uncase my ankle knife.

"Try it and you'll be minus a thumb."

"You need rest."

"Then bring me a couple more blankets. I'm staying."

I fell back and closed my eyes.

Someone was shaking me. Gloom and cold. Spotlights
bled yellow on the deck. I was in a jury-rigged bunk, bulked
against the center blister. Swaddled in wool, I still shivered.

"It's been eleven hours. You're not going to see anything
now."

I tasted blood.

"Drink this."

Water. I had a remark but I couldn't mouth it.

"Don't ask how I feel," I croaked. "I know that comes
next, but don't ask me. Okay?"

"Okay. Want to go below now?"

"No. Just get me my jacket."

"Right here."

"What's he doing?"

"Nothing. He's deep, he's doped but he's staying down."

"How long since last time he showed?"

"Two hours, about."

"Jean?"

"She won't let anyone in the Slider. Listen, Mike says come on in. He's right behind you in the blister."

I sat up and turned. Mike was watching. He gestured; I gestured back.

I swung my feet over the edge and took a couple of deep breaths. Pains in my stomach. I got to my feet and made it into the blister.

"Howza gut?" queried Mike.

I checked the scope. No Ikky. Too deep.

"You buying?"

"Yeah, coffee."

"Not coffee."

"You're ill. Also, coffee is all that's allowed in here."

"Coffee is a brownish liquid that burns your stomach. You have some in the bottom drawer."

"No cups. You'll have to use a glass."

"Tough."

He poured.

"You do that well. Been practicing for that job?"

"What job?"

"The one I offered you—"

A blot on the scope!

"Rising, ma'am! Rising!" he yelled into the box.

"Thanks, Mike. I've got it in here," she crackled.

"Jean!"

"Shut up! She's busy!"

"Was that Carl?"

"Yeah," I called. "Talk later," and I cut it.

Why did I do that?

"Why did you do that?"

I didn't know.

"I don't know."

Damned echoes! I got up and walked outside.

Nothing. Nothing.

Something?

Tensquare actually rocked! He must have turned when he saw the hull and started downward again. White water to my left, and boiling. An endless spaghetti of cable roared hotly into the belly of the deep.

I stood awhile, then turned and went back inside.

Two hours sick. Four, and better.

"The dope's getting to him."

"Yeah."

"What about Miss Luharich?"

"What about her?"

"She must be half dead."

"Probably."

"What are you going to do about it?"

"She signed the contract for this. She knew what might happen. It did."

"I think you could land him."

"So do I."

"So does she."

"Then let her ask me."

Ikky was drifting lethargically, at thirty fathoms.

I took another walk and happened to pass behind the Slider. She wasn't looking my way.

"Carl, come in here!"

Eyes of Picasso, that's what, and a conspiracy to make me Slide . . .

"Is that an order?"

"Yes—No! Please."

I dashed inside and monitored. He was rising.

"Push or pull?"

I slammed the "wind" and he came like a kitten.

"Make up your own mind now."

He balked at ten fathoms.

"Play him?"

"No!"

She wound him upwards—five fathoms, four . . .

She hit the extensors at two, and they caught him. Then the graffles.

Cries without and a heat lightning of flashbulbs.

The crew saw Ikky.

He began to struggle. She kept the cables tight, raised the graffles . . .

Up.

Another two feet and the graffles began pushing.

Screams and fast footfalls.

Giant beanstalk in the wind, his neck, waving. The green hills of his shoulders grew.

"He's big, Carl!" she cried.

And he grew, and grew, and grew uneasy . . .

"Now!"

He looked down.

He looked down, as the god of our most ancient ancestors

might have looked down. Fear, shame, and mocking laughter rang in my head. Her head, too?

"Now!"

She looked up at the nascent earthquake.

"I can't!"

It was going to be so damnably simple this time, now the rabbit had died. I reached out.

I stopped.

"Push it yourself."

"I can't. You do it. Land him, Carl!"

"No. If I do, you'll wonder for the rest of your life whether you could have. You'll throw away your soul finding out. I know you will, because we're alike, and I did it that way. Find out now!"

She stared.

I gripped her shoulders.

"Could be that's me out there," I offered. "I am a green sea serpent, a hateful, monstrous beast, and out to destroy you. I am answerable to no one. Push the Inject."

Her hand moved to the button, jerked back.

"Now!"

She pushed it.

I lowered her still form to the floor and finished things up with Ikky.

It was a good seven hours before I awakened to the steady, sea-chewing grind of Tensquare's blades.

"You're sick," commented Mike.

"How's Jean?"

"The same."

"Where's the beast?"

"Here."

"Good." I rolled over. ". . . Didn't get away this time."

So that's the way it was. No one is born a baitman, I don't think, but the rings of Saturn sing epithalamium the seabeast's dower.

STUDENT BODY

BY F. L. WALLACE

The first morning that they were fully committed to the planet, the executive officer stepped out of the ship. It was not quite dawn. Executive Hafner squinted in the early light; his eyes opened wider, and he promptly went back inside. Three minutes later, he reappeared with the biologist in tow.

"Last night you said there was nothing dangerous," said the executive. "Do you still think it's so?"

Dano Marin stared. "I do." What his voice lacked in conviction, it made up in embarrassment. He laughed uncertainly.

"This is no laughing matter. I'll talk to you later."

The biologist stood by the ship and watched as the executive walked to the row of sleeping colonists.

"Mrs. Athyl," said the executive as he stopped beside the sleeping figure.

She yawned, rubbed her eyes, rolled over, and stood up. The covering that should have been there, however, wasn't. Neither was the garment she had on when she had gone to sleep. She assumed the conventional position of a woman who is astonished to find herself unclad without her knowledge or consent.

"It's all right, Mrs. Athyl. I'm not a voyeur myself. Still, I think you should get some clothing on." Most of the colonists were awake now. Executive Hafner turned to them. "If you haven't any suitable clothing in the ship, the commissary will issue you some. Explanations will be given later."

The colonists scattered. There was no compulsive mod-

206

esty among them, for it couldn't have survived a year and a half in crowded spaceships. Nevertheless, it was a shock to awaken with no clothing on and not know who or what had removed it during the night. It was surprise more than anything else that disconcerted them.

On his way back to the spaceship, Executive Hafner paused. "Any ideas about it?"

Dano Marin shrugged. "How could I have? The planet is as new to me as it is to you."

"Sure. But you're the biologist."

As the only scientist in a crew of rough-and-ready colonists and builders, Marin was going to be called on to answer a lot of questions that weren't in his field.

"Nocturnal insects, most likely," he suggested. That was pretty weak, though he knew that in ancient times locusts had stripped fields in a matter of hours. Could they do the same with the clothing of humans and not awaken them? "I'll look into the matter. As soon as I find anything, I'll let you know."

"Good." Hafner nodded and went into the spaceship.

Dano Marin walked to the grove in which the colonists had been sleeping. It had been a mistake to let them bed down there, but at the time the request had been made, there had seemed no reason not to grant it. After eighteen months in crowded ships everyone naturally wanted fresh air and the rustle of leaves overhead.

Marin looked out through the grove. It was empty now; the colonists, both men and women, had disappeared inside the ship, dressing, probably.

The trees were not tall and the leaves were dark bottle-green. Occasional huge white flowers caught sunlight that made them seem larger than they were. It wasn't Earth and therefore the trees couldn't be magnolias. But they reminded Marin of magnolia trees and thereafter he always thought of them as that.

The problem of the missing clothing was ironic. Biological Survey never made a mistake—yet obviously they had. They listed the planet as the most suitable for Man of any so far discovered. Few insects, no dangerous animals, a most equitable climate. They had named it Glade because that was the word which fitted best. The whole land mass seemed to be one vast and pleasant meadow.

Evidently there were things about the planet that Biological Survey had missed.

Marin dropped to his knees and began to look for clues. If insects had been responsible, there ought to be a few dead ones, crushed, perhaps, as the colonists rolled over in their sleep. There were no insects, either live or dead.

He stood up in disappointment and walked slowly through the grove. It might be the trees. At night they could exude a vapor which was capable of dissolving the material from which the clothing had been made. Far-fetched, but not impossible. He crumbled a leaf in his hand and rubbed it against his sleeve. A pungent smell, but nothing happened. That didn't disprove the theory, of course.

He looked out through the trees at the blue sun. It was bigger than Sol, but farther away. At Glade, it was about equal to the Sun on Earth.

He almost missed the bright eyes that regarded him from the underbrush. Almost, but didn't—the domain of biology begins at the edge of the atmosphere; it includes the brush and the small creatures that live in it.

He swooped down on it. The creature fled squealing. He ran it down in the grass outside the grove. It collapsed into quaking flesh as he picked it up. He talked to it gently and the terror subsided.

It nibbled contentedly on his jacket as he carried it back to the ship.

Executive Hafner stared unhappily into the cage. It was an undistinguished animal, small and something like an undeveloped rodent. Its fur was sparse and stringy, unglamorous; it would never be an item in the fur export trade.

"Can we exterminate it?" asked Hafner. "Locally, that is."

"Hardly. It's ecologically basic."

The executive looked blank. Dano Marin added the explanation: "You know how Biological Control works. As soon as a planet has been discovered that looks suitable, they send out a survey ship loaded with equipment. The ship flies low over a good part of the planet and the instruments in the ship record the neural currents of the animals below. The instruments can distinguish the characteristic neural patterns of anything that has a brain, including insects.

"Anyway, they have a pretty good idea of the kinds of animals on the planet and their relative distribution. Naturally, the survey party takes a few specimens. They have to in order to correlate the pattern with the actual animal, otherwise the neural pattern would be merely a meaningless squiggle on a microfilm.

"The survey shows that this animal is one of only four species of mammals on the planet. It is also the most numerous."

Hafner grunted. "So if we kill them off here, others will swarm in from surrounding areas?"

"That's about it. There are probably millions of them on this peninsula. Of course, if you want to put a barrier across the narrow connection to the mainland, you might be able to wipe them out locally."

The executive scowled. A barrier was possible, but it would involve more work than he cared to expend.

"What do they eat?" he asked truculently.

"A little bit of everything, apparently. Insects, fruits, berries, nuts, succulents, and grain." Dano Marin smiled. "I guess it could be called an omnivore—now that our clothing is handy, it eats that, too."

Hafner didn't smile. "I thought our clothing was supposed to be verminproof."

Marin shrugged. "It is, on twenty-seven planets. On the twenty-eighth, we meet up with a little fella that has better digestive fluids, that's all."

Hafner looked pained. "Are they likely to bother the crops we plant?"

"Offhand, I would say they aren't. But then I would have said the same about our clothing."

Hafner made up his mind. "All right. You worry about the crops. Find some way to keep them out of the fields. Meanwhile, everyone sleeps in the ship until we can build dormitories."

Individual dwelling units would have been more appropriate in the colony at this stage, thought Marin. But it wasn't for him to decide. The executive was a man who regarded a schedule as something to be exceeded.

"The omnivore—" began Marin.

Hafner nodded impatiently. "Work on it," he said, and walked away.

The biologist sighed. The omnivore really was a queer little creature, but it was by no means the most important thing on Glade. For instance, why were there so few species of land animals on the planet? No reptiles, numerous birds, and only four kinds of mammals.

Every comparable planet teemed with a wild variety of

life. Glade, in spite of seemingly ideal conditions, hadn't developed. Why?

He had asked Biological Controls for this assignment because it had seemed an interesting problem. Now, apparently, he was being pressed into service as an exterminator.

He reached in the cage and picked up the omnivore. Mammals on Glade were not unexpected. Parallel development took care of that. Given roughly the same kind of environment, similar animals would usually evolve.

In the Late Carboniferous forest on Earth, there had been creatures like the omnivore, the primitive mammal from which all others had evolved. On Glade, that kind of evolution just hadn't taken place. What had kept nature from exploiting its evolutionary potentialities? There was the real problem, not how to wipe them out.

Marin stuck a needle in the omnivore. It squealed and then relaxed. He drew out the blood and set it back in the cage. He could learn a lot about the animal from trying to kill it.

The quartermaster was shouting, though his normal voice carried quite well.

"How do you know it's mice?" the biologist asked him.

"Look," said the quartermaster angrily.

Marin looked. The evidence did indicate mice.

Before he could speak, the quartermaster snapped, "Don't tell me they're only micelike creatures. I know that. The question is: how can I get rid of them?"

"Have you tried poison?"

"Tell me what poison to use and I'll use it."

It wasn't the easiest question to answer. What was poisonous to an animal he had never seen and knew nothing about? According to Biological Survey, the animal didn't exist.

It was unexpectedly serious. The colony could live off the land, and was expected to. But another group of colonists was due in three years. The colony was supposed to accumulate a surplus of food to feed the increased numbers. If they couldn't store the food they grew any better than the concentrates, that surplus was going to be scanty.

Marin went over the warehouse thoroughly. It was the usual early construction on a colonial world. Not esthetic, it was sturdy enough. Fused dirt floor, reinforced foot-thick walls, a ceiling slab of the same. The whole was bound together with a molecular cement that made it practically airtight. It had no windows; there were two doors. Certainly it should keep out rodents.

A closer examination revealed an unexpected flaw. The floor was as hard as glass; no animal could gnaw through it, but, like glass, it was also brittle. The crew that had built the warehouse had evidently been in such a hurry to get back to Earth that they hadn't been as careful as they should have been, for here and there the floor was thin. Somewhere under the heavy equipment piled on it, the floor had cracked. There a burrowing animal had means of entry.

Short of building another warehouse, it was too late to do anything about that. Micelike animals were inside and had to be controlled where they were.

The biologist straightened up. "Catch me a few of them alive and I'll see what I can do."

In the morning, a dozen live specimens were delivered to the lab. They actually did resemble mice.

Their reactions were puzzling. No two of them were affected by the same poison. A compound that stiffened one in a matter of minutes left the others hale and hearty, and the poison he had developed to control the omnivores was completely ineffective.

The depredations in the warehouse went on. Black mice, white ones, gray and brown, short-tailed and long-eared, or the reverse, they continued to eat the concentrates and spoil what they didn't eat.

Marin conferred with the executive, outlined the problem as he saw it and his ideas on what could be done to combat the nuisance.

"But we can't build another warehouse," argued Hafner. "Not until the atomic generator is set up, at any rate. And then we'll have other uses for the power." The executive rested his head in his hands. "I like the other solution better. Build one and see how it works."

"I was thinking of three," said the biologist.

"One," Hafner insisted. "We can't spare the equipment until we know how it works."

At that he was probably right. They had equipment, as much as three ships could bring. But the more they brought, the more was expected of the colony. The net effect was that equipment was always in short supply.

Marin took the authorization to the engineer. On the way, he privately revised his specifications upward. If he couldn't get as many as he wanted, he might as well get a better one.

In two days, the machine was ready.

It was delivered in a small crate to the warehouse. The crate was opened and the machine leaped out and stood there, poised.

"A cat!" exclaimed the quartermaster, pleased. He stretched out his hand toward the black fuzzy robot.

"If you've touched anything a mouse may have, get your hand away," warned the biologist. "It reacts to smell as well as sight and sound."

Hastily, the quartermaster withdrew his hand. The robot disappeared silently into the maze of stored material.

In one week, though there were still some mice in the warehouse, they were no longer a danger.

The executive called Marin into his office, a small sturdy building located in the center of the settlement. The colony was growing, assuming an aspect of permanency. Hafner sat in his chair and looked out over that growth with satisfaction.

"A good job on the mouse plague," he said.

The biologist nodded. "Not bad, except there shouldn't be any mice here. Biological Survey—"

"Forget it," said the exec. "Everybody makes mistakes, even B. S." He leaned back and looked seriously at the biologist. "I have a job I need done. Just now I'm short of men. If you have no objections . . ."

The exec was always short of men, would be until the planet was overcrowded, and he would try to find someone to do the work his own men should have done. Dano Marin was not directly responsible to Hafner; he was on loan to the expedition from Biological Controls. Still, it was a good idea to cooperate with the executive. He sighed.

"It's not as bad as you think," said Hafner, interpreting the sound correctly. He smiled. "We've got the digger together. I want you to run it."

Since it tied right in with his investigations, Dano Marin looked relieved and showed it.

"Except for food, we have to import most of our supplies," Hafner explained. "It's a long haul, and we've got to make use of everything on the planet we can. We need oil. There are going to be a lot of wheels turning, and everyone of them will have to have oil. In time we'll set up a synthetic plant, but if we can locate a productive field now, it's to our advantage."

"You're assuming the geology of Glade is similar to Earth?"

Hafner waggled his hand. "Why not? It's a nicer twin of Earth."

Why not? Because you couldn't always tell from the surface, thought Marin. It *seemed* like Earth, but was it? Here was a good chance to find out the history of Glade.

Hafner stood up. "Any time you're ready, a technician will check you out on the digger. Let me know before you go."

Actually, the digger wasn't a digger. It didn't move or otherwise displace a gram of dirt or rock. It was a means of looking down below the surface, to any practical depth. A large crawler, it was big enough for a man to live in without discomfort for a week.

It carried an outsize ultrasonic generator and a device for directing the beam into the planet. That was the sending apparatus. The receiving end began with a large sonic lens which picked up sound beams reflected from any desired depth, converted it into electrical energy and thence into an image which was flashed onto a screen.

At the depth of ten miles, the image was fuzzy, though good enough to distinguish the main features of the strata. At three miles, it was better. It could pick up the sound reflection of a buried coin and convert it into a picture on which the date could be seen.

It was to a geologist as a microscope is to a biologist. Being a biologist, Dano Marin could appreciate the analogy.

He started at the tip of the peninsula and zigzagged across, heading toward the isthmus. Methodically, he covered the territory, sleeping at night in the digger. On the morning of the third day, he discovered oil traces, and by that afternoon he had located the main field.

He should probably have turned back at once, but now that he had found oil, he investigated more deliberately. Starting at the top, he let the image range downward below the top strata.

It was the reverse of what it should have been. In the top few feet, there were plentiful fossil remains, mostly of the four species of mammals. The squirrel-like creature and the far larger grazing animal were the forest dwellers. Of the plains animals, there were only two, in size fitting neatly between the extremes of the forest dwellers.

After the first few feet, which correspond to approximately twenty thousand years, he found virtually no fossils.

Not until he reached a depth which he could correlate to the Late Carboniferous age on Earth did fossils reappear. Then they were of animals appropriate to the epoch. At that depth and below, the history of Glade was quite similar to Earth's.

Puzzled, he checked again in a dozen widely scattered localities. The results were always the same—fossil history for the first twenty thousand years, then none for roughly a hundred million. Beyond that, it was easy to trace the thread of biological development.

In that period of approximately one hundred million years, something unique had happened to Glade. What was it?

On the fifth day his investigations were interrupted by the sound of the keyed-on radio.

"Marin."

"Yes?" He flipped on the sending switch.

"How soon can you get back?"

He looked at the photo-map. "Three hours. Two if I hurry."

"Make it two. Never mind the oil."

"I've found oil. But what's the matter?"

"You can see it better than I can describe it. We'll discuss it when you get back."

Reluctantly, Marin retracted the instruments into the digger. He turned it around and, with not too much regard for the terrain, let it roar. The treads tossed dirt high in the air. Animals fled squealing from in front of him. If the grove was small enough, he went around it, otherwise he went through and left matchsticks behind.

He skidded the crawler ponderously to halt near the edge of the settlement. The center of activity was the warehouse. Pickups wheeled in and out, transferring supplies to a cleared area outside. He found Hafner in a corner of the warehouse, talking to the engineer.

Hafner turned around when he came up. "Your mice have grown, Marin."

Marin looked down. The robot cat lay on the floor. He knelt and examined it. The steel skeleton hadn't broken; it had been bent, badly. The tough plastic skin had been torn off and, inside, the delicate mechanism had been chewed into an unrecognizable mass.

Around the cat were rats, twenty or thirty of them, huge by any standards. The cat had fought; the dead animals were headless or disemboweled, unbelievably battered. But the robot had been outnumbered.

Biological Survey had said there weren't any rats on Glade. They had also said that about mice. What was the key to their errors?

The biologist stood up. "What are you going to do about it?"

"Build another warehouse, two-foot-thick fused dirt floors, monolithic construction. Transfer all perishables to it."

Marin nodded. That would do it. It would take time, of course, and power, all they could draw out of the recently set up atomic generator. All other construction would have to be suspended. No wonder Hafner was disturbed.

"Why not build more cats?" Marin suggested.

The executive smiled nastily. "You weren't here when we opened the doors. The warehouse was swarming with rats. How many robot cats would we need—five, fifteen? I don't know. Anyway the engineer tells me we have enough parts to build three more cats. The one lying there can't be salvaged."

It didn't take an engineer to see that, thought Marin.

Hafner continued, "If we need more, we'll have to rob the computer in the spaceship. I refuse to permit that."

Obviously he would. The spaceship was the only link with Earth until the next expedition brought more colonists. No exec in his right mind would permit the ship to be crippled.

But why had Hafner called him back? Merely to keep him informed of the situation?

Hafner seemed to guess his thoughts. "At night we'll floodlight the supplies we remove from the warehouse. We'll post a guard armed with decharged rifles until we can move the food into the new warehouse. That'll take about ten days. Meanwhile, our fast crops are ripening. It's my guess the rats will turn to them for food. In order to protect our future food supply, you'll have to activate your animals."

The biologist started. "But it's against regulations to loose any animal on a planet until a complete investigation of the possible ill effects is made."

"That takes ten or twenty years. This is an emergency and I'll be responsible—in writing, if you want."

The biologist was effectively countermanded. Another rabbit-infested Australia or the planet that the snails took over might be in the making, but there was nothing he could do about it.

"I hardly think they'll be of any use against rats this size," he protested.

"You've got hormones. Apply them." The executive turned and began discussing construction with the engineer.

Marin had the dead rats gathered up and placed in the freezer for further study.

After that, he retired to the laboratory and worked out a course of treatment for the domesticated animals that the colonists had brought with them. He gave them the first injections and watched them carefully until they were safely through the initial shock phase of growth. As soon as he saw they were going to survive, he bred them.

Next he turned to the rats. Of note was the wide variation in size. Internally, the same thing was true. They had the usual organs, but the proportions of each varied greatly, more than is normal. Nor were their teeth uniform. Some carried huge fangs set in delicate jaws; others had tiny teeth that didn't match the massive bone structure. As a species, they were the most scrambled the biologist had ever encountered.

He turned the microscope on their tissues and tabulated the results. There was less difference here between individual specimens, but it was enough to set him pondering. The reproductive cells were especially baffling.

Late in the day, he felt rather than heard the soundless whoosh of the construction machinery. He looked out of the laboratory and saw smoke rolling upward. As soon as the vegetation was charred, the smoke ceased and heat waves danced into the sky.

They were building on a hill. The little creatures that crept and crawled in the brush attacked in the most vulnerable spot, the food supply. There was no brush, not a blade of grass, on the hill when the colonists finished.

Terriers. In the past, they were the hunting dogs of the agricultural era. What they lacked in size they made up in ferocity toward rodents. They had earned their keep originally in granaries and fields, and, for a brief time, they were doing it again on colonial worlds where conditions were repeated.

The dogs the colonists brought had been terriers. They were still as fast, still with the same anti-rodent disposition, but they were no longer small. It had been a difficult job, yet Marin had done it well, for the dogs had lost none of their skill and speed in growing to the size of a great dane.

The rats moved in on the fields of fast crops. Fast crops were made to order for a colonial world. They could be planted, grown, and harvested in a matter of weeks. After four such plantings, the fertility of the soil was destroyed, but that meant nothing in the early years of a colonial planet, for land was plentiful.

The rat tide grew in the fast crops, and the dogs were loosed on the rats. They ranged through the fields, hunting. A rush, a snap of their jaws, the shake of a head, and the rat was tossed aside, its back broken. The dogs went on to the next.

Until they could not see, the dogs prowled and slaughtered. At night they came in bloody, most of it not their own, and exhausted. Marin pumped them full of antibiotics, bandaged their wounds, fed them through their veins, and shot them into sleep. In the morning he awakened them with an injection of stimulant and sent them tingling into battle.

It took the rats two days to learn they could not feed during the day. Not so numerous, they came at night. They climbed on the vines and nibbled the fruit. They gnawed growing grain and ravaged vegetables.

The next day the colonists set up lights. The dogs were with them, discouraging the few rats who were still foolish enough to forage while the sun was overhead.

An hour before dusk, Marin called the dogs in and gave them an enforced rest. He brought them out of it after dark and took them to the fields, staggering. The scent of rats revived them; they were as eager as ever, if not quite so fast.

The rats came from the surrounding meadows, not singly, or in twos and threes, as they did before; this time they came together. Squealing and rustling the grass, they moved toward the fields. It was dark, and though he could not see them, Marin could hear them. He ordered the great lights turned on in the area of the fields.

The rats stopped under the glare, milling around uneasily. The dogs quivered and whined. Marin held them back. The rats resumed their march, and Marin released the dogs.

The dogs charged in to attack, but didn't dare brave the main mass. They picked off the stragglers and forced the rats into a tighter formation. After that the rats were virtually unassailable.

The colonists could have burned the bunched-up rats with

the right equipment, but they didn't have it and couldn't get it for years. Even if they'd had it, the use of such equipment would endanger the crops, which they had to save if they could. It was up to the dogs.

The rat formation came to the edge of the fields, and broke. They could face a common enemy and remain united, but in the presence of food, they forgot that unity and scattered—hunger was the great divisor. The dogs leaped joyously in pursuit. They hunted down the starved rodents, one by one, and killed them as they ate.

When daylight came, the rat menace had ended.

The next week the colonists harvested and processed the food for storage and immediately planted another crop.

Marin sat in the lab and tried to analyze the situation. The colony was moving from crisis to crisis, all of them involving food. In itself, each critical situation was minor, but lumped together they could add up to failure. No matter how he looked at it, they just didn't have the equipment they needed to colonize Glade.

The fault seemed to lie with Biological Survey; they hadn't reported the presence of pests that were endangering the food supply. Regardless of what the exec thought about them, Survey knew their business. If they said there were no mice or rats on Glade, then there hadn't been any—*when the survey was made.*

The question was: when did they come and how did they get here?

Marin sat and stared at the wall, turning over hypotheses in his mind, discarding them when they failed to make sense.

His gaze shifted from the wall to the cage of the omnivores, the squirrel-size forest creature. The most numerous animal on Glade, it was a commonplace sight to the colonists.

And yet it was a remarkable animal, more than he had realized. Plain, insignificant in appearance, it might be the most important of any animal Man had encountered on the many worlds he had settled on. The longer he watched, the more Marin became convinced of it.

He sat silent, observing the creature, not daring to move. He sat until it was dark and the omnivore resumed its normal activity.

Normal? The word didn't apply on Glade.

The interlude with the omnivore provided him with one

answer. He needed another one; he thought he knew what it was, but he had to have more data, additional observations.

He set up his equipment carefully on the fringes of the settlement. There and in no other place existed the information he wanted.

He spent time in the digger, checking his original investigations. It added up to a complete picture.

When he was certain of his facts, he called on Hafner.

The executive was congenial; it was a reflection of the smoothness with which the objectives of the colony were being achieved.

"Sit down," he said affably. "Smoke?"

The biologist sat down and took a cigarette.

"I thought you'd like to know where the mice came from," he began.

Hafner smiled. "They don't bother us any more."

"I've also determined the origin of the rats."

"They're under control. We're doing nicely."

On the contrary, thought Marin. He searched for the proper beginning.

"Glade has an Earth-type climate and topography," he said. "Has had for the past twenty thousand years. Before that, about a hundred million years ago, it was also like Earth of the comparable period."

He watched the look of polite interest settle on the executive's face as he stated the obvious. Well, it *was* obvious, up to a point. The conclusions weren't, though.

"Between a hundred million years and twenty thousand years ago, something happened to Glade," Marin went on. "I don't know the cause; it belongs to cosmic history and we may never find out. Anyway, whatever the cause—fluctuations in the sun, unstable equilibrium of forces within the planet, or perhaps an encounter with an interstellar dust cloud of variable density—the climate on Glade changed.

"It changed with inconceivable violence and it kept on changing. A hundred million years ago, plus or minus, there was carboniferous forest on Glade. Giant reptiles resembling dinosaurs and tiny mammals roamed through it. The first great change wiped out the dinosaurs, as it did on Earth. It didn't wipe out the still more primitive ancestor of the omnivore, because it could adapt to changing conditions.

"Let me give you an idea how the conditions changed. For a few years a given area would be a desert; after that it would turn into a jungle. Still later a glacier would begin to form. And then the cycle would be repeated, with wild variations. All this might happen—did happen—within a span covered by the lifetime of a single omnivore. This occurred many times. For roughly a hundred million years, it was the norm of existence on Glade. This condition was hardly conducive to the preservation of fossils."

Hafner saw the significance and was concerned. "You mean these climatic fluctuations suddenly stopped, twenty thousand years ago? Are they likely to begin again?"

"I don't know," confessed the biologist. "We can probably determine it if we're interested."

The exec nodded grimly. "We're interested, all right."

Maybe we are, thought the biologist. He said, "The point is that survival was difficult. Birds could and did fly to more suitable climates; quite a few of them survived. Only one species of mammals managed to come through."

"Your facts are not straight," observed Hafner. "There are four species, ranging in size from a squirrel to a water buffalo."

"One species," Marin repeated doggedly. "They're the same. If the food supply for the largest animal increases, some of the smaller so-called species grow up. Conversely, if food becomes scarce in any category, the next generation, which apparently can be produced almost instantly, switches to a form which does have an adequate food supply."

"The mice," Hafner said slowly.

Marin finished the thought for him. "The mice weren't here when we got here. They were born of the squirrel-size omnivore."

Hafner nodded. "And the rats?"

"Born of the next larger size. After all, we're environment, too—perhaps the harshest the beasts have yet faced."

Hafner was a practical man, trained to administer a colony. Concepts were not his familiar ground. "Mutations, then? But I thought—"

The biologist smiled. It was thin and cracked at the edges of his mouth. "On Earth, it would be mutation. Here it is merely normal evolutionary adaptation." He shook his head. "I never told you, but omnivores, though they could be mistaken for an animal from Earth, have no genes or chromosomes. Obviously they do have heredity, but how it is passed down, I don't know. However it functions, it responds to external conditions far faster than anything we've ever encountered."

Hafner nodded to himself. "Then we'll never be free from pests." He clasped and unclasped his hands. "Unless, of course, we rid the planet of all animal life."

"Radioactive dust?" asked the biologist. "They have survived worse."

The exec considered alternatives. "Maybe we should leave the planet and leave it to the animals."

"Too late," said the biologist. "They'll be on Earth, too, and all the planets we've settled on."

Hafner looked at him. The same pictures formed in his mind that Marin had thought of. Three ships had been sent to colonize Glade. One had remained with the colonists, survival insurance in case anything unforeseen happened. Two had gone back to Earth to carry the report that all was well and that more supplies were needed. They had also carried specimens from the planet.

The cages those creatures were kept in were secure. But a smaller species could get out, must already be free, inhabiting, undetected, the cargo spaces of the ships.

There was nothing they could do to intercept those ships. And once they reached Earth, would the biologists suspect? Not for a long time. First a new kind of rat would appear. A mutation could account for that. Without specific knowledge, there would be nothing to connect it with the specimens picked up from Glade.

"We have to stay," said the biologist. "We have to study them and we can do it best here."

He thought of the vast complex of buildings on Earth. There was too much invested to tear them down and make them verminproof. Billions of people could not be moved off the planet while the work was being done.

They were committed to Glade not as a colony, but as a gigantic laboratory. They had gained one planet and lost the equivalent of ten, perhaps more when the destructive properties of the omnivores were finally assessed.

A rasping animal cough interrupted the biologist's thoughts. Hafner jerked his head and glanced at the window. Lips tight, he grabbed a rifle off the wall and ran out. Marin followed him.

The exec headed toward the fields where the second fast crop was maturing. On top of a knoll, he stopped and knelt. He flipped the dial to *extreme charge,* aimed, and fired. It was high; he missed the animal in the field. A neat strip of smoking brown appeared in the green vegetation.

He aimed more carefully and fired again. The charge screamed out of the muzzle. It struck the animal on the forepaw. The beast leaped high in the air and fell down, dead and broiled.

They stood over the animal Hafner had killed. Except for the lack of markings, it was a good imitation of a tiger. The exec prodded it with his toe.

"We chase the rats out of the warehouse and they go to the fields," he muttered. "We hunt them down in the fields with dogs and they breed tigers."

"Easier than rats," said Marin. "We can shoot tigers." He bent down over the slain dog near which they had surprised the big cat.

The other dog came whining from the far corner of the field to which he had fled in terror. He was a courageous dog, but he could not face the great carnivore. He whimpered and licked the face of his mate.

The biologist picked up the mangled dog and headed toward the laboratory.

"You can't save her," said Hafner morosely. "She's dead."

"But the pups aren't. We'll need them. The rats won't disappear merely because tigers have showed up."

The head drooped limply over his arm and blood seeped into his clothing as Hafner followed him up the hill.

"We've been here three months," the exec said suddenly. "The dogs have been in the fields only two. And yet the tiger was mature. How do you account for something like that?"

Marin bent under the weight of the dog. Hafner never would understand his bewilderment. As a biologist, all his categories were upset. What did evolution explain? It was a history of organic life on a particular world. Beyond that world, it might not apply.

Even about himself there were many things Man didn't know, dark patches in his knowledge which theory simply had to pass over. About other creatures, his ignorance was sometimes limitless.

Birth was simple; it occurred on countless planets. Meek grazing creatures, fierce carnivores—the most unlikely animals gave birth to their young. It happened all the time. And the young grew up, became mature and mated.

He remembered that evening in the laboratory. It was

accidental—what if he had been elsewhere and not witnessed it? They would not know what little they did.

He explained it carefully to Hafner. "If the survival factor is high and there's a great disparity in size, the young need not ever be young. They may be born as fully functioning adults!"

Although not at the rate it had initially set, the colony progressed. The fast crops were slowed down and a more diversified selection was planted. New buildings were constructed and the supplies that were stored in them were spread out thin, for easy inspection.

The pups survived and within a year shot up to maturity. After proper training, they were released to the fields where they joined the older dogs. The battle against the rats went on; they were held in check, though the damage they caused was considerable.

The original animal, unchanged in form, developed an appetite for electrical insulation. There was no protection except to keep the power on at all times. Even then there were unwelcome interruptions until the short was located and the charred carcass was removed. Vehicles were kept tightly closed or parked only in verminproof buildings. While the plague didn't increase in numbers, it couldn't be eliminated, either.

There was a flurry of tigers, but they were larger animals and were promptly shot down. They prowled at night, so the colonists were assigned to guard the settlement around the clock. Where lights failed to reach, the infra-red 'scope did. As fast as they came, the tigers died. Except for the first one, not a single dog was lost.

The tigers changed, though not in form. Externally, they were all big and powerful killers. But as the slaughter went on, Marin noticed one astonishing fact—the internal organic structure became progressively more immature.

The last one that was brought to him for examination was the equivalent of a newly born cub. That tiny stomach was suited more for the digestion of milk than meat. How it had furnished energy to drive those great muscles was something of a miracle. But drive it had, for a murderous fifteen minutes before the animal was brought down. No lives were lost, though sick bay was kept busy for a while.

That was the last tiger they shot. After that, the attacks ceased.

The seasons passed and nothing new occurred. A space-ship civilization or even that fragment of it represented by the colony was too much for the creature, which Marin by now had come to think of as the "Omnimal." It had evolved out of a cataclysmic past, but it could not meet the challenge of the harshest environment.

Or so it seemed.

Three months before the next colonists were due, a new animal was detected. Food was missing from the fields. It was not another tiger; they were carnivorous. Nor rats, for vines were stripped in a manner that no rodent could manage.

The food was not important. The colony had enough in storage. But if the new animal signaled another plague, it was necessary to know how to meet it. The sooner they knew what the animal was, the better defense they could set up against it.

Dogs were useless. The animal roamed the field they were loose in, and they did not attack nor even seem to know it was there.

The colonists were called upon for guard duty again, but it evaded them. They patrolled for a week and they still did not catch sight of it.

Hafner called them in and rigged up an alarm system in the field most frequented by the animal. It detected that, too, and moved its sphere of operations to a field in which the alarm system had not been installed.

Hafner conferred with the engineer, who devised an alarm that would react to body radiation. It was buried in the original field and the old alarm was moved to another.

Two nights later, just before dawn, the alarm rang.

Marin met Hafner at the edge of the settlement. Both carried rifles. They walked; the noise of any vehicle was likely to frighten the animal. They circled around and approached the field from the rear. The men in the camp had been alerted. If they needed help, it was ready.

They crept silently through the underbrush. It was feeding in the field, not noisily, yet they could hear it. The dogs hadn't barked.

They inched nearer. The blue sun of Glade came up and shone full on their quarry. The gun dropped in Hafner's hand. He clenched his teeth and raised it again.

Marin put out a restraining arm. "Don't shoot," he whispered.

"I'm the exec here. I say it's dangerous."

"Dangerous," agreed Marin, still in a whisper. "That's why you can't shoot. It's more dangerous than you know."

Hafner hesitated and Marin went on. "The omnimal couldn't compete in the changed environment and so it evolved mice. We stopped the mice and it countered with rats. We turned back the rat and it provided the tiger.

"The tiger was easiest of all for us and so it was apparently stopped for a while. But it didn't really stop. Another animal was being formed, the one you see there. It took the omnimal two years to create it—how, I don't know. A million years were required to evolve it on Earth."

Hafner hadn't lowered the rifle and he showed no signs of doing so. He looked lovingly into the sights.

"Can't you see?" urged Marin. "We can't destroy the omnimal. It's on Earth now, and on the other planets, down in the storage areas of our big cities, masquerading as rats. And we've never been able to root out even our own terrestrial rats, so how can we exterminate the omnimal?"

"All the more reason to start now." Hafner's voice was flat.

Marin struck the rifle down. "Are their rats better than ours?" he asked wearily. "Will their pests win or ours be stronger? Or will the two make peace, unite and interbreed, make war on us? It's not impossible; the omnimal could do it if interbreeding had a high survival factor.

"Don't you still see? There is a progression. After the tiger, it bred this. If this evolution fails, if we shoot it down, what will it create next? This creature I think we can compete with. *It's the one after this that I do not want to face.*"

It heard them. It raised its head and looked around. Slowly it edged away and backed toward a nearby grove.

The biologist stood up and called softly. The creature scurried to the trees and stopped just inside the shadows among them.

The two men laid down their rifles. Together they approached the grove, hands spread open to show they carried no weapons.

It came out to meet them. Naked, it had had no time to learn about clothing. Neither did it have weapons. It plucked a large white flower from the tree and extended this mutely as a sign of peace.

"I wonder what it's like," said Marin. "It seems adult, but can it be, all the way through? What's inside that body?"

"I wonder what's in his head," Hafner said worriedly.

It looked very much like a man.

BLACK DESTROYER

BY A. E. VAN VOGT

On and on Coeurl prowled! The black, moonless, almost starless night yielded reluctantly before a grim reddish dawn that crept up from his left. A vague, dull light it was, that gave no sense of approaching warmth, no comfort, nothing but a cold, diffuse lightness, slowly revealing a nightmare landscape.

Black, jagged rock and black, unliving plain took form around him, as a pale-red sun peered at last above the grotesque horizon. It was then Coeurl recognized suddenly that he was on familiar ground.

He stopped short. Tenseness flamed along his nerves. His muscles pressed with sudden, unrelenting strength against his bones. His great forelegs—twice as long as his hindlegs—twitched with a shuddering movement that arched every razor-sharp claw. The thick tentacles that sprouted from his shoulders ceased their weaving undulation, and grew taut with anxious alertness.

Utterly appalled, he twisted his great cat head from side to side, while the little hairlike tendrils that formed each ear vibrated frantically, testing every vagrant breeze, every throb in the ether.

But there was no response, no swift tingling along his intricate nervous system, not the faintest suggestion anywhere of the presence of the all-necessary id. Hopelessly, Coeurl crouched, an enormous catlike figure silhouetted against the dim reddish skyline, like a distorted etching of a black tiger resting on a black rock in a shadow world.

He had known this day would come. Through all the centuries of restless search, this day had loomed ever nearer,

227

blacker, more frightening—this inevitable hour when he must return to the point where he began his systematic hunt in a world almost depleted of id-creatures.

The truth struck in waves like an endless, rhythmic ache at the seat of his ego. When he had started, there had been a few id-creatures in every hundred square miles, to be mercilessly rooted out. Only too well Coeurl knew in this ultimate hour that he had missed none. There were no id-creatures left to eat. In all the hundreds of thousands of square miles that he had made his own by right of ruthless conquest—until no neighboring coeurl dared to question his sovereignty—there was no id to feed the otherwise immortal engine that was his body.

Square foot by square foot he had gone over it. And now—he recognized the knoll of rock just ahead, and the black rock bridge that formed a queer, curling tunnel to his right. It was in that tunnel he had lain for days, waiting for the simple-minded, snakelike id-creature to come forth from its hole in the rock to bask in the sun—his first kill after he had realized the absolute necessity of organized extermination.

He licked his lips in brief gloating memory of the moment his slavering jaws tore the victim into precious toothsome bits. But the dark fear of an idless universe swept the sweet remembrance from his consciousness, leaving only certainty of death.

He snarled audibly, a defiant, devilish sound that quavered on the air, echoed and re-echoed among the rocks, and shuddered back along his nerves—instinctive and hellish expression of his will to live.

And then—abruptly—it came.

He saw it emerge out of the distance on a long downward slant, a tiny glowing spot that grew enormously into a metal ball. The great shining globe hissed by above Coeurl, slowing visibly in quick deceleration. It sped over a black line of hills to the right, hovered almost motionless for a second, then sank down out of sight.

Coeurl exploded from his startled immobility. With tiger speed, he flowed down among the rocks. His round, black eyes burned with the horrible desire that was an agony within him. His ear tendrils vibrated a message of id in such tremendous quantities that his body felt sick with the pangs of his abnormal hunger.

The little red sun was a crimson ball in the purple-black heavens when he crept up from behind a mass of rock and

gazed from its shadows at the crumbling, gigantic ruins of
the city that sprawled below him. The silvery globe, in spite
of its great size, looked strangely inconspicuous against that
vast, fairylike reach of ruins. Yet about it was a leashed
aliveness, a dynamic quiescence that, after a moment, made
it stand out, dominating the foreground. A massive, rock-
crushing thing of metal, it rested on a cradle made by its
own weight in the harsh, resisting plain which began abruptly
at the outskirts of the dead metropolis.

Coeurl gazed at the strange, two-legged creatures who
stood in little groups near the brilliantly lighted opening that
yawned at the base of the ship. His throat thickened with
the immediacy of his need; and his brain grew dark with the
first wild impulse to burst forth in furious charge and smash
these flimsy, helpless-looking creatures whose bodies emit-
ted the id-vibrations.

Mists of memory stopped that mad rush when it was still
only electricity surging through his muscles. Memory that
brought fear in an acid stream of weakness, pouring along
his nerves, poisoning the reservoirs of his strength. He had
time to see that the creatures wore things over their real
bodies, shimmering transparent material that glittered in
strange, burning flashes in the rays of the sun.

Other memories came suddenly. Of dim days when the
city that spread below was the living, breathing heart of an
age of glory that dissolved in a single century before flaming
guns whose wielders knew only that for the survivors there
would be an ever-narrowing supply of id.

It was the remembrance of those guns that held him
there, cringing in a wave of terror that blurred his reason.
He saw himself smashed by balls of metal and burned by
searing flame.

Came cunning—understanding of the presence of these
creatures. This, Coeurl reasoned for the first time, was a
scientific expedition from another star. In the older days,
the coeurls had thought of space travel, but disaster came
too swiftly for it ever to be more than a thought.

Scientist meant investigation, not destruction. Scientists in
their way were fools. Bold with his knowledge, he emerged
into the open. He saw the creatures become aware of him.
They turned and stared. One, the smallest of the group,
detached a shining metal rod from a sheath, and held it
casually in one hand. Coeurl loped on, shaken to his core by
the action; but it was too late to turn back.

Commander Hal Morton heard little Gregory Kent, the chemist, laugh with the embarrassed half gurgle with which he invariably announced inner uncertainty. He saw Kent fingering the spindly metalite weapon.

Kent said: "I'll take no chances with anything as big as that."

Commander Morton allowed his own deep chuckle to echo along the communicators. "That," he grunted finally, "is one of the reasons why you're on this expedition, Kent—because you never leave anything to chance."

His chuckle trailed off into silence. Instinctively, as he watched the monster approach them across that black rock plain, he moved forward until he stood a little in advance of the others, his huge form bulking the transparent metalite suit. The comments of the men pattered through the radio communicator into his ears:

"I'd hate to meet that baby on a dark night in an alley."

"Don't be silly. This is obviously an intelligent creature. Probably a member of the ruling race."

"It looks like nothing else than a big cat, if you forget those tentacles sticking our from its shoulders, and make allowances for those monster forelegs."

"Its physical development," said a voice, which Morton recognized as that of Siedel, the psychologist, "presupposes an animal-like adaptation to surroundings, not an intellectual one. On the other hand, its coming to us like this is not the act of an animal but of a creature possessing a mental awareness of our possible identity. You will notice that its movements are stiff, denoting caution, which suggests fear and consciousness of our weapons. I'd like to get a good look at the end of its tentacles. If they taper into handlike appendages that can really grip objects, then the conclusion would be inescapable that it is a descendant of the inhabitants of this city. It would be a great help if we could establish communication with it, even though appearances indicate that it has degenerated into a historyless primitive."

Coeurl stopped when he was still ten feet from the foremost creature. The sense of id was so overwhelming that his brain drifted to the ultimate verge of chaos. He felt as if his limbs were bathed in molten liquid; his very vision was not quite clear, as the sheer sensuality of his desire thundered through his being.

The men—all except the little one with the shining metal rod in his fingers—came closer. Coeurl saw that they were frankly and curiously examining him. Their lips were moving, and their voices beat in a monotonous, meaningless rhythm on his ear tendrils. At the same time he had the sense of waves of a much higher frequency—his own communication level—only it was a machinelike clicking that jarred his brain. With a distinct effort to appear friendly, he broadcast his name from his ear tendrils, at the same time pointing at himself with one curving tentacle.

Gourlay, chief of communications, drawled: "I got a sort of static in my radio when he wiggled those hairs, Morton. Do you think—"

"Looks very much like it," the leader answered the unfinished question. "That means a job for you, Gourlay. If it speaks by means of radio waves, it might not be altogether impossible that you can create some sort of television picture of its vibrations, or teach him the Morse code."

"Ah," said Siedel. "I was right. The tentacles each develop into seven strong fingers. Provided the nervous system is complicated enough, those fingers could, with training, operate any machine."

Morton said: "I think we'd better go in and have some lunch. Afterward, we've got to get busy. The material men can set up their machines and start gathering data on the planet's metal possibilities, and so on. The others can do a little careful exploring. I'd like some notes on architecture and on the scientific development of this race, and particularly what happened to wreck the civilization. On earth civilization after civilization crumbled, but always a new one sprang up in its dust. Why didn't that happen here? Any questions?"

"Yes. What about pussy? Look, he wants to come in with us."

Commander Morton frowned, an action that emphasized the deep-space pallor of his face. "I wish there was some way we could take it in with us, without forcibly capturing it. Kent, what do you think?"

"I think we should first decide whether it's an it or a him, and call it one or the other. I'm in favor of him. As for taking him in with us—" The little chemist shook his head decisively. "Impossible. This atmosphere is twenty-eight percent chlorine. Our oxygen would be pure dynamite to his lungs."

The commander chuckled. "He doesn't believe that, apparently." He watched the catlike monster follow the first two men through the great door. The men kept an anxious distance from him, then glanced at Morton questioningly. Morton waved his hand. "O.K. Open the second lock and let him get a whiff of the oxygen. That'll cure him."

A moment later, he cursed his amazement. "By Heaven, he doesn't even notice the difference! That means he hasn't any lungs, or else the chlorine is not what his lungs use. Let him in! You bet he can go in! Smith, here's a treasure house for a biologist—harmless enough if we're careful. We can always handle him. But what a metabolism!"

Smith, a tall, thin, bony chap with a long, mournful face, said in an oddly forceful voice: "In all our travels, we've found only two higher forms of life. Those dependent on chlorine, and those who need oxygen—the two elements that support combustion. I'm prepared to stake my reputation that no complicated organism could ever adapt itself to both gases in a natural way. At first thought I should say here is an extremely advanced form of life. This race long ago discovered truths of biology that we are just beginning to suspect. Morton, we mustn't let this creature get away if we can help it."

"If his anxiety to get inside is any criterion," Commander Morton laughed, "then our difficulty will be to get rid of him."

He moved into the lock with Coeurl and the two men. The automatic machinery hummed; and in a few minutes they were standing at the bottom of a series of elevators that led up to the living quarters.

"Does that go up?" One of the men flicked a thumb in the direction of the monster.

"Better send him up alone, if he'll go in."

Coeurl offered no objection, until he heard the door slam behind him; and the closed cage shot upward. He whirled with a savage snarl, his reason swirling into chaos. With one leap, he pounced at the door. The metal bent under his plunge, and the desperate pain maddened him. Now, he was all trapped animal. He smashed at the metal with his paws, bending it like so much tin. He tore great bars loose with his thick tentacles. The machinery screeched; there were horrible jerks as the limitless power pulled the cage along in spite of projecting pieces of metal that scraped the outside walls. And then the cage stopped, and he snatched off the rest of the door and hurtled into the corridor.

He waited there until Morton and the men came up with

drawn weapons. "We're fools," Morton said. "We should have shown him how it works. He thought we'd double-crossed him."

He motioned to the monster, and saw the savage glow fade from the coal-black eyes as he opened and closed the door with elaborate gestures to show the operation.

Coeurl ended the lesson by trotting into the large room to his right. He lay down on the rugged floor, and fought down the electric tautness of his nerves and muscles. A very fury of rage against himself for his fright consumed him. It seemed to his burning brain that he had lost the advantage of appearing a mild and harmless creature. His strength must have startled and dismayed them.

It meant greater danger in the task which he now knew he must accomplish: To kill everything in the ship, and take the machine back to their world in search of unlimited id.

With unwinking eyes, Coeurl lay and watched the two men clearing away the loose rubble from the metal doorway of the huge old building. His whole body ached with the hunger of his cells for id. The craving tore through his palpitant muscles, and throbbed like a living thing in his brain. His every nerve quivered to be off after the men who had wandered into the city. One of them, he knew, had gone—alone.

The dragging minutes fled; and still he restrained himself, still he lay there watching, aware that the men knew he watched. They floated a metal machine from the ship to the rock mass that blocked the great half-open door, under the direction of a third man. No flicker of their fingers escaped his fierce stare, and slowly, as the simplicity of the machinery became apparent to him, contempt grew upon him.

He knew what to expect finally, when the flame flared in incandescent violence and ate ravenously at the hard rock beneath. But in spite of his preknowledge, he deliberately jumped and snarled as if in fear as that white heat burst forth. His ear tendrils caught the laughter of the men, their curious pleasure at his simulated dismay.

The door was released, and Morton came over and went inside with the third man. The latter shook his head.

"It's a shambles. You can catch the drift of the stuff. Obviously, they used atomic energy, but . . . but it's in wheel form. That's a peculiar development. In our science, atomic energy brought in the nonwheel machine. It's possible that here they've progressed—*further* to a new type of wheel mechanics. I hope their libraries are better preserved than this, or we'll never know. What could have happened to a civilization to make it vanish like this?"

A third voice broke through the communicators: "This is Siedel. I heard your question, Pennons. Psychologically and sociologically speaking, the only reason why a territory becomes uninhabited is lack of food."

"But they're so advanced scientifically, why didn't they develop space flying and go elsewhere for their food?"

"Ask Gunlie Lester," interjected Morton. "I heard him expounding some theory even before we landed."

The astronomer answered the first call. "I've still got to verify all my facts, but this desolate world is the only planet revolving around that miserable red sun. There's nothing else. No moon, not even a planetoid. And the nearest star system is *nine hundred light-years* away.

"So tremendous would have been the problem of the ruling race of this world, that in one jump they would not only have had to solve interplanetary but interstellar space traveling. When you consider how slow our own development was—first the moon, then Venus—each success leading to the next, and after centuries to the nearest stars; and last of all to the anti-accelerators that permitted galactic travel. Considering all this, I maintain it would be impossible for any race to create such machines without practical experience. And, with the nearest star so far away, they had no incentive for the space adventuring that makes for experience."

Coeurl was trotting briskly over to another group. But now, in the driving appetite that consumed him, and in the frenzy of his high scorn, he paid no attention to what they were doing. Memories of past knowledge, jarred into activity by what he had seen, flowed into his consciousness in an ever developing and more vivid stream.

From group to group he sped, a nervous dynamo—jumpy, sick with his awful hunger. A little car rolled up, stopping in front of him, and a formidable camera whirred as it took a picture of him. Over on a mound of rock, a gigantic telescope was rearing up toward the sky. Nearby, a disintegrating machine drilled its searing fire into an ever-deepening hole, down and down, straight down.

Coeurl's mind became a blur of things he watched with half attention. And ever more imminent grew the moment when he knew he could no longer carry on the torture of

acting. His brain strained with an irresistible impatience; his
body burned with the fury of his eagerness to be off after
the man who had gone alone into the city.

He could stand it no longer. A green foam misted his
mouth, maddening him as he saw that, for the bare moment,
nobody was looking.

Like a shot from a gun, he was off. He floated along in
great, gliding leaps, a shadow among the shadows of the
rocks. In a minute, the harsh terrain hid the spaceship and
the two-legged beings.

Coeurl forgot the ship, forgot everything but his purpose,
as if his brain had been wiped clear by a magic, memory-
erasing brush. He circled widely, then raced into the city,
along deserted streets, taking short cuts with the ease of
familiarity, through gaping holes in time-weakened walls,
through long corridors of moldering buildings. He slowed to
a crouching lope as his ear tendrils caught the id vibrations.

Suddenly, he stopped and peered from a scatter of fallen
rock. The man was standing at what must once have been a
window, sending the glaring rays of his flashlight into the
gloomy interior. The flashlight clicked off. The man, a heavy-
set, powerful fellow, walked off with quick, alert steps.
Coeurl didn't like that alertness. It presaged trouble; it
meant lightning reaction to danger.

Coeurl waited till the human being had vanished around a
corner, then he padded into the open. He was running now,
tremendously faster than a man could walk, because his
plan was clear in his brain. Like a wraith, he slipped down
the next street, past a long block of buildings. He turned the
first corner at top speed; and then, with dragging belly,
crept into the hall-darkness between the building and a huge
chunk of débris. The street ahead was barred by a solid line
of loose rubble that made it like a valley, ending in a
narrow, bottlelike neck. The neck had its outlet just below
Coeurl.

His ear tendrils caught the log-frequency waves of whistling. The sound throbbed through his being; and suddenly
terror caught with icy fingers at his brain. The man would
have a gun. Suppose he leveled one burst of atomic energy—
one burst—before his own muscles could whip out in murder
fury.

A little shower of rocks streamed past. And then the man
was beneath him. Coeurl reached out and struck a single
crushing blow at the shimmering transparent headpiece of

the spacesuit. There was a tearing sound of metal and a gushing of blood. The man doubled up as if part of him had been telescoped. For a moment, his bones and legs and muscles combined miraculously to keep him standing. Then he crumpled with a metallic clank of his space armor.

Fear completely evaporated, Coeurl leaped out of hiding. With ravenous speed, he smashed the metal and the body within it to bits. Great chunks of metal, torn piecemeal from the suit, sprayed the ground. Bones cracked. Flesh crunched.

It was simple to tune in on the vibrations of the id, and to create the violent chemical disorganization that freed it from the crushed bone. The id was, Coeurl discovered, mostly in the bone.

He felt revived, almost reborn. Here was more food than he had had in the whole past year.

Three minutes, and it was over, and Coeurl was off like a thing fleeing dire danger. Cautiously, he approached the glistening globe from the opposite side to that by which he had left. The men were all busy at their tasks. Gliding noiselessly, Coeurl slipped unnoticed up to a group of men.

Morton stared down at the horror of tattered flesh, metal and blood on the rock at his feet, and felt a tightening in his throat that prevented speech. He heard Kent say:

"He *would* go alone, damn him!" The little chemist's voice held a sob imprisoned; and Morton remembered that Kent and Jarvey had chummed together for years in the way only two men can.

"The worst part of it is," shuddered one of the men, "it looks like a senseless murder. His body is spread out like little lumps of flattened jelly, but it seems to be all there. I'd almost wager that if we weighed everything here, there'd still be one hundred and seventy-five pounds by earth gravity. That'd be about one hundred and seventy pounds here."

Smith broke in, his mournful face lined with gloom: "The killer attacked Jarvey, and then discovered his flesh was alien—uneatable. Just like our big cat. Wouldn't eat anything we set before him—" His words died out in sudden, queer silence. Then he said slowly: "Say, what about that creature? He's big enough and strong enough to have done this with his own little paws."

Morton frowned. "It's a thought. After all, he's the only living thing we've seen. We can't just execute him on suspicion, of course—"

"Besides," said one of the men, "he was never out of my sight."

Before Morton could speak, Siedel, the psychologist, snapped, "Positive about that?"

The man hesitated. "Maybe he was for a few minutes. He was wandering around so much, looking at everything."

"Exactly," said Siedel with satisfaction. He turned to Morton. "You see, commander, I, too, had the impression that he was always around; and yet, thinking back over it, I find gaps. There were moments—probably long minutes—when he was completely out of sight."

Morton's face was dark with thought, as Kent broke in fiercely: "I say, take no chances. Kill the brute on suspicion before he does any more damage."

Morton said slowly: "Korita, you've been wandering around with Cranessy and Van Horne. Do you think pussy is a descendant of the ruling class of this planet?"

The tall Japanese archeologist stared at the sky as if collecting his mind. "Commander Morton," he said finally, respectfully, "there is a mystery here. Take a look, all of you, at that majestic skyline. Notice the almost Gothic outline of the architecture. In spite of the megalopolis which they created, these people were close to the soil. The buildings are not simply ornamented. They are ornamental in themselves. Here is the equivalent of the Doric column, the Egyptian pyramid, the Gothic cathedral, growing out of the ground, earnest, big with destiny. If this lonely, desolate world can be regarded as a mother earth, then the land had a warm, spiritual place in the hearts of the race.

"The effect is emphasized by the winding streets. Their machines prove they were mathematicians, but they were artists first; and so they did not create the geometrically designed cities of the ultra-sophisticated world metropolis. There is a genuine artistic abandon, a deep joyous emotion written in the curving and unmathematical arrangements of houses, buildings and avenues; a sense of intensity, of divine belief in an inner certainty. This is not a decadent, hoary-with-age civilization, but a young and vigorous culture, confident, strong with purpose.

"There it ended. Abruptly, as if at this point culture had its Battle of Tours, and began to collapse like the ancient Mohammedan civilization. Or as if in one leap it spanned the centuries and entered the period of contending states. In the Chinese civilization that period occupied 480-230 B.C., at

the end of which the State of Tsin saw the beginning of the
Chinese Empire. This phase Egypt experienced between
1780-1580 B.C., of which the last century was the 'Hyksos'—
unmentionable—time. The classical experienced it from
Chæronea—338—and, at the pitch of horror, from the
Gracchi—133—to Actium—31 B.C. The West European
Americans were devastated by it in the nineteenth and
twentieth centuries, and modern historians agree that, nom-
inally, we entered the same phase fifty years ago; though, of
course, we have solved the problem.

"You may ask, commander, what has all this to do with
your question? My answer is: there is no record of a culture
entering abruptly into the period of contending states. It is
always a slow development; and the first step is a merciless
questioning of all that was once held sacred. Inner certain-
ties cease to exist, are dissolved before the ruthless probings
of scientific and analytic minds. The skeptic becomes the
highest type of being.

"I say that this culture ended abruptly in its most flourish-
ing age. The sociological effects of such a catastrophe would
be a sudden vanishing of morals, a reversion to almost
bestial criminality, unleavened by any sense of ideal, a cal-
lous indifference to death. If this . . . this pussy is a descendant of such a race, then he will be a cunning creature, a
thief in the night, a cold-blooded murderer, who would cut
his own brother's throat for gain."

"That's enough!" It was Kent's clipped voice. "Commander, I'm willing to act the rôle of executioner."

Smith interrupted sharply: "Listen, Morton, you're not
going to kill that cat yet, even if he is guilty. He's a biological treasure house."

Kent and Smith were glaring angrily at each other. Morton frowned at them thoughtfully, then said: "Korita, I'm
inclined to accept your theory as a working basis. But one
question: Pussy comes from a period earlier than our own?
That is, we are entering the highly civilized area of our
culture, while he became suddenly historyless in the most
vigorous period of his. *But* it is possible that his culture is a
later one on this planet than ours is in the galactic-wide
system we have civilized?"

"Exactly. His may be the middle of the tenth civilization
of his world; while ours is the end of the eighth sprung from
earth, each of the ten, of course, having been builded on the
ruins of the one before it."

"In that case, pussy would not know anything about the skepticism that made it possible for us to find him out so positively as a criminal and murderer?"

"No; it would be literally magic to him."

Morton was smiling grimly. "Then I think you'll get your wish, Smith. We'll let pussy live; and if there are any fatalities, now that we know him, it will be due to rank carelessness. There's just the chance, of course, that we're wrong. Like Siedel, I also have the impression that he was always around. But now—we can't leave poor Jarvey here like this. We'll put him in a coffin and bury him."

"No, we won't!" Kent barked. He flushed. "I beg your pardon, commander. I didn't mean it that way. I maintain pussy wanted something from that body. It looks to be all there, but something must be missing. I'm going to find out what, and pin this murder on him so that you'll have to believe it beyond the shadow of a doubt."

It was late night when Morton looked up from a book and saw Kent emerge through the door that led from the laboratories below.

Kent carried a large, flat bowl in his hands; his tired eyes flashed across at Morton, and he said in a weary, yet harsh, voice: "Now watch!"

He started toward Coeurl, who lay sprawled on the great rug, pretending to be asleep.

Morton stopped him. "Wait a minute, Kent. Any other time, I wouldn't question your actions, but you look ill; you're overwrought. What have you got there?"

Kent turned, and Morton saw that his first impression had been but a flashing glimpse of the truth. There were dark pouches under the little chemist's gray eyes—eyes that gazed feverishly from sunken cheeks in an ascetic face.

"I've found the missing element," Kent said. "It's phosphorus. There wasn't so much as a square millimeter of phosphorus left in Jarvey's bones. Every bit of it had been drained out—by what superchemistry I don't know. There are ways of getting phosphorus out of the human body. For instance, a quick way was what happened to the workman who helped build this ship. Remember, he fell into fifteen tons of molten metalite—at least, so his relatives claimed— but the company wouldn't pay compensation until the metalite, on analysis, was found to contain a high percentage of phosphorus—"

"What about the bowl of food?" somebody interrupted. Men were putting away magazines and books, looking up with interest.

"It's got organic phosphorus in it. He'll get the scent, or whatever it is that he uses instead of scent—"

"I think he gets the vibrations of things," Gourlay interjected lazily. "Sometimes, when he wiggles those tendrils, I get a distinct static on the radio. And then, again, there's no reaction, just as if he's moved higher or lower on the wave scale. He seems to control the vibrations at will."

Kent waited with obvious impatience until Gourlay's last word, then abruptly went on: "All right, then, when he gets the vibration of the phosphorus and reacts to it like an animal, then—well, we can decide what we've proved by his reaction. Can I go ahead, Morton?"

"There are three things wrong with your plan," Morton said. "In the first place, you seem to assume that he is only animal; you seem to have forgotten he may not be hungry after Jarvey; you seem to think that he will not be suspicious. But set the bowl down. His reaction may tell us something."

Coeurl stared with unblinking black eyes as the man set the bowl before him. His ear tendrils instantly caught the id-vibrations from the contents of the bowl—and he gave it not even a second glance.

He recognized this two-legged being as the one who had held the weapon that morning. Danger! With a snarl, he floated to his feet. He caught the bowl with the fingerlike appendages at the end of one looping tentacle, and emptied its contents into the face of Kent, who shrank back with a yell.

Explosively, Coeurl flung the bowl aside and snapped a hawser-thick tentacle around the cursing man's waist. He didn't bother with the gun that hung from Kent's belt. It was only a vibration gun, he sensed—atomic powered, but not an atomic disintegrator. He tossed the kicking Kent onto the nearest couch—and realized with a hiss of dismay that he should have disarmed the man.

Not that the gun was dangerous—but, as the man furiously wiped the gruel from his face with one hand, he reached with the other for his weapon. Coeurl crouched back as the gun was raised slowly and a white beam of flame was discharged at his massive head.

His ear tendrils hummed as they canceled the efforts of

the vibration gun. His round, black eyes narrowed as he caught the movement of men reaching for their metalite guns. Morton's voice lashed across the silence.

"Stop!"

Kent clicked off his weapon; and Coeurl crouched down, quivering with fury at this man who had forced him to reveal something of his power.

"Kent," said Morton coldly, "you're not the type to lose your head. You deliberately tried to kill pussy, knowing that the majority of us are in favor of keeping him alive. You know what our rule is: If anyone objects to my decisions, he must say so *at the time*. If the majority object, my decisions are overruled. In this case, no one but you objected, and, therefore, your action in taking the law into your own hands is most reprehensible, and automatically debars you from voting for a year."

Kent stared grimly at the circle of faces. "Korita was right when he said ours was a highly civilized age. It's decadent." Passion flamed harshly in his voice. "My God, isn't there a man here who can see the horror of the situation? Jarvey dead only a few hours and this creature, whom we all know to be guilty, lying there unchained, planning his next murder; and the victim is right here in this room. What kind of men are we—fools, cynics, ghouls—or is it that our civilization is so steeped in reason that we can contemplate a murderer sympathetically?"

He fixed brooding eyes on Coeurl. "You were right, Morton, that's no animal. That's a devil from the deepest hell of this forgotten planet, whirling its solitary way around a dying sun."

"Don't go melodramatic on us," Morton said. "Your analysis is all wrong, so far as I am concerned. We're not ghouls or cynics; we're simply scientists, and pussy here is going to be studied. Now that we suspect him, we doubt his ability to trap any of us. One against a hundred hasn't a chance." He glanced around. "Do I speak for all of us?"

"Not for me, commander!" It was Smith who spoke, and, as Morton stared in amazement, he continued: "In the excitement and momentary confusion, no one seems to have noticed that when Kent fired his vibration gun, the beam hit this creature squarely on his cat head—and didn't hurt him."

Morton's amazed glance went from Smith to Coeurl, and back to Smith again. "Are you certain it hit home? As you say, it all happened so swiftly—when pussy wasn't hurt I simply assumed that Kent had missed him."

"He hit him in the face," Smith said positively. "A vibration gun, of course, can't even kill a man right away—but it can injure him. There's no sign of injury on pussy, though, not even a singed hair."

"Perhaps his skin is a good insulation against heat of any kind."

"Perhaps. But in view of our uncertainty, I think we should lock him up in the cage."

While Morton frowned darkly in thought, Kent spoke up. "Now you're talking sense, Smith."

Morton asked: "Then you would be satisfied, Kent, if we put him in the cage?"

Kent considered, finally: "Yes. If four inches of micro-steel can't hold him, we'd better give him the ship."

Coeurl followed the men as they went out into the corridor. He trotted docilely along as Morton unmistakably motioned him through a door he had not hitherto seen. He found himself in a square, solid metal room. The door clanged metallically behind him; he felt the flow of power as the electric lock clicked home.

His lips parted in a grimace of hate, as he realized the trap, but he gave no other outward reaction. It occurred to him that he had progressed a long way from the sunk-into-primitiveness creature who, a few hours before, had gone incoherent with fear in an elevator cage. Now, a thousand memories of his powers were reawakened in his brain; ten thousand cunnings were, after ages of disuse, once again part of his very being.

He sat quite still for a moment on the short, heavy haunches into which his body tapered, his ear tendrils examining his surroundings. Finally, he lay down, his eyes glowing with contemptuous fire. The fools! The poor fools!

It was about an hour later when he heard the man—Smith—fumbling overhead. Vibrations poured upon him, and for just an instant he was startled. He leaped to his feet in pure terror—and then realized that the vibrations were vibrations, not atomic explosions. Somebody was taking pictures of the inside of his body.

He crouched down again, but his ear tendrils vibrated, and he thought contemptuously: the silly fool would be surprised when he tried to develop those pictures.

After a while the man went away, and for a long time

there were noises of men doing things far sway. That, too, died away slowly.

Coeurl lay waiting, as he felt the silence creep over the ship. In the long ago, before the dawn of immortality, the coeurls, too, had slept at night; and the memory of it had been revived the day before when he saw some of the men dozing. At last, the vibration of two pairs of feet, pacing, pacing endlessly, was the only human-made frequency that throbbed on his ear tendrils.

Tensely, he listened to the two watchmen. The first one walked slowly past the cage door. Then about thirty feet behind him came the second. Coeurl sensed the alertness of these men; knew that he could never surprise either while they walked separately. It meant—he must be double careful!

Fifteen minutes, and they came again. The moment they were past, he switched his senses from their vibrations to a vastly higher range. The pulsating violence of the atomic engines stammered its soft story to his brain. The electric dynamos hummed their muffled song of pure power. He felt the whisper of that flow through the wires in the walls of his cage, and through the electric lock of his door. He forced his quivering body into straining immobility, his senses seeking, searching to tune in on that sibilant tempest of energy. Suddenly, his ear tendrils vibrated in harmony—he caught the surging change into shrillness of that rippling force wave.

There was a sharp click of metal on metal. With a gentle touch of one tentacle, Coeurl pushed open the door, and glided out into the dully gleaming corridor. For just a moment, he felt contempt, a glow of superiority, as he thought of the stupid creatures who dared to match their wit against a coeurl. And in that moment, he suddenly thought of other coeurls. A queer, exultant sense of race pounded through his being; the driving hate of centuries of ruthless competition yielded reluctantly before pride of kinship with the future rulers of all space.

Suddenly, he felt weighed down by his limitations, his need for other coeurls, his aloneness—one against a hundred, with the stake all eternity; the starry universe itself beckoned his rapacious, vaulting ambition. If he failed, there would never be a second chance—no time to revive long-rotted machinery, and attempt to solve the secret of space travel.

He padded along on tensed paws—through the salon—into the next corridor—and came to the first bedroom door.

It stood half open. One swift flow of synchronized muscles, one swiftly lashing tentacle that caught the unresisting throat of the sleeping man, crushing it; and the lifeless head rolled crazily, the body twitched once.

Seven bedrooms; seven dead men. It was the seventh taste of murder that brought a sudden return of lust, a pure, unbounded desire to kill, return of a millennium-old habit of destroying everything containing the precious id.

As the twelfth man slipped convulsively into death, Coeurl emerged abruptly from the sensuous joy of the kill to the sound of footsteps.

They were not near—that was what brought wave after wave of fright swirling into the chaos that suddenly became his brain.

The watchmen were coming slowly along the corridor toward the door of the cage where he had been imprisoned. In a moment, the first man would see the open door—and sound the alarm.

Coeurl caught at the vanishing remnants of his reason. With frantic speed, careless now of accidental sounds, he raced—along the corridor with its bedroom doors—through the salon. He emerged into the next corridor, cringing in awful anticipation of the atomic flame he expected would stab into his face.

The two men were together, standing side by side. For one single instant, Coeurl could scarcely believe his tremendous good luck. Like a fool the second had come running when he saw the other stop before the open door. They looked up, paralyzed, before the nightmare of claws and tentacles, the ferocious cat head and hate-filled eyes.

The first man went for his gun, but the second, physically frozen before the doom he saw, uttered a shriek, a shrill cry of horror that floated along the corridors—and ended in a curious gurgle, as Coeurl flung the two corpses with one irresistible motion the full length of the corridor. He didn't want the dead bodies found near the cage. That was his one hope.

Shaking in every nerve and muscle, conscious of the terrible error he had made, unable to think coherently, he plunged into the cage. The door clicked softly shut behind him. Power flowed once more through the electric lock.

He crouched tensely, simulated sleep, as he heard the rush of many feet, caught the vibration of excited voices. He knew when somebody actuated the cage audioscope and looked in. A few moments now, and the other bodies would be discovered.

"Siedel gone!" Morton said numbly. "What are we going to do without Siedel? And Breckenridge! And Coulter and—Horrible!"

He covered his face with his hands, but only for an instant. He looked up grimly, his heavy chin outthrust as he stared into the stern faces that surrounded him. "If anybody's got so much as a germ of an idea, bring it out."

"Space madness!"

"I've thought of that. But there hasn't been a case of a man going mad for fifty years. Dr. Eggert will test everybody, of course, and right now he's looking at the bodies with that possibility in mind."

As he finished, he saw the doctor coming through the door. Men crowded aside to make way for him.

"I heard you, commander," Dr. Eggert said, "and I think I can say right now that the space-madness theory is out. The throats of these men have been squeezed to a jelly. No human being could have exerted such enormous strength without using a machine."

Morton saw that the doctor's eyes kept looking down the corridor, and he shook his head and groaned:

"It's no use suspecting pussy, doctor. He's in his cage, pacing up and down. Obviously heard the racket and— Man alive! You can't suspect him. That cage was built to hold literally *anything*—four inches of micro-steel—and there's not a scratch on the door. Kent, even you won't say, 'Kill him on suspicion,' because there can't be any suspicion, unless there's a new science here. Beyond anything we can imagine—"

"On the contrary," said Smith flatly, "we have all the evidence we need. I used the telefluor on him—you know the arrangement we have on top of the cage—and tried to take some pictures. They just blurred. Pussy jumped when the telefluor was turned on, as if he felt the vibrations.

"You all know what Gourlay said before? This beast can apparently receive and send vibrations of any lengths. The way he dominated the power of Kent's gun is final proof of his special ability to interfere with energy."

"What in the name of all the hells have we got here?" One of the men groaned. "Why, if he can control that power, and send it out in any vibrations, there's nothing to stop him killing all of us."

"Which proves," snapped Morton, "that he isn't invincible, or he would have done it long ago."

Very deliberately, he walked over to the mechanism that controlled the prison cage.

"You're not going to open the door!" Kent gasped, reaching for his gun.

"No, but if I pull this switch, electricity will flow through the floor, and electrocute whatever's inside. We've never had to use this before, so you had probably forgotten about it."

He jerked the switch hard over. Blue fire flashed from the metal, and a bank of fuses above his head exploded with a single bang.

Morton frowned. "That's funny. Those fuses shouldn't have blown! Well, we can't even look in, now. That wrecked the audios, too."

Smith said: "If he could interfere with the electric lock, enough to open the door, then he probably probed every possible danger and was ready to interfere when you threw that switch."

"At least, it proves he's vulnerable to our energies!" Morton smiled grimly. "Because he rendered them harmless. The important thing is, we've got him behind four inches of the toughest of metal. At the worst we can open the door and ray him to death. But first, I think we'll try to use the telefluor power cable—"

A commotion from inside the cage interrupted his words. A heavy body crushed against a wall, followed by a dull thump.

"He knows what we were trying to do!" Smith grunted to Morton. "And I'll bet it's a very sick pussy in there. What a fool he was to go back into that cage and does he realize it!"

The tension was relaxing; men were smiling nervously, and there was even a ripple of humorless laughter at the picture Smith drew of the monster's discomfiture.

"What I'd like to know," said Pennons, the engineer, "is, why did the telefluor meter dial jump and waver at full power when pussy made that noise? It's right under my nose here, and the dial jumped like a house afire!"

There was silence both without and within the cage, then Morton said: "It may mean he's coming out. Back, everybody, and keep your guns ready. Pussy was a fool to think he could conquer a hundred men, but he's by far the most formidable creature in the galactic system. He may come out of that door, rather than die like a rat in a trap. And he's just tough enough to take some of us with him—if we're not careful."

The men backed slowly in a solid body; and somebody said: "That's funny. I thought I heard the elevator."

"Elevator!" Morton echoed. "Are you sure, man?"

"Just for a moment I was!" The man, a member of the crew, hesitated. "We were all shuffling our feet—"

"Take somebody with you, and go look. Bring whoever dared to run off back here—"

There was a jar, a horrible jerk, as the whole gigantic body of the ship careened under them. Morton was flung to the floor with a violence that stunned him. He fought back to consciousness, aware of the other men lying all around him. He shouted: "Who the devil started those engines!"

The agonizing acceleration continued; his feet dragged with awful exertion, as he fumbled with the nearest audioscope, and punched the engine-room number. The picture that flooded onto the screen brought a deep bellow to his lips:

"It's pussy! He's in the engine room—and we're heading straight out into space."

The screen went black even as he spoke, and he could see no more.

It was Morton who first staggered across the salon floor to the supply room where the spacesuits were kept. After fumbling almost blindly into his own suit, he cut the effects of the body-torturing acceleration, and brought suits to the semiconscious men on the floor. In a few moments, other men were assisting him; and then it was only a matter of minutes before everybody was clad in metalite, with anti-acceleration motors running at half power.

It was Morton then who, after first looking into the cage, opened the door and stood, silent as the others crowded about him, to stare at the gaping hole in the real wall. The hold was a frightful thing of jagged edges and horribly bent metal, and it opened upon another corridor.

"I'll swear," whispered Pennons, "that it's impossible. The ten-ton hammer in the machine shops couldn't more than dent four inches of micro with one blow—and we only heard one. It would take at least a minute for an atomic disintegrator to do the job. Morton, this is a super-being."

Morton saw that Smith was examining the break in the

wall. The biologist looked up. "If only Breckenridge weren't dead! We need a metallurgist to explain this. Look!"

He touched the broken edge of the metal. A piece crumbled in his finger and slithered away in a fine shower of dust to the floor. Morton noticed for the first time that there was a little pile of metallic débris and dust.

"You've hit it." Morton nodded. "No miracle of strength here. The monster merely used his special powers to interfere with the electronic tensions holding the metal together. That would account, too, for the drain on the telefluor power cable that Pennons noticed. The thing used the power with his body as a transforming medium, smashed through the wall, ran down the corridor to the elevator shaft, and so down to the engine room."

"In the meantime, commander," Kent said quietly, "we are faced with a super-being in control of the ship, completely dominating the engine room, and its almost unlimited power, and in possession of the best part of the machine shops."

Morton felt the silence, while the men pondered the chemist's words. Their anxiety was a tangible thing that lay heavily upon their faces; in every expression was the growing realization that here was the ultimate situation in their lives; their very existence was at stake, and perhaps much more. Morton voiced the thought in everybody's mind:

"Suppose he wins. He's utterly ruthless, and he probably sees galactic power within his grasp."

"Kent is wrong," barked the chief navigator. "The thing doesn't dominate the engine room. We've still got the control room, and that gives us, *first* control of all the machines. You fellows may not know the mechanical set-up we have; but, though he can eventually disconnect us, we can cut off all the switches in the engine room *now*. Commander, why didn't you just shut off the power instead of putting us into spacesuits? At the very least you could have adjusted the ship to the acceleration."

"For two reasons," Morton answered. "Individually, we're safer within the force fields of our spacesuits. And we can't afford to give up our advantages in panicky moves."

"Advantages. What other advantages have we got?"

"We know things about him," Morton replied. "And right now, we're going to make a test. Pennons, detail five men to each of the four approaches to the engine room.

Take atomic disintegrators to blast through the big doors. They're all shut, I noticed. He's locked himself in.

"Selenski, you go up to the control room and shut off everything except the drive engines. Gear them to the master switch, and shut them off all at once. One thing though— leave the acceleration on full blast. No anti-acceleration must be applied to the ship. Understand?"

"Aye, sir!" The pilot saluted.

"And report to me through the communicators if any of the machines start to run again." He faced the men. "I'm going to lead the main approach. Kent, you take No. 2; Smith, No. 3, and Pennons, No. 4. We're going to find out right now if we're dealing with unlimited science, or a creature limited like the rest of us. I'll bet on the last possibility."

Morton had an empty sense of walking endlessly, as he moved, a giant of a man in his transparent space armor, along the glistening metal tube that was the main corridor of the engine-room floor. Reason told him the creature had already shown feet of clay, yet the feeling that here was an invincible being persisted.

He spoke into the communicator: "It's no use trying to sneak up on him. He can probably hear a pin drop. So just wheel up your units. He hasn't been in that engine room long enough to do anything.

"As I've said, this is largely a test attack. In the first place, we could never forgive ourselves if we didn't try to conquer him now, before he's had time to prepare against us. But, aside from the possibility that we can destroy him immediately, I have a theory.

"The idea goes something like this: Those doors are built to withstand accidental atomic explosions, and it will take fifteen minutes for the atomic disintegrators to smash them. During that period the monster will have no power. True, the drive will be on, but that's straight atomic explosion. My theory is, he can't touch stuff like that; and in a few minutes you'll see what I mean—I hope."

His voice was suddenly crisp: "Ready, Selenski?"

"Aye, ready."

"Then cut the master switch."

The corridor—the whole ship, Morton knew—was abruptly plunged into darkness. Morton clicked on the dazzling light of his spacesuit; the other men did the same, their faces pale and drawn.

"Blast!" Morton barked into his communicator.

The mobile units throbbed; and then pure atomic flame ravened out and poured upon the hard metal of the door. The first molten droplet rolled reluctantly, not down, but up the door. The second was more normal. It followed a shaky downward course. The third rolled sideways—for this was pure force, not subject to gravitation. Other drops followed until a dozen streams of hellish, sparkling fire, bright as fairy gems, alive with the coruscating fury of atoms suddenly tortured, and running blindly, crazy with pain.

The minutes ate at time like a slow acid. At last Morton asked huskily:

"Selenski?"

"Nothing yet, commander."

Morton half whispered: "But he must be doing something. He can't be just waiting in there like a cornered rat. Selenski?"

"Nothing, commander."

Seven minutes, eight minutes, then twelve.

"Commander!" It was Selenski's voice, taut. "He's got the electric dynamo running."

Morton drew a deep breath, and heard one of his men say:

"That's funny. We can't get any deeper. Boss, take a look at this."

Morton looked. The little scintillating streams had frozen rigid. The ferocity of the disintegrators vented in vain against metal grown suddenly invulnerable.

Morton sighed. "Our test is over. Leave two men guarding every corridor. The others come up to the control room."

He seated himself a few minutes later before the massive control keyboard. "So far as I'm concerned the test was a success. We know that of all the machines in the engine room, the most important to the monster was the electric dynamo. He must have worked in a frenzy of terror while we were at the doors."

"Of course, it's easy to see what he did," Pennons said. "Once he had the power he increased the electronic tensions of the door to their ultimate."

"The main thing is this," Smith chimed in. "He works with vibrations only so far as his special powers are concerned, and the energy must come from outside himself. Atomic energy in its pure form, not being vibration, he can't handle any differently than we can."

Kent said glumly: "The main point in my opinion is that

he stopped us cold. What's the good of knowing that his control over vibrations did it? If we can't break through those doors with our atomic disintegrators, we're finished."

Morton shook his head. "Not finished—but we'll have to do some planning. First, though, I'll start these engines. It'll be harder for him to get control of them when they're running."

He pulled the master switch back into place with a jerk. There was a hum, as scores of machines leaped into violent life in the engine room a hundred feet below. The noises sank to a steady vibration of throbbing power.

Three hours later, Morton paced up and down before the men gathered in the salon. His dark hair was uncombed; the space pallor of his strong face emphasized rather than detracted from the outthrust aggressiveness of his jaw. When he spoke, his deep voice was crisp to the point of sharpness:

"To make sure that our plans are fully co-ordinated, I'm going to ask each expert in turn to outline his part in the overpowering of this creature. Pennons first!"

Pennons stood up briskly. He was not a big man, Morton thought, yet he looked big, perhaps because of his air of authority. This man knew engines, and the history of engines. Morton had heard him trace a machine through its evolution from a simple toy to the highly complicated modern instrument. He had studied machine development on a hundred planets; and there was literally nothing fundamental that he didn't know about mechanics. It was almost weird to hear Pennons, who could have spoken for a thousand hours and still only have touched upon his subject, say with absurd brevity:

"We've set up a relay in the control room to start and stop every engine rhythmically. The trip lever will work a hundred times a second, and the effect will be to create vibrations of every description. There is just a possibility that one or more of the machines will burst, on the principle of soldiers crossing a bridge in step—you've heard that old story, no doubt—but in my opinion there is no real danger of a break of that tough metal. The main purpose is simply to interfere with the interference of the creature, and smash through the doors."

"Gourlay next!" barked Morton.

Gourlay climbed lazily to his feet. He looked sleepy, as if he was somewhat bored by the whole proceedings, yet Morton knew he loved people to think him lazy, a good-for-

nothing slouch, who spent his days in slumber and his nights
catching forty winks. His title was chief communication engineer, but his knowledge extended to every vibration field;
and he was probably, with the possible exception of Kent,
the fastest thinker on the ship. His voice drawled out, and—
Morton noted—the very deliberate assurance of it had a
soothing effect on the men—anxious faces relaxed, bodies
leaned back more restfully:

"Once inside," Gourlay said, "we've rigged up vibration
screens of pure force that should stop nearly everything he's
got on the ball. They work on the principle of reflection, so
that everything he sends will be reflected back to him. In
addition, we've got plenty of spare electric energy that we'll
just feed him from mobile copper cups. There must be a
limit to his capacity for handling power with those insulated
nerves of his."

"Selenski!" called Morton.

The chief pilot was already standing, as he had anticipated Morton's call. And that, Morton reflected, was the
man. His nerves had that rocklike steadiness which is the
first requirement of the master controller of a great ship's
movements; yet that very steadiness seemed to rest on dynamite ready to explode at its owner's volition. He was not a
man of great learning, but he "reacted" to stimuli so fast
that he always seemed to be anticipating.

"The impression I've received of the plan is that it must
be cumulative. Just when the creature thinks that he can't
stand any more, another thing happens to add to his trouble
and confusion. When the uproar's at its height, I'm supposed to cut in the anti-accelerators. The commander thinks
with Gunlie Lester that these creatures will know nothing
about anti-acceleration. It's a development, pure and simple, of the science of interstellar flight, and couldn't have
been developed in any other way. We think when the creature feels the first effects of the anti-acceleration—you all
remember the caved-in feeling you had the first month—it
won't know what to think or do."

"Korita next."

"I can only offer you encouragement," said the archeologist, "on the basis of my theory that the monster has all the
characteristics of a criminal of the early ages of any civilization, complicated by an apparent reversion to primitiveness.
The suggestion has been made by Smith that his knowledge
of science is puzzling, and could only mean that we are

dealing with an actual inhabitant, not a descendant of the inhabitants of the dead city we visited. This would ascribe a virtual immortality to our enemy, a possibility which is borne out by his ability to breathe both oxygen and chlorine—or neither—but even that makes no difference. He comes from a certain age in his civilization; and he has sunk so low that his ideas are mostly memories of that age.

"In spite of all the powers of his body, he lost his head in the elevator the first morning, until he remembered. He placed himself in such a position that he was forced to reveal his special powers against vibrations. He bungled the mass murders a few hours ago. In fact, his whole record is one of the low cunning of the primitive, egotistical mind which has little or no conception of the vast organization with which it is confronted.

"He is like the ancient German soldier who felt superior to the elderly Roman scholar, yet the latter was part of a mighty civilization of which the Germans of that day stood in awe.

"You may suggest that the sack of Rome by the Germans in later years defeats my argument; however, modern historians agree that the 'sack' was an historical accident, and not history in the true sense of the word. The movement of the 'Sea-peoples' which set in against the Egyptian civilization from 1400 B.C. succeeded only as regards the Cretan island-realm—their mighty expeditions against the Libyan and Phœnician coasts, with the accompaniment of Viking fleets, failed as those of the Huns failed against the Chinese Empire. Rome would have been abandoned in any event. Ancient, glorious Samarra was desolate by the tenth century; Pataliputra, Asoka's great capital, was an immense and completely uninhabited waste of houses when the Chinese traveler Hsinan-tang visited it about A.D. 635.

"We have, then, a primitive, and that primitive is now far out in space, completely outside of his natural habitat. I say, let's go in and win."

One of the men grumbled, as Korita finished: "You can talk about the sack of Rome being an accident, and about this fellow being a primitive, but the facts are facts. It looks to me as if Rome is about to fall again; and it won't be no primitive that did it, either. This guy's got plenty of what it takes."

Morton smiled grimly at the man, a member of the crew. "We'll see about that—right now!"

*   *   *

In the blazing brilliance of the gigantic machine shop, Coeurl slaved. The forty-foot, cigar-shaped spaceship was nearly finished. With a grunt of effort, he completed the laborious installation of the drive engines, and paused to survey his craft.

Its interior, visible through the one aperture in the outer wall, was pitifully small. There was literally room for nothing but the engines—and a narrow space for himself.

He plunged frantically back to work as he heard the approach of the men, and the sudden change in the tempestlike thunder of the engines—a rhythmical off-and-on hum, shriller in tone, sharper, more nerve-racking than the deepthroated, steady throb that had preceded it. Suddenly, there were the atomic disintegrators again at the massive outer doors.

He fought them off, but never wavered from his task. Every mighty muscle of his powerful body strained as he carried great loads of tools, machines and instruments, and dumped them into the bottom of his makeshift ship. There was no time to fit anything into place, no time for anything— no time—no time.

The thought pounded at his reason. He felt strangely weary for the first time in his long and vigorous existence. With a last, tortured heave, he jerked the gigantic sheet of metal into the gaping aperture of the ship—and stood there for a terrible minute, balancing it precariously.

He knew the doors were going down. Half a dozen disintegrators concentrating on one point were irresistibly, though slowly, eating away the remaining inches. With a gasp, he released his mind from the doors and concentrated every ounce of his mind on the yard-thick outer wall, toward which the blunt nose of his ship was pointing.

His body cringed from the surging power that flowed from the electric dynamo through his ear tendrils into that resisting wall. The whole inside of him felt on fire, and he knew that he was dangerously close to carrying his ultimate load.

And still he stood there, shuddering with the awful pain, holding the unfastened metal plate with hard-clenched tentacles. His massive head pointed as in dread fascination at that bitterly hard wall.

He heard one of the engine-room doors crash inward. Men shouted; disintegrators rolled forward, their raging power unchecked. Coeurl heard the floor of the engine room hiss in protest, as those beams of atomic energy tore everything in their path to bits. The machines rolled closer; cautious footsteps sounded behind them. In a minute they would be at the flimsy doors separating the engine room from the machine shop.

Suddenly, Coeurl was satisfied. With a snarl of hate, a vindictive glow of feral eyes, he ducked into his little craft, and pulled the metal plate down into place as if it were a hatchway.

His ear tendrils hummed, as he softened the edges of the surrounding metal. In an instant, the plate was more than welded—it was part of his ship, a seamless, rivetless part of a whole that was solid opaque metal except for two transparent areas, one in the front, one in the rear.

His tentacle embraced the power drive with almost sensuous tenderness. There was a forward surge of his fragile machine, straight at the great outer wall of the machine shops. The nose of the forty-foot craft touched—and the wall dissolved in a glittering shower of dust.

Coeurl felt the barest retarding movement; and then he kicked the nose of the machine out into the cold of space, twisted it about, and headed back in the direction from which the big ship had been coming all these hours.

Men in space armor stood in the jagged hold that yawned in the lower reaches of the gigantic globe. The men and the great ship grew smaller. Then the men were gone; and there was only the ship with its blaze of a thousand blurring portholes. The ball shrank incredibly, too small now for individual portholes to be visible.

Almost straight ahead, Coeurl saw a tiny, dim, reddish ball—his own sun, he realized. He headed toward it at full speed. There were caves where he could hide and with other coeurls build secretly a spaceship in which they could reach other planets safely—now that he knew how.

His body ached from the agony of acceleration, yet he dared not let up for a single instant. He glanced back, half in terror. The globe was still there, a tiny dot of light in the immense blackness of space. Suddenly it twinkled and was gone.

For a brief moment, he had the empty, frightened impression that just before it disappeared, it moved. But he could see nothing. He could not escape the belief that they had shut off all their lights, and were sneaking up on him in the darkness. Worried and uncertain, he looked through the forward transparent plate.

A tremor of dismay shot through him. The dim red sun toward which he was heading was not growing larger. *It was becoming smaller* by the instant, and it grew visibly tinier during the next five minutes, became a pale-red dot in the sky—and vanished like the ship.

Fear came then, a blinding surge of it, that swept through his being and left him chilled with the sense of the unknown. For minutes, he stared frantically into the space ahead, searching for some landmark. But only the remote stars glimmered there, unwinking points against a velvet background of unfathomable distance.

Wait! One of the points was growing larger. With every muscle and nerve tense, Coeurl watched the point becoming a dot, a round ball of light—red light. Bigger, bigger, it grew. Suddenly, the red light shimmered and turned white— and there, before him, was the great globe of the spaceship, lights glaring from every porthole, the very ship which a few minutes before he had watched vanish behind him.

Something happened to Coeurl in that moment. His brain was spinning like a flywheel, faster, faster, more incoherently. Suddenly, the wheel flew apart into a million aching fragments. His eyes almost started from their sockets as, like a maddened animal, he raged in his small quarters.

His tentacles clutched at precious instruments and flung them insensately; his paws smashed in fury at the very walls of his ship. Finally, in a brief flash of sanity, he knew that he couldn't face the inevitable fire of atomic disintegrators.

It was a simple thing to create the violent disorganization that freed every drop of id from his vital organs.

They found him lying dead in a little pool of phosphorus.

"Poor pussy," said Morton. "I wonder what he thought when he saw us appear ahead of him, after his own sun disappeared. Knowing nothing of anti-accelerators, he couldn't know that we could stop short in space, whereas it would take him more than three hours to decelerate; and in the meantime he'd be drawing farther and farther away from where he wanted to go. He couldn't know that by stopping, we flashed past him at millions of miles a second. Of course, he didn't have a chance once he left our ship. The whole world must have seemed topsy-turvy."

"Never mind the sympathy," he heard Kent say behind

him. "We've got a job—to kill every cat in that miserable world."

Korita murmured softly: "That should be simple. They are but primitives; and we have merely to sit down, and they will come to us, cunningly expecting to delude us."

Smith snapped: "You fellows make me sick! Pussy was the toughest nut we ever had to crack. He had everything he needed to defeat us—"

Morton smiled as Korita interrupted blandly: "Exactly, my dear Smith, except that he reacted according to the biological impulses of his type. His defeat was already foreshadowed when we unerringly analyzed him as a criminal from a certain era of his civilization.

"It was history, honorable Mr. Smith, our knowledge of history that defeated him," said the Japanese archeologist, reverting to the ancient politeness of his race.

MOTHER

BY PHILIP JOSÉ FARMER

I

"Look, Mother. The clock is running backward."

Eddie Fetts pointed to the hands on the pilot room dial.

Dr. Paula Fetts said, "The crash must have reversed it."

"How could it do that?"

"I can't tell you. I don't know everything, Son."

"Oh!"

"Well, don't look at me so disappointedly. I'm a pathologist, not an electronician."

"Don't be so cross, Mother. I can't stand it. Not now."

He walked out of the pilot room. Anxiously, she followed him. The burial of the crew and her fellow scientists had been very trying for him. Spilled blood had always made him dizzy and sick; he could scarcely control his hands enough to help her sack the scattered bones and entrails.

He had wanted to put the corpses in the nuclear furnace, but she had forbidden that. The Geigers amidships were ticking loudly, warning that there was invisible death in the stern.

The meteor that struck the moment the ship came out of Translation into normal space had probably wrecked the engine room. So she had understood from the incoherent high-pitched phrases of a colleague before he fled to the pilot room. She had hurried to find Eddie. She feared his cabin door would still be locked, as he had been making a tape of the aria "Heavy Hangs the Albatross" from Gianelli's *Ancient Mariner*.

Fortunately, the emergency system had automatically

258

thrown out the locking circuits. Entering, she had called out his name in fear he'd been hurt. He was laying half unconscious on the floor, but it was not the accident that had thrown him there. The reason lay in the corner, released from his lax hand; a quart free-fall thermos, rubber-nippled. From Eddie's open mouth charged a breath of rye that not even Nodor pills had been able to conceal.

Sharply she had commanded him to get up and onto the bed. Her voice, the first he had ever heard, pierced through the phalanx of Old Red Star. He struggled up, and she, though smaller, had thrown every ounce of her weight into getting him up and onto the bed.

There she had lain down with him and strapped them both in. She understood that the lifeboat had been wrecked also, and that it was up to the captain to bring the yacht down safely to the surface of this charted but unexplored planet, Baudelaire. Everybody else had gone to sit behind the captain, strapped in crashchairs, unable to help except with their silent backing.

Moral support had not been enough. The ship had come in on a shallow slant. Too fast. The wounded motors had not been able to hold her up. The prow had taken the brunt of the punishment. So had those seated in the nose.

Dr. Fetts had held her son's head on her bosom and prayed out loud to her God. Eddie had snored and muttered. Then there was a sound like the clashing of the gates of doom—a tremendous bong as if the ship were a clapper in a gargantuan bell tolling the most frightening message human ears may hear—a blinding blast of light—and darkness and silence.

A few moments later Eddie began crying out in a childish voice, "Don't leave me to die, Mother! Come back! Come back!"

Mother was unconscious by his side, but he did not know that. He wept for a while, then he lapsed back into his rye-fogged stupor—if he had ever been out of it—and slept. Again, darkness and silence.

It was the second day since the crash, if "day" could describe that twilight state on Baudelaire. Dr. Fetts followed her son wherever he went. She knew he was very sensitive and easily upset. All his life she had known it and had tried to get between him and anything that would cause

trouble. She had succeeded, she thought, fairly well until
three months ago when Eddie had eloped.

The girl was Polina Fameux, the ash-blond long-legged
actress whose tridi image, taped, had been shipped to frontier stars where a small acting talent meant little and a large
and shapely bosom much. Since Eddie was a well-known
Metro tenor, the marriage made a big splash whose ripples
ran around the civilized Galaxy.

Dr. Fetts had felt very bad about the elopement, but she
had, she hoped, hidden her grief very well beneath a smiling
mask. She didn't regret having to give him up; after all, he
was a full-grown man, no longer her little boy. But, really,
aside from the seasons at the Met and his tours, he had not
been parted from her since he was eight.

That was when she went on a honeymoon with her second
husband. And then she and Eddie had not been separated
long, for Eddie had gotten very sick, and she'd had to hurry
back and take care of him, as he had insisted she was the
only one who could make him well.

Moreover, you couldn't count his days at the opera as a
total loss, for he vised her every noon and they had a long
talk—no matter how high the vise bills ran.

The ripples caused by her son's marriage were scarcely a
week old before they were followed by even bigger ones.
They bore the news of the separation of Eddie and his wife.
A fortnight later, Polina applied for divorce on grounds of
incompatibility. Eddie was handed the papers in his mother's apartment. He had come back to her the day he and
Polina had agreed they "couldn't make a go of it," or, as he
phrased it to his mother, "couldn't get together."

Dr. Fetts was, of course, very curious about the reason
for their parting, but, as she explained to her friends, she
"respected" his silence. What she didn't say was that she
had told herself the time would come when he would tell
her all.

Eddie's "nervous breakdown" started shortly afterward.
He had been very irritable, moody, and depressed, but he
got worse the day a so-called friend told Eddie that whenever Polina heard his name mentioned, she laughed loud
and long. The friend added that Polina had promised to tell
some day the true story of their brief merger.

That night his mother had to call in a doctor.

In the days that followed, she thought of giving up her
position as research pathologist at De Kruif and taking all

her time to help him "get back on his feet." It was a sign of the struggle going on in her mind that she had not been able to decide within a week's time. Ordinarily given to swift consideration and resolution of a problem, she could not agree to surrender her beloved quest into tissue regeneration.

Just as she was on the verge of doing what was for her the incredible and the shameful, tossing a coin, she had been vised by her superior. He told her she had been chosen to go with a group of biologists on a research cruise to ten preselected planetary systems.

Joyfully, she had thrown away the papers that would turn Eddie over to a sanatorium. And, since he was quite famous, she had used her influence to get the government to allow him to go along. Ostensibly, he was to make a survey of the development of opera on planets colonized by Terrans. That the yacht was not visiting any colonized globes seemed to have been missed by the bureaus concerned. But it was not the first time in the history of a government that its left hand knew not what its right was doing.

Actually, he was to be "rebuilt" by his mother, who thought herself much more capable of curing him than any of the prevalent A, F, J, R, S, K, or H therapies. True, some of her friends reported amazing results with some of the symbol-chasing techniques. On the other hand, two of her close companions had tried them all and had gotten no benefits from any of them. She was his mother; she could do more for him than any of those "alphabatties"; he was flesh of her flesh, blood of her blood. Besides, he wasn't so sick. He just got awfully blue sometimes and made theatrical but insincere threats of suicide or else just sat and stared into space. But she could handle him.

II

So now it was that she followed him from the backward-running clock to his room. And saw him step inside, look for a second, and then turn to her with a twisted face.

"Neddie is ruined, Mother. Absolutely ruined."

She glanced at the piano. It had torn loose from the wall-racks at the moment of impact and smashed itself against the opposite wall. To Eddie it wasn't just a piano; it was Neddie. He had a pet name for everything he contacted for more than a brief time. It was as if he hopped from one appellation to the next, like an ancient sailor who felt lost unless he was close to the familiar and designated points of the shoreline. Otherwise, Eddie seemed to be drifting helplessly in a chaotic ocean, one that was anonymous and amorphous.

Or, analogy more typical of him, he was like the nightclubber who feels submerged, drowning, unless he hops from table to table, going from one well-known group of faces to the next, avoiding the featureless and unnamed dummies at the strangers' tables.

He did not cry over Neddie. She wished he would. He had been so apathetic during the voyage. Nothing, not even the unparalleled splendor of the naked stars nor the inexpressible alienness of strange planets had seemed to lift him very long. If he would only weep or laugh loudly or display some sign that he was reacting violently to what was happening. She would even have welcomed his striking her in anger or calling her "bad" names.

But no, not even during the gathering of the mangled corpses, when he looked for a while as if he were going to vomit, would he give way to his body's demand for expression. She understood that if he were to throw up, he would be much better for it, would have gotten rid of much of the psychic disturbance along with the physical.

He would not. He had kept on raking flesh and bones into the large plastic bags and kept a fixed look of resentment and sullenness.

She hoped now that the loss of his piano would bring tears and shaking shoulders. Then she could take him in her arms and give him sympathy. He would be her little boy again, afraid of the dark, afraid of the dog killed by a car, seeking her arms for the sure safety, the sure love.

"Never mind, Baby," she said. "When we're rescued, we'll get you a new one."

"When—!"

He lifted his eyebrows and sat down on the bed's edge.

"What do we do now?"

She became very brisk and efficient.

"The ultrad automatically started working the moment the meteor struck. It it's survived the crash, it's still sending SOS's. If not, then there's nothing we can do about it. Neither of us knows how to repair it.

"However, it's possible that in the last five years since this planet was located, other expeditions may have landed here. Not from Earth but from some of the colonies. Or from nonhuman globes. Who knows? It's worth taking a chance. Let's see."

A single glance was enough to wreck their hopes. The ultrad had been twisted and broken until it was no longer recognizable as the machine that sent swifter-than-light waves through the noether.

Dr Fetts said with false cheeriness, "Well, that's that! So what? It makes things too easy. Let's go into the storeroom and see what we can see."

Eddie shrugged and followed her. There she insisted that each take a panrad. If they had to separate for any reason, they could always communicate and also, using the DF's— the built-in direction finders—locate each other. Having used them before, they knew the instruments' capabilities and how essential they were on scouting or camping trips.

The panrads were lightweight cylinders about two feet high and eight inches in diameter. Crampacked, they held the mechanisms of two dozen different utilities. Their batteries lasted a year without recharging, they were practically indestructible and worked under almost any conditions.

Keeping away from the side of the ship that had the huge hole in it, they took the panrads outside. The long-wave bands were searched by Eddie while his mother moved the dial that ranged up and down the shortwaves. Neither really expected to hear anything, but to search was better than doing nothing.

Finding the modulated wave-frequencies empty of any significant noises, he switched to the continuous waves. He was startled by a dot-dashing.

"Hey, Mom! Something in the 1000 kilocycles! Unmodulated!"

"Naturally, Son," she said with some exasperation in the midst of her elation. "What would you expect from a radio-telegraphic signal?"

She found the band on her own cylinder. He looked blankly at her. "I know nothing about radio, but that's not Morse."

"What? You must be mistaken!"

"I—I don't think so."

"Is it or isn't it? Good God, Son, can't you be certain of *anything!*"

She turned the amplifier up. As both of them had learned Galacto-Morse through sleeplearn techniques, she checked him at once.

"You're right. What do you make of it?"

His quick ear sorted out the pulses.

"No simple dot and dash. Four different time-lengths."

He listened some more.

"They've got a certain rhythm, all right. I can make out definite groupings. Ah! That's the sixth time I've caught that particular one. And there's another. And another."

Dr. Fetts shook her ash-blond head. She could make out nothing but a series of zzt-zzt-zzt's.

Eddie glanced at the DF needle.

"Coming from NE by E. Should we try to locate?"

"Naturally," she replied. "But we'd better eat first. We don't know how far away it is, or what we'll find there. While I fix a hot meal, you get our field trip stuff ready."

"O.K.," he said with more enthusiasm than he had shown for a long time.

When he came back he ate everything in the large dish his mother had prepared on the unwrecked galley stove.

"You always did make the best stew," he said.

"Thank you. I'm glad you're eating again, Son. I am surprised. I thought you'd be sick about all this."

He waved vaguely but energetically.

"The challenge of the unknown. I have a sort of feeling this is going to turn out much better than we thought. Much better."

She came close and sniffed his breath. It was clean, innocent even of stew. That meant he'd taken Nodor, which probably meant he'd been sampling some hidden rye. Otherwise, how explain his reckless disregard of the possible dangers? It wasn't like him.

She said nothing, for she knew that if he tried to hide a bottle in his clothes or field sack while they were tracking down the radio signals, she would soon find it. And take it away. He wouldn't even protest, merely let her lift it from his limp hand while his lips swelled with resentment.

III

They set out. Both wore knapsacks, and carried the panrads. He carried a gun over his shoulder, and she had snapped onto her sack her small black bag of medical and lab supplies.

High noon of late autumn was topped by a weak red sun that barely managed to make itself seen through the eternal double layer of clouds. Its companion, an even smaller blob of lilac, was setting on the northwestern horizon. They walked in a sort of bright twilight, the best that Baudelaire ever achieved. Yet, despite the lack of light, the air was warm. It was a phenomenon common to certain planets behind the Horsehead Nebula, one being investigated but as yet unexplained.

The country was hilly, with many deep ravines. Here and there were prominences high enough and steep-sided enough to be called embryo mountains. Considering the roughness of the land, however, there was a surprising amount of vegetation. Pale green, red, and yellow bushes, vines, and little trees clung to every bit of ground, horizontal or vertical. All had comparatively broad leaves that turned with the sun to catch the light.

From time to time, as the two Terrans strode noisily through the forest, small multicolored insect-like and mammal-like creatures scuttled from hiding place to hiding place. Eddie decided to carry his gun in the crook of his arm. Then, after they were forced to scramble up and down ravines and hills and fight their way through thickets that became unexpectedly tangled, he put it back over his shoulder, where it hung from a strap.

Despite their exertions, they did not tire quickly. They weighed about twenty pounds less than they would have on Earth and, though the air was thinner, it was richer in oxygen.

Dr. Fetts kept up with Eddie. Thirty years the senior of the twenty-three-year-old, she passed even at close inspection for his older sister. Longevity pills took care of that. However, he treated her with all the courtesy and chivalry that one gave one's mother and helped her up the steep inclines, even though the climbs did not appreciably cause her deep chest to demand more air.

They paused once by a creek bank to get their bearings.

"The signals have stopped," he said.

"Obviously," she replied.

At that moment the radar-detector built into the panrad began to ping. Both of them automatically looked upward.

"There's no ship in the air."

"It can't be coming from either of those hills," she pointed out. "There's nothing but a boulder on top of each one. Tremendous rocks."

"Nevertheless, it's coming from there, I think. Oh! Oh!

Did you see what I saw? Looked like a tall stalk of some kind being pulled down behind that big rock."

She peered through the dim light. "I think you were imagining things, Son. I saw nothing."

Then, even as the pinging kept up, the zzting started again. But after a burst of noise, both stopped.

"Let's go up and see what we shall see," she said.

"Something screwy," he commented. She did not answer.

They forded the creek and began the ascent. Halfway up, they stopped to sniff in puzzlement at a gust of some heavy odor coming downwind.

"Smells like a cageful of monkeys," he said.

"In heat," she added. If his was the keener ear, hers was the sharper nose.

They went on up. The RD began sounding its tiny hysterical gonging. Nonplused, Eddie stopped. The DF indicated the radar pulses were not coming from the top of the hill they were climbing, as formerly, but from the other hill across the valley. Abruptly, the panrad fell silent.

"What do we do now?"

"Finish what we started. This hill. Then we go to the other one."

He shrugged and then hastened after her tall slim body in its long-legged coveralls. She was hot on the scent, literally, and nothing could stop her. Just before she reached the bungalow-sized boulder topping the hill, he caught up with her. She had stopped to gaze intently at the DF needle, which swung wildly before it stopped at neutral. The monkey-cage odor was very strong.

"Do you suppose it could be some sort of radio-generating mineral?" she asked, disappointedly.

"No. Those groupings were semantic. And that smell. . ."

"Then what—?"

He didn't know whether to feel pleased or not that she had so obviously and suddenly thrust the burden of responsibility and action on him. Both pride and a curious shrinking affected him. But he did feel exhilarated. Almost, he thought, he felt as if he were on the verge of discovering what he had been looking for for a long time. What the object of his search had been, he could not say. But he was excited and not very much afraid.

He unslung his weapon, a two-barreled combination shotgun and rifle. The panrad was still quiet.

"Maybe the boulder is camouflage for a spy outfit," he said. He sounded silly, even to himself.

Behind him, his mother gasped and screamed. He whirled and raised his gun, but there was nothing to shoot. She was pointing at the hilltop across the valley, shaking, and saying something incoherent.

He could make out a long slim antenna seemingly projecting from the monstrous boulder crouched there. At the same time, two thoughts struggled for first place in his mind: one, that it was more than a coincidence that both hills had almost identical stone structures on their brows, and, two, that the antenna must have been recently stuck out, for he was sure he had not seen it the last time he looked.

He never got to tell her his conclusions, for something thin and flexible and irresistible seized him from behind. Lifted into the air, he was borne backward. He dropped the gun and tried to grab the bands or tentacles around him and tear them off with his bare hands. No use.

He caught one last glimpse of his mother running off down the hillside. Then a curtain snapped down, and he was in total darkness.

IV

Eddie sensed himself, still suspended, twirled around. He could not know for sure, of course, but he thought he was facing in exactly the opposite direction. Simultaneously, the tentacles binding his legs and arms were released. Only his waist was still gripped. It was pressed so tightly that he cried out with pain.

Then, boot-toes bumping on some resilient substance, he was carried forward. Halted, facing he knew not what horrible monster, he was suddenly assailed—not by a sharp beak or tooth or knife or some other cutting or mangling instrument—but by a dense cloud of that same monkey perfume.

In other circumstances, he might have vomited. Now his stomach was not given the time to consider whether it should clean house or not. The tentacle lifted him higher and thrust him against something soft and yielding—something fleshlike and womanly—almost breastlike in texture and smoothness and warmth and in its hint of gentle curving.

He put his hands and feet out to brace himself, for he

thought for a moment he was going to sink in and be covered up—enfolded—ingested. The idea of a gargantuan amoeba-thing hiding within a hollow rock—or a rocklike shell—made him writhe and yell and shove at the protoplasmic substance.

But nothing of the kind happened. He was not plunged into a smothering and slimy jelly that would strip him of his skin and then his flesh and then dissolve his bones. He was merely shoved repeatedly against the soft swelling. Each time, he pushed or kicked or struck at it. After a dozen of these seemingly purposeless acts, he was held away, as if whatever was doing it was puzzled by his behavior.

He had quit screaming. The only sounds were his harsh breathing and the zzzts and pings from the panrad. Even as he became aware of them, the zzzts changed tempo and settled into a recognizable pattern of bursts—three units that crackled out again and again.

"Who are you? Who are you?"

Of course, if could just as easily have been, "What are you?" or "What the hell!" or "Nov smoz ka pop?"

Or nothing—semantically speaking.

But he didn't think the latter. And when he was gently lowered to the floor, and the tentacle went off to only-God-knew-where in the dark, he was sure that the creature was communicating—or trying to—with him.

It was this thought that kept him from screaming and running around in the lightless and fetid chamber, brainlessly seeking an outlet. He mastered his panic and snapped open a little shutter in the panrad's side and thrust in his right-hand index finger. There he poised it above the key and in a moment, when the thing paused in transmitting, he sent back, as best he could, the pulses he had received. It was not necessary for him to turn on the light and spin the dial that would put him on the 1000 kc band. The instrument would automatically key that frequency in with the one he had just received.

The oddest part of the whole procedure was that his whole body was trembling almost uncontrollably—one part excepted. That was his index finger, his one unit that seemed to him to have a definite function in this otherwise meaningless situation. It was the section of him that was helping him to survive—the only part that knew how—at that moment. Even his brain seemed to have no connection with his finger. That digit was himself, and the rest just happened to be linked to it.

When he paused, the transmitter began again. This time the units were unrecognizable. There was a certain rhythm to them, but he could not know what they meant. Meanwhile, the RD was pinging. Something somewhere in the dark hole had a beam held tightly on him.

He pressed a button on the panrad's top, and the built-in flashlight illuminated the area just in front of him. He saw a wall of reddish-gray rubbery substance. On the wall was a roughly circular, light gray swelling about four feet in diameter. Around it, giving it a Medusa appearance, were coiled twelve very long, very thin tentacles.

Though he was afraid that if he turned his back to them the tentacles would seize him once more, his curiosity forced him to wheel about and examine his surroundings with the bright beam. He was in an egg-shaped chamber about thirty feet long, twelve wide, and eight to ten high in the middle. It was formed of a reddish-gray material, smooth except for irregular intervals of blue or red pipes. Veins and arteries?

A door-sized portion of the wall had a vertical slit running down it. Tentacles fringed it. He guessed it was a sort of iris and that it had opened to drag him inside. Starfish-shaped groupings of tentacles were scattered on the walls or hung from the ceiling. On the wall opposite the iris was a long and flexible stalk with a cartilaginous ruff around its free end. When Eddie moved, it moved, its blind point following him as a radar antenna tracks the thing it is locating. That was what it was. And unless he was wrong, the stalk was also a C.W. transmitter-receiver.

He shot the light around. When it reached the end farthest from him, he gasped. Ten creatures were huddled together facing him! About the size of half-grown pigs, they looked like nothing so much as unshelled snails; they were eyeless, and the stalk growing from the forehead of each was a tiny duplicate of that on the wall. They didn't look dangerous. Their open mouths were little and toothless, and their rate of locomotion must be slow, for they moved like snails, on a large pedestal of flesh—a foot-muscle.

Nevertheless, if he were to fall asleep they could overcome him by force of numbers, and those mouths might drip an acid to digest him, or they might carry a concealed poisonous sting.

His speculations were interrupted violently. He was seized,

lifted, and passed on to another group of tentacles. He was
carried beyond the antenna-stalk and toward the snail-beings.
Just before he reached them, he was halted, facing the wall.
As it is, hitherto invisible, opened. His light shone into it,
but he could see nothing but convolutions of flesh.

His panrad gave off a new pattern of dit-dot-deet-dats.
The iris widened until it was large enough to admit his body,
if he were shoved in head first. Or feet first. It didn't
matter. The convolutions straightened out and became a
tunnel. Or a throat. From thousands of little pits emerged
thousands of tiny, razor sharp teeth. They flashed out and
sank back in, and before they had disappeared thousands of
other wicked little spears darted out and past the receding
fangs.

Meat-grinder.

Beyond the murderous array, at the end of the throat,
was a huge pouch of water. Steam came from it, and with it
an odor like that of his mother's stew. Dark bits, presumably
meat, and pieces of vegetables floated on the seething surface.

Then the iris closed, and he was turned around to face the
slugs. Gently, but unmistakably, a tentacle spanked his but-
tocks. And the panrad zzzted a warning.

Eddie was not stupid. He knew now that the ten creatures
were not dangerous unless he molested them. In which case
he had just seen where he would go if he did not behave.

Again he was lifted and carried along the wall until he
was shoved against the light gray spot. The monkey-cage
odor, which had died out, became strong again. Eddie identified its source with a very small hole which appeared in the
wall.

When he did not respond—he had no idea yet how he was
supposed to act—the tentacles dropped him so unexpectedly
that he fell on his back. Unhurt by the yielding flesh, he
rose.

What was the next step? Exploration of his resources.
Itemization: The panrad. A sleeping-bag, which he wouldn't
need as long as the present too-warm temperature kept up.
A bottle of Old Red Star capsules. A free-fall thermos with
attached nipple. A box of A-2-Z rations. A Foldstove. Car-
tridges for his double-barrel, now lying outside the creature's boulderish shell. A roll of toilet paper. Toothbrush.
Paste. Soap. Towel. Pills: Nodor, hormone, vitamin, longevity, reflex, and sleeping. And a thread-thin wire, a hundred feet long when uncoiled, that held prisoner in its

molecular structure a hundred symphonies, eighty operas, a thousand different types of musical pieces, and two thousand great books ranging from Sophocles and Dostoyevsky to the latest bestseller. It could be played inside the panrad.

He inserted it, pushed a button, and spoke. "Eddie Fett's recording of Puccini's *Che gelida manina*, please."

And while he listened approvingly to his own magnificent voice, he zipped open a can he had found in the bottom of the sack. His mother had put into it the stew left over from their last meal in the ship.

Not knowing what was happening, yet for some reason sure he was for the present safe, he munched meat and vegetables with a contented jaw. Transition from abhorrence to appetite sometimes came easily for Eddie.

He cleaned out the can and finished with some crackers and a chocolate bar. Rationing was out. As long as the food lasted, he would eat well. Then, if nothing turned up, he would . . . But then, he reassured himself as he licked his fingers, his mother, who was free, would find some way to get him out of his trouble.

She always had.

V

The panrad, silent for a while, began signaling. Eddie spotlighted the antenna and saw it was pointing at the snail-beings, which he had, in accordance with his custom, dubbed familiarly. Sluggos he called them.

The Sluggos crept toward the wall and stopped close to it. Their mouths, placed on the tops of their heads, gaped like so many hungry young birds. The iris opened, and two lips formed into a spout. Out of it streamed steaming-hot water and chunks of meat and vegetables. Stew! Stew that fell exactly into each waiting mouth.

That was how Eddie learned the second phrase of Mother Polyphema's language. The first message had been, "What are you?" This was, "Come and get it!"

He experimented. He tapped out a repetition of what he'd last heard. As one, the Sluggos—except the one then being fed—turned to him and crept a few feet before halting, puzzled.

Inasmuch as Eddie was broadcasting, the Sluggos must have had some sort of built-in DF. Otherwise they wouldn't have been able to distinguish between his pulses and their Mother's.

Immediately after, a tentacle smote Eddie across the shoulders and knocked him down. The panrad zzzted its third intelligible message: "Don't ever do that!"

And then a fourth, to which the ten young obeyed by wheeling and resuming their former positions.

"This way, children."

Yes, they were the offspring, living, eating, sleeping, playing, and learning to communicate in the womb of their mother—the Mother. They were the mobile brood of this vast immobile entity that had scooped up Eddie as a frog scoops up a fly. This Mother. She who had once been just such a Sluggo until she had grown hog-size and had been pushed out of her Mother's womb. And who, rolled into a tight ball, had free-wheeled down her natal hill, straightened out at the bottom, inched her way up the next hill, rolled down, and so on. Until she found the empty shell of an adult who had died. Or, if she wanted to be a first class citizen in her society and not a prestigeless *occupée* she found the bare top of a tall hill—or any eminence that commanded a big sweep of territory—and there squatted.

And there she put out many thread-thin tendrils into the soil and into the cracks in the rocks, tendrils that drew sustenance from the fat of her body and grew and extended downward and ramified into other tendrils. Deep underground the rootlets worked their instinctive chemistry; searched for and found the water, the calcium, the iron, the copper, the nitrogen, the carbons, fondled earthworms and grubs and larvae, teasing them for the secrets of their fats and proteins; broke down the wanted substance into shadowy colloidal particles; sucked them up the thready pipes of the tendrils and back to the pale and slimming body crouching on a flat space atop a ridge, a hill, a peak.

There, using the blueprints stored in the molecules of the cerebellum, her body took the building blocks of elements and fashioned them into a very thin shell of the most available material, a shield large enough so she could expand to fit it while her natural enemies—the keen and hungry predators that prowled twilighted Baudelaire—nosed and clawed it in vain.

Then, her evergrowing bulk cramped, she would resorb the hard covering. And if no sharp tooth found her during that process of a few days, she would cast another and a larger. And so on through a dozen or more.

Until she had become the monstrous and much reformed body of an adult and virgin female. Outside would be the stuff that so much resembled a boulder, that was, actually, rock: either granite, diorite, marble, basalt, or maybe just plain limestone. Or sometimes iron, glass, or cellulose.

Within was the centrally located brain, probably as large as a man's. Surrounding it, the tons of organs: the nervous system, the mighty heart, or hearts, the four stomachs, the microwave and longwave generators, the kidneys, bowels, tracheae, scent and taste organs, the perfume factory which made odors to attract animals and birds close enough to be seized, and the huge womb. And the antennae—the small one inside for teaching and scanning the young, and a long and powerful stalk on the outside, projecting from the shelltop, retractable if danger came.

The next step was from virgin to Mother, lower-case to upper-case as designated in her pulse-language by a longer pause before a word. Not until she was deflowered could she take a high place in her society. Immodest, unblushing, she herself made the advances, the proposals, and the surrender.

After which, she ate her mate.

The clock in the panrad told Eddie he was in his thirtieth day of imprisonment when he found out that little bit of information. He was shocked, not because it offended his ethics, but because he himself had been intended to be the mate. And the dinner.

His finger tapped, "Tell me, Mother, what you mean."

He had not wondered before how a species that lacked males could reproduce. Now he found that, to the Mothers, all creatures except themselves were male. Mothers were immobile and female. Mobiles were male. Eddie had been mobile. He was, therefore, a male.

He had approached this particular Mother during the mating season, that is, midway through raising a litter of young. She had scanned him as he came along the creekbanks at the valley bottom. When he was at the foot of the hill, she had detected his odor. It was new to her. The closest she could come to it in her memory banks was that of a beast similar to him. From her description, he guessed it to be an ape. So she had released from her repertoire its rut stench. When he seemingly fell into the trap, she had caught him.

He was supposed to attack the conception-spot, that light gray swelling on the wall. After he had ripped and torn it enough to begin the mysterious workings of pregnancy, he would have been popped into her stomach-iris.

Fortunately, he had lacked the sharp beak, the fang, the claw. And she had received her own signals back from the panrad.

Eddie did not understand why it was necessary to use a mobile for mating. A Mother was intelligent enough to pick up a sharp stone and mangle the spot herself.

He was given to understand that conception would not start unless it was accompanied by a certain titillation of the nerves—a frenzy and its satisfaction. Why this emotional state was needed, Mother did not know.

Eddie tried to explain about such things as genes and chromosomes and why they had to be present in highly developed species.

Mother did not understand.

Eddie wondered if the number of slashes and rips in the spot corresponded to the number of young. Or if there were a large number of potentialities in the heredity-ribbons spread out under the conception-skin. And if the haphazard irritation and consequent stimulation of the genes paralleled the chance combining of genes in human male-female mating. Thus resulting in offspring with traits that were combinations of their parents.

Or did the inevitable devouring of the mobile after the act indicate more than an emotional and nutritional reflex? Did it hint that the mobile caught up scattered genenodes, like hard seeds, along with the torn skin, in its claws and tusks, that these genes survived the boiling in the stew-stomach, and were later passed out in the feces? Where animals and birds picked them up in beak, tooth, or foot, and then, seized by other Mothers in this oblique rape, transmitted the heredity-carrying agents to the conception-spots while attacking them, the nodules being scraped off and implanted in the skin and blood of the swelling even as others were harvested? Later, the mobiles were eaten, digested, and ejected in the obscure but ingenious and never-ending cycle? Thus ensuring the continual, if haphazard, recombining of genes, chances for variations in offspring, opportunities for mutations, and so on?

Mother pulsed that she was nonplused.

Eddie gave up. He'd never know. After all, did it matter?

He decided not, and rose from his prone position to request water. She pursed up her iris and spouted a tepid quartful into his thermos. He dropped in a pill, swished it around till it dissolved, and drank a reasonable facsimile of Old Red Star. He preferred the harsh and powerful rye, though he could have afforded the smoothest. Quick results were what he wanted. Taste didn't matter, as he disliked all liquor tastes. Thus he drank what the Skid Row bums drank and shuddered even as they did, renaming it Old Rotten Tar and cursing the fate that had brought them so low they had to gag such stuff down.

The rye glowed in his belly and spread quickly through his limbs and up to his head, chilled only by the increasing scarcity of the capsules. When he ran out—then what? It was at times like this that he most missed his mother.

Thinking about her brought a few large tears. He snuffled and drank some more and when the biggest of the Sluggos nudged him for a back-scratching, he gave it instead a shot of Old Red Star. A slug for Sluggo. Idly, he wondered what effect a taste for rye would have on the future of the race when these virgins became Mothers.

At that moment he was shaken by what seemed a life-saving idea. These creatures could suck up the required elements from the earth and with them duplicate quite complex molecular structures. Provided, of course, they had a sample of the desired substance to brood over in some cryptic organ.

Well, what easier to do than give her one of the cherished capsules? One could become any number. Those, plus the abundance of water pumped up through hollow underground tendrils from the nearby creek, would give enough to make a master-distiller green!

He smacked his lips and was about to key her his request when what she was transmitting penetrated his mind.

Rather cattily, she remarked that her neighbor across the valley was putting on airs because she, too, held prisoner a communicating mobile.

VI

The Mothers had a society as hierarchical as table-protocol in Washington or peck-order in a barnyard. Prestige was what counted, and prestige was determined by the broadcasting power, the height of the eminence on which the Mother sat, which governed the extent of her radar-territory, and the abundance and novelty and wittiness of her gossip. The creature that had snapped Eddie up was a queen. She had precedence over thirty-odd of her kind; they all had to let her broadcast first, and none dared start pulsing until she quit. Then, the next in order began, and so on down the line. Any of them could be interrupted at any time by Number One, and if any of the lower echelon had something interesting to transmit, she could break in on the one then speaking and get permission from the queen to tell her tale.

Eddie knew this, but he could not listen in directly to the hilltop-gabble. The thick pseudo-granite shell barred him from that and made him dependent upon her womb-stalk for relayed information.

Now and then Mother opened the door and allowed her young to crawl out. There they practiced beaming and broadcasting at the Sluggos of the Mother across the valley. Occasionally that Mother deigned herself to pulse the young, and Eddie's keeper reciprocated to her offspring.

Turnabout.

The first time the children had inched through the exit-iris, Eddie had tried, Ulysses-like, to pass himself off as one of them and crawl out in the midst of the flock. Eyeless, but no Polyphemus, Mother had picked him out with her tentacles and hauled him back in.

It was following that incident that he had named her Polyphema.

He knew she had increased her own already powerful prestige tremendously by possession of that unique thing—a transmitting mobile. So much had her importance grown that the Mothers on the fringes of her area passed on the news to others. Before he had learned her language, the entire continent was hooked up. Polyphema had become a veritable gossip columnist; tens of thousands of hillcrouchers listened in eagerly to her accounts of her dealings with the walking paradox: a semantic male.

That had been fine. Then, very recently, the Mother across the valley had captured a similar creature. And in one bound she had become Number Two in the area and would, at the slightest weakness on Polyphema's part, wrest the top position away.

Eddie became wildly excited at the news. He had often

day-dreamed about his mother and wondered what she was doing. Curiously enough, he ended many of his fantasies with lip-mutterings, reproaching her almost audibly for having left him and for making no try to rescue him. When he became aware of his attitude, he was ashamed. Nevertheless, the sense of desertion colored his thoughts.

Now that he knew she was alive and had been caught, probably while trying to get him out, he rose from the lethargy that had lately been making him doze the clock around. He asked Polyphema if she would open the entrance so he could talk directly with the other captive. She said yes. Eager to listen in on a conversation between two mobiles, she was very cooperative. There would be a mountain of gossip in what they would have to say. The only thing that dented her joy was that the other Mother would also have access.

Then, remembering she was still Number One and would broadcast the details first, she trembled so with pride and ecstasy that Eddie felt the floor shaking.

Iris open, he walked through it and looked across the valley. The hillsides were still green, red, and yellow, as the plants on Baudelaire did not lose their leaves during winter. But a few white patches showed that winter had begun. Eddie shivered from the bite of cold air on his naked skin. Long ago he had taken off his clothes. The womb-warmth had made garments too uncomfortable; moreover, Eddie, being human, had had to get rid of waste products. And Polyphema, being a Mother, had had periodically to flush out the dirt with warm water from one of her stomachs. Every time the tracheae-vents exploded streams that swept the undesirable elements out through her door-iris, Eddie had become soaked. When he abandoned dress, his clothes had gone floating out. Only by sitting on his pack did he keep it from a like fate.

Afterward, he and the Sluggos had been dried off by warm air pumped through the same vents and originating from the mighty battery of lungs. Eddie was comfortable enough—he'd always like showers—but the loss of his garments had been one more thing that kept him from escaping. He would soon freeze to death outside unless he found the yacht quickly. And he wasn't sure he remembered the path back.

So now, when he stepped outside, he retreated a pace or

two and let the warm air from Polyphema flow like a cloak from his shoulders.

Then he peered across the half-mile that separated him from his mother, but he could not see her. The twilight state and the dark of the unlit interior of her captor hid her.

He tapped in Morse, "Switch to the talkie, same frequency." Paula Fetts did so. She began asking him frantically if he were all right.

He replied he was fine.

"Have you missed me terribly, Son?"

"Oh, very much."

Even as he said this he wondered vaguely why his voice sounded so hollow. Despair at never again being able to see her, probably.

"I've almost gone crazy, Eddie. When you were caught I ran away as fast as I could. I had no idea what horrible monster it was that was attacking us. And then, halfway down the hill, I fell and broke my leg . . ."

"Oh, no, Mother!"

"Yes. But I managed to crawl back to the ship. And there, after I'd set it myself, I gave myself B.K. shots. Only, my system didn't react like it's supposed to. There are people that way, you know, and the healing took twice as long.

"But when I was able to walk, I got a gun and a box of dynamite. I was going to blow up what I thought was a kind of rock-fortress, an outpost for some kind of extee. I'd no idea of the true nature of these beasts. First, though, I decided to reconnoiter. I was going to spy on the boulder from across the valley. But I was trapped by this thing.

"Listen, Son. Before I'm cut off, let me tell you not to give up hope. I'll be out of here before long and over to rescue you."

"How?"

"If you remember, my lab kit holds a number of carcinogens for field work. Well, you know that sometimes a Mother's conception-spot when it is torn up during mating, instead of begetting young, goes into cancer—the opposite of pregnancy. I've injected a carcinogen into the spot and a beautiful carcinoma has developed. She'll be dead in a few days."

"Mom! You'll be buried in that rotting mass!"

"No. This creature has told me that when one of her species dies, a reflex opens the labia. That's to permit their young—if any—to escape. Listen, I'll—"

A tentacle coiled about him and pulled him back through the iris, which shut.

When he switched back to C.W., he heard, "Why didn't you communicate? What were you doing? Tell me! Tell me!"

Eddie told her. There was a silence that could only be interpreted as astonishment. After Mother had recovered her wits, she said, "From now on, you will talk to the other male through me."

Obviously, she envied and hated his ability to change wavebands, and, perhaps, had a struggle to accept the idea.

"Please," he persisted, not knowing how dangerous were the waters he was wading in, "please let me talk to my mother di—"

For the first time, he heard her stutter.

"Wha-wha-what? You Mo-Mo-Mother?"

"Yes. Of course."

The floor heaved violently beneath his feet. He cried out and braced himself to keep from falling and then flashed on the light. The walls were pulsating like shaken jelly, and the vascular columns had turned from red and blue to gray. The entrance-iris sagged open, like a lax mouth, and the air cooled. He could feel the drop in temperature in her flesh with the soles of his feet.

It was some time before he caught on.

Polyphema was in a state of shock.

What might have happened had she stayed in it, he never knew. She might have died and thus forced him out into the winter before his mother could escape. If so, and he couldn't find the ship, he would die. Huddled in the warmest corner of the egg-shaped chamber, Eddie contemplated that idea and shivered to a degree for which the outside air couldn't account.

VII

However, Polyphema had her own method of recovery. It consisted of spewing out the contents of her stew-stomach, which had doubtless become filled with the poisons draining out of her system from the blow. Her ejection of the stuff was the physical manifestation of the physical catharsis. So furious was the flood that her foster son was almost swept out in the hot tide, but she, reacting instinctively, had coiled tentacles about him and the Sluggos. Then she followed the first upchucking by emptying her other three water-pouches, the second hot and the third luke-warm and the fourth, just filled, cold.

Eddie yelped as the icy water doused him.

Polphema's irises closed again. The floor and walls gradually quit quaking; the temperature rose; and her veins and arteries regained their red and blue. She was well again. Or so she seemed.

But when, after waiting twenty-four hours, he cautiously approached the subject, he found she not only would not talk about it, she refused to acknowledge the existence of the other mobile.

Eddie, giving up hope of conversation, thought for quite a while. The only conclusion he could come to, and he was sure he'd grasped enough of her psychology to make it valid, was that the concept of a mobile female was utterly unacceptable.

Her world was split into two: mobile and her kind, the immobile. Mobile meant food and mating. Mobile meant— male. The Mothers were—female.

How the mobiles reproduced had probably never entered the hillcrouchers' minds. Their science and philosophy were on the instinctive body-level. Whether they had some notion of spontaneous generation or amoeba-like fission being responsible for the continued population of mobiles, or they'd just taken for granted they "growed," like Topsy, Eddie never found out. To them, they were female and the rest of the protoplasmic cosmos was male.

That was that. Any other idea was more than foul and obscene and blasphemous. It was—unthinkable.

Polyphema had received a deep trauma from his words. And though she seemed to have recovered, somewhere in those tons of unimaginably complicated flesh a bruise was buried. Like a hidden flower, dark purple, it bloomed, and the shadow it cast was one that cut off a certain memory, a certain tract, from the light of consciousness. That bruise-stained shadow covered that time and event which the Mother, for reasons unfathomable to the human being, found necessary to mark KEEP OFF.

Thus, though Eddie did not word it, he understood in the cells of his body, he felt and knew, as if his bones were prophesying and his brain did not hear, what came to pass.

Sixty-six hours later by the panrad clock, Polyphema's

entrance-lips opened. Her tentacles darted out. They came
back in, carrying his helpless and struggling mother.

Eddie, roused out of a doze, horrified, paralyzed, saw her
toss her lab kit at him and heard an inarticulate cry from
her. And saw her plunged, headforemost, into the stomach-iris.

Polyphema had taken the one sure way of burying the
evidence.

Eddie lay face down, nose mashed against the warm and
faintly throbbing flesh of the floor. Now and then his hands
clutched spasmodically as if he were reaching for something
that someone kept putting just within his reach and then
moving away.

How long he was there he didn't know, for he never again
looked at the clock.

Finally, in the darkness, he sat up and giggled inanely.
"Mother always did make good stew."

That set him off. He leaned back on his hands and threw
his head back and howled like a wolf under a full moon.

Polyphema, of course, was dead-deaf, but she could radar
his posture, and her keen nostrils deduced from his body-
scent that he was in terrible fear and anguish.

A tentacle glided out and gently enfolded him.

"What is the matter?" zzted the panrad.

He stuck his finger in the keyhole.

"I have lost my mother!"

"?"

"She's gone away, and she'll never come back."

"I don't understand. *Here I am.*"

Eddie quit weeping and cocked his head as if he were
listening to some inner voice. He snuffled a few times and
wiped away the tears, slowly disengaged the tentacle, patted
it, walked over to his pack in a corner, and took out the
bottle of Old Red Star capsules. One he popped into the
thermos; the other he gave to her with the request she
duplicate it, if possible. Then he stretched out on his side,
propped on one elbow like a Roman in his sensualities,
sucked the rye through the nipple, and listened to a medley
of Beethoven, Moussorgsky, Verdi, Strauss, Porter, Feinstein,
and Waxworth.

So the time—if there were such a thing there—flowed
around Eddie. When he was tired of music or plays or
books, he listened in on the area hookup. Hungry, he rose
and walked—or often just crawled—to the stew-iris. Cans of
rations lay in his pack; he had planned to eat those until he

was sure that—what was it he was forbidden to eat? Poison? Something had been devoured by Polyphema and the Sluggos. But sometime during the music-rye orgy, he had forgotten. He now ate quite hungrily and with thought for nothing but the satisfaction of his wants.

Sometimes the door-iris opened, and Billy Greengrocer hopped in. Billy looked like a cross between a cricket and a kangaroo. He was the size of a collie, and he bore in a marsupialian pouch vegetables and fruit and nuts. These he extracted with shiny green, chitinous claws and gave to Mother in return for meals of stew. Happy symbiote, he chirruped merrily while his many-faceted eyes, revolving independently of each other, looked one at the Sluggos and the other at Eddie.

Eddie, on impulse, abandoned the 1000 kc band and roved the frequencies until he found that both Polyphema and Billy were emitting a 108 wave. That, apparently, was their natural signal. When Billy had his groceries to deliver, he broadcast. Polyphema, in turn, when she needed them, sent back to him. There was nothing intelligent on Billy's part; it was just his instinct to transmit. And the Mother was, aside from the "semantic" frequency, limited to that one band. But it worked out fine.

VIII

Everything was fine. What more could a man want? Free food, unlimited liquor, soft bed, air-conditioning, shower-baths, music, intellectual works (on the tape), interesting conversation (much of it was about him), privacy, and security.

If he had not already named her, he would have called her Mother Gratis.

Nor were creature comforts all. She had given him the answers to all his questions, all . . .

Except one.

That was never expressed vocally by him. Indeed, he would have been incapable of doing so. He was probably unaware that he had such a question.

But Polyphema voiced it one day when she asked him to do her a favor.

Eddie reacted as if outraged.

"One does not—! One does not—!"

He choked, and then he thought, how ridiculous! She is not—

And looked puzzled, and said, "But she is."

He rose and opened the lab kit. While he was looking for a scalpel, he came across the carcinogens. He threw them through the half-opened labia far out and down the hillside.

Then he turned and, scalpel in hand, leaped at the light gray swelling on the wall. And stopped, staring at it, while the instrument fell from his hand. And picked it up and stabbed feebly and did not even scratch the skin. And again let it drop.

"What is it? What is it?" crackled the panrad hanging from his wrist.

Suddenly, a heavy cloud of human odor—mansweat—was puffed in his face from a nearby vent.

"????"

And he stood, bent in a half-crouch, seemingly paralyzed. Until tentacles seized him in fury and dragged him toward the stomach-iris, yawning man-sized.

Eddie screamed and writhed and plunged his finger in the panrad and tapped, "All right! All right!"

And once back before the spot, he lunged with a sudden and wild joy; he slashed savagely; he yelled. "Take that! And that, P . . ." and the rest was lost in a mindless shout.

He did not stop cutting, and he might have gone on and on until he had quite excised the spot had not Polyphema interfered by dragging him toward her stomach-iris again. For ten seconds he hung there, helpless and sobbing with a mixture of fear and glory.

Polyphema's reflexes had almost overcome her brain. Fortunately, a cold spark of reason lit up a corner of the vast, dark, and hot chapel of her frenzy.

The convolutions leading to the steaming, meat-laden pouch closed and the foldings of flesh rearranged themselves. Eddie was suddenly hosed with warm water from what he called the "sanitation" stomach. The iris closed. He was put down. The scalpel was put back in the bag.

For a long time Mother seemed to be shaken by the thought of what she might have done to Eddie. She did not trust herself to transmit until her nerves were settled. When they were, she did not refer to his narrow escape. Nor did he.

He was happy. He felt as if a spring, tight-coiled against his bowels since he and his wife had parted, was now, for some reason, released. The dull vague pain of loss and discontent, the slight fever and cramp in his entrails, and the apathy that sometimes afflicted him, were gone. He felt fine.

Meanwhile, something akin to deep affection had been lighted, like a tiny candle under the drafty and overtowering roof of a cathedral. Mother's shell housed more than Eddie; it now curved over an emotion new to her kind. This was evident by the event that filled him with terror.

For the wounds in the spot healed and the swelling increased into a large bag. Then the bag burst and ten mouse-sized Sluggos struck the floor. The impact had the same effect as a doctor spanking a newborn baby's bottom; they drew in their first breath with shock and pain; their uncontrolled and feeble pulses filled the ether with shapeless SOS's.

When Eddie was not talking with Polyphema or listening in or drinking or sleeping or eating or bathing or running off the tape, he played with the Sluggos. He was, in a sense, their father. Indeed, as they grew to hog-size, it was hard for their female parent to distinguish him from her young. As he seldom walked any more, and was often to be found on hands and knees in their midst, she could not scan him too well. Moreover, something in the heavy-wet air or in the diet had caused every hair on his body to drop off. He grew very fat. Generally speaking, he was one with the pale, soft, round, and bald offspring. A family likeness.

There was one difference. When the time came for the virgins to be expelled, Eddie crept to one end, whimpering, and stayed there until he was sure Mother was not going to thrust him out into the cold, hard, and hungry world.

The final crisis over, he came back to the center of the floor. The panic in his breast had died out, but his nerves were still quivering. He filled his thermos and then listened for a while to his own tenor singing the "Sea Things" aria from his favorite opera, Gianelli's *Ancient Mariner*. Suddenly he burst out and accompanied himself, finding himself thrilled as never before by the concluding words.

> And from my neck so free
> The Albatross fell off, and sank
> Like lead into the sea.

Afterward, voice silent but heart singing, he switched off the wire and cut in on Polyphema's broadcast.

Mother was having trouble. She could not precisely describe to the continent-wide hookup this new and almost inexpressible emotion she felt about the mobile. It was a concept her language was not prepared for. Nor was she helped any by the gallons of Old Red Star in her bloodstream.

Eddie sucked at the plastic nipple and nodded sympathetically and drowsily at her search for words. Presently, the thermos rolled out of his hand.

He slept on his side, curled in a ball, knees on his chest and arms crossed, neck bent forward. Like the pilot room chronometer whose hands reversed after the crash, the clock of his body was ticking backward, ticking backward . . .

In the darkness, in the moistness, safe and warm, well fed, much loved.

EXPLORATION TEAM

BY MURRAY LEINSTER

I

The nearer moon went by overhead. It was jagged and irregular in shape, and was probably a captured asteroid. Huyghens had seen it often enough, so he did not go out of his quarters to watch it hurtle across the sky with seemingly the speed of an atmosphere-flier, occulting the stars as it went. Instead, he sweated over paper work, which should have been odd because he was technically a felon and all his labors on Loren Two felonious. It was odd, too, for a man to do paper work in a room with steel shutters and a huge bald eagle—untethered—dozing on a three-inch perch set in the wall. But paper work was not Huyghens' real task. His only assistant had tangled with a nightwalker and the furtive Kodius Company ships had taken him away to where Kodius Company ships came from. Huyghens had to do two men's work in loneliness. To his knowledge, he was the only man in this solar system.

Below him, there were snufflings. Sitka Pete got up heavily and padded to his water pan. He lapped the refrigerated water and sneezed violently. Sourdough Charley waked and complained in a rumbling growl. There were divers other rumblings and mutterings below. Huyghens called reassuringly, "Easy there!" and went on with his work. He finished a climate report, and fed figures to a computer, and while it hummed over them he entered the inventory totals in the station log, showing what supplies remained. Then he began to write up the log proper.

"*Sitka Pete,*" he wrote, "*has apparently solved the prob-*

lem of killing individual sphexes. He has learned that it doesn't do to hug them and that his claws can't penetrate their hide—not the top hide, anyhow. Today Semper notified us that a pack of sphexes had found the scent-trail to the station. Sitka hid downwind until they arrived. Then he charged from the rear and brought his paws together on both sides of a sphex's head in a terrific pair of slaps. It must have been like two twelve-inch shells arriving from opposite directions at the same time. It must have scrambled the sphex's brains as if they were eggs. It dropped dead. He killed two more with such mighty pairs of wallops. Sourdough Charley watched, grunting, and when the sphexes turned on Sitka, he charged in his turn. I, of course, couldn't shoot too close to him, so he might have fared badly but that Faro Nell came pouring out of the bear quarters to help. The diversion enabled Sitka Pete to resume the use of his new technic, towering on his hind legs and swinging his paws in the new and grisly fashion. The fight ended promptly. Semper flew and screamed above the scrap, but as usual did not join in. Note: Nugget, the cub, tried to mix in but his mother cuffed him out of the way. Sourdough and Sitka ignored him as usual. Kodius Champion's genes are sound!"

The noises of the night went on outside. There were notes like organ tones—song lizards. There were the tittering giggling cries of nightwalkers—not to be tittered back at. There were sounds like tack hammers, and doors closing, and from every direction came noises like hiccups in various keys. These were made by the improbable small creatures which on Loren Two took the place of insects.

Huyghens wrote out:

"Sitka seemed ruffled when the fight was over. He painstakingly used his trick on every dead or wounded sphex, except those he'd killed with it, lifting up their heads for his pile-driver-like blows from two directions at once, as if to show Sourdough how it was done. There was much grunting as they hauled the carcasses to the incinerator. It almost seemed—"

The arrival bell clanged, and Huyghens jerked up his head to stare at it. Semper, the eagle, opened icy eyes. He blinked.

Noises. There was a long, deep, contented snore from below. Something shrieked, out in the jungle. Hiccups. Clatterings, and organ notes—

The bell clanged again. It was a notice that a ship aloft somewhere had picked up the beacon beam—which only Kodius Company ships should know about—and was communicating for a landing. But there shouldn't be any ships in this solar system just now! This was the only habitable planet of the sun, and it had been officially declared uninhabitable by reason of inimical animal life. Which meant sphexes. Therefore no colony was permitted, and the Kodius Company broke the law. And there were few graver crimes than unauthorized occupation of a new planet.

The bell clanged a third time. Huyghens swore. His hand went out to cut off the beacon—but that would be useless. Radar would have fixed it and tied it in with physical features like the nearby sea and the Sere Plateau. The ship could find the place, anyhow, and descend by daylight.

"The devil!" said Huyghens. But he waited yet again for the bell to ring. A Kodius Company ship would double-ring to reassure him. But there shouldn't be a Kodius Company ship for months.

The bell clanged singly. The space phone dial flickered and a voice came out of it, tinny from stratospheric distortion:

"*Calling ground! Calling ground! Crete Line ship* Odysseus *calling ground on Loren Two. Landing one passenger by boat. Put on your field lights.*"

Huyghens' mouth dropped open. A Kodius Company ship would be welcome. A Colonial Survey ship would be extremely unwelcome, because it would destroy the colony and Sitka and Sourdough and Faro Nell and Nugget—and Semper—and carry Huyghens off to be tried for unauthorized colonization and all that it implied.

But a commercial ship, landing one passenger by boat—There was simply no circumstances under which that would happen. Not to an unknown, illegal colony. Not to a furtive station!

Huyghens flicked on the landing-field lights. He saw the glare in the field outside. Then he stood up and prepared to take the measures required by discovery. He packed the paper work he'd been doing into the disposal safe. He gathered up all personal documents and tossed them in. Every record, every bit of evidence that the Kodius Company maintained this station went into the safe. He slammed the door. He touched his finger to the disposal button, which would destroy the contents and melt down even the ashes past their possible use for evidence in court.

Then he hesitated. If it were a Survey ship, the button had to be pressed and he must resign himself to a long term in prison. But a Crete Line ship—if the space phone told the truth—was not threatening. It was simply unbelievable.

He shook his head. He got into travel garb and armed himself. He went down into the bear quarters, turning on lights as he went. There were startled snufflings and Stika Pete reared himself very absurdly to a sitting position to blink at him. Sourdough Charley lay on his back with his legs in the air. He'd found it cooler, sleeping that way. He rolled over with a thump. He made snorting sounds which somehow sounded cordial. Faro Nell padded to the door of her separate apartment—assigned her so that Nugget would not be underfoot to irritate the big males.

Huyghens, as the human population of Loren Two, faced the work force, fighting force, and—with Nugget—four-fifths of the terrestrial nonhuman population of the planet. They were mutated Kodiak bears, descendants of the Kodius Champion for whom the Kodius Company was named. Sitka Pete was a good twenty-two hundred pounds of lumbering, intelligent carnivore. Sourdough Charley would weigh within a hundred pounds of that figure. Faro Nell was eighteen hundred pounds of female charm—and ferocity. Then Nugget poked his muzzle around his mother's furry rump to see what was toward, and he was six hundred pounds of ursine infancy. The animals looked at Huyghens expectantly. If he'd had Semper riding on his shoulder, they'd have known what was expected of them.

"Let's go," said Huyghens. "It's dark outside, but somebody's coming. And it may be bad!"

He unfastened the outer door of the bear quarters. Sitka Pete went charging clumsily through it. A forthright charge was the best way to develop any situation—if one was an oversized male Kodiak bear. Sourdough went lumbering after him. There was nothing hostile immediately outside. Sitka stood up on his hind legs—he reared up a solid twelve feet—and sniffed the air. Sourdough methodically lumbered to one side and then the other, sniffing in his turn. Nell came out, nine-tenths of a ton of daintiness, and rumbled admonitorily at Nugget, who trailed her closely. Huyghens stood in the doorway, his night-sighted gun ready. He felt uncomfortable at sending the bears ahead into a Loren Two jungle at night. But they were qualified to scent danger, and he was not.

The illumination of the jungle in a wide path toward the landing field made for weirdness in the look of things. There were arching giant ferns and columnar trees which grew above them, and the extraordinary lanceolate underbrush of the jungle. The flood lamps, set level with the ground, lighted everything from below. The foliage, then, was brightly lit against the black night-sky—brightly lit enough to dim-out the stars. There were astonishing contrasts of light and shadow everywhere.

"On ahead!" commanded Huyghens, waving. "Hup!"

He swung the bear-quarters door shut. He moved toward the landing field through the lane of lighted forest. The two giant male Kodiaks lumbered ahead. Sitka Pete dropped to all fours and prowled. Sourdough Charley followed closely, swinging from side to side. Huyghens came alertly behind the two of them, and Faro Nell brought up the rear with Nugget following her closely.

It was an excellent military formation for progress through dangerous jungle. Sourdough and Sitka were advance-guard and point, respectively, while Faro Nell guarded the rear. With Nugget to look after, she was especially alert against attack from behind. Huyghens was, of course, the striking force. His gun fired explosive bullets which would discourage even sphexes, and his night-sight—a cone of light which went on when he took up the trigger-slack—told exactly where they would strike. It was not a sportsmanlike weapon, but the creatures of Loren Two were not sportsmanlike antagonists. The night-walkers, for example— But night-walkers feared light. They attacked only in a species of hysteria if it were too bright.

Huyghens moved toward the glare at the landing field. His mental state was savage. The Kodius Company station on Loren Two was completely illegal. It happened to be necessary, from one point of view, but it was still illegal. The tinny voice on the space phone was not convincing, in ignoring that illegality. But if a ship landed, Huyghens could get back to the station before men could follow, and he'd have the disposal safe turned on in time to protect those who'd sent him here.

But he heard the faraway and high harsh roar of a landing-boat rocket—not a ship's bellowing tubes—as he made his way through the unreal-seeming brush. The roar grew louder as he pushed on, the three big Kodiaks padding here and there, sniffing thoughtfully, making a perfect defensive-offensive formation for the particular conditions of this planet.

He reached the edge of the landing field, and it was blindingly bright, with the customary divergent beams slanting skyward so a ship could check its instrument landing by sight. Landing fields like this had been standard, once upon a time. Nowadays all developed planets had landing grids—monstrous structures which drew upon ionospheres for power and lifted and drew down star ships with remarkable gentleness and unlimited force. This sort of landing field would be found where a survey-team was at work, or where some strictly temporary investigation of ecology or bacteriology was under way, or where a newly authorized colony had not yet been able to build its landing grid. Of course it was unthinkable that anybody would attempt a settlement in defiance of the law!

Already, as Huyghens reached the edge of the scorched open space, the night-creatures had rushed to the light like moths on Earth. The air was misty with crazily gyrating, tiny flying things. They were innumerable and of every possible form and size, from the white midges of the night and multi-winged flying worms to those revoltingly naked-looking larger creatures which might have passed for plucked flying monkeys if they had not been carnivorous and worse. The flying things soared and whirred and danced and spun insanely in the glare. They made peculiarly plaintive humming noises. They almost formed a lamp-lit ceiling over the cleared space. They did hide the stars. Staring upward, Huyghens could just barely make out the blue-white flame of the space-boat's rocket through the fog of wings and bodies.

The rocket-flame grew steadily in size. Once, apparently, it tilted to adjust the boat's descending course. It went back to normal. A speck of incandescence at first, it grew until it was like a great star, and then a more-than-brilliant moon, and then it was a pitiless glaring eye. Huyghens averted his gaze from it. Sitka Pete sat lumpily—more than a ton of him—and blinked wisely at the dark jungle away from the light. Sourdough ignored the deepening, increasing rocket roar. He sniffed the air delicately. Faro Nell held Nugget firmly under one huge paw and licked his head as if tidying him up to be seen by company. Nugget wriggled.

The roar became that of ten thousand thunders. A warm

breeze blew outward from the landing-field. The rocket
boat hurled downward, and its flame touched the mist of
flying things, and they shriveled and burned and were hot.
Then there were churning clouds of dust everywhere, and
the center of the field blazed terribly—and something slid
down a shaft of fire, and squeezed it flat, and sat on it—and
the flame went out. The rocket boat sat there, resting on its
tail fins, pointing toward the stars from which it came.

There was a terrible silence after the tumult. Then, very
faintly, the noises of the night came again. There were
sounds like those of organ pipes, and very faint and apolo-
getic noises like hiccups. All these sounds increased, and
suddenly Huyghens could hear quite normally. Then a side-
port opened with a quaint sort of clattering, and something
unfolded from where it had been inset into the hull of the
space boat, and there was a metal passageway across the
flame-heated space on which the boat stood.

A man came out of the port. He reached back in and
shook hands very formally. He climbed down the ladder
rungs to the walkway. He marched above the steaming
baked area, carrying a traveling bag. He reached the end of
the walk and stepped gingerly to the ground. He moved
hastily to the edge of the clearing. He waved to the space
boat. There were ports. Perhaps someone returned the gesture. The walkway folded briskly back up to the hull and
vanished in it. A flame exploded into being under the tail
fins. There were fresh clouds of monstrous, choking dust
and a brightness like that of a sun. There was noise past the
possibility of endurance. Then the light rose swiftly through
the dust cloud, and sprang higher and climbed more swiftly
still. When Huyghens' ears again permitted him to hear
anything, there was only a diminishing mutter in the heavens and a small bright speck of light ascending to the sky
and swinging eastward as it rose to intercept the ship which
had let it descend.

The night noises of the jungle went on. Life on Loren
Two did not need to heed the doings of men. But there was
a spot of incandescence in the day-bright clearing, and a
short, brisk man looked puzzledly about him with a traveling bag in his hand.

Huyghens advanced toward him as the incandescence
dimmed. Sourdough and Sitka preceded him. Faro Nell
trailed faithfully, keeping a maternal eye on her offspring.
The man in the clearing stared at the parade they made. It

would be upsetting, even after preparation, to land at night on a strange planet, and to have the ship's boat and all links with the rest of the cosmos depart, and then to find one's self approached—it might seem stalked—by two colossal male Kodiak bears, with a third bear and a cub behind them. A single human figure in such company might seem irrelevant.

The new arrival gazed blankly. He moved, startled. Then Huyghens called:

"Hello, there! Don't worry about the bears! They're friends!"

Sitka reached the newcomer. He went warily downwind from him and sniffed. The smell was satisfactory. Man-smell. Sitka sat down with the solid impact of more than a ton of bear-meat landing on packed dirt. He regarded the man amiably. Sourdough said *"Whoosh!"* and went on to sample the air beyond the clearing. Huyghens approached. The newcomer wore the uniform of the Colonial Survey. That was bad. It bore the insignia of a senior officer. Worse.

"Hah!" said the just-landed man. "Where are the robots? What in all the nineteen hells are these creatures? Why did you shift your station? I'm Roane, here to make a progress report on your colony."

Huyghens said:

"What colony?"

"Loren Two Robot Installation—" Then Roane said indignantly, "Don't tell me that that idiot skipper dropped me at the wrong place! This is Loren Two, isn't it? And this is the landing field. But where are your robots You should have the beginning of a grid up! What the devil's happened here and what are these beasts?"

Huyghens grimaced.

"This," he said politely, "is an illegal, unlicensed settlement. I'm a criminal. These beasts are my confederates. If you don't want to associate with criminals you needn't, of course, but I doubt if you'll live till morning unless you accept my hospitality while I think over what to do about your landing. In reason, I ought to shoot you."

Faro Nell came to a halt behind Huyghens, which was her proper post in all out-door movement. Nugget, however, saw a new human. Nugget was a cub, and, therefore, friendly. He ambled forward ingratiatingly. He was four feet high at the shoulders, on all fours. He wriggled bashfully as he approached Roane. He sneezed, because he was embarrassed.

His mother overtook him swiftly and cuffed him to one side. He wailed. The wail of a six-hundred-pound Kodiak bear-cub is a remarkable sound. Roane gave ground a pace.

"I think," he said carefully, "that we'd better talk things over. But if this is an illegal colony, of course you're under arrest and anything you say will be used against you."

Huyghens grimaced again.

"Right," he said. "But now if you'll walk close to me, we'll head back to the station. I'd have Sourdough carry your bag—he likes to carry things—but he may need his teeth. We've half a mile to travel." He turned to the animals. "Let's go!" he said commandingly. "Back to the station! Hup!"

Grunting, Sitka Pete arose and took up his duties as advanced point of a combat team. Sourdough trailed, swinging widely to one side and another. Huyghens and Roane moved together. Faro Nell and Nugget brought up the rear. Which, of course, was the only relatively safe way for anybody to travel on Loren Two, in the jungle, a good half mile from one's fortresslike residence.

But there was only one incident on the way back. It was a night-walker, made hysterical by the lane of light. It poured through the underbrush, uttering cries like maniacal laughter.

Sourdough brought it down, a good ten yards from Huyghens. When it was all over, Nugget bristled up to the dead creature, uttering cub-growls. He feigned to attack it.

His mother whacked him soundly.

II

There were comfortable, settling-down noises below. The bears grunted and rumbled, but ultimately were still. The glare from the landing field was gone. The lighted lane through the jungle was dark again. Huyghens ushered the man from the space boat up into his living quarters. There was a resulting stir, and Semper took his head from under his wing. He stared coldly at the two humans. He spread monstrous, seven-foot wings and fluttered them. He opened his beak and closed it with a snap.

"That's Semper," said Huyghens. "Semper Tyrannis. He's the rest of the terrestrial population here. Not being a fly-by-night sort of creature, he didn't come out to welcome you."

Roane blinked at the huge bird, perched on a three-inch-thick perch set in the wall.

"An eagle?" he demanded. "Kodiak bears—mutated ones you say, but still bears—and now an eagle? You've a very nice fighting unit in the bears."

"They're pack animals, too," said Huyghens. "They can carry some hundreds of pounds without losing too much combat efficiency. And there's no problem of supply. They live off the jungle. Not sphexes, though. Nothing will eat a sphex, even if it can kill one."

He brought out glasses and a bottle. He indicated a chair. Roane put down his traveling bag. He took a glass.

"I'm curious," he observed. "Why Sempter Tyrannis? I can understand Sitka Pete and Sourdough Charley as names. The home of their ancestors makes them fitting. But why Semper?"

"He was bred for hawking," said Huyghens. "You sic a dog on something. You sic Semper Tyrannis. He's too big to ride on a hawking glove, so the shoulders of my coats are padded to let him ride there. He's a flying scout. I've trained him to notify us of sphexes, and in flight he carries a tiny television camera. He's useful, but he hasn't the brains of the bears."

Roane sat down and sipped at his glass.

"Interesting . . . very interesting! But this is an illegal settlement. I'm a Colonial Survey officer. My job is reporting on progress according to plan, but nevertheless I have to arrest you. Didn't you say something about shooting me?"

Huyghens said doggedly:

"I'm trying to think of a way out. Add up all the penalties for illegal colonization and I'd be in a very bad fix if you got away and reported this set-up. Shooting you would be logical."

"I see that," said Roane reasonably. "But since the point has come up—I have a blaster trained on you from my pocket."

Huyghens shrugged.

"It's rather likely that my human confederates will be back here before your friends. You'd be in a very tight fix if my friends came back and found you more or less sitting on my corpse."

Roane nodded.

"That's true, too. Also it's probable that your fellow terrestrials wouldn't co-operate with me as they have with you. You seem to have the whip hand, even with my blaster trained on you. On the other hand, you could have killed me quite easily after the boat left, when I'd first landed. I'd have been quite unsuspicious. So you may not really intend to murder me."

Huyghens shrugged again.

"So," said Roane, "since the secret of getting along with people is that of postponing quarrels—suppose we postpone the question of who kills whom? Frankly, I'm going to send you to prison if I can. Unlawful colonization is very bad business. But I suppose you feel that you have to do something permanent about me. In your place I probably should, too. Shall we declare a truce?"

Huyghens indicated indifference. Roane said vexedly:

"Then I do! I have to! So—"

He pulled his hand out of his pocket and put a pocket blaster on the table. He leaned back, defiantly.

"Keep it," said Huyghens. "Loren Two isn't a place where you live long unarmed." He turned to a cupboard. "Hungry?"

"I could eat," admitted Roane.

Huyghens pulled out two mealpacks from the cupboard and inserted them in the readier below. He set out plates.

"Now—what happened to the official, licensed, authorized colony here?" asked Roane briskly. "License issued eighteen months ago. There was a landing of colonists with a drone fleet of equipment and supplies. There've been four ship-contacts since. There should be several thousand robots being industrious under adequate human supervision. There should be a hundred-mile-square clearing, planted with food plants for later human arrivals. There should be a landing grid at least half-finished. Obviously there should be a space beacon to guide ships to a landing. There isn't. There's no clearing visible from space. That Crete Line ship has been in orbit for three days, trying to find a place to drop me. Her skipper was fuming. Your beacon is the only one on the planet, and we found it by accident. What happened?"

Huyghens served the food. He said dryly:

"There could be a hundred colonies on this planet without any one knowing of any other. I can only guess about your robots, but I suspect they ran into sphexes."

Roane paused, with his fork in his hand.

"I read up on this planet, since I was to report on its colony. A sphex is part of the inimical animal life here. Cold-blooded belligerent carnivore, not a lizard but a genus all its own. Hunts in packs. Seven to eight hundred pounds, when adult. Lethally dangerous and simply too numerous to fight. They're why no license was ever granted to human colonists. Only robots could work here, because they're machines. What animal attacks machines?"

Huyghens said:

"What machine attacks animals? The sphexes wouldn't bother robots, of course, but would robots bother the sphexes?"

Roane chewed and swallowed.

"Hold it! I'll agree that you can't make a hunting-robot. A machine can discriminate, but it can't decide. That's why there's no danger of a robot revolt. They can't decide to do something for which they have no instructions. But this colony was planned with full knowledge of what robots can and can't do. As ground was cleared, it was enclosed in an electric fence which no sphex could touch without frying."

Huyghens thoughtfully cut his food. After a moment:

"The landing was in the wintertime," he observed. "It must have been, because the colony survived awhile. And at a guess, the last ship-landing was before thaw. The years are eighteen months long here, you know."

Roane admitted:

"It was in winter that the landing was made. And the last ship-landing was before spring. The idea was to get mines in operation for material, and to have ground cleared and enclosed in sphex-proof fence before the sphexes came back from the tropics. They winter there, I understand."

"Did you ever see a sphex?" Huyghens asked. Then added, "No, of course not. But if you took a spitting cobra and crossed it with a wildcat, painted it tan-and-blue and then gave it hydrophobia and homicidal mania at once— why you might have one sphex. But not the race of sphexes. They can climb trees, by the way. A fence wouldn't stop them."

"An electrified fence," said Roane. "Nothing could climb that!"

"No one animal," Huyghens told him. "But sphexes are a race. The smell of one dead sphex brings others running with blood in their eyes. Leave a dead sphex alone for six hours and you've got them around by the dozen. Two days and there are hundreds. Longer, and you've got thousands of them! They gather to caterwaul over their dead pal and hunt for whoever or whatever killed him."

He returned to his meal. A moment later he said:

"No need to wonder what happened to your colony. During the winter the robots burned out a clearing and put up an electrified fence according to the book. Come spring, the sphexes came back. They're curious, among their other madnesses. A sphex would try to climb the fence just to see what was behind it. He'd be electrocuted. His carcass would bring others, raging because a sphex was dead. Some of them would try to climb the fence—and die. And their corpses would bring others. Presently the fence would break down from the bodies hanging on it, or a bridge of dead beasts' carcasses would be built across it—and from as far downwind as the scent carried there'd be loping, raging, scent-crazed sphexes racing to the spot. They'd pour into the clearing through or over the fence, squalling and screeching for something to kill. I think they'd find it."

Roane ceased to eat. He looked sick.

"There were . . . pictures of sphexes in the data I read. I suppose that would account for . . . everything."

He tried to lift his fork. He put it down again.

"I can't eat," he said abruptly.

Huyghens made no comment. He finished his own meal, scowling. He rose and put the plates into the top of the cleaner. There was a whirring. He took them out of the bottom and put them away.

"Let me see those reports, eh?" he asked dourly. "I'd like to see what sort of a set-up they had—those robots."

Roane hesitated and then opened his traveling bag. There was a microviewer and reels of films. One entire reel was labeled "Specifications of Construction, Colonial Survey," which would contain detailed plans and all requirements of material and workmanship for everything from desks, office, administrative personnel, for use of, to landing grids, heavy-gravity planets, lift-capacity one hundred thousand Earth-tons. But Huyghens found another. He inserted it and spun the control swiftly here and there, pausing only briefly at index frames until he came to the section he wanted. He began to study the information with growing impatience.

"Robots, robots, robots!" he snapped. "Why don't they

leave them where they belong—in cities to do the dirty work, and on airless planets where nothing unexpected ever happens! Robots don't belong in new colonies! Your colonists depended on them for defense! Dammit, let a man work with robots long enough and he thinks all nature is as limited as they are! This is a plan to set up a controlled environment! On Loren Two! Controlled environment—" He swore, luridly. "Complacent, idiotic, desk-bound half-wits!"

"Robots are all right," said Roane. "We couldn't run civilization without them."

"But you can't tame a wilderness with 'em!" snapped Huyghens. "You had a dozen men landed, with fifty assembled robots to start with. There were parts for fifteen hundred more—and I'll bet anything I've got that the ship-contacts landed more still."

"They did," admitted Roane.

"I despise 'em!" growled Huyghens. "I feel about 'em the way the old Greeks and Romans felt about slaves. They're for menial work—the sort of work a man will perform for himself, but that he won't do for another man for pay. Degrading work!"

"Quite aristocratic!" said Roane with a touch of irony. "I take it that robots clean out the bear quarters downstairs."

"No!" snapped Huyghens. "I do! They're my friends! They fight for me! They can't understand the necessity and no robot would do the job right!"

He growled, again. The noises of the night went on outside. Organ tones and hiccupings and the sound of tack hammers and slamming doors. Somewhere there was a singularly exact replica of the discordant squeaking of a rusty pump.

"I'm looking," said Huyghens at the micro-viewer, "for the record of their mining operations. An open-pit operation wouldn't mean a thing. But if they had driven a tunnel, and somebody was there supervising the robots when the colony was wiped out, there's an off-chance he survived a while."

Roane regarded him with suddenly intent eyes.

"And—"

"Dammit," snapped Huyghens, "if so I'll go see! He'd . . . they'd have no chance at all, otherwise. Not that the chance is good in any case!"

Roane raised his eyebrows.

"I'm a Colonial Survey officer," he said. "I've told you

I'll send you to prison if I can. You've risked the lives of millions of people, maintaining non-quarantined communication with an unlicensed planet. If you did rescue somebody from the ruins of the robot colony, does it occur to you that they'd be witnesses to your unauthorized presence here?"

Huyghens spun the viewer again. He stopped. He switched back and forth and found what he wanted. He muttered in satisfaction: "They did run a tunnel!" Aloud he said, "I'll worry about witnesses when I have to."

He pushed aside another cupboard door. Inside it were the odds and ends a man makes use of to repair the things about his house that he never notices until they go wrong. There was an assortment of wires, transistors, bolts, and similar stray items that a man living alone will need. When to his knowledge he's the only inhabitant of a solar system, he especially needs such things.

"What now?" asked Roane mildly.

"I'm going to try to find out if there's anybody left alive over there. I'd have checked before if I'd known the colony existed. I can't prove they're all dead, but I may prove that somebody's still alive. It's barely two weeks' journey away from here! Odd that two colonies picked spots so near!"

He absorbedly picked over the oddments he'd selected. Roane said vexedly:

"Confound it! How can you check whether somebody's alive some hundreds of miles away—when you didn't know he existed half an hour ago?"

Huyghens threw a switch and took down a wall panel, exposing electronic apparatus and circuits behind. He busied himself with it.

"Ever think about hunting for a castaway?" he asked over his shoulder. "There's a planet with some tens of millions of square miles on it. You know there's a ship down. You've no idea where. You assume the survivors have power—no civilized man will be without power very long, so long as he can smelt metals!—but making a space beacon calls for high-precision measurements and workmanship. It's not to be improvised. So what will your ship-wrecked civilized man do, to guide a rescue ship to the one or two square miles he occupies among some tens of millions on the planet?"

Roane fretted visibly.

"What?"

"He's had to go primitive, to begin with," Roane explained. "He cooks his meat over a fire, and so on. He has to make a strictly primitive signal. It's all he can do without gauges and micrometers and very special tools. But he can fill all the planet's atmosphere with a signal that searchers for him can't miss. You see?"

Roane thought irritably. He shook his head.

"He'll make," said Huyghens, "a spark transmitter. He'll fix its output at the shortest frequency he can contrive—it'll be somewhere in the five-to-fifty-meter wave-band, but it will tune very broad—and it will be a plainly human signal. He'll start it broadcasting. Some of those frequencies will go all around the planet under the ionosphere. Any ship that comes in under the radio roof will pick up his signal, get a fix on it, move and get another fix, and then go straight to where the castaway is waiting placidly in a hand-braided hammock, sipping whatever sort of drink he's improvised out of the local vegetation."

Roane said grudgingly:

"Now that you mention it, of course—"

"My space phone picks up microwaves," said Huyghens, "I'm shifting a few elements to make it listen for longer stuff. It won't be efficient, but it will pick up a distress signal if one's in the air. I don't expect it, though."

He worked. Roane sat still a long time, watching him. Down below, a rhythmic sort of sound arose. It was Sourdough Charley, snoring. He lay on his back with his legs in the air. He'd discovered that he slept cooler that way. Sitka Pete grunted in his sleep. He was dreaming. In the general room of the station Semper, the eagle, blinked his eyes rapidly and then tucked his head under a gigantic wing and went to sleep. The noises of the Loren Two jungle came through the steel-shuttered windows. The nearer moon—which had passed overhead not long before the ringing of the arrival bell—again came soaring over the eastern horizon. It sped across the sky at the apparent speed of an atmosphere-flier. Overhead, it could be seen to be a jagged irregular mass of rock or metal, plunging blindly about the great planet forever.

Inside the station, Roane said angrily:

"See here, Huyghens! You've reason to kill me. Apparently you don't intend to. You've excellent reason to leave that robot colony strictly alone. But you're preparing to help, if there's anybody alive to need it. And yet you're a criminal—and I mean a criminal! There've been plenty of lives lost in consequence, and you're risking more! Why do you do it? Why do you do something that could produce monstrous results to other beings?"

Huyghens grunted.

"You're only assuming there are no sanitary and quarantine precautions taken in my communications. As a matter of fact, there are. They're taken, all right! As for the rest, you wouldn't understand."

"I don't understand," snapped Roane, "but that's no proof I can't! Why are you a criminal?"

Huyghens painstakingly used a screwdriver inside the wall panel. He delicately lifted out a small electronic assembly. He carefully began to fit in a spaghettied new assembly with larger units.

"I'm cutting my amplification here to hell-and-gone," he observed, "but I think it'll do. I'm doing what I'm doing," he added calmly, "I'm being a criminal because it seems to me befitting what I think I am. Everybody acts according to his own real notion of himself. You're a conscientious citizen, and a loyal official, and a well-adjusted personality. You consider yourself an intelligent rational animal. But you don't act that way! You're reminding me of my need to shoot you or something similar, which a merely rational animal would try to make me forget. You happen, Roane, to be a man. So am I. But I'm aware of it. Therefore, I deliberately do things a merely rational animal wouldn't, because they're my notion of what a man who's more than a rational animal should do."

He very carefully tightened one small screw after another. Roane said annoyedly:

"Oh. Religion."

"Self-respect," corrected Huyghens. "I don't like robots. They're too much like rational animals. A robot will do whatever it can that its supervisor requires it to do. A merely rational animal will do whatever it can that circumstances require it to do. I wouldn't like a robot unless it had some idea of what was befitting it and would spit in my eye if I tried to make it do something else. The bears downstairs, now—They're no robots! They are loyal and honorable beasts, but they'd turn and tear me to bits if I tried to make them do something against their nature. Faro Nell would fight me and all creation together, if I tried to harm

Nugget. It would be unintelligent and unreasonable and irrational. She'd lose out and get killed. But I like her that way! And I'll fight you and all creation when you make me try to do something against my nature. I'll be stupid and unreasonable and irrational about it." Then he grinned over his shoulder. "So will you. Only you don't realize it."

He turned back to his task. After a moment he fitted a manual-control knob over a shaft in his haywire assembly.

"What did somebody try to make you do?" asked Roane shrewdly. "What was demanded of you that turned you into a criminal? What are you in revolt against?"

Huyghens threw a switch. He began to turn the knob which controlled the knob of his makeshift-modified receiver.

"Why," he said amusedly, "when I was young the people around me tried to make me into a conscientious citizen and a loyal employee and a well-adjusted personality. They tried to make me into a highly intelligent rational animal and nothing more. The difference between us, Roane, is that I found it out. Naturally, I rev—"

He stopped short. Faint, crackling, crisp frying sounds came from the speaker of the space phone now modified to receive what once were called short waves.

Huyghens listened. He cocked his head intently. He turned the knob very, very slowly. Then Roane made an arrested gesture, to call attention to something in the sibilant sound. Huyghens nodded. He turned the knob again, with infinitesimal increments.

Out of the background noise came a patterned mutter. As Huyghens shifted the tuning, it grew louder. It reached a volume where it was unmistakable. It was a sequence of sounds like discordant buzzing. There were three half-second buzzings with half-second pauses between. A two-second pause. Three full-second buzzings with half-second pauses between. Another two-second pause and three half-second buzzings, again. Then silence for five seconds. Then the pattern repeated.

"The devil!" said Huyghens. "That's a human signal! Mechanically made, too! In fact, it used to be a standard distress-call. It was termed an S O S, though I've no idea what that meant. Anyhow, somebody must have read old-fashioned novels, some time, to know about it. And so someone is still alive over at your licensed, but now smashed-up, robot colony. And they're asking for help. I'd say they're likely to need it."

He looked at Roane.

"The intelligent thing to do is sit back and wait for a ship—either of my friends or yours. A ship can help survivors or castaways much better than we can. A ship can even find them more easily. But maybe time is important to the poor devils! So I'm going to take the bears and see if I can reach them. You can wait here, if you like. What say? Travel on Loren Two isn't a picnic! I'll be fighting nearly every foot of the way. There's plenty of 'inimical animal life' here!"

Roane snapped angrily:

"Don't be a fool! Of course I'm coming! What do you take me for? And two of us should have four times the chance of one!"

Huyghens grinned.

"Not quite. You forget Sitka Pete and Sourdough Charley and Faro Nell. There'll be five of us if you come, instead of four. And, of course, Nugget has to come—and he'll be no help—but Semper may make up for him. You won't quadruple our chances, Roane, but I'll be glad to have you if you want to be stupid and unreasonable and not at all rational—and come along."

III

There was a jagged spur of stone looming precipitously over a river-valley. A thousand feet below, a broad stream ran westward to the sea. Twenty miles to the east, a wall of mountains rose sheer against the sky. Its peaks seemed to blend to a remarkable evenness of height. There was rolling, tumbled ground between for as far as the eye could see.

A speck in the sky came swiftly downward. Great pinions spread, and flapped, and icy eyes surveyed the rocky space. With more great flappings, Semper the eagle came to ground. He folded his huge wings and turned his head jerkily, his eyes unblinking. A tiny harness held a miniature camera against his chest. He strutted over the bare stone to the highest point. He stood there, a lonely and arrogant figure in the vastness.

There came crashings and rustlings, and then snuffling sounds. Sitka Pete came lumbering out into the clear space. He wore a harness too, and a pack. The harness was complex, because it had not only to hold a pack in normal travel, but, when he stood on his hind legs, it must not hamper the use of his forepaws in combat.

He went cagily all over the open area. He peered over the edge of the spur's farthest tip. He prowled to the other side and looked down. He scouted carefully. Once he moved close to Semper and the eagle opened his great curved beak and uttered an indignant noise. Sitka paid no attention.

He relaxed, satisfied. He sat down untidily, his hind legs sprawling. He wore an air approaching benevolence as he surveyed the landscape about and below him.

More snufflings and crashings. Sourdough Charley came into view with Huyghens and Roane behind him. Sourdough carried a pack, too. Then there was a squealing and Nugget scurried up from the rear, impelled by a whack from his mother. Faro Nell appeared, with the carcass of a staglike animal lashed to her harness.

"I picked this place from a space photo," said Huyghens, "to make a directional fix from. I'll get set up."

He swung his pack from his shoulders to the ground. He extracted an obviously self-constructed device which he set on the ground. It had a whip aerial, which he extended. Then he plugged in a considerable length of flexible wire and unfolded a tiny, improvised directional aerial with an even tinier booster at its base. Roane slipped his pack from his shoulders and watched. Huyghens slipped headphones over his ears. He looked up and said sharply:

"Watch the bears, Roane. The wind's blowing up the way we came. Anything that trails us—sphexes, for example— will send its scent on before. The bears will tell us."

He busied himself with the instruments he'd brought. He heard the hissing, frying, background noise which could be anything at all except a human signal. He reached out and swung the small aerial around. Rasping, buzzing tones came in, faintly and then loudly. This receiver, though, had been made for this particular wave band. It was much more efficient than the modified space phone had been. It picked up three short buzzes, three long ones, and three short ones again. Three dots, three dashes, and three dots. Over and over again. S O S. S O S. S O S.

Huyghens took a reading and moved the directional aerial a carefully measured distance. He took another reading. He shifted it yet again and again, carefully marking and measuring each spot and taking notes of the instrument readings.

When he finished, he had checked the direction of the signal not only by loudness but by phase—he had as accurate a fix as could possibly be had with portable apparatus.

Sourdough growled softly. Sitka Pete whiffed the air and arose from his sitting position. Faro Nell whacked Nugget, sending him whimpering to the farthest corner of the flea place. She stood bristling, facing down-hill the way they'd come.

"Damn!" said Huyghens.

He got up and waved his arm at Semper, who had turned his head at the stirrings. Semper squawked in a most un-eaglelike fashion and dived off the spur and was immediately fighting the down-draught beyond it. As Huyghens reached his weapon, the eagle came back overhead. He went magnificently past, a hundred feet high, careening and flapping in the tricky currents. He screamed, abruptly, and circled and screamed again. Huyghens swung a tiny vision plate from its strap to where he could look into it. He saw, of course, what the little camera on Semper's chest could see—reeling, swaying terrain as Semper saw it, though without his breadth of field. There were moving objects to be seen through the shifting trees. Their coloring was unmistakable.

"Sphexes," said Huyghens dourly. "Eight of them. Don't look for them to follow our track, Roane. They run parallel to a trail on either side. That way they attack in breadth and all at once when they catch up. And listen! The bears can handle anything they tangle with! It's our job to pick off the loose ones! And aim for the body! The bullets explode."

He threw off the safety of his weapon. Faro Nell, uttering thunderous growls, went padding to a place between Sitka Pete and Sourdough. Sitka glanced at her and made a whuffing noise, as if derisive of her blood-curdling sounds. Sourdough grunted in a somehow solid fashion. He and Sitka moved farther away from Nell to either side. They would cover a wider front.

There was no other sign of life than the shrillings of the incredibly tiny creatures which on this planet were birds, and Faro Nell's deep-bass, raging growls, and then the click of Roane's safety going off as he got ready to use the weapon Huyghens had given him.

Semper screamed again, flapping low above the treetops, following parti-colored, monstrous shapes beneath.

Eight blue-and-tan fiends came racing out of the under-brush. They had spiny fringes, and horns, and glaring eyes, and they looked as if they had come straight out of hell. On the instant of their appearance they leaped, emitting squalling, spitting squeals that were like the cries of fighting tomcats ten thousand times magnified. Huyghens' rifle cracked, and its sound was wiped out in the louder detonation of its bullet in sphexian flesh. A tan-and-blue monster tumbled over, shrieking. Faro Nell charged, the very impersonation of white-hot fury. Roane fired, and his bullet exploded against a tree. Sitka Pete brought his massive forepaws in a clapping, monstrous ear-boxing motion. A sphex died.

Then Roane fired again. Sourdough Charley whuffed. He fell forward upon a spitting bi-colored fiend, rolled him over, and raked with his hind claws. The belly-hide of the sphex was tenderer than the rest. The creature rolled away, snapping at its own wounds. Another sphex found itself shaken loose from the tumult about Sitka Pete. It whirled to leap on him from behind—and Huyghens fired very coldly—and two plunged upon Faro Nell and Roane blasted one and Faro Nell disposed of the other in truly awesome fury. Then Sitka Pete heaved himself erect—seeming to drip sphexes—and Sourdough waddled over and pulled one off and killed it and went back for another. And both rifles cracked together and there was suddenly nothing left to fight.

The bears prowled from one to another of the corpses. Sitka Pete rumbled and lifted up a limp head. Crash! Then another. He went over the lot, whether or not they showed signs of life. When he had finished, they were wholly still.

Semper came flapping down out of the sky. He had screamed and fluttered overhead as the fight went on. Now he landed with a rush. Huyghens went soothingly from one bear to another, calming them with his voice. It took longest to calm Faro Nell, licking Nugget with impassioned solicitude and growling horribly as she licked.

"Come along, now," said Huyghens, when Sitka showed signs of intending to sit down again. "Heave these carcasses over a cliff. Come along! Sitka! Sourdough! Hup!"

He guided them as the two big males somewhat fastidiously lifted up the nightmarish creatures they and the guns together had killed, and carried them to the edge of the spur of stone. They let the dead beasts go bouncing and sliding down into the valley.

"That," said Huyghens, "is so their little pals will gather

round them and caterwaul their woe where there's no trail
of ours to give them ideas. If we'd been near a river, I'd
have dumped them in to float downriver and gather mourn-
ers wherever they stranded. Around the station I incinerate
them. If I had to leave them, I'd make tracks away. About
fifty miles upwind would be a good idea."

He opened the pack Sourdough carried and extracted
giant-sized swabs and some gallons of antiseptic. He tended
the three Kodiaks in turn, swabbing not only the cuts and
scratches they'd received, but deeply soaking their fur where
there could be suspicion of spilled sphex blood.

"This antiseptic deodorizes, too," he told Roane. "Or
we'd be trailed by any sphex who passed to leeward of us.
When we start off, I'll swab the bears' paws for the same
reason."

Roane was very quiet. He'd missed his first shot with a
bullet-firing weapon—a beam hasn't the stopping-power of
an explosive bullet—but he'd seemed to grow savagely angry with himself. The last few seconds of the fight, he'd
fired very deliberately and every bullet hit. Now he said
bitterly:

"If you're instructing me so I can carry on should you be
killed, I doubt that it's worth while!"

Huyghens felt in his pack and unfolded the enlargements
he'd made of the space photos of this part of the planet. He
carefully oriented the map with distant landmarks. He drew
a painstakingly accurate line across the photo.

"The S O S signal comes from somewhere close to the
robot colony," he reported. "I think a little to the south of
it. Probably from a mine they'd opened up, on the far
side—of course—of the Sere Plateau. See how I've marked
this map? Two fixes, one from the station and one from
here. I came away off-course to get a fix here so we'd have
two position-lines to the transmitter. The signal could have
come from the other side of the planet. But it doesn't."

"The odds would be astronomical against other castaways,"
protested Roane.

"No-o-o-o," said Huyghens. "Ships have been coming
here. To the robot-colony. One could have crashed. And I
have friends, too."

He repacked his apparatus and gestured to the bears. He
led them beyond the scene of combat and very carefully
swabbed off their paws, so they could not possibly leave a

trail of sphex-blood scent behind them. He waved Semper, the eagle, aloft.

"Let's go," he told the Kodiaks. "Yonder! Hup!"

The party headed downhill and into the jungle again. Now it was Sourdough's turn to take the lead, and Sitka Pete prowled more widely behind him. Faro Nell trailed the men, with Nugget. She kept an extremely sharp eye upon the cub. He was a baby, still. He only weighed six hundred pounds. And of course she watched against danger from the rear.

Overhead, Semper fluttered and flew in giant circles and spirals, never going very far away. Huyghens referred constantly to the screen which showed what the air-borne camera saw. The image tilted and circled and banked and swayed. It was by no means the best air-reconnaissance that could be imagined. But it was the best that would work. Presently Huyghens said:

"We swing to the right, here. The going's bad straight ahead, and it looks like a pack of sphexes has killed and is feeding."

Roane was upset. He was dissatisfied with himself. So he said:

"It's against reason for carnivores to be as thick as you say! There has to be a certain amount of other animal life for every meat-eating beast! Too many of them would eat all the game and starve!"

"They're gone all winter," explained Huyghens, "which around here isn't as severe as you might think. And a good many animals seem to breed just after the sphexes go south. Also, the sphexes aren't around all the warm weather. There's a sort of peak, and then for a matter of weeks you won't see a one of them, and suddenly the jungle swarms with them again. Then, presently, they head south. Apparently they're migratory in some fashion, but nobody knows." He said dryly: "There haven't been many naturalists around on this planet. The animal life is inimical."

Roane fretted. He was a senior officer in the Colonial Survey, and he was accustomed to arrival at a partly or completely-finished colonial set-up, and to pass upon the completion or non-completion of the planned installation as designed. Now he was in an intolerably hostile environment, depending upon an illegal colonist for his life, engaged upon a demoralizingly indefinite enterprise—because the mechan-

ical spark-signal could be working long after its constructors
were dead—and his ideas about a number of matters were
shaken. He was alive, for example, because of three giant
Kodiak bears and a bald eagle. He and Huyghens could
have been surrounded by ten thousand robots, and they'd
have been killed. Sphexes and robots would have ignored
each other, and sphexes would have made straight for the
men, who'd have had less than four seconds in which to
discover for themselves that they were attacked, prepare to
defend themselves, and kill eight sphexes.

Roane's convictions as a civilized man were shaken. Robots were marvelous contrivances for doing the expected:
accomplishing the planned; coping with the predicted. But
they also had defects. Robots could only follow instructions—if
this thing happens, do this, if that thing happens do that.
But before something else, neither this nor that, robots
were helpless. So a robot civilization worked only in an
environment where nothing unanticipated ever turned up,
and human supervisors never demanded anything unexpected.
Roane was appalled. He'd never encountered the truly
unpredictable before in all his life and career.

He found Nugget, the cub, ambling uneasily in his wake.
The cub flattened his ears miserably when Roane glanced at
him. It occurred to the man that Nugget was receiving a lot
of disciplinary thumpings from Faro Nell. He was knocked
about physically, pretty much as Roane was being knocked
about psychologically. His lack of information and unfitness
for independent survival in this environment was being ham-
mered into him.

"Hi, Nugget," said Roane ruefully. "I feel just about the
way you do!"

Nugget brightened visibly. He frisked. He tended to gam-
bol. He looked very hopefully up into Roane's face—and he
stood four feet high at the shoulder and would overtop
Roane if he stood erect.

Roane reached out and patted Nugget's head. It was the
first time in all his life that he'd ever petted an animal.

He heard a snuffling sound behind him. Skin crawled at
the back of his neck. He whirled.

Faro Nell regarded him—eighteen hundred pounds of
she-bear only ten feet away and looking into his eyes. For
one panicky instant Roane went cold all over. Then he
realized that Faro Nell's eyes were not burning. She was not
snarling. She did not emit those blood-curdling sounds which

the bare prospect of danger to Nugget had produced up on the rocky spur. She looked at him blandly. In fact, after a moment she swung off on some independent investigation of a matter that had aroused her curiosity.

The traveling party went on, Nugget frisking beside Roane and tending to bump into him out of pure cub-clumsiness. Now and again he looked adoringly at Roane, in the instant and overwhelming affection of the very young.

Roane trudged on. Presently he glanced behind again. Faro Nell was now ranging more widely. She was well satisfied to have Nugget in the immediate care of a man. From time to time he got on her nerves.

A little while later, Roane called ahead.

"Huyghens! Look here! I've been appointed nursemaid to Nugget!" Huyghens looked back.

"Oh, slap him a few times and he'll go back to his mother."

"The devil I will!" said Roane querulously. "I like it!"

The traveling party went on.

When night fell, they camped. There could be no fire, of course, because all the minute night-things about would come eagerly to dance in the glow. But there could not be darkness, equally, because night-walkers hunted in the dark. So Huyghens set out the barrier lamps which made a wall of twilight about their halting place, and the staglike creature Faro Nell had carried became their evening meal. Then they slept—at least the men did—and the bears dozed and snorted and waked and dozed again. But Semper sat immobile with his head under his wing on a tree limb. And presently there was a glorious cool hush and all the world glowed in morning light diffused through the jungle by a newly risen sun. And they arose, and traveled again.

This day they stopped stock-still for two hours while sphexes puzzled over the trail the bears had left. Huyghens discoursed calmly on the need for an anti-scent, to be used on the boots of men and the paws of bears, which would make the following of their trails unpopular with sphexes. And Roane seized upon the idea and absorbedly suggested that a sphex-repellent odor might be worked out, which would make a human revolting to a sphex. If that were done—why— humans could go freely about unmolested.

"Like stink-bugs," said Huyghens, sardonically. "A very intelligent idea! Very rational! You can feel proud!"

And suddenly Roane, very obscurely, was not proud of
the idea at all.

They camped again. On the third night they were at the
base of that remarkable formation, the Sere Plateau, which
from a distance looked like a mountain-range but was actually a desert tableland. And it was not reasonable for a
desert to be raised high, while lowlands had rain, but on the
fourth morning they found out why. They saw, far, far
away, a truly monstrous mountain-mass at the end of the
long-way expanse of the plateau. It was like the prow of a
ship. It lay, so Huyghens observed, directly in line with the
prevailing winds, and divided them as a ship's prow divides
the waters. The moisture-bearing air-currents flowed beside
the plateau, not over it, and its interior was pure sere desert
in the unscreened sunshine of high altitudes.

It took them a full day to get halfway up the slope. And
here, twice as they climbed, Semper flew screaming over
aggregations of sphexes to one side of them or the other.
These were much larger groups than Huyghens had ever
seen before—fifty to a hundred monstrosities together, where
a dozen was a large hunting-pack elsewhere. He looked in
the screen which showed him what Semper saw, four to five
miles away. The sphexes padded uphill toward the Sere
Plateau in a long line. Fifty—sixty—seventy tan-and-azure
beasts out of hell.

"I'd hate to have that bunch jump us," he said candidly to
Roane. "I don't think we'd stand a chance."

"Here's where a robot tank would be useful," Roane
observed.

"Anything armored," conceded Huyghens. "One man in
an armored station like mine would be safe. But if he killed
a sphex he'd be besieged. He'd have to stay holed up,
breathing the smell of dead sphex, until the odor had gone
away. And he mustn't kill any others or he'd be besieged
until winter came."

Roane did not suggest the advantages of robots in other
directions. At that moment, for example, they were working
their way up a slope which averaged fifty degrees. The bears
climbed without effort despite their burdens. For the men it
was infinite toil. Semper, the eagle, manifested impatience
with bears and men alike, who crawled so slowly up an
incline over which he soared.

He went ahead up the mountainside and steered in the

air-currents at the plateau's edge. Huyghens looked in the visionplate by which he reported.

"How the devil," panted Roane—they had stopped for a breather, and the bears waited patiently for them—"do you train bears like these? I can understand Semper."

"I don't train them," said Huyghens, staring into the plate. "They're mutations. In heredity the sex-linkage of physical characteristics is standard stuff. But there's been some sound work done on the gene-linkage of psychological factors. There was need, on my home planet, for an animal who could fight like a fiend, live off the land, carry a pack and get along with men at least as well as dogs do. In the old days they'd have tried to breed the desired physical properties into an animal who already had the personality they wanted. Something like a giant dog, say. But back home they went at it the other way about. They picked the wanted physical characteristics and bred for the personality— the psychology. The job got done over a century ago—a Kodiak bear named Kodius Champion was the first real success. He had everything that was wanted. These bears are his descendants."

"They look normal," commented Roane.

"They are!" said Huyghens warmly. "Just as normal as an honest dog! They're not trained, like Semper. They train themselves!" He looked back into the plate in his hands, which showed the ground five and six and seven thousand feet higher. "Semper, now, is a trained bird without too much brains. He's educated—a glorified hawk. But the bears want to get along with men. They're emotionally dependent on us! Like dogs. Semper's a servant, but they're companions and friends. He's trained, but they're loyal. He's conditioned. They love us. He'd abandon me if he ever realized he could—he thinks he can only eat what men feed him. But the bears wouldn't want to. They like us. I admit that I like them. Maybe because they like me."

Roane said deliberately:

"Aren't you a trifle loose-tongued, Huyghens? I'm a Colonial Survey officer. I have to arrest you sooner or later. You've told me something that will locate and convict the people who set you up here. It shouldn't be hard to find where bears were bred for psychological mutations, and where a bear named Kodius Champion left descendants! I can find out where you came from now, Huyghens!"

Huyghens looked up from the plate with its tiny swaying

television image, relayed from where Semper floated impatiently in mid-air.

"No harm done," he said amiably. "I'm a criminal there,
too. It's officially on record that I kidnapped these bears
and escaped with them. Which, on my home planet, is
about as heinous a crime as a man can commit. It's worse
than horse-theft back on Earth in the old days. The kin and
cousins of my bears are highly thought of. I'm quite a
criminal, back home."

Roane stared.

"Did you steal them?" he demanded.

"Confidentially," said Huyghens, "no. But prove it!" Then
he said: "Take a look in this plate. See what Semper can see
up at the plateau's edge."

Roane squinted aloft, where the eagle flew in great sweeps
and dashes. Somehow, by the experience of the past few
days, Roane knew that Semper was screaming fiercely as he
flew. He made a dart toward the plateau's border.

Roane looked at the transmitter picture. It was only four
inches by six, but it was perfectly without grain and in
accurate color. It moved and turned as the camera-bearing
eagle swooped and circled. For an instant the screen showed
the steeply sloping mountainside, and off at one edge the
party of men and bears could be seen as dots. Then it swept
away and showed the top of the plateau.

There were sphexes. A pack of two hundred trotted toward
the desert interior. They moved at leisure, in the open. The
viewing camera reeled, and there were more. As Roane
watched and as the bird flew higher, he could see still other
sphexes moving up over the edge of the plateau from a
small erosion-defile here and another one there. The Sere
Plateau was alive with the hellish creatures. It was inconceivable that there should be game enough for them to live
on. They were visible as herds of cattle would be visible on
grazing planets.

It was simply impossible.

"Migrating," observed Huyghens. "I said they did. They're
headed somewhere. Do you know, I doubt that it would be
healthy for us to try to cross the plateau through such a
swarm of sphexes?"

Roane swore, in abrupt change of mood.

"But the signal's still coming through! Somebody's alive

over at the robot colony! Must we wait till the migration's over?"

"We don't know," Huyghens pointed out, "that they'll stay alive. They may need help badly. We have to get to them. But at the same time—"

He glanced at Sourdough Charley and Sitka Pete, clinging patiently to the mountainside while the men rested and talked. Sitka had managed to find a place to sit down, though one massive paw anchored him in his place.

Huyghens waved his arm, pointing in a new direction.

"Let's go!" he called briskly. "Let's go! Yonder! Hup!"

IV

They followed the slopes of the Sere Plateau, neither ascending to its level top—where sphexes congregated—nor descending into the foothills where sphexes assembled. They moved along hillsides and mountain-flanks which sloped anywhere from thirty to sixty degrees, and they did not cover much distance. They practically forgot what it was to walk on level ground. Semper, the eagle, hovered overhead during the daytime, not far away. He descended at nightfall for his food from the pack of one of the bears.

"The bears aren't doing too well for food," said Huyghens dryly. "A ton of bear needs a lot to eat. But they're loyal to us. Semper hasn't any loyalty. He's too stupid. But he's been conditioned to think that he can only eat what men feed him. The bears know better, but they stick to us regardless. I rather like these bears."

It was the most self-evident of understatements. This was at an encampment on the top of a massive boulder which projected from a mountainous stony wall. This was six days from the start of their journey. There was barely room on the boulder for all the party. And Faro Nell fussily insisted that Nugget should be in the safest part, which meant near the mountain-flank. She would have crowded the men outward, but Nugget whimpered for Roane. Wherefore, when Roane moved to comfort him, Faro Nell contentedly drew back and snorted at Sitka and Sourdough and they made room for her near the edge.

It was a hungry camp. They had come upon tiny rills upon occasion, flowing down the mountain side. Here the bears had drunk deeply and the men had filled canteens. But this was the third night, and there had been no game at all.

Huyghens made no move to bring out food for Roane or himself. Roane made no comment. He was beginning to participate in the relationship between bears and men, which was not the slavery of the bears but something more. It was two-way. He felt it.

"It would seem," he said fretfully, "that since the sphexes don't seem to hunt on their way uphill, that there should be some game. They ignore everything as they file uphill."

This was true enough. The normal fighting formation of sphexes was line abreast, which automatically surrounded anything which offered to flee and outflanked anything which offered fight. But here they ascended the mountain in long lines, one after the other, following apparently long-established trails. The wind blew along the slopes and carried scent only sidewise. But the sphexes were not diverted from their chosen paths. The long processions of hideous blue-and-tawny creatures—it was hard to think of them as natural beasts, male and female and laying eggs like reptiles on other planets—simply climbed.

"There've been other thousands of beasts before them," said Huyghens. "They must have been crowding this way for days or even weeks. We've seen tens of thousands in Semper's camera. They must be uncountable, altogether. The first-comers ate all the game there was, and the last-comers have something else on whatever they use for minds."

Roane protested: "But so many carnivores in one place is impossible! I know they are here, but they can't be!"

"They're cold-blooded," Huyghens pointed out. "They don't burn food to sustain body-temperature. After all, lots of creatures go for long periods without eating. Even bears hibernate. But this isn't hibernation—or estivation, either."

He was setting up the radiation-wave receiver in the darkness. There was no point in attempting a fix here. The transmitter was on the other side of the Sere Plateau, which inexplicably swarmed with the most ferocious and deadly of all the creatures of Loren Two. The men and bears would commit suicide by crossing here.

But Huyghens turned on the receiver. There came the whispering, scratchy sound of background-noise. Then the signal. Three dots, three dashes, three dots. It went on and on and on. Huyghens turned it off. Roane said:

"Shouldn't we have answered that signal before we left the station? To encourage them?"

"I doubt they have a receiver," said Huyghens. "They

won't expect an answer for months, anyhow. They'd hardly listen all the time, and if they're living in a mine-tunnel and trying to sneak out for food to stretch their supplies—why, they'll be too busy to try to make complicated recorders or relays."

Roane was silent for a moment or two.

"We've got to get food for the bears," he said presently. "Nugget's weaned, and he's hungry."

"We will," Huyghens promised. "I may be wrong, but it seems to me that the number of sphexes climbing the mountain is less than yesterday and the day before. We may have just about crossed the path of their migration. They're thinning out. When we're past their trail, we'll have to look out for night-walkers and the like again. But I think they wiped out all animal life on their migration-route."

He was not quite right. He was waked in darkness by the sound of slappings and the grunting of bears. Feather-light puffs of breeze beat upon his face. He struck his belt-lamp sharply and the world was hidden by a whitish film which snatched itself away. Something flapped. Then he saw the stars and the emptiness on the edge of which they camped. Then big white things flapped toward him.

Sitka Pete whuffed mightily and swatted. Faro Nell grunted and swung. She caught something in her claws. She crunched. The light went off as Huyghens realized. Then he said:

"Don't shoot, Roane!" He listened, and heard the sounds of feeding in the dark. It ended. "Watch this!" said Huyghens.

The belt-light came on again. Something strangely-shaped and pallid like human skin reeled and flapped crazily toward him. Something else. Four. Five—ten—twenty—more . . .

A huge hairy paw reached up into the light-beam and snatched a flying thing out of it. Another great paw. Huyghens shifted the light and the three great Kodiaks were on their hind legs, swatting at creatures which flittered insanely, unable to resist the fascination of the glaring lamp. Because of their wild gyrations it was impossible to see them in detail, but they were those unpleasant night-creatures which looked like plucked flying monkeys but were actually something quite different.

The bears did not snarl or snap. They swatted, with a remarkable air of businesslike competence and purpose. Small mounds of broken things built up about their feet.

Suddenly there were no more. Huyghens snapped off the light. The bears crunched and fed busily in the darkness.

"Those things are carnivores *and* blood-suckers, Roane,"
said Huyghens calmly. "They drain their victims of blood
like vampire bats—they've some trick of not waking them—
and when they're dead the whole tribe eats. But bears have
thick furs, and they wake when they're touched. And they're
omnivorous—they'll eat anything but sphexes, and like it.
You might say that those night-creatures came to lunch. But
they stayed. They are it—for the bears, who are living off
the country as usual."

Roane uttered a sudden exclamation. He made a tiny
light, and blood flowed down his hand. Huyghens passed
over his pocket kit of antiseptic and bandages. Roane
staunched the bleeding and bound up his hand. Then he
realized that Nugget chewed on something. When he turned
the light, Nugget swallowed convulsively. It appeared that
he had caught and devoured the creature which had drawn
blood from Roane. But Roane had lost none to speak of, at
that.

In the morning they started along the sloping scarp of the
plateau once more. During the morning, Roane said painfully:

"Robots wouldn't have handled those vampire-things,
Huyghens."

"Oh, they could be built to watch for them," said
Huyghens, tolerantly. "But you'd have to swat for yourself.
I prefer the bears."

He led the way on. Here their jungle-formation could not
apply. On a steep slope the bears ambled comfortably, the
tough pads of their feet holding fast on the slanting rock,
but the men struggled painfully. Twice Huyghens halted to
examine the ground about the mountains' bases through
binoculars. He looked encouraged as they went on. The
monstrous peak which was like the bow of a ship at the end
of the Sere Plateau was visibly nearer. Toward midday,
indeed, it looked high above the horizon, no more than
fifteen miles away. And at midday Huyghens called a final
halt.

"No more congregations of sphexes down below," he said
cheerfully, "and we haven't seen a climbing line of them in
miles." The crossing of a sphex-trail meant simply waiting
until one party had passed, and then crossing before another
came in view. "I've a hunch we've crossed their migration-
route. Let's see what Semper tells us!"

He waved the eagle aloft. And Semper, like all creatures
other than men, normally functioned only for the satisfac-

tion of his appetite, and then tended to loaf or sleep. He had ridden the last few miles perched on Sitka Pete's pack. Now he soared upward and Huyghens watched in the small vision-plate.

Semper went soaring—and the image on the plate swayed and turned and turned—and in minutes was above the plateau's edge. And here there was some vegetation and the ground rolled somewhat, and there were even patches of brush. But as Semper towered higher still, the inner desert appeared. But nearby it was clear of beasts. Only once, when the eagle banked sharply and the camera looked along the long dimension of the plateau, did Huyghens see any sign of the blue-and-tan beasts. There he saw what looked like masses amounting to herds. But, of course, carnivores do not gather in herds.

"We go straight up," said Huyghens in satisfaction. "We cross the plateau here—and we can edge downwind a bit, even. I think we'll find something interesting on our way to your robot colony."

He waved to the bears to go ahead uphill.

They reached the top hours later—barely before sunset. And they saw game. Not much, but game at the grassy, brushy border of the desert. Huyghens brought down a shaggy ruminant which surely would not live on a desert. When night fell there was an abrupt chill in the air. It was much colder than night-temperatures on the slopes. The air was thin. Roane thought confusedly and presently guessed at the cause. In the lee of the prow-mountain the air was calm. There were no clouds. The ground radiated its heat to empty space. It could be bitterly cold in the nighttime, here.

"And hot by day," Huyghens agreed when he mentioned it. "The sunshine's terrifically hot where the air is thin, but on most mountains there's wind. By day, here, the ground will tend to heat up like the surface of a planet without atmosphere. It may be a hundred and forty or fifty degrees on the sand at midday. But it should be cold at night."

It was. Before midnight Huyghens built a fire. There could be no danger of night-walkers when the temperature dropped to freezing.

In the morning the men were stiff with cold, but the bears snorted and moved about briskly. They seemed to revel in the morning chill. Sitka and Sourdough Charley, in fact, became festive and engaged in a mock fight, whacking each other with blows that were only feigned, but would have crushed in the skull of any man. Nugget sneezed with excitement as he watched them. Faro Nell regarded them with female disapproval.

They went on. Semper seemed sluggish. After a single brief flight he descended and rode on Sitka's pack, as on the previous day. He perched there, surveying the landscape as it changed from semi-arid to pure desert in their progress. His air was arrogant. But he would not fly. Soaring birds do not like to fly when there are no winds to make currents of which to take advantage. On the way, Huyghens painstakingly pointed out to Roane exactly where they were on the enlarged photograph taken from space, and the exact spot from which the distress-signal seemed to come.

"You're doing it in case something happens to you," said Roane. "I admit it's sense, but—what could I do to help those survivors even if I got to them, without you?"

"What you've learned about sphexes would help," said Huyghens. "The bears would help. And we left a note back at my station. Whoever grounds at the landing field back there—and the beacon's working again—will find instructions to come to the place we're trying to reach."

Roane plodded alongside him. The narrow non-desert border of the Sere Plateau was behind them, now. They marched across powdery desert sand.

"See here," said Roane. "I want to know something! You tell me you're listed as a bear-thief on your home planet. You tell me it's a lie—to protect your friends from prosecution by the Colonial Survey. You're on your own, risking your life every minute of every day. You took a risk in not shooting me. Now you're risking more in going to help men who'd have to be witnesses that you were a criminal. What are you doing it for?"

Huyghens grinned.

"Because I don't like robots. I don't like the fact that they're subduing men—making men subordinate to them."

"Go on," insisted Roane. "I don't see why disliking robots should make you a criminal. Nor men subordinating themselves to robots, either!"

"But they are," said Huyghens mildly. "I'm a crank, of course. But—I live like a man on this planet. I go where I please and do what I please. My helpers, the bears, are my friends. If the robot colony had been a success, would the humans in it have lived like men? Hardly! They'd have to live the way the robots let them! They'd have to stay inside a fence the robots built. They'd have to eat foods that robots could raise, and no others. Why—a man couldn't move his bed near a window, because if he did the house-tending robots couldn't work! Robots would serve them—the way the robots determined—but all they'd get out of it would be jobs servicing the robots!"

Roane shook his head.

"As long as men want robot service, they have to take the service that robots can give. If you don't want those services—"

"I want to decide what I want," said Huyghens, again mildly, "instead of being limited to choose among what I'm offered. On my home planet we halfway tamed it with dogs and guns. Then we developed the bears, and we finished the job with them. Now there's population-pressure and the room for bears and dogs—and men—is dwindling. More and more people are being deprived of the power of decision, and being allowed only the power of choice among the things robots allow. The more we depend on robots, the more limited those choices become. We don't want our children to limit themselves to wanting what robots can provide! We don't want them shriveling to where they abandon everything robots can't give—or won't! We want them to be men—and women. Not damned automations who live *by* pushing robot-controls so they can live *to* push robot-controls. If that's not subordination to robots—"

"It's an emotional argument," protested Roane. "Not everybody feels that way."

"But I feel that way," said Huyghens. "And so do a lot of others. This is a big galaxy and it's apt to contain some surprises. The one sure thing about a robot and a man who depends on them is that they can't handle the unexpected. There's going to come a time when we need men who can. So on my home planet, some of us asked for Loren Two, to colonize. It was refused—too dangerous. But men can colonize anywhere if they're men. So I came here to study the planet. Especially the sphexes. Eventually, we expected to ask for a license again, with proof that we could handle even those beasts. I'm already doing it in a mild way. But the Survey licensed a robot colony—and where is it?"

Roane made a sour face.

"You picked the wrong way to go about it, Huyghens. It was illegal. It is. It was the pioneer spirit, which is admirable enough, but wrongly directed. After all, it was pioneers who left Earth for the stars. But—"

Sourdough raised up on his hind legs and sniffed the air. Huyghens swung his rifle around to be handy. Roane slipped off the safety-catch of his own. Nothing happened.

"In a way," said Roane vexedly, "you're talking about liberty and freedom, which most people think is politics. You say it can be more. In principle, I'll concede it. But the way you put it, it sounds like a freak religion."

"It's self-respect," corrected Huyghens.

"You may be—"

Faro Nell growled. She bumped Nugget with her nose, to drive him closer to Roane. She snorted at him. She trotted swiftly to where Sitka and Sourdough faced toward the broader, sphex-filled expanse of the Sere Plateau. She took up her position between them.

Huyghens gazed sharply beyond them and then all about.

"This could be bad!" he said softly. "But luckily there's no wind. Here's a sort of hill. Come along, Roane!"

He ran ahead, Roane following and Nugget plumping heavily with him. They reached the raised place—actually a mere hillock no more than five or six feet above the surrounding sand, with a distorted cactus-like growth protruding from the ground. Huyghens stared again. He used his binoculars.

"One sphex," he said curtly. "Just one! And it's out of all reason for a sphex to be alone! But it's not rational for them to gather in hundreds of thousands, either!" He wetted his finger and held it up. "No wind at all."

He used the binoculars again.

"It doesn't know we're here," he added. "It's moving away. Not another one in sight—" He hesitated, biting his lips. "Look here, Roane! I'd like to kill that one lone sphex and find out something. There's a fifty per cent chance I could find out something really important. But—I might have to run. If I'm right—" Then he said grimly, "It'll have to be done quickly. I'm going to ride Faro Nell—for speed. I doubt Sitka or Sourdough would stay behind. But Nugget can't run fast enough. Will you stay here with him?"

Roane drew in his breath. Then he said calmly:

"You know what you're doing. Of course."

"Keep your eyes open. If you see anything, even at a distance, shoot and we'll be back—fast! Don't wait until something's close enough to hit. Shoot the instant you see anything—if you do!"

Roane nodded. He found it peculiarly difficult to speak again. Huyghens went over to the enbattled bears. He climbed up on Faro Nell's back, holding fast by her shaggy fur.

"Let's go!" he snapped. "That way! Hup!"

The three Kodiaks plunged away at a dead run, Huyghens lurching and swaying on Faro Nell's back. The sudden rush dislodged Semper from his perch. He flapped wildly and got aloft. Then he followed effortlessly, flying low.

It happened very quickly. A Kodiak bear can travel as fast as a race horse on occasion. These three plunged arrow-straight for a spot perhaps half a mile distant, where a blue-and-tawny shape whirled to face them. There was the crash of Huyghens' weapon from where he rode on Faro Nell's back—the explosion of the weapon and the bullet was one sound. The somehow unnatural spiky monster leaped and died.

Huyghens jumped down from Faro Nell. He became feverishly busy at something on the ground—where the particolored sphex had fallen. Semper banked and whirled and came down to the ground. He watched, with his head on one side.

Roane stared, from a distance. Huyghens was doing something to the dead sphex. The two male bears prowled about. Faro Nell regarded Huyghens with intense curiosity. Back at the hillock, Nugget whimpered a little. Roane patted him roughly. Nugget whimpered more loudly. In the distance, Huyghens straightened up and took three steps toward Faro Nell. He mounted. Sitka turned his head back toward Roane. He seemed to see or sniff something dubious. He reared upward. He made a noise, apparently, because Sourdough ambled to his side. The two great beasts began to trot back. Semper flapped wildly and—lacking wind—lurched crazily in the air. He landed on Huyghens' shoulder and his talons clung there.

Then Nugget howled hysterically and tried to swarm up Roane, as a cub tries to swarm up the nearest tree in time of danger. Roane collapsed, and the cub upon him—and there was a flash of stinking scaly hide, while the air was filled with the snarling, spitting squeals of a sphex in full leap. The beast had overjumped, aiming at Roane and the cub while both were upright and arriving when they had fallen. It went tumbling.

Roane heard nothing but the fiendish squalling, but in the distance Sitka and Sourdough were coming at rocketship speed. Faro Nell let out a roar and fairly split the air. And then there was a furry cub streaking toward her, bawling, while Roane rolled to his feet and snatched up his gun. He raged through pure instinct. The sphex crouched to pursue the cub and Roane swung his weapon as a club. He was literally too close to shoot—and perhaps the sphex had only seen the fleeing bear-cub. But he swung furiously.

And the sphex whirled. Roane was toppled from his feet. An eight-hundred-pound monstrosity straight out of hell— half wildcat and half spitting cobra with hydrophobia and homicidal mania added—such a monstrosity is not to be withstood when in whirling its body strikes one in the chest.

That was when Sitka arrived, bellowing. He stood on his hind legs, emitting roars like thunder, challenging the sphex to battle. He waddled forward. Huyghens arrived, but he could not shoot with Roane in the sphere of an explosive bullet's destructiveness. Faro Nell raged and snarled, torn between the urge to be sure that Nugget was unharmed, and the frenzied fury of a mother whose offspring has been endangered.

Mounted on Faro Nell, with Semper clinging idiotically to his shoulder, Huyghens watched helplessly as the sphex spat and squalled at Sitka, having only to reach out one claw to let out Roane's life.

V

They got away from there, though Sitka seemed to want to lift the limp carcass of his victim in his teeth and dash it repeatedly to the ground. He seemed doubly raging because a man—with whom all Kodius Champion's descendants had an emotional relationship—had been mishandled. But Roane was not grievously hurt. He bounced and swore as the bears raced for the horizon. Huyghens had flung him up on Sourdough's pack and snapped for him to hold on. He bumped and chattered furiously:

"Dammit, Huyghens! This isn't right! Sitka got some deep scratches! That horror's claws may be poisonous!"

But Huyghens snapped, "Hup! Hup!" to the bears, and they continued their race against time. They went on for a good two miles, when Nugget wailed despairingly of his exhaustion and Faro Nell halted firmly to nuzzle him.

"This may be good enough," said Huyghens. "Considering that there's no wind and the big mass of beasts is down the plateau and there were only those two around here. Maybe they're too busy to hold a wake, even! Anyhow—"

He slid to the ground and extracted the antiseptic and swabs.

"Sitka first," snapped Roane. "I'm all right!"

Huyghens swabbed the big bear's wounds. They were trivial, because Sitka Pete was an experienced sphex-fighter. Then Roane grudgingly let the curiously-smelling stuff—it reeked of ozone—be applied to the slashes on his chest. He held his breath as it stung. Then he said dourly:

"It was my fault, Huyghens. I watched you instead of the landscape. I couldn't imagine what you were doing."

"I was doing a quick dissection," Huyghens told him. "By luck, that first sphex was a female, as I hoped. And she was just about to lay her eggs. Ugh! And now I know why the sphexes migrate, and where, and how it is that they don't need game up here."

He slapped a quick bandage on Roane. He led the way eastward, still putting distance between the dead sphexes and his party. It was a crisp walk, only, but Semper flapped indignantly overhead, angry that he was not permitted to ride again.

"I'd dissected them before," said Huyghens. "Not enough's been known about them. Some things needed to be found out if men were ever to be able to live here."

"With bears?" asked Roane ironically.

"Oh, yes," said Huyghens. "But the point is that sphexes come to the desert here to breed—to mate and lay their eggs for the sun to hatch. It's a particular place. Seals return to a special place to mate—and the males at least don't eat for weeks on end. Salmon return to their native streams to spawn. They don't eat, and they die afterward. And eels—I'm using Earth examples, Roane—travel some thousands of miles to the Sargasso to mate and die. Unfortunately, sphexes don't appear to die, but it's clear that they have an ancestral breeding place and that they come here to the Sere Plateau to deposit their eggs!"

Roane plodded onward. He was angry: angry with himself because he hadn't taken elementary precautions; because he'd felt too safe, as a man in a robot-served civilization forms the habit of doing; because he hadn't used his brain when Nugget whimpered, in even a bear-cub's awareness that danger was near.

"And now," Huyghens added, "I need some equipment that the robot colony had. With it, I think we can make a start toward making this a planet that men can live like men on!"

Roane blinked.

"What's that?"

"Equipment," said Huyghens impatiently. "It'll be at the robot colony. Robots were useless because they wouldn't pay attention to sphexes. They'd still be. But take out the robot controls and the machines will do! They shouldn't be ruined by a few months' exposure to weather!"

Roane marched on and on. Presently he said:

"I never thought you'd want anything that came from that colony, Huyghens!"

"Why not?" demanded Huyghens impatiently. "When men make machines do what they want, that's all right. Even robots—when they're where they belong. But men will have to handle flame-casters in the job I want them for. There have to be some, because there was a hundred-mile clearing to be burned off. And Earth-sterilizers—intended to kill the seeds of any plants that robots couldn't handle. We'll come back up here, Roane, and at the least we'll destroy the spawn of these infernal beasts! If we can't do more than that—just doing that every year will wipe out the race in time. There are probably other hordes than this, with other breeding places. But we'll find them, too. We'll make this planet into a place where men from my world can come— and still be men!"

Roane said sardonically:

"It was sphexes that beat the robots. Are you sure you aren't planning to make this world safe for robots?"

Huyghens laughed shortly.

"You've only seen one night-walker," he said. "And how about those things on the mountain-slope—which would have drained you of blood and then feasted? Would you care to wander about this planet with only a robot body-guard, Roane? Hardly! Men can't live on this planet with only robots to help them—and stop them from being fully men! You'll see!"

*   *   *

They found the colony after only ten days more of travel and after many sphexes and more than a few staglike creatures and shaggy ruminants had fallen to their weapons and the bears. But first they found the survivors of the colony.

There we.e three of them, hard-bitten and bearded and deeply embittered. When the electrified fence went down, two of them were away at a mine-tunnel, installing a new control-panel for the robots who worked in it. The third was in charge of the mining operation. They were alarmed by the stopping of communication with the colony and went back in a tank-truck to find out what had happened, and only the fact that they were unarmed saved them. They found sphexes prowling and caterwauling about the fallen colony, in numbers they still did not wholly believe. And the sphexes smelled men inside the armored vehicle, but couldn't break in. In turn, the men couldn't kill them, or they'd have been trailed to the mine and besieged there for as long as they could kill an occasional monster.

The survivors stopped all mining—of course—and tried to use remote-controlled robots for revenge and to get supplies for them. Their mining-robots were not designed for either task. And they had no weapons. They improvised miniature throwers of burning rocket-fuel, and they sent occasional prowling sphexes away screaming with scorched hides. But this was useful only because it did not kill the beasts. And it cost fuel. In the end they barricaded themselves and used the fuel only to keep a spark-signal going against the day when another ship came to seek the colony. They stayed in the mine as in a prison, on short rations, waiting without real hope. For diversion they could only contemplate the mining-robots they could not spare fuel to run and which could not do anything but mine.

When Huyghens and Roane reached them, they wept. They hated robots and all things robotic only a little less than they hated sphexes. But Huyghens explained, and armed them with weapons from the packs of the bears, and they marched to the dead colony with the male Kodiaks as point and advance-guard, and with Faro Nell bringing up the rear. They killed sixteen sphexes on the way. In the now overgrown clearing there were four more. In the shelters of the colony they found only foulness and the fragments of what had been men. But there was some food—not much, because the sphexes clawed at anything that smelled of men, and had ruined the plastic packets of radiation-sterilized

food. But there were some supplies in metal containers
which were not destroyed.

And there was fuel, which men could dispense when they
got to the control-panels of the equipment. There were
robots everywhere, bright and shining and ready for operation, but immobile, with plants growing up around and over
them.

They ignored those robots. But lustfully they fueled tracked
flame-casters—adapting them to human rather than robot
operation—and the giant soil-sterilizer which had been built
to destroy vegetation that robots could not be made to weed
out or cultivate. And they headed back for the Sere Plateau,
burning-eyed and filled with hate.

But Nugget became a badly spoiled bear-cub, because the
freed men approved passionately of anything that would
even grow up to kill sphexes. They petted him to excess,
when they camped.

And they reached the plateau by a sphex-trail to the top.
And Semper scouted for sphexes, and the giant Kodiaks
disturbed them and the sphexes came squalling and spitting
to destroy them—and while Roane and Huyghens fired steadily, the great machines swept up with their special weapons.
The Earth-sterilizer, it was found, was deadly against animal
life as well as seeds, when its diathermic beam was raised
and aimed. But it had to be handled by a man. No robot
could decide just when it was to be used, and against what
target.

Presently the bears were not needed, because the scorched
corpses of sphexes drew live ones from all parts of the
plateau even in the absence of noticeable breezes. The
official business of the sphexes was presumably finished, but
they came to caterwaul and seek vengeance—which they did
not find. Presently the survivors of the robot colony drove
machines—as men needed to do, here—in great circles around
the hugest heap of slaughtered fiends, destroying new arrivals as they came. It was such a killing as men had never
before made on any planet, but there would not be many
left of the sphex-horde which had bred in this particular
patch of desert. There might be other hordes elsewhere, and
other breeding places, but the normal territory of this mass
of monsters would see few of them this year.

Or next year, either. Because the soil-sterilizer would go
over the dug-up sand where the sphex-spawn lay hidden for
the sun to hatch. And the sun would never hatch them.

But Huyghens and Roane, by that time, were camped on the edge of the plateau with the Kodiaks. They were technically upwind from the scene of slaughter—and somehow it seemed more befitting for the men of the robot colony to conduct it. After all, it was those men whose companions had been killed.

There came an evening when Huyghens amiably cuffed Nugget away from where he sniffed too urgently at a stag-steak cooking on the campfire. Nugget ambled dolefully behind the protecting form of Roane and sniveled.

"Huyghens," said Roane painfully, "we've got to come to a settlement of our affairs. I'm a Colonial Survey officer. You're an illegal colonist. It's my duty to arrest you."

Huyghens regarded him with interest.

"Will you offer me lenience if I tell on my confederates," he asked mildly, "or may I plead that I can't be forced to testify against myself?"

Roane said vexedly:

"It's irritating! I've been an honest man all my life, but—I don't believe in robots as I did, except in their place. And their place isn't here. Not as the robot colony was planned, anyhow. The sphexes are nearly wiped out, but they won't be extinct and robots can't handle them. Bears and men will have to live here or—the people who do will have to spend their lives behind sphex-proof fences, accepting only what robots can give them. And there's much too much on this planet for people to miss it! To live in a robot-managed controlled environment on a planet like Loren Two wouldn't . . . it wouldn't be self-respecting!"

"You wouldn't be getting religious, would you?" asked Huyghens dryly. "That was your term for self-respect before."

Semper, the eagle, squawked indignantly as Sitka Pete almost stepped on him, approaching the fire. Sitka Pete sniffed, and Huyghens spoke to him sharply, and he sat down with a thump. He remained sitting in an untidy lump, looking at the steak and drooling.

"You don't let me finish!" protested Roane querulously. "I'm a Colonial Survey officer, and it's my job to pass on the work that's done on a planet before any but the first-landed colonists may come there to live. And of course to see that specifications are followed. Now—the robot colony I was sent to survey was practically destroyed. As designed, it wouldn't work. It couldn't survive."

Huyghens grunted. Night was falling. He turned the meat over the fire.

"Now, in emergencies," said Roane carefully, "colonists have the right to call on any passing ship for aid. Naturally! So— I've always been an honest man before, Huyghens—my report will be that the colony as designed was impractical, and that it was overwhelmed and destroyed except for three survivors who holed up and signaled for help. They did, you know!"

"Go on," grunted Huyghens.

"So," said Roane querulously, "it just happened—just happened, mind you—that a ship with you and Sitka and Sourdough and Faro Nell on board—and Nugget and Semper, too, of course—picked up the distress-call. So you landed to help the colonists. And you did. That's the story. Therefore it isn't illegal for you to be here. It was only illegal for you to be here when you were needed. But we'll pretend you weren't."

Huyghens glanced over his shoulder in the deepening night. He said calmly:

"I shouldn't believe that if I told it myself. Do you think the Survey will?"

"They're not fools," said Roane tartly. "Of course they won't! But when my report says that because of this unlikely series of events it is practical to colonize the planet, whereas before it wasn't—and when my report proves that a robot colony alone is stark nonsense, but that with bears and men from your world added, so many thousand colonists can be received per year— And when that much is true, anyhow—"

Huyghens seemed to shake a little as a dark silhouette against the flames. A little way off, Sourdough sniffed the air hopefully. With a bright light like the fire, presently naked-looking flying things might appear to be slapped down out of the air. They were succulent—to a bear.

"My reports carry weight," insisted Roane. "The deal will be offered, anyhow! The robot colony organizers will have to agree or they'll have to hold up. It's true! And your people can hold them up for nearly what terms they choose."

Huyghens' shaking became understandable. It was laughter.

"You're a lousy liar, Roane," he said, chuckling. "Isn't it unintelligent and unreasonable and irrational to throw away a lifetime of honesty just to get me out of a jam? You're not acting like a rational animal, Roane. But I thought you wouldn't, when it came to the point."

Roane squirmed.

"That's the only solution I can think of. But it'll work."

"I accept it," said Huyghens, grinning. "With thanks. If only because it means another few generations of men living like men on a planet that is going to take a lot of taming. And—if you want to know—because it keeps Sourdough and Sitka and Nell and Nugget from being killed because I brought them here illegally."

Something pressed hard against Roane. Nugget, the cub, pushed urgently against him in his desire to get closer to the fragrantly cooking meat. He edged forward. Roane toppled from where he squatted on the ground. He sprawled. Nugget sniffed luxuriously.

"Slap him," said Huyghens. "He'll move back."

"I won't!" said Roane indignantly from where he lay. "I won't do it! He's my friend!"

ALL THE WAY BACK

BY MICHAEL SHAARA

Great were the Antha, so reads the One Book of
history, greater perhaps than any of the Galactic Peoples, and they were brilliant and fair, and their reign
was long, and in all things they were great and proud,
even in the manner of their dying—
Preface to Loab: History of the Master Race.

The huge red ball of a sun hung glowing upon the screen.

Jansen adjusted the traversing knob, his face tensed and
weary. The sun swung off the screen to the right, was
replaced by the live black of space and the million speckled
lights of the farther stars. A moment later the sun glided
silently back across the screen and went off at the left.
Again there was nothing but space and the stars.

'Try it again?' Cohn asked.

Jansen mumbled: 'No. No use,' and he swore heavily.
'Nothing. Always nothing. Never a blessed thing.'

Cohn repressed a sigh, began to adjust the controls.

In both of their minds was the single, bitter thought that
there would be only one more time, and then they would go
home. And it was a long way to come to go home with
nothing.

When the controls were set there was nothing left to do.
The two men walked slowly aft to the freeze room. Climbing up painfully on to the flat steel of the beds, they lay
back and waited for the mechanism to function, for the
freeze to begin.

Turned in her course, the spaceship bore off into the open

332

emptiness. Her ports were thrown open, she was gathering speed as she moved away from the huge red star.

The object was sighted upon the last leg of the patrol, as the huge ship of the Galactic Scouts came across the edge of the Great Desert of the Rim, swinging wide in a long slow curve. It was there on the massometer as a faint *blip*, and, of course, the word went directly to Roymer.

'Report,' he said briefly, and Lieutenant Goladan—a young and somewhat pompous Higiandrian—gave the Higiandrian equivalent of a cough and then reported.

'Observe,' said Lieutenant Goladan, 'that it is not a meteor, for the speed of it is much too great.'

Roymer nodded patiently.

'And again, the speed is decreasing'—Goladan consulted his figures—'at the rate of twenty-four dines per segment. Since the orbit appears to bear directly upon the star Mina, and the decrease in speed is of a certain arbitrary origin, we must conclude that the object is a spaceship.'

Roymer smiled.

'Very good, lieutenant.' Like a tiny nova, Goladan began to glow and expand.

A good man, thought Roymer tolerantly, his is a race of good men. They have been two million years in achieving space flight; a certain adolescence is to be expected.

'Would you call Mind-Search, please?' Roymer asked.

Goladan sped away, to return almost immediately with the heavy-headed non-human Trian, chief of the Mind-Search Section.

Trian cocked an eyelike thing at Roymer, with grave inquiry.

'Yes, commander?'

The abrupt change in course was noticeable only on the viewplate, as the stars slid silently by. The patrol vessel veered off, swinging around and into the desert, settled into a parallel course with the strange new craft, keeping a discreet distance of—approximately—a light-year.

The scanners brought the object into immediate focus, and Goladan grinned with pleasure. A spaceship, yes, Alien, too. Undoubtedly a primitive race. He voiced these thoughts to Roymer.

'Yes,' the commander said, staring at the strange, small, projectilelike craft. 'Primitive type. It is to be wondered what they are doing in the desert.'

Goladan assumed an expression of intense curiosity.

'Trian,' said Roymer pleasantly, 'would you contact?'

The huge head bobbed up and down once and then stared into the screen. There was a moment of profound silence. Then Trian turned back to stare at Roymer, and there was a distinctly human expression of surprise in his eyelike things.

'Nothing,' came the thought. 'I can detect no presence at all.'

Roymer raised an eyebrow.

'Is there a barrier?'

'No'—Trian had turned to gaze back into the screen—'a barrier I could detect. But there is nothing at all. There is no sentient activity on board that vessel.'

Trian's word had to be taken, of course, and Roymer was disappointed. A spaceship empty of life—Roymer shrugged. A derelict, then. But why the decreasing speed? Pre-set controls would account for that, of course, but why? Certainly, if one abandoned a ship, one would not arrange for it to—

He was interrupted by Trian's thought:

'Excuse me, but there is nothing. May I return to my quarters?'

Roymer nodded and thanked him, and Trian went ponderously away. Goladan said:

'Shall we prepare to board it, sir?'

'Yes.'

And then Goladan was gone to give his proud orders.

Roymer continued to stare at the primitive vessel which hung on the plate. Curious. It was very interesting, always, to come upon derelict ships. The stories that were old, the silent tombs that had been drifting perhaps, for millions of years in the deep sea of space. In the beginning Roymer had hoped that the ship would be manned, and alien, but—nowadays, contact with an isolated race was rare, extremely rare. It was not to be hoped for, and he would be content with this, this undoubtedly empty, ancient ship.

And then, to Roymer's complete surprise, the ship at which he was staring shifted abruptly, turned on its axis, and flashed off like a live thing upon a new course.

When the defrosters activated and woke him up, Jansen lay for a while upon the steel table, blinking. As always with the freeze, it was difficult to tell at first whether anything had actually happened. It was like a quick blink and no more, and then you were lying, feeling exactly the same, thinking the same thoughts even, and if there was anything at all different it was maybe that you were a little numb. And yet in the blink time took a great leap, and the months went by like—Jansen smiled—like fenceposts.

He raised a languid eye to the red bulb in the ceiling. Out. He sighed. The freeze had come and gone. He felt vaguely cheated, reflected that this time, before the freeze, he would take a little nap.

He climbed down from the table, noted that Cohn had already gone to the control room. He adjusted himself to the thought that they were approaching a new sun, and it came back to him suddenly that this would be the last one, now they would go home.

Well then, let this one have planets. To have come all this way, to have been gone from home for eleven years, and yet to find nothing—

He was jerked out of the old feeling of despair by a lurch of the ship. That would be Cohn taking her off the auto. And now, he thought, we will go in and run out the telescope and have a look, and there won't be a thing.

Wearily, he clumped off over the iron deck, going up to the control room. He had no hope left now, and he had been so hopeful at the beginning. As they are all hopeful, he thought, as they have been hoping now for three hundred years. And they will go on hoping, for a little while, and then men will become hard to get, even with the freeze, and then the starships won't go out any more. And Man will be doomed to the System for the rest of his days.

Therefore, he asked humbly, silently, let this one have planets.

Up in the dome of the control cabin, Cohn was bent over the panel, pouring power into the board. He looked up, nodded briefly as Jansen came in. It seemed to both of them that they had been apart for five minutes.

'Are they all hot yet?' asked Jansen.

'No, not yet.'

The ship had been in deep space with her ports thrown open. Absolute cold had come in and gone to the core of her, and it was always a while before the ship was reclaimed and her instruments warmed. Even now there was a sharp chill in the air of the cabin.

Jansen sat down idly, rubbing his arms.

'Last time around, I guess.'

'Yes,' said Cohn, and added laconically, 'I wish Weizsäcker was here.'

Jansen grinned. Weizsäcker, poor old Weizsäcker. He was long dead and it was a good thing, for he was the most maligned human being in the System.

For a hundred years his theory on the birth of planets, that every sun necessarily gave birth to a satellite family, had been an accepted part of the knowledge of Man. And then, of course, there had come space flight.

Jansen chuckled wryly. Lucky man, Weizsäcker. Now, two hundred years and a thousand stars later, there had been discovered just four planets. Alpha Centauri had one: a barren, ice-crusted mote no larger than the Moon; and Pollux had three, all dead lumps of cold rock and iron. None of the other stars had any at all. Yes, it would have been a great blow to Weizsäcker.

A hum of current broke into Jansen's thought as the telescope was run out. There was a sudden beginning of light upon the screen.

In spite of himself and the wry, hopeless feeling that had been in him, Jansen arose quickly, with a thin trickle of nervousness in his arms. There is always a chance, he thought, after all, there is always a chance. We have only been to a thousand suns, and in the Galaxy a thousand suns are not anything at all. So there is always a chance.

Cohn, calm and methodical, was manning the radar.

Gradually, condensing upon the center of the screen, the image of the star took shape. It hung at last, huge and yellow and flaming with an awful brilliance, and the prominences of the rim made the vast circle uneven. Because the ship was close and the filter was in, the stars of the background were invisible, and there was nothing but the one great sun.

Jansen began to adjust for observation.

The observation was brief.

They paused for a moment before beginning the tests, gazing upon the face of the alien sun. The first of their race to be here and to see, they were caught up for a time in the ancient, deep thrill of space and the unknown Universe.

They watched, and into the field of their vision, breaking in slowly upon the glaring edge of the sun's disk, there came a small black ball. It moved steadily away from the edge, in toward the center of the sun. It was unquestionably a planet in transit.

* * *

When the alien ship moved, Roymer was considerably rattled.

One does not question Mind-Search, he knew, and so there could not be any living thing aboard that ship. Therefore, the ship's movement could be regarded only as a peculiar aberration in the still-functioning drive. Certainly, he thought, and peace returned to his mind.

But it did pose an uncomfortable problem. Boarding that ship would be no easy matter, not if the thing was inclined to go hopping away like that, with no warning. There were two hundred years of conditioning in Roymer, it would be impossible for him to put either his ship or his crew into an unnecessarily dangerous position. And wavery, erratic spaceships could undoubtedly be classified as dangerous.

Therefore, the ship would have to be disabled.

Regretfully, he connected with Fire Control, put the operation into the hands of the Firecon officer, and settled back to observe the results of the actions against the strange craft.

And the alien moved again.

Not suddenly, as before, but deliberately now, the thing turned once more from its course, and its speed decreased even more rapidly. It was still moving in upon Mina, but now its orbit was tangential and no longer direct. As Roymer watched the ship come about, he turned up the magnification for a larger view, checked the automatic readings on the board below the screen. And his eyes were suddenly directed to a small, conical projection which had begun to rise up out of the ship, which rose for a short distance and stopped, pointed in on the orbit towards Mina at the center.

Roymer was bewildered, but he acted immediately. Firecon was halted, all protective screens were re-established, and the patrol ship back-tracked quickly into the protection of deep space.

There was no question in Roymer's mind that the movements of the alien had been directed by a living intelligence, and not by any mechanical means. There was also no doubt in Roymer's mind that there was no living being on board that ship. The problem was acute.

Roymer felt the scalp of his hairless head beginning to crawl. In the history of the galaxy, there had been discovered but five nonhuman races, yet never a race which did not betray its existence by the telepathic nature of its thinking. Roymer could not conceive of a people so alien that even the fundamental structure of their thought process was entirely different from the Galactics.

Extra-Galactics? He observed the ship closely and shook his head. No. Not an extra-Galactic ship certainly, much too primitive a type.

Extraspatial? His scalp crawled again.

Completely at a loss as to what to do, Roymer again contacted Mind-Search and requested that Trian be sent to him immediately.

Trian was preceded by a puzzled Goladan. The orders to alien contact, then to Firecon, and finally for a quick retreat, had affected the lieutenant deeply. He was a man accustomed to a strictly logical and somewhat ponderous course of events. He waited expectantly for some explanation to come from his usually serene commander.

Roymer, however, was busily occupied in tracking the alien's new course. An orbit about Mina, Roymer observed, with that conical projection laid on the star; a device of war; or some measuring instrument?

The stolid Trian appeared—walking would not quite describe how—and was requested to make another attempt at contact with the alien. He replied with his usual eerie silence and in a moment, when he turned back to Roymer, there was surprise in the transmitted thought.

'I cannot understand. There is life there now.'

Roymer was relieved, but Goladan was blinking.

Trian went on, turning again to gaze at the screen.

'It is very remarkable. There are two life-beings. Human-type race. Their presence is very clear, they are'—he paused briefly—'explorers, it appears. But they were not there before. It is extremely unnerving.'

So it is, Roymer agreed. He asked quickly: 'Are they aware of us?'

'No. They are directing their attention on the star. Shall I contact?'

'No. Not yet. We will observe them first.'

The alien ship floated upon the screen before them, moving in slow orbit about the star Mina.

Seven. There were seven of them. Seven planets, and three at least had atmospheres, and two might even be inhabitable. Jansen was so excited he was hopping around the control room. Cohn did nothing, but grin widely with a wondrous joy, and the two of them repeatedly shook hands and gloated.

'Seven!' roared Jansen. 'Old lucky seven!'

Quickly then, and with extreme nervousness, they ran spectrograph analyses of each of those seven fascinating worlds. They began with the central planets, in the favorable temperature belt where life conditions would be most likely to exist, and they worked outwards.

For reasons which were as much sentimental as they were practical, they started with the third planet of this fruitful sun. There was a thin atmosphere, fainter even than that of Mars, and no oxygen. Silently they went on to the fourth. It was cold and heavy, perhaps twice as large as Earth, had a thick envelope of noxious gases. They saw with growing fear that there was no hope there, and they turned quickly inwards toward the warmer area nearer the sun.

On the second planet—as Jansen put it—they hit the jackpot.

A warm, green world it was, of an Earthlike size and atmosphere; oxygen and water vapor lines showed strong and clear in the analysis.

'This looks like it,' said Jansen, grinning again.

Cohn nodded, left the screen and went over to man the navigating instruments.

'Let's go down and take a look.'

'Radio check first.' It was the proper procedure. Jansen had gone over it in his mind a thousand times. He clicked on the receiver, waited for the tubes to function, and then scanned for contact. As they moved in toward the new planet he listened intently, trying all lengths, waiting for any sound at all. There was nothing but the rasping static of open space.

'Well,' he said finally, as the green planet grew large upon the screen, 'if there's any race there, it doesn't have radio.'

Cohn showed his relief.

'Could be a young civilization.'

'Or one so ancient and advanced that it doesn't *need* radio.'

Jansen refused to let his deep joy be dampened. It was impossible to know what would be there. Now it was just as it had been three hundred years ago, when the first Earth ship was approaching Mars. And it will be like this—Jansen thought—in every other system to which we go. How can you picture what there will be? There is nothing at all in your past to give you a clue. You can only hope.

The planet was a beautiful green ball on the screen.

* * *

The thought which came out of Trian's mind was tinged with relief.

'I see how it was done. They have achieved a complete statis, a perfect state of suspended animation which they produce by an ingenious usage of the absolute zero of outer space. Thus, when they are—frozen, is the way they regard it—their minds do not function, and their lives are not detectable. They have just recently revived and are directing their ship.'

Roymer digested the new information slowly. What kind of a race was this? A race which flew in primitive star ships, yet it had already conquered one of the greatest problems in Galactic history, a problem which had baffled the Galactics for millions of years. Roymer was uneasy.

'A very ingenious device,' Trian was thinking, 'they use it to alter the amount of subjective time consumed in their explorations. Their star ship has a very low maximum speed. Hence, without this—freeze—their voyage would take up a good portion of their lives.'

'Can you classify the mind-type?' Roymer asked with growing concern.

Trian reflected silently for a moment.

'Yes,' he said, 'although the type is extremely unusual. I have never observed it before. General classification would be Human-Four. More specifically, I would place them at the Ninth level.'

Roymer started. 'The Ninth level?'

'Yes. As I say, they are extremely unusual.'

Roymer was now clearly worried. He turned away and paced the deck for several moments. Abruptly, he left the room and went to the files of alien classification. He was gone for a long time, while Goladan fidgeted and Trian continued to gather information plucked across space from the alien minds. Roymer came back at last.

'What are they doing?'

'They are moving in on the second planet. They are about to determine whether the conditions are suitable there for an establishment of a colony of their kind.'

Gravely, Roymer gave his orders to navigation. The patrol ship swung into motion, sped off swiftly in the direction of the second planet.

* * *

There was a single, huge blue ocean which covered an
entire hemisphere of the new world. And the rest of the
surface was a young jungle, wet and green and empty of any
kind of people, choked with queer growths of green and
orange. They circled the globe at a height of several thousand feet, and to their amazement and joy, they never saw a
living thing; not a bird or a rabbit or the alien equivalent, in
fact nothing alive at all. And so they stared in happy
fascination.

'This is it,' Jansen said again, his voice uneven.

'What do you think we ought to call it?' Cohn was speaking absently. 'New Earth? Utopia?'

Together they watched the broken terrain slide by beneath them.

'No people at all. It's ours.' And after a while Jansen
said: 'New Earth. That's a good name.'

Cohn was observing the features of the ground intently.

'Do you notice the kind of . . . circular appearance of
most of those mountain ranges? Like on the Moon, but
grown over and eroded. They're all almost perfect circles.'

Pulling his mind away from the tremendous visions he had
of the colony which would be here, Jansen tried to look at
the mountains with an objective eye. Yes, he realized with
faint surprise, they were round, like Moon craters.

'Peculiar,' Cohn muttered. 'Not natural, I don't think.
Couldn't be. Meteors not likely in this atmosphere. What
in—?'

Jansen jumped. 'Look there,' he cried suddenly, 'a round
lake!'

Off toward the northern pole of the planet, a lake which
was a perfect circle came slowly into view. There was no
break in the rim other than that of a small stream which
flowed in from the north.

'That's not natural,' Cohn said briefly, 'someone built
that.'

They were moving on to the dark side now, and Cohn
turned the ship around. The sense of exhilaration was too
new for them to be let down, but the strange sight of a huge
number of perfect circles, existing haphazardly like the remains of great splashes on the surface of the planet, was
unnerving.

It was the sight of one particular crater, a great barren
hole in the midst of a wide red desert, which rang a bell in
Jansen's memory, and he blurted:

'A war! There was a war here. That one there looks just like a fusion bomb crater.'

Cohn stared, then raised his eyebrows.

'I'll bet you're right.'

'A bomb crater, do you see? Pushes up hills on all sides in a circle, and kills—' A sudden, terrible thought hit Jansen. Radioactivity. Would there be radioactivity here?

While Cohn brought the ship in low over the desert, he tried to calm Jansen's fears.

'There couldn't be much. Too much plant life. Jungles all over the place. Take it easy, man.'

'But there's not a living thing on the planet. I'll bet that's why there was a war. It got out of hand, the radioactivity got everything. We might have done this to Earth!'

They glided in over the flat emptiness of the desert, and the counters began to click madly.

'That's it,' Jansen said conclusively, 'still radioactive. It might not have been too long ago.'

'Could have been a million years, for all we know.'

'Well, most places are safe, apparently. We'll check before we go down.'

As he pulled the ship up and away, Cohn whistled.

'Do you suppose there's really not a living thing? I mean, not a bug or a germ or even a virus? Why, it's like a clean new world, a nursery!' He could not take his eyes from the screen.

They were going down now. In a very little while they would be out and walking in the sun. The lust of the feeling was indescribable. They were Earthmen freed forever from the choked home of the System, Earthmen gone out to the stars, landing now upon the next world of their empire.

Cohn could not control himself.

'Do we need a flag?' he said grinning. 'How do we claim this place?'

'Just set her down, man,' Jansen roared.

Cohn began to chuckle.

'Oh, brave new world,' he laughed, 'that has *no* people in it.'

'But why do we have to contact them?' Goladan asked impatiently. 'Could we not just—'

Roymer interrupted without looking at him.

'The law requires that contact be made and the situation

explained before action is taken. Otherwise it would be a barbarous act.'

Goladan brooded.

The patrol ship hung in the shadow of the dark side, tracing the alien by its radioactive trail. The alien was going down for a landing on the daylight side.

Trian came forward with the other members of the Alien Contact Crew, reported to Roymer, 'The aliens have landed.'

'Yes,' said Roymer, 'we will let them have a little time. Trian, do you think you will have any difficulty in the transmission?'

'No. Conversation will not be difficult. Although the confused and complex nature of their thought-patterns does make their inner reactions somewhat obscure. But I do not think there will be any problem.'

'Very well. You will remain here and relay the messages.'
'Yes.'

The patrol ship flashed quickly up over the north pole, then swung inward toward the equator, circling the spot where the alien had gone down. Roymer brought his ship in low and with the silence characteristic of a Galactic, landed her in a wooded spot a mile east of the alien. The Galactics remained in their ship for a short while as Trian continued his probe for information. When at last the Alien Contact Crew stepped out, Roymer and Goladan were in the lead. The rest of the crew faded quietly into the jungle.

As he walked through the young orange brush, Roymer regarded the world around him. Almost ready for repopulation, he thought, in another hundred years the radiation will all be gone, and we will come back. One by one the worlds of that war will be reclaimed.

He felt Trian's directions pop into his mind.

'You are approaching them. Proceed with caution. They are just beyond the next small rise. I think you had better wait, since they are remaining close to their ship.'

Roymer sent back a silent yes. Motioning Goladan to be quiet, Roymer led the way up the last rise. In the jungle around him the Galactic crew moved silently.

The air was perfect; there was no radiation. Except for the wild orange color of the vegetation, the spot was a Garden of Eden. Jansen felt instinctively that there was no danger here, no terrible blight or virus or any harmful thing. He felt a violent urge to get out of his spacesuit and run and

breathe, but it was forbidden. Not on the first trip. That
would come later, after all the tests and experiments had
been made and the world pronounced safe.

One of the first things Jansen did was get out the recorder
and solemnly claim this world for the Solar Federation,
recording the historic words for the archives of Earth. And
he and Cohn remained for a while by the air lock of their
ship, gazing around at the strange yet familiar world into
which they had come.

'Later on we'll search for ruins,' Cohn said. 'Keep an eye
out for anything that moves. It's possible that there are
some of them left and who knows what they'll look like.
Mutants, probably, with five heads. So keep an eye open.'

'Right.'

Jansen began collecting samples of the ground, of the air,
of the nearer foliage. The dirt was Earth-dirt, there was no
difference. He reached down and crumbled the soft moist
sod with his fingers. The flowers may be a little peculiar—
probably mutated, he thought—but the dirt is honest to
goodness dirt, and I'll bet the air is Earth-air.

He rose and stared into the clear open blue of the sky,
feeling again an almost overpowering urge to throw open his
helmet and breathe, and as he stared at the sky and at the
green and orange hills, suddenly, a short distance from
where he stood, a little old man came walking over the hill.

They stood facing each other across the silent space of a
foreign glade. Roymer's face was old and smiling; Jansen
looked back at him with absolute astonishment.

After a short pause, Roymer began to walk out onto the
open soil, with Goladan following, and Jansen went for his
heat gun.

'Cohn!' he yelled, in a raw brittle voice, 'Cohn!'

And as Cohn turned and saw and froze, Jansen heard
words being spoken in his brain. They were words coming
from the little old man.

'Please do not shoot,' the old man said, his lips unmoving.

'No, don't shoot,' Cohn said quickly. 'Wait. Let him
alone.' The hand of Cohn, too, was at his heat gun.

Roymer smiled. To the two Earth-men his face was incredibly old and wise and gentle. He was thinking: Had I
been a nonhuman they would have killed me.

He sent a thought back to Trian. The Mind-Searcher
picked it up and relayed it into the brains of the Earthmen,
sending it through their cortical centers and then up into

their conscious minds, so that the words were heard in the language of Earth. 'Thank you,' Roymer said gently. Jansen's hand held the heat gun leveled on Roymer's chest. He stared, not knowing what to say.

'Please remain where you are,' Cohn's voice was hard and steady.

Roymer halted obligingly. Goladan stopped at his elbow, peering at the Earthmen with mingled fear and curiosity. The sight of fear helped Jansen very much.

'Who are you?' Cohn said clearly, separating the words.

Roymer folded his hands comfortably across his chest, he was still smiling.

'With your leave, I will explain our presence.'

Cohn just stared.

'There will be a great deal to explain. May we sit down and talk?'

Trian helped with the suggestion. They sat down.

The sun of the new world was setting, and the conference went on. Roymer was doing most of the talking. The Earthmen sat transfixed.

It was like growing up suddenly, in the space of a second.

The history of Earth and of all Mankind just faded and dropped away. They heard of great races and worlds beyond number, the illimitable government which was the Galactic Federation. The fiction, the legends, the dreams of a thousand years had come true in a moment, in the figure of a square little old man who was not from Earth. There was a great deal for them to learn and accept in the time of a single afternoon, on an alien planet.

But it was just as new and real to them that they had discovered an uninhabited, fertile planet, the first to be found by Man. And they could not help but revolt from the sudden realization that the planet might well be someone else's property—that the Galactics owned everything worth owning.

It was an intolerable thought.

'How far,' asked Cohn, as his heart pushed up in his throat, 'does the Galactic League extend?'

Roymer's voice was calm and direct in their minds.

'Only throughout the central regions of the galaxy. There are millions of stars along the rim which have not yet been explored.'

Cohn relaxed, bowed down with relief. There was room then, for Earthmen.

'This planet. Is it part of the Federation?'

'Yes,' said Roymer, and Cohn tried to mask his thought. Cohn was angry, and he hoped that the alien could not read his mind as well as he could talk to it. To have come this far—

'There was a race here once,' Roymer was saying, 'a humanoid race which was almost totally destroyed by war. This planet has been uninhabitable for a very long time. A few of its people who were in space at the time of the last attack were spared. The Federation established them elsewhere. When the planet is ready, the descendants of those survivors will be brought back. It is their home.'

Neither of the Earthmen spoke.

'It is surprising,' Roymer went on, 'that your home world is in the desert. We had thought that there were no habitable worlds—'

'The desert?'

'Yes. The region of the galaxy from which you have come is that which we call the desert. It is an area almost entirely devoid of planets. Would you mind telling me which star is your home?'

Cohn stiffened.

'I'm afraid our government would not permit us to disclose any information concerning our race.'

'As you wish. I am sorry you are disturbed. I was curious to know—' He waved a negligent hand to show that the information was important. We will get it later, he thought, when we decipher their charts. He was coming to the end of the conference, he was about to say what he had come to say.

'No doubt you have been exploring the stars about your world?'

The Earthmen both nodded. But for the question concerning Sol, they long ago would have lost all fear of this placid old man and his wide-eyed, silent companion.

'Perhaps you would like to know,' said Roymer, 'why your area is a desert.'

Instantly, both Jansen and Cohn were completely absorbed. This was it, the end of three hundred years of searching. They would go home with the answer.

Roymer never relaxed.

'Not too long ago,' he said, 'approximately thirty thousand years by your reckoning, a great race ruled the desert, a race which was known as the Antha, and it was not a desert then. The Antha ruled hundreds of worlds. They were perhaps the greatest of all the Galactic peoples; certainly they were as brilliant a race as the galaxy has ever known.

'But they were not a good race. For hundreds of years, while they were still young, we tried to bring them into the Federation. They refused, and of course we did not force them. But as the years went by the scope of their knowledge increased amazingly; shortly they were the technological equals of any other race in the galaxy. And then the Antha embarked upon an era of imperialistic expansion.

'They were superior, they knew it and were proud. And so they pushed out and enveloped the races and worlds of the area now known as the desert. Their rule was a tyranny unequaled in Galactic history.'

The Earthmen never moved, and Roymer went on.

'But the Antha were not members of the Federation, and, therefore, they were not answerable for their acts. We could only stand by and watch as they spread their vicious rule from world to world. They were absolutely ruthless.

'As an example of their kind of rule, I will tell you of their crime against the Apectans.

'The planet of Apectus not only resisted the Antha, but somehow managed to hold out against their approach for several years. The Antha finally conquered and then, in retaliation for the Apectans' valor, they conducted the most brutal of their mass experiments.

'They were a brilliant people. They had been experimenting with the genes of heredity. Somehow they found a way to alter the genes of the Apectans, who where humanoids like themselves, and they did it on a mass scale. They did not choose to exterminate the race, their revenge was much greater. Every Apectan born since the Antha invasion, has been born without one arm.'

Jansen sucked in his breath. It was a very horrible thing to hear, and a sudden memory came into his brain. Caesar did that, he thought. He cut off the right hands of the Gauls. Peculiar coincidence. Jansen felt uneasy.

Roymer paused for a moment.

'The news of what happened to the Apectans set the Galactic peoples up in arms, but it was not until the Antha attacked a Federation world that we finally moved against them. It was the greatest war in the history of Life.

'You will perhaps understand how great a people the

Antha were when I tell you that they alone, unaided, dependent entirely upon their own resources, fought the rest of the Galactics, and fought them to a standstill. As the terrible years went by we lost whole races and planets—like this one, which was one the Antha destroyed—and yet we could not defeat them.

'It was only after many years, when a Galactic invented the most dangerous weapon of all, that we won. The invention—of which only the Galactic Council has knowledge—enabled us to turn the suns of the Antha into novae, at a long range. One by one we destroyed the Antha worlds. We hunted them through all the planets of the desert; for the first time in history the edict of the Federation was death, death for an entire race. At last there were no longer any habitable worlds where the Antha had been. We burned their worlds, and ran them down in space. Thirty thousand years ago, the civilization of the Antha perished.'

Roymer had finished. He looked at the Earthmen out of grave, tired old eyes.

Cohn was staring in open-mouth fascination, but Jansen—unaccountably felt a chill. The story of Caesar remained uncomfortably in his mind. And he had a quick, awful suspicion.

'Are you sure you got all of them?'

'No. Some surely must have escaped. There were too many in space, and space is without limits.'

Jansen wanted to know: 'Have any of them been heard of since?'

Roymer's smile left him as the truth came out. 'No. Not until now.'

There were only a few more seconds. He gave them time to understand. He could not help telling them that he was sorry, he even apologized. And then he sent the order with his mind.

The Antha died quickly and silently, without pain.

Only thirty thousand years, Roymer was thinking, but thirty thousand years, and they came back out to the stars. They have no memory now of what they were or what they have done. They started all over again, the old history of the race has been lost, and in thirty thousand years they came all the way back.

Roymer shook his head with sad wonder and awe. The most brilliant people of all.

Goladan came in quietly with the final reports.

'There are no charts,' he grumbled, 'no maps at all. We will not be able to trace them to their home star.'

Roymer did not know, really, what was right, to be disappointed or relieved. We cannot destroy them now, he thought, not right away. He could not help being relieved. Maybe this time there will be a way, and they will not have to be destroyed. They could be—

He remembered the edict—the edict of death. The Antha had forged it for themselves and it was just. He realized that there wasn't much hope.

The reports were on his desk and he regarded them with a wry smile. There was indeed no way to trace them back. They had no charts, only a regular series of course-check coordinates which were preset on their home planet and which were not decipherable. Even at this stage of their civilization they had already anticipated the consequences of having their ship fall into alien hands. And this although they lived in the desert.

Goladan startled him with an anxious question:

'What can we do?'

Roymer was silent.

We can wait, he thought. Gradually, one by one, they will come out of the desert, and when they come we will be waiting. Perhaps one day we will follow one back and destroy their world, and perhaps before then we will find a way to save them.

Suddenly, as his eyes wandered over the report before him and he recalled the ingenious mechanism of the freeze, a chilling, unbidden thought came into his brain.

And perhaps, he thought calmly, for he was a philosophical man, they will come out already equipped to rule the galaxy.

ABOUT THE EDITORS

ISAAC ASIMOV has been called "one of America's treasures." Born in the Soviet Union, he was brought to the United States at the age of three (along with his family) by agents of the American government in a successful attempt to prevent him from working for the wrong side. He quickly established himself as one of this country's foremost science fiction writers and writer about everything, and although now approaching middle age, he is going stronger than ever. He long ago passed his age and weight in books, and with some 250 to his credit threatens to close in on his I.Q. His sequel to *The Foundation Trilogy—Foundation's Edge*—was one of the bestselling books of 1982 and 1983.

MARTIN H. GREENBERG has been called (in *The Science Fiction and Fantasy Book Review*) "The King of the Anthologists"; to which he replied—"It's good to be the King!" He has produced more than 150 of them, usually in collaboration with a multitude of co-conspirators, most frequently the two who have given you MONSTERS. A professor of Regional Analysis and Political Science at the University of Wisconsin—Green Bay, he is still trying to publish his weight.

CHARLES G. WAUGH is a professor of Psychology and Communications at the University of Maine at Augusta who is still trying to figure out how he got himself into all this. He has also worked with many collaborators, since he is basically a very friendly fellow. He has done some fifty anthologies and single-author collections, and especially enjoys locating unjustly ignored stories. He also claims that he met his wife via computer dating—her choice was an entire fraternity or him, and she has only minor regrets.

ORDER FORM

If you cannot find these titles in your bookshop, they can be obtained directly from the publisher. Please indicate the number of copies required and fill in the form overleaf in block letters.

The Mammoth Book of Short Science Fiction Novels
___ Presented by Isaac Asimov   £4.95

The Mammoth Book of Short Fantasy Novels
___ Presented by Isaac Asimov   £4.95

The Mammoth Book of Short Crime Novels
___ Edited by Bill Pronzini and Martin H. Greenberg   £4.95

The Mammoth Book of Short Spy Novels
___ Edited by Bill Pronzini and Martin H. Greenberg   £4.95

The Mammoth Book of Modern Crime Stories
___ Edited by George Hardinge   £4.95

The Mammoth Book of Classic Fantasy
___ Edited by Cary Wilkins   £4.95

The Mammoth Book of Classic Science Fiction
___ Presented by Isaac Asimov   £4.95

The Mammoth Book of Best New Science Fiction
___ Edited by Gardner Dozois   £4.95

Mythic Beasts
___ Edited by Isaac Asimov, C. Waugh and M. Greenberg   £3.50

Spells
___ Edited by Isaac Asimov, C. Waugh and M. Greenberg   £3.50

Intergalactic Empires
___ Edited by Isaac Asimov, C. Waugh and M. Greenberg
   £2.95

Please fill in the form below in block letters:

NAME_____

ADDRESS_____

_____

_____

_____

Send to Robinson Publishing Cash Sales,
P.O. Box 11, Falmouth, Cornwall TR10 9EN

Please enclose cheque or postal order to the value of the cover price plus:

In UK only – 55p for the first book, 22p for the second book, and 14p for each additional book to a maximum £1.75.

BFPO – 55p for the first book, 22p for the second book, and 14p for the next seven books and 8p for each book thereafter.

Overseas – £1.25 for the first book, 31p per copy for each additional book.

Whilst every effort is made to keep prices low, it is sometimes necessary to increase prices at short notice. Robinson Publishing reserve the right to show on covers, and charge, new retail prices which may differ from those advertised in text or elsewhere.